Our Lady of West Hollywood

Susan Roether

FT

Fellow Travelers Media
www.fellow-travelers.com

ISBN-13:
978-0615522739 (Fellow Travelers)

ISBN-10:
0615522734

For my sisters and L.A. friends who provided
inspiration and encouragement:

Anne, Catherine, Deb, Debbie, Esther, Francoise,
Jamie, Jeanney, Julie, Kim, Laurie, Lee, Lisa,
Mimi, Pat, Patty, Pituka, Regina, Rena, Rosie,
Therese and Virginia

CHAPTER ONE

October 14, 1998

Nora wished she could get the image out of her head, out of her imagination, but it lingered: the way the girl got out of the car, the door to the big American sedan flung open. The girl's hair disheveled and the man inside the car leaning back, behind the wheel, looking at nothing. The man very clearly handed over some money-- the gesture of payment was unmistakable. The worst thing though, the thing Nora wished she hadn't seen, happened before the girl got out of the car: the sight of her head suddenly appearing next to the man in the driver's seat. The girl's head suddenly rising from the man's lap. It all happened so fast-- when Ginger drove her Volvo into the pot-holed alley behind the liquor store on Melrose Avenue, the entire scene played out in front of their headlights and the two women watched it, stunned.

"I can't believe it" Ginger said. " In this neighborhood? Look at her, she's so young!" Nora and Ginger were on their way from West Hollywood to the valley at rush hour. Nora really didn't want to look—but there was no way she could not see what happened.

Ginger was trying to avoid the gridlock by taking a shortcut. She knew the city; this was her neighborhood. Nora, after two years in Los Angeles, often said the city didn't "make sense" to her-- the sheer gargantuan sprawl of it, the lack of any real center or landmarks. The choked thoroughfares overflowed regularly onto side streets in a twice-daily flood of cars. To Nora it felt like an emergency evacuation was taking place--like the aftermath of a natural disaster. In many ways, Nora herself felt like a refugee here because she had only a temporary home and few friends. She felt she had left her real life behind in New York and found herself in Los Angeles on a temporary, exploratory visit that had been extended indefinitely.

Rounding the corner, Ginger stopped at a red light and waited as pedestrians crossed. "Oh my god," Ginger said, "that's her! See? That's her --the same girl we saw in the alley."

"She doesn't look like a prostitute."

Nora watched the girl cross the street, the tousled hair was unmistakable. She was very thin with long pale bare legs. A short dark-haired girl who wore tight jeans and high heels walked beside her. The two young faces appeared to glow, gilded with the electric street light; they walked with a casual, offhand gait, in no hurry. The girl they'd seen get out of the car in the alley looked like a suburban high school student; her friend had curly black hair and a curvaceous figure.

"She doesn't look over fifteen," Ginger said, following the other cars through the intersection and turning her head to watch the girls as they disappeared into the traffic of the street.

"What time does the thing start?" Nora asked and Ginger told her seven o'clock. Ginger was determined not to be late to Marie's baby shower, she was looking forward to this evening. Before long the Volvo was traveling on the Hollywood freeway, the 101, accelerating and braking with the mass of cars slowly moving northward. Freeways had vestigial place names as well as more efficient numbers.

"Do they know if it's a boy or girl?"

"Boy."

The mother-to-be was one of Ginger's closest friends, but Nora had met her only a couple of times at large gatherings.

"When's it due?"

"December I think," Ginger said.

"They're still together, right? Marie and Doug?"

"Definitely. No, he's really into it."

"How old is she?"

"She's close to forty I think," Ginger said. "She's been at Universal for at least twelve years. Marie has a great job in distribution, but I know she's always wanted a baby."

"Doesn't he have kids with his first wife?"

"Yes, she just got re-married to that actor. What's his name? He's on one of those cop shows."

"Which one?"

"I forget...Scott something. He has very short hair, tall?"

Nora settled back into the passenger seat and said nothing. She probably knew the actor, Ginger thought, if I could only think of his name. Nora kept up on all that because she was in "the industry" as it was called in L.A. It seemed that most of the people Ginger knew were working in some ambitious career or trying to get a foothold in "the industry." In her family therapy practice, Ginger offered support to the overwhelmed and the wanna-be's. She saw women obsessed with body weight and aging; the children without fathers; the alcoholism and drug-dependence of the highly stressed. Ginger knew the pathology of ambition, but she was still impressed by the people who played and won.

Nora had produced, for three years, a television show from New York that Ginger watched every week. When the show was cancelled, Nora moved to Los Angeles and rented a spare room in Ginger's house.

"Look, there's the Moorpark exit coming up." Nora pointed at the green and white sign. Ginger steered towards the right lane as quickly as possible, afraid she'd miss the exit, but then the lane of cars slowed to a crawl and she was caught for a half mile traveling at ten miles an hour. Nora didn't say anything, but Tim would have. Her ex-husband never missed an opportunity to criticize, Ginger recalled, hearing in her memory Tim's precise tone of voice and his impatience--he would have driven into the faster lane, sped past the cars in front, and cut back into the lane at the last minute to make the exit.

Nora pulled down the mirrored flap that hung above the windshield and with a few careful strokes applied lipstick. She then rubbed a little color from the tube unto her finger and rouged her cheekbones. Ginger seldom remembered to wear makeup. On special occasions she tried, but the effect was never what she hoped. Nora, with her pale skin and dark hair, was visibly brightened by the red lipstick she wore. The spot of color gave her face instant definition and spark. Even in the dark, Ginger thought, Nora's carefully made-up eyes seemed large and vivid. Like a photograph Ginger remembered seeing of Maria Callas-- those wide, almond-shaped eyes.

Satisfied with her face, Nora flipped up the mirror and read the address out loud to Ginger -- 23414 Buena Vista Circle-- and the Volvo turned down a quiet street lined with low-lying suburban houses.

CHAPTER TWO

Marie, expansively pregnant, held up the little garment for her guests to admire--a baby sailor suit smaller than a dinner napkin, complete with snaps at the crotch and a square navy blue collar.

"So tiny. Oh my god..."

Nora worried that Marie might start crying. Must be hormones, she thought. Ginger had obviously chosen the perfect gift.

"And a little hat!"

Marie twirled a saucer-sized white sailor hat on her index finger. Ginger looked pleased. Her eyes were tearing up too, Nora noticed. The gift opening had gone on and on. Each gift was ceremoniously exhibited to be oohed and aahed over by the assembled girlfriends.

Nora really wanted a cigarette but knew it was impossible, even more impossible than usual in Los Angeles. She was stuck between Ginger and a blonde woman on a small sofa against the wall with her exit blocked by a glass coffee table in front and two overstuffed chairs on either side, both occupied.

"That happened to my sister," the woman on Nora's left was saying to Ginger.

"Sometimes they make a mistake. They told her she was having a boy, then it turned out to be a girl. Her husband was really upset--I mean, think about it, that could be very upsetting."

Nora plunged in. "But don't they see it on an x-ray or something?"

"It's sound waves," the blonde woman explained. "Ultrasound-- but, you know, they see this tiny thing hanging between the legs. Sometimes they can't see it very well...or they think they see a penis but it's something else. Could be a finger or something." The speaker paused briefly and asked Nora " Do you have kids?"

Nora was expecting the question. She answered no, in a neutral tone.

The tall athletic-looking guest across the coffee table put down her fork and cake plate. "My astrologer says you can affect the sex of the baby by what you eat."

"Oh, I've heard of that--some kind of yin-yang thing," said the blonde.

"If you want a boy you drink lots of coffee and, well it also depends on the frequency of intercourse. We had one daughter and then two boys. Boys are easier, believe me."

"But girls learn faster. They're less aggressive too."

"Yeah, but when they get to be teenagers..."

The tall woman, after another bite of carrot cake, shook her head vigorously as she simultaneously swallowed and found her voice. "A nightmare."

There was general agreement on that, Nora noted, both to the left and right. She stood up then and made an unobtrusive move towards the kitchen, as the mother-to-be said, "It won't have my genes but I'm sure we'll bond and everything."

Nora found another clutch of guests gathered near the refrigerator in the kitchen. Someone was pouring white wine from a frosted green bottle.

"And then my water broke."

A woman's voice rose dramatically, signaling the next chapter of a familiar tale.

As the kitchen chorus murmured and exclaimed, Nora sought the back door but there was a table blocking it. Nora could tell, though she'd never seen the speaker before, that the petite brown-eyed woman enjoyed telling her story as she paused with an eager glance around at her audience

"In the car?" one of the women prompted

"On the 405!" In a triumphant tone, "My neighbor was driving."

Nora tried to position herself in a posture of relaxed attention while at the same time reaching for the bottle of wine uncorked on the counter. As she poured a tall glass she turned towards the storyteller with a look that she hoped conveyed sympathy and interest.

"I was in the back seat. I told her, Lisa, don't turn around and look, just get into the fast lane!"

The punch line elicited shrill squeals of commiseration...the mood was of a victorious battle, oft remembered. The audience couldn't have been more involved, Nora noted. Two others spoke at once...

"I had a home birth..." a fifty-something woman began. Nora drank and listened. "After seventeen hours of labor, I was still only three millimeters..."

"Dilated..." someone in the chorus offered.

Nora noticed a swift movement behind her and looked around to see Marie's husband Doug, the father-to-be, in sweatpants and undershirt, running upstairs barefoot clutching a sandwich in his hand. He's probably watching the basketball game, Nora thought, he looked like he didn't want to be noticed. She imagined the men in a room upstairs with a large TV. She felt a strong urge to run upstairs and join that party but she knew it was completely out of the question.

Nora had met a few of the women in the room before. Sidnie Talphen was in the kitchen putting more ice in her Perrier. She was remarkably thin, and wore a very slim skirt of exactly the correct length and her pale blue cashmere sweater was tied just so around her shoulders. Someone asked Sidnie about the new Spielberg picture that she'd been working on.

"I think it's one of his best," she said with a reverent tone. "It's really outstanding."

The women standing in her vicinity all nodded approvingly. Sidnie had seen the recently completed film and she felt so clearly, so sincerely, that it was exceptional. There was nothing else for anyone in the little clump to say. No one even asked what it was about, Nora noticed.

Patty McCray was sitting at the kitchen table, which was piled with used paper plates and pink cardboard bakery boxes. She had three other women laughing at something she said. Nora sat down in the remaining chair. Patty, plump and boisterous, was a successful casting agent who knew almost everyone in the room. Nora's sister had introduced them not long ago and Patty greeted Nora with genuine friendliness and launched into a story.

"You all know Kelly Urbansky, right?" Patty spoke to the assembled. "You know she got a job working for Richard Bremerton, right?

Nora recognized the name of a director known for his out-of-control ego and abusive rages. He'd won an Academy Award two years before. "I rule the universe" he'd said, in front of the Hollywood audience and some fifty million other TV viewers around the world.

"Well, he was going out of town and before he left he told Kelly to get his car washed. He has one of those giant Humvee military jeeps. It's like double-wide and has huge tires."

"A Humvee? He drives that in L.A.?

"Oh yeah, lots of people have them now," Patty said. "Anyway, Kelly just started working there and she doesn't want to make a mistake, right? She has to get the hummer washed and she wants it to be perfect. So, she takes it to that place on Santa Monica, you know, and they do the hand wash number and all, but when it's finished there's still like dirt on the wheel wells or whatever. So, Kelly thinks, you know, the ruler of the universe always wants everything perfect. Mr. Perfect, right ? So, he's out of town and she has plenty of time so Kelly drives the Humvee over to the best detailer in the valley."

"Detailer?" Nora was puzzled.

"That's where they clean everything on your car with like toothbrushes," Patty explained. "It takes hours and costs a couple hundred dollars, they shine every inch of the car. She wants to make sure it's totally perfect, right? And the guys go to work on it and when they're finished it is immaculate--like every bumper and knob is sparkling, right?"

"Well, when Bremerton gets back home and sees what Kelly's done, he goes ballistic. He screams at her, calls her every name in the book. She was in tears. Turns out..." Patty paused and chuckled as she caught her breath "he tried for months to get the Humvee dirty enough so it looked authentic--like he was macho man driving around in the wilderness or something."

"So Kelly got fired?"

"Yeah, but I think she's starting another job over at Warner Brothers."

"Unbelievable."

"That's just incredible."

Nora often noticed how frequently people in L.A. expressed incredulity. About events that were good (amazingly beautiful) or bad (I just can't believe this could happen). As though people are always being caught off-guard-- unprepared to comprehend daily events or behavior. As though they had no way to prepare themselves for the daunting multiplicity of life's possibilities. Nora tried to picture a city full of people constantly amazed. Any deviation from the usual or any occurrence not planned or predicted or specifically expected causing open-mouthed wide-eyed awe. In reality, she thought, life is all too predictable.

Nora stood in the entrance to the rectangular living where Ginger seemed to be engrossed in a conversation with a young Black woman wearing a stylish grey pantsuit and pearls. Those who had children were telling the ones who didn't what it was like.

Nora knew Ginger's only daughter lived in Toronto and she saw her once a year at Christmas. As far as Nora knew there had been some kind of rift after the divorce. Still, this didn't affect the significance of Ginger's role as mother, the personal significance that had nothing to do with the actual outcome or success of the child-producing operation. It seemed to Nora that the event of initiation, the advent, was the important thing--that was what the celebration was about. Nora imagined that the actual production of a child would be an interesting experience, it was everything afterward that she had no talent for.

"I'm glad it's just women aren't you?" A middle-aged woman with graying hair wearing no make-up joined Nora leaning against the wall. Without asking, she filled Nora's glass from a bottle of chardonnay she was carrying with her right hand. With her left she drank from a tumbler half-full of wine. Nora wondered if the older woman was a relative of the mother-to-be.

"It's more fun when it's just women--I don't think men should be invited to baby showers, you know what I mean?"

Nora nodded "I went to one last summer that was like a cocktail party. The men talked business."

"That's not the way it should be," the older woman said. There's a different vibe when it's just women; there's a deeper connection; the energy is more nurturing."

Nora had once felt contemptuous of the California-speak she encountered when she first came to Los Angeles but now she was used to it.

"I think it's because men tend to take up more space, you know, psychic space," the woman continued. And then women who aren't with...a partner...feel, I don't know, less..."

"Disempowered," said Nora.

"Right. And the ones who are with a man can't really ...you know...the energy is different."

"No, it's not the same" Nora agreed, taking a long swallow of the wine. She usually didn't like California chardonnay but she liked it tonight.

She wanted to like this plain-looking overweight woman who didn't seem to fit into the career-in-the-motion-picture-industry mold. Although she was wearing a blue and yellow flowered T-shirt and blue polyester slacks, Nora saw that she was a perceptive person.

"How do you know Marie?" Nora asked.

"I'm her neighbor, I live next door. Where are you from? You have kind of an accent."

"I'm from New York."

Nora had begun to shorten the longer version of where she'd lived in her life. She was an ex-New Yorker now.

"You like it out here?"

"I miss my friends but, yeah, the climate is great." Nora looked over at Ginger, hoping to see her get up from the sofa but she seemed engrossed in conversation.

"Do you work at Universal?"

"No," said Nora, dreading the tedious next question.

"What do you do?"

"I'm a writer."

"What do you write?"

"I'm working on a film script at the moment. I worked as a producer in New York."

"You produced movies? "

"No, television."

"Have I seen any movies you've written?"

"No," said Nora.

"What's it about? " The neighbor looked genuinely interested. "The story?"

Nora felt a fight or flight mechanism clicking on somewhere deep in her cerebellum. She wanted to dart out the door but she was stuck. They always asked that. At least there was no one to overhear. A faint note of hostility crept into Nora's voice.

"It's about a man and a woman."

"Kind of a love story?"

"Kind of."

"Is it a younger man?" the neighbor asked. "My best friend just got a divorce after twenty-two years. She's dating an electrician who does therapeutic shiatsu massage."

"Amazing," said Nora flatly.

"You can use that," said the woman. "He's twenty-eight and she's forty-five. I see that happening more and more now."

"Really?" Nora said, "Hey, is there any more wine in..." The woman didn't hesitate to empty the last of the Chardonnay into her glass. "Thanks. Are you in the Industry, um..."

"Carol--with a K. Sort of, I do catering--for events. I do a lot of work at the studios. You know, for screenings, things like that."

"That's interesting" Nora lied.

Finally, Ginger was slowly rising from the gift-littered sofa. She moved carefully but not gracefully around the coffee table and half-tripped into the center of the room. Nora gave her a hopeful wave as Karol continued asking questions.

The show Nora had co-produced in New York turned out to be one of Karol's favorites. Nora was sorry she'd mentioned it--she should have kept this encounter simple, impersonal. She realized she had a need to define herself, to get approval, and this made her feel childish and silly. Then Karol produced a card which read "Kare-free Katering" and said "Listen, if you ever need someone to do a party or just some snacks or finger food with drinks, please call me, okay? Here's my home number."

Nora caught Ginger's eye and made a motion with her chin towards the door. Ginger smiled a conciliatory smile; she knew it was time to leave but the conversation had stimulated her. Her face was animated and flushed--Ginger rarely drank more than one glass of wine. Nora's impatience increased when Karol turned her business card over and placed it on a table to write on the back.

"Here, I'll put my cell phone number in case you need to get in touch with me in a hurry."

Nora couldn't imagine a situation in which she would appreciate this favor, but she nodded in a polite way. "Okay, fine."

"I have five women working with me," Karol continued in her sales promotion voice.

"I'm not involved with producing right now," Nora repeated, "I don't really..."

"You never know" Karol was firm. "Please give us a call, you won't be sorry."

As Nora and Ginger made their way to the door, Nora found herself wishing she could just leave without the requisite goodbye kisses and hugs. She knew, from past experience in Los Angeles, that a display of emotional involvement was mandatory.

A display that was far more effusive than she felt comfortable with. Maybe because so many people she met here were trained as actors, Nora thought their style of social interaction seemed very theatrical. Any encounter in this city inspired, if not overt insincerity, a kind of exaggerated cordiality; but when babies, children, anything with a sentimental quotient was part of the scenario, it became instant opera. Soap, not grand, Nora noted.

Ginger was already enfolding Marie in the obligatory bear hug. They separated, looked into each other's moist eyes and embraced again as though they dreaded the thought of parting.

"You look so beautiful" Ginger told the mother-to-be, patting her extended belly. "You are just glowing, Marie. I can't believe you're going to be a mother. I'm so happy for you. You're going to have a sweet perfect little boy."

As Ginger and Marie embraced, Nora felt apprehensive because her turn was next and she knew that whatever she said could only seem lukewarm in comparison. She didn't want to be lukewarm.

Nora felt a surge of compassion for this woman who was close to forty and swollen into a larger pinker version of herself.

When it was her turn to hug Marie, Nora said "I hope..." then in a sudden flash she realized she was about to say "everything comes out all right" but she stopped herself and said to Marie "you enjoy this experience as much as possible."

Once on the street, Ginger dug in her heavy handbag for the car keys and Nora was struck by the stillness of Buena Vista Circle. Each of its pastel houses sat back from the street on an identical lot. Each lot had its private rectangle of lawn and its private dark shadows. She heard a rain-like patter and swish and realized that it was the sound of lawn sprinklers watering dozens of lawns in the dark.

Nora wanted to switch on the radio in the Volvo but Ginger felt like talking as she drove.

"Marie is so sweet. You know what she told me? They plan to name the baby Lawrence--that was my father's name."

Nora almost said "So what?" But she didn't, she could guess what was coming next.

"I've been thinking about my father so much lately. He died five years ago. I mean, isn't it strange that Marie would pick that name?"

Nora knew the answer: "There are no coincidences."

Ginger gripped the steering wheel tightly, excited by new possibilities. "That's right! I feel like maybe I have some special connection to this baby or something, I don't know. I mean, how many people are named Lawrence?"

"Right."

Nora was used to Ginger's California mysticism. Ginger wasn't the only one, Nora knew that many studio executives consulted psychics about personal and business decisions. In New York, people who needed help went to psychiatrists, they believed in science. Out here they had astrologers and seers—there was a general belief in systems more arcane, metaphysical.

Nora liked driving at night in Los Angeles. Four hours after the frantic evening rush, the wide boulevards and streaming freeways were practically abandoned. It was a different city after darkness obliterated the smog and the ugly buildings and the cheap advertising. After ten o'clock it was just colored lights and easy speed over smooth concrete. In fifteen minutes, the women were in a familiar Hollywood neighborhood. Ginger stopped at a traffic light on Melrose Avenue.

"Nora! She's still here! Look ! I don't believe it!"

"What? Who is? " Nora didn't know what Ginger was talking about.

"That girl we saw earlier--in the car--and her friend."

Ginger was stopped behind another car, waiting to turn at an intersection with a liquor store on one side and a gas station on the opposite corner. Then Nora saw the two teenaged girls--they were talking to some men in a car parked behind the liquor store.

"Look at them. Have they been here all this time?" Ginger sounded upset.

"Those girls are way too young, they shouldn't be here, they can't stay out on the street all night. They don't know what they're doing."

"Maybe they do know," Nora told her. In the bright light from the street she could clearly see their faces--they didn't look over sixteen years old.

Ginger was getting more and more agitated. "We have to do something."

"What can we...there's nothing we can do except call the police."

"They wouldn't even come." Ginger shook her head. "We haven't got proof of a crime or anything." She turned right at the light then rounded another corner and drove around to the liquor store intersection again.

"They obviously don't know what they're doing" Ginger couldn't take her eyes off the girls. The tall thin one did most of the talking. Her friend kept watching the sidewalk. The men in the car drove away.

There was no question about the girls' occupation at this late hour. Most of the streetwalkers stayed further east on Sunset Blvd.; these two had strayed into a residential area.

"They just don't look like prostitutes. My guess is they're runaways--probably don't know anybody in the city and have no way to get home."

"Come on Ginger, you don't know what they..."

"We can't let them stay out here" Nora had never seen Ginger
so distressed, "they don't know what they're getting into. Their
families are probably worried about them."

"You don't know that--maybe they..."

"Look how young they are." Ginger's eyes were fixed on the
two girls.

They stood casually under the bright streetlight, eyeing each car
as it came their way; their young faces seemed somehow hopeful
and engaged--not at all like the furtive, wary streetwalkers Nora
had seen in New York.

"They're drug addicts probably," Nora said.

"But they don't look strung-out; they look healthy. They must
be running away from their parents. I can tell they're nice girls.
Maybe they just don't have any idea how dangerous this is. We
can give them a ride home, or maybe call their families to come
and get them."

Ginger was now speaking in what Nora thought of as her
"therapist voice" which was a particular tone that signaled her
conviction that she knew what was good for someone else.

"Ginger, you have no idea who those girls are or what they're
into. We don't know anything about them--they're not our
responsibility. We're not in a position to help them. Really, what
can we do? " Nora tried to sound supportive and reasonable even
though she was impatient to get home.

Ginger turned to Nora "Look, the bottom line is--if we take
them off the street tonight we could be saving their lives. Nobody
else is going to help them." Ginger used her therapist voice again-
-she knew for certain what should be done.

"But you don't know who..." Nora tried to think of how to talk
her out of it. If Ginger wanted to play Mother Theresa she
couldn't stop her. It was her home she was offering as shelter;
Nora was only renting a room there.

"You want to see on the news tomorrow that they're found
dead?" Ginger had the last word, then got out of the car and began
walking towards the girls.

"What are you thinking?" Nora mouthed the words silently as
she watched tall, broad-shouldered slow-moving Ginger lumber
into the yellow glare of the streetlight where the girls were facing
the approaching traffic. Nora could see Ginger pointing at her car.

The two girls backed away from her and moved closer to each other. Nora rolled down the window so she could hear what was going on.

The taller girl seemed to be doing most of the talking. Her voice was loudly defiant. "What do you want?"

Ginger answered calmly, reassuring her "I don't want anything. But you shouldn't stay out here at this hour--it's too dangerous. You could get hurt."

"Leave us alone," the girl answered, "we have a right to be here."

"A right?" Ginger's voice was louder now, on edge. "A right? What you're doing is illegal."

The tiny brunette with the long curly hair spoke up "Are you a cop?"

Face to face with the girls now, Ginger answered, "No, I'm not a cop--I'm a psychologist."

"Shit! Leave us alone."

"Listen to me" Ginger, said, "If you two need a place to sleep tonight, I'm offering--I mean here's a chance to get off the street. I'll take you to my house."

As Ginger spoke, Nora saw a late-model convertible drive up to the curb near the corner. The smaller girl saw it first. She touched her friend's arm and pointed. Both girls eyed the convertible when it stopped.

"You girls looking for a good time?" Two middle-aged men leaned towards the curb. "We like to party."

The driver was driving with one hand, smoking a cigarette with his left elbow propped in front of the side mirror. The young girls walked closer to the convertible, hips swinging.

Just when they got within negotiating distance, Ginger stepped into the street behind the convertible and yelled at the top of her voice. "Hey you--I got your license number--I'm calling the police--I'm calling! That's 4D713--I got your number!"

The men spun around in their seats. The driver said something to his passenger and tossed his cigarette into the street. The other man held up his middle finger in a violent choppy gesture towards Ginger as the car took off with a loud squeal of tires.

"Why are you doing this to us? The shorter girl asked, a whining child's voice.

"I want to help you" Ginger glanced plaintively back at Nora, who saw that she would be required to get out of the car.

"We don't want your help."

"Where are you going to sleep tonight?" Ginger asked them.

"We don't know," the petite curly-haired girl admitted.

"Shut up, Michelle!" Her friend sounded exasperated.

"I'm offering you two a place to stay--no obligation--we just want to help."

As Ginger spoke, Nora approached and stood beside her. The night had turned cold and windy.

The tall girl looked even younger up close. Her light brown hair was baby fine. She was dressed for warm weather in a skimpy halter-top, which barely covered her small undeveloped breasts.

"What's your name?" Ginger asked her. She didn't answer.

"Michelle," Ginger asked the brunette, "what's your friend's name?"

"Jennifer."

Jennifer folded her bare arms in front of her. She was shivering slightly from the cold. She wouldn't look at Ginger.

"Don't be afraid Jennifer, we just want to help." Ginger spoke with the practiced reassuring voice of a professional therapist.

Nora suddenly felt tired and impatient "It's getting late, we can't stand here all night."

Michelle whispered something inaudible to her friend, who suddenly looked less sure of herself. In a quick dash, Jennifer grabbed Michelle's hand and the two girls ran down an alley.

"No!" Ginger shouted and ran after them.

Nora followed more slowly, reluctant to let Ginger disappear into the darkness.

"Why are you doing this?" Nora asked her, but Ginger didn't answer.

Just then, from behind a wide metal dumpster, Jennifer and little Michelle walked towards them, each carrying an overnight bag.

Ginger opened the trunk of the Volvo and the girls threw their lightweight cloth bags inside; Michelle's was pink and decorated with yellow mermaids. As they stood beside the car, Jennifer slumped in a sullen posture like she was being punished. Michelle seemed eager to go with them, maybe slightly relieved.

"Is this all you have?" Ginger asked, like she was surprised, Nora thought.

CHAPTER THREE

"Y ou mean," Ginger was looking at Jennifer, "both your parents--yours too, right Michelle --are dead?"

Jennifer and Michelle sat at the round table in Ginger's kitchen in West Hollywood with their hands around warm cups of cocoa. Jennifer was still shivering a little. Nora noticed that her bare legs were pink from the cold and both girls wore nothing but high-heeled sandals on their feet.

Jennifer stared down into her steaming cup and nodded yes.

"All four of your parents?"

Nora was tired. There was no point in asking so many questions. They obviously didn't want to talk about themselves.

"Where did you go to school?" Ginger asked the question with what sounded like sudden burning curiosity.

Michelle took a deep breath. "Jennifer grew up in Omaha. I went to school in Oxnard and the Valley and Lancaster."

Ginger nodded encouragingly "The San Fernando Valley?"

"I'm really tired" Michelle looked directly into Ginger's eyes with her wide brown eyes.

Ginger wanted the girls to feel comfortable. She leaned forward and spoke in a quiet soothing voice. "If you just tell us about…a little bit about yourselves. Maybe we can…we want to try to help."

Michelle nodded, her hands clutching the warm cup. She darted a glance at Jennifer, then looked into the cup again.

"Please tell us where you live," Ginger continued, trying to make eye contact with Jennifer who didn't, who wouldn't look up.

Jennifer kept her eyes on the steaming cup in front of her, took a small sip. Nora squirmed on the wooden kitchen chair. What did Ginger expect to find out?

"Can I just ask one more question?" Ginger looked at Jennifer.

"Go ahead" Michelle answered, eyeing her friend, then Ginger.

"Why were you…I mean, why?"

"We need money." Jennifer spoke up immediately, without hesitation. Michelle nodded in agreement.

Nora met Ginger's eyes across the table. "They need money," she told her.

Ginger nodded and got up from the table to find the extra bedding she kept in the hall closet. In the living room, Michelle and Jennifer watched as Ginger and Nora pulled open the sofa bed. The metal frame resisted like a stiff pocketknife, then sprang open with a loud thump.

"There's a bathroom right here" Ginger pointed to the door off the living room. Ginger smoothed sheets onto the thin mattress.

"Sorry we only have this one bed--but it's queen size. Bring some towels." Ginger called to Nora when she left the room.

Jennifer and Michelle went into the bathroom together, carrying their little overnight bags. Ginger could hear them giggling and talking, she was relieved that the two girls were off the street. She didn't want to think about what they might be doing now if they hadn't found their way to this room, this bed. Nora came back carrying a stack of towels.

"I'm going to sleep," she told Ginger.

Just then, Jennifer emerged from the bathroom in her nightgown--it was transparent red nylon and resembled a very short slip with ruffled top and bottom. Michelle followed, wearing a short yellow satin gown cut very low in front. She must be about a 36 D Ginger couldn't help noticing, the size Ginger had been before she'd gained weight. Ginger saw Nora's eyes widen when the girls appeared in their sleeping attire. She hoped Nora wouldn't say something snide or sarcastic because the girls needed to feel secure about themselves, not self-conscious. Ginger avoided looking at Nora and didn't react at all to what the girls were wearing. It's sad, really, she thought, they are so young. Nora made a short snorting sound which she turned into a cough-- she caught Ginger's eye and raised her eyebrows.

"Baby dolls" Nora said under her breath to Ginger as the two guests got settled into the fold out bed. Ginger hoped they didn't hear.

"Isn't that what they're called?' Nora kept her voice low. " It's a classic look--Fredericks of Hollywood circa nineteen-sixty."

How would Jennifer and Michelle feel if they thought we were ridiculing them, Ginger worried. It really isn't funny. Ginger hoped Nora would be more sensitive to the girls' feelings.

She watched as Michelle made herself comfortable in the bed. With her two tiny forearms she spread her thick dark hair over the sides of the pillow in a gesture quick and graceful as a ballerina. Ginger stood beside the bed and looked down at Michelle looking up at her; she felt a strong impulse to bend down and kiss the girl goodnight.

"Can we watch TV?" Jennifer didn't sound tired.

"Okay," Ginger said, "but just for a little while--you two need your sleep." Ginger turned on the television, which was not far from the foot of the bed.

"I'll turn the lights off" and Ginger left the room in darkness lit by the flicker of talking faces, the cackling of audience.

From her own bedroom on the other side of the wall, Ginger could hear the sound of the television. She considered going back and turning the sound down but she thought probably they wouldn't keep it on long; she could wait for a while. She searched in her bedside drawer for some diazepam--just a half tablet to help her sleep.

Nora had trouble getting used to how quiet the neighborhood was at night. In Manhattan, traffic and ambulances provided a constant nighttime soundtrack; but her upstairs bedroom in the house on Westborne Street was so quiet, even the hum of the refrigerator was audible. Nora got out of bed and put on her robe and walked quietly down the stairs to the kitchen. As she felt for the light switch she heard noises and caught sight of movement--

she froze and stopped breathing for a second--then she saw Jennifer.

"I couldn't sleep. I'm not tired," the girl said, standing in the bright kitchen light in her red nylon nightie.

Nora said "Oh" then "I can't sleep either."

Nora saw the pack of cigarettes in Jennifer's hand. "Can I have one of those?"

"You smoke?" Jennifer asked, surprised.

"No, I quit" Nora said. That explained not having cigarettes.

Jennifer took a Camel filter out of her pack and handed it to Nora; then she put another cigarette into her mouth and clicked a plastic lighter into flame.

"Wait," Nora put her hand on Jennifer's, you can't light that in here. This is a no-smoking house."

"Shit," said Jennifer.

Nora opened the narrow back door which led from the kitchen into a small laundry room leading to the back yard.

"We can sit out here."

Jennifer found an old blanket on the washing machine and wrapped it around her shoulders. She followed Nora outside. They sat on rusty lawn chairs under a tall tree. Nora caught a whiff of the sweet citrus smell of the Magnolia tree's white flowers. Huge leathery leaves littered the small yard.

"It's cold", Jennifer said, wrapping the blanket around her shoulders like an Indian. In the dim electric glare of the streetlights, the dark shapes behind the house gradually came into focus.

"When I moved in I told Ginger I was a non-smoker," Nora explained to Jennifer.

"Why?"

"She's really against it. I mean, I didn't lie. I'm not a chain smoker or anything. Sometimes I just like…"

"So this is her house?"

"Yeah. She used to live here with her husband." Nora took a long drag on the cigarette. "After the divorce she had to buy him out."

"She has to pay her ex-husband?" Jennifer was curious. "How long have you lived here?"

"Almost a year.   My sister knew that Ginger needed a roommate. She used to be her therapist."

"Your sister's?"

"Right.   So when I left New York and wanted to move here, I needed a place to stay and…"

"How come you didn't get your own place?"

"To save money." Nora hated being interrogated.

"It costs a lot to live," Jennifer said sympathetically.

"Yeah, it does. Are you and Michelle thinking of getting a place of your own?

"Maybe." Jennifer didn't waste words.

"Where have you been staying--I mean, before tonight?"   Nora tried to sound casual, not parental.   "Last night, for example."

"It just depends." The hostility was gone from Jennifer's voice. Maybe she was too tired to maintain her defensive stance. "Where ever we end up--you know, at the end of the night.   It just depends."

"With friends?"

"Sort of."

"Do you know many people in L.A.?" Nora tried to imagine Jennifer's daily routine.

"What do you think?"

"I think you might be running away from something," Nora told Jennifer.

"So?" Now the anger was back in her voice. She'd pushed too far. Jennifer was defensive again. "That's not your problem."

"Are you in some kind of trouble?"

"Look, we just don't have any money, all right?   That's our trouble--it's a big problem. Is that so hard to understand?"

"No" said Nora quickly, "it isn't."

They let that float for a minute as they smoked. Jennifer sat very still as though she was thinking or very angry. Nora couldn't tell. Probably Jennifer had a problem trusting anyone; Nora didn't take it personally. Ginger said they showed her I.D. and they were both eighteen.   They could have forged driving licenses. Maybe they were younger than that.

Nora rubbed her cigarette out in the wet grass. "I'm going to bed," she told Jennifer.

"I think I'll just stay here for a while."

Nora couldn't see the girl's face; she was bundled up with the blanket hooded over her head. "You'll freeze out here," Nora said, then she thought--I'm acting like her mother. "I'll leave the door unlocked—be sure to lock the bolt when you come in, okay?"

CHAPTER FOUR

Ginger woke up early the next morning because she wanted to be the first one in the kitchen. She always began the day by reading the Los Angeles Times with her breakfast. Ginger measured six cups of water into the coffee maker, wondering if the girls drank coffee and whether there was enough milk in the refrigerator. As she filled the circular paper filter with finely ground beans she noticed Jennifer's scuffed brown handbag left hanging on a kitchen chair. Ginger lifted Jennifer's bag onto the table, sat down in her usual chair with her back to the stove and opened the paper. The front page featured an aerial photograph of a desert car chase. The police had caught the man who abducted a junior high school girl last week.

Ginger remembered her first year of living in L.A. She got lost on the freeway one day and drove so far in the wrong direction that gradually there was no more city, and fewer and fewer cars until she found herself alone on a two-lane highway in the desert. If you drove East, she knew, after a while there was just nothing--a dry hot expanse of sandy dirt, barren of vegetation, trees, houses, any sign of life. The city was bordered by the empty desert on the east, the cold Pacific Ocean on the west and identical featureless suburbs all the way up the coast to Santa Barbara and south to San Diego.

Ginger could see from the kitchen table that the living room door was closed. They're still asleep, she thought; they must have been exhausted.

Ginger always felt a little sad after reading the paper, but it was a habit. She thought it was important to know what was going on in the city. Her mother had been president of the League of Women Voters in Philadelphia. She felt a tug of guilt when she realized that she had begun to skip the Metro Section, which almost daily featured a large full-color picture of a grieving or angry relative on the front page. The child, parent, spouse or sibling of the aggrieved would be described in the story below the photograph as shot by police; shot by a family member; burned alive in sub-standard unsafe housing; or killed by a deranged classmate or fellow worker in a school/ workplace where such a thing had never happened before. There were always a multitude of victims. The dead ones whose violent deaths were described graphically in print; and the live ones photographed in contorted undignified close-ups. One picture is worth a thousand words, Ginger thought, steeling herself to examine a photo of several weeping black teenagers placing flowers and candles on a sidewalk somewhere in south-central where a policeman had accidentally shot a young girl. She felt grateful that the editorial policy of the Times seemed to prohibit publishing photographs of bleeding corpses.

Ginger carried the newspaper into the small bathroom off the kitchen. It was very fortunate, she realized now, that they had added this extra bathroom when Tim...when they had remodeled the house. At the same time, they had re-finished all the wood floors and enlarged the kitchen and re-tiled the upstairs bathroom. Ginger couldn't help but feel a little twinge of victory that all the renovation on the house had been done before Tim...before he left. Before the divorce, when there were two incomes, when she had hopes that they might one day sell this house and move to a larger place-- she knew that was unlikely to happen now.

Ginger spent her childhood in Philadelphia in a two-story brick house which had a full attic and four bedrooms on the second floor with a wide front porch shaded by ancient tall trees,.   Ginger thought about the tall elms and lush maple trees of Pennsylvania. She missed those trees. The vegetation in California seemed stunted and brown in comparison to those towering trees whose shapes she remembered like architecture. When Ginger finished washing her hands and walked back into the kitchen she was genuinely shocked.

"What are you doing?"

Nora kept her voice low, with a glance towards the living room. "I'm looking through Jennifer's stuff."

Ginger saw the contents of Jennifer's purse spread out upon the table: A disposable lighter, a pack of cigarettes, a smeared tube of lipstick, chewing gum, two condoms, a round plastic dispenser of birth control pills, some rolled-up articles of dirty underwear, a chipped pink compact, white sunglasses, tampons, used Kleenex.

"You can't do this. It's an invasion of privacy. I can't believe you'd..."

"I'm looking for drugs," Nora told her as she unzipped a red billfold.

"Don't!" Ginger stopped her. "You are violating her right to privacy."

Nora wasn't deterred. "What if she had heroin in here? We'd be liable, wouldn't we?"

Ginger looked anxiously in the direction of the sleeping guests, then at the table strewn with Jennifer's belongings. She gingerly picked up a circle of black nylon which at first appeared to be a headband until she saw it was thong underwear. Ginger thought she heard a sound from the living room and dropped the undergarment.

"This just isn't right, Nora, put it all back please."

Nora casually examined the various objects as she replaced them in Jennifer's bag. She held up a foil-wrapped condom and considered the fine print on the package.

Ginger was impatient--she wanted all of Jennifer's things replaced in the bag as soon as possible. She glanced nervously towards the living room and back at the pile of things on the table.

"Please," she said to Nora in a low tense voice, "we have no right."

Nora put everything back and closed the bag. She poured some coffee and glanced at the front page of the newspaper.

"I have a dentist appointment at nine-thirty," Ginger continued. "And after that I have two clients at the office. Promise me you won't let her know you did this. We have to earn their trust."

"I'm wondering who they are," Nora said "why won't they tell us anything?"

Ginger hurried to find her briefcase and her jacket. "I'll be back around one." She stood looking down at Nora who continued reading the Calendar section of the Times with her feet propped on a chair.

"Please Nora, this is just a temporary situation. Let's try to, you know, treat them with a little respect."

After Ginger left, Nora took the newspaper and piled it carefully on the floor near the wastebasket. She decided not to read any more of the morning paper because it interfered with her work. Her mind was at its best when she woke up, Nora thought, she didn't want to get depressed. She needed to get at least one scene finished before dinner tonight. She planned to go to the Beverly Hills library and write; she liked the atmosphere there, it was cool and quiet. It reminded her of her university days when she was an art history major. Some vestigial part of her brain wanted to slow down and enjoy the hot cloudless day. But it was already October--summer was over. There was no transition in sight; no sign of a shifting season. Nora looked forward to the first rain of the year. People really didn't slow down at all here during the summer, she thought. In New York, you feel the affects of weather--you move a little slower in the heat, relax a little. Then you feel the city speed up again in the fall when the first cool days …Nora didn't want to think about New York. She didn't want to remember Tony, he was out of her life forever. She got ready to leave the house and wrote a note on a file card: "Ginger back at one p.m.: help yourself to coffee." She propped the note next to the glass sugar bowl on the table.

March Redhill looked out her front window at two people on the sidewalk. Earlier, she'd watched her neighbor's Volvo pull out of the driveway next door; then the white BMW on the street in front had driven away. Two teenaged girls were walking past her front yard. She'd seen them come out of the house next door and stand still for a minute, the two of them, looking down one end of the street and up the other, like they couldn't make up their mind which way to go. Some of the neighbors walked their dogs, but these girls didn't have a dog. Also, they were wearing very high heels, noted March, wondering if they were Ginger Wilson's relatives.

March stood peeking through the pink and yellow curtains framing her picture window in her small tidy living room. "Wonder who those girls are?" she asked Leonardo, the parrot, whose large domed cage was near the window. "It's not Ginger's daughter, she's older than that."

March had lived on Westborne street since1968; longer than anyone she knew except old Mr. Tebby across the way. His dog died several years ago. She remembered when the Wilsons had moved in next door with their young daughter. Ginger's husband Tim had often helped March wheel the heavy garbage can out to the curb on collection days and she missed him; ex-husband now. March was sorry he'd left; she'd never been friends with Ginger. Maybe because March was aware of a faint scent of disapproval when Ginger occasionally spoke to her on the street. Ginger thought she knew what was best for other people, March could see it in her eyes. Like that Hilary Clinton woman--thought she knew better than anyone else. Other people, a large group, March thought, there are more of them all the time.

The two young girls walked slowly past March's house carrying little duffel bags on straps over their shoulders. She watched through the window looking out over her small garden planted with flat-leaved banana palms, overgrown jade plants and fuzzy cacti.

"In those high heels they won't be going far" March said to Leonardo. "Look how they're dressed,"

She made tssking noises with her tongue. The parrot cocked his green head in the bright morning light.

"I wonder where those girls are going."

CHAPTER FIVE

Michelle's foot hurt.   The back strap of her shoe was rubbing against the thin part of her heel and it was already blistered. If she kept on walking like this, in a minute it would be bleeding.

"Jennifer, she said she'd be back soon. I think we should at least say goodbye."

"What for?" Jennifer didn't look at her friend.

"These shoes are killing my feet. Where are we going anyway?"

Jennifer didn't slow her determined pace. "Did you notice which way we came last night? Wasn't Sunset that way?" She indicated the direction several blocks distant where the concrete sidewalk blurred and shimmered in the heat.

"No." Michelle answered, "I don't know. It's too far to walk."

"How do you know?"

"I can't walk any further than that next stop sign," Michelle declared, and Jennifer knew it was no use trying to get her to change her mind.

Michelle always wants to quit when she has a problem, Jennifer thought; she's not a fighter, she always wants to quit. I'm not afraid of anything, Jennifer thought, but she didn't say it out loud, she said it inside herself.

Out loud she said, "So your foot hurts, big deal."

They stopped at an intersection and Michelle sat down on the curb near a parked car. There was no traffic on the street and nobody walking in the ripening heat of the day. Jennifer saw a man in shorts standing beside a tree with a black poodle on a leash. He was only a block away; she thought maybe they could ask him for directions.

"Come on Michelle, it can't be that much further."

"No Jennifer." Now she was whining. "I don't want to walk. I'm going back. Ginger will give us a ride."

"Where to?" asked Jennifer. She preferred to move until there was a good reason to stop; to let the destination find them when the time was right.

"I don't know."

"You want to go back and stay with your aunt?" Jennifer asked.

"No!" Michelle almost wailed. She didn't like to make decisions. Jennifer knew Michelle needed to have decisions made for her. Michelle took off her shoe and touched her heel--there was blood on her hand.

"Look at my foot--I'm bleeding. Jennifer, can't we go back ? Please ?"

Jennifer sighed and helped Michelle to stand up. "Just one more block," she suggested.

"No!" Michelle's brown eyes had tears in them now.

Jennifer didn't want her to start crying. They turned around and went back the way they'd come without further discussion.

When they reached Ginger's house, Jennifer remembered--the door had locked behind them. There was no one at home.

"We don't have a key--shit."

The two girls sat down to wait on the concrete steps that led to the door to Ginger's stucco house. Tall clumps of spiky flowers that exactly resembled alert orange birds with long pointed beaks and sharp purple tongues grew beside the doorway. The sky was a glare of white; it had been six months since a heavy rain had fallen on West Hollywood. The woody shrubbery in the garden looked parched and dusty; the lawn was patched with brown.

"I'm thirsty," said Jennifer.

"You'll have to wait 'til we can get back inside," Michelle told her.

Jennifer saw a garden hose hooked up to a faucet at the side of the house. She turned on the water, letting it run warm for a while until it cooled enough to drink. She had just lifted the hose to her mouth when Ginger's Volvo pulled into the driveway. Michelle jumped up and clapped her hands. Like it's a big treat all of a sudden, Jennifer thought, to see Ginger again. Still, the possibility of cooling off and getting something cold to drink and maybe a free lunch had a calming effect on Jennifer's morning irritation. Michelle never thought about money because Michelle had never had to work at a job because her mother…But Jennifer knew how much things cost. Even to buy a hamburger would deplete their cash supply--even if we eat at Mickey D's, Jennifer calculated, as she watched Ginger hurry up the walk, keys jangling.

" I'm sorry you had to wait," Ginger said, "have you been here long?"

"Yeah, I'm really thirsty," Jennifer told her.

"I think we have some cold drinks in the refrigerator, help yourself. I need to make some phone calls." Ginger went to her room and Michelle and Jennifer looked at each other and smiled.

Suddenly, Jennifer was glad they'd come back. The kitchen was clean and sunny with comfortable wooden chairs pulled up to a round table. Michelle opened a can of root beer and put her feet up on a chair.

"They have an ice maker," Michelle pointed to a chrome apparatus on the refrigerator door.

"A nice maker?" asked Jennifer, and Michelle's laugh burbled and burst.

"Ice!"she told her friend, giggling.

Jennifer pushed down on the lever and ice cubes dropped out of the door onto the little grate below. She held one against the middle of her forehead and moved it over her eyebrows and temples.

"Can I have one?" Michelle held out her hand for ice.

Jennifer gave her some and Michelle rubbed the ice cube on her sore foot. Jennifer got another ice cube and rubbed the sole of Michelle's other foot, roughly tickling her.

"Stop," Michelle, shrieked, giggling, "Stop."

Jennifer rubbed the ice cube over Michelle's small plump toes, which curled up and kicked. "Stop it" Michelle was squirming and giggling but Jennifer persisted. After a brief struggle, Michelle kicked Jennifer against the table, spilling her drink.

"Now look what you did" Michelle searched for a paper towel and wiped up the spilled liquid quickly, as if afraid of being caught.

Ginger was on the phone for a while. When she returned to the kitchen she told Michelle and Ginger she wanted to take them to a clinic for tests.

"Why?" Jennifer asked.

"I want to make sure you're okay," Ginger explained in a reassuring voice. "It's for your own good."

Ginger leaned out the car window trying to see down Santa Monica Boulevard where four lanes of traffic had come to a standstill. "What's the problem, I wonder." Ginger's hands clutching the steering wheel of the Volvo felt damp with perspiration. "Nothing's moving."

"Looks like there's an accident" Michelle stuck her head out the right window so she could see better.

Jennifer was sprawled in the back seat, her head propped on the armrest as she wedged her bare feet against the opposite window.

"How long will this take?" She asked in a bored voice.

Ginger turned briefly to look at Jennifer. She doesn't like me sitting like this, Jennifer thought, but Ginger spoke calmly.

"The clinic is only a few blocks from here. They told me we can just walk in, no appointment necessary. It's a simple blood test. You need to know."

The traffic began moving again. Jennifer shifted up onto one arm to look at the street ahead.

"Doing this will help you feel you're in control" Ginger kept her eyes on the street as she talked. "I want you to take responsibility for your own decisions." To her left, Ginger saw the Clinic sign in a crowded row of storefronts, next to a dry cleaners. She drove down the block to the next intersection and signaled left, waiting for the oncoming traffic to pause; then she saw the No Left Turn sign.

"I'll have to turn left at the next street I guess." Ginger kept up this running commentary in a cheery voice, like she wanted to reassure her passengers.

She's the one who's worried, Jennifer thought, I'm not afraid to get a blood test.

Ginger took a right at the next light, then drove around the block and approached the storefront again.

"There it is, " Ginger said, "If I can find a parking place."

She swiveled her head to look at the street behind her, then sped up and turned down a side street.

"Are you getting stressed?" Michelle asked.

"I'm just afraid they'll close before we get in there." Ginger kept her eyes on the street.

"You should take a pill," Jennifer crossed her arms to pillow her head against the door and lifted her feet against the cool glass of the car window.

"Prozac anyone?" Both girls giggled at that.

"I'm doing this to help you." Ginger didn't think it was funny.

"Thanks Ginger." Michelle couldn't handle somebody being mad at her.

"Unbelievable, there's a parking place. Amazing." Ginger's voice reverted to cheerful again. We're going to make it, I think."

An hour and a half later, Jennifer held the door open and Michelle and Ginger walked out of the clinic onto Santa Monica Boulevard.

"That wasn't so bad was it?" Ginger was in charge now.

The clinic was air-conditioned and efficient. Ginger helped Michelle and Jennifer with the forms and waited while the test was performed. After an hour, they walked back to the car parked on the street around the corner.

"I feel a little dizzy" Jennifer said.

"Do you want some orange juice?" Ginger took everything so seriously.

"Don't worry about me," Jennifer told her, "I'll be okay."

When they got to where the Volvo was parked, Ginger found a blue envelope stuck under the windshield wiper. "We were five minutes past the expiration time and they gave me a ticket." Ginger announced.

"A parking ticket? That sucks," said Michelle.

Driving home, Ginger was quiet for a few blocks. She stopped at a red light behind eight other cars. "The important thing to remember is that you own your life, know what I mean? You can make choices that work for you or work against you. You're in charge."

Jennifer kicked off her shoes and stretched out on the back seat. She felt like going to sleep.

"Like getting a parking ticket," Ginger continued. "That's a consequence of my actions. Everything we do has consequences. We all have to be aware of that."

"Everything?" Jennifer piped up from the back seat.

Ginger's voice rose: "Every choice we make is determined by our world-view--how you feel about yourself. If you feel you're worthless, you'll act that way."

Jennifer sat up and rolled down the car window and eased her head into the moving stream of warm air. The street smelled pungently greasy after the stale air-conditioned clinic. Her eyes watered and her hair lifted off her neck.

"Air-conditioning doesn't work with the window open, Jennifer; roll it up please."

Ginger spoke looking straight ahead as she drove, glancing in the rear-view mirror.

"So you mean," said Jennifer, looking at the back of Ginger's head, "We are what we think we are--is that it?"

"Yes, basically." Ginger was so sure of herself.

"I'm a joke." Jennifer announced, just to see what Ginger would say.

Michelle turned around and looked at Jennifer and laughed.

Jennifer's mouth twisted into a smile that she suppressed. "I'm a saint." she said. Michelle giggled and punched Jennifer's upper arm. Then they both giggled for a while as Ginger drove home.

CHAPTER SIX

Mr. Martinelli looked at his watch. It was eight-thirty and the dining room of his cozy restaurant was almost filled. He sat at a small table near the bar sipping espresso beside his wife, a small-boned woman in a fashionable dress who rarely spoke. The light of many red-shaded lamps filled the room with a rosy glow. Mr. Martinelli watched white-jacketed waiters carry plates and bottles of wine across the flowered carpeting amid the muted clatter of silverware and conversation while a Puccini aria played in the background.

Luigi Martinelli spent every evening except Sunday at his table near the door to Martinelli's, his restaurant. He greeted many of his patrons by name; after the third or fourth visit they were embraced as friends. The restaurateur said something to his wife, which made her smile; then he walked over to table number twelve near the corner and offered his congratulations.

"Happy Birthday, Mr. Downing."

Dan Downing was having dinner with Nora Gregorian, who had made the reservations in her name. Mr. Martinelli bowed slightly and kissed Nora's hand. She wore her hair pinned up for this occasion and large silver and coral earrings.

Nora saw that Dan was enjoying the attention. "Did you like the wine?' Mr. M. asked and both Dan and Nora answered: "wonderful...yes."

Nora smiled benevolently at both men and they both looked admiringly at her.

After the amiable Mr. Martinelli returned to his station, Dan looked at Nora and said: "You want commitment? I'll dedicate myself to you heart and soul, tooth and eye; hands, stomach, knees, thighs, all yours. My dedication is for life, our lives. Nothing, nobody, can separate us. I'm willing to work for you darling, for us. Always."

For a few seconds, Nora considered Dan's words. She was directly opposite him at the small table. The lighting couldn't have been more flattering to his face. He had such long dark lashes over his earnest blue eyes. Unfortunately, he'd recently cut his hair very short. It pleased Nora that Dan didn't cultivate a tan like so many California males. His complexion was pale, emphasizing his eyes; though now, with much of his hair gone, she thought his scalp looked a little too white.

"Wait...stomach? Did you say stomach?"

Dan looked down at the sheet of paper he held "You don't like it?" He asked her.

"Would he say stomach?" Nora's voice was dubious, pained. She tried not to reject things arbitrarily but...

"Gut?" Dan offered, taking a pen out of his inside jacket pocket.

"Just cross out stomach," Nora directed.

"I know this isn't a good time to get into the script--I just wanted to tell you about my idea for the hospital scene. You know--where he goes to her room and she's just regained consciousness?"

"Yeah?"

"What if..." Dan began, but Nora interrupted.

"He takes all his clothes off and jumps into the hospital bed with her. She pulls the I.V. tubes out of her arms and they fuck like rabbits." Nora looked into Dan's eyes as she finished the sentence.

A smile played on the corners of Dan's lips but he kept his face straight. He quickly glanced at the diners at the next table to see if they'd overheard Nora's comment. He sipped some wine and replied dryly "No, that's not what I had in mind."

He's embarrassed, Nora thought, it's so easy to shock him, too easy.

"Go on" she said to Dan.

"No more script talk" Dan put away the notebook he had opened. "This can wait until later."

Nora raised her glass "Happy Birthday, Dan."

"Thanks Nora, you've been...grand. You didn't have to do this."

"You'd do the same for me if I was stuck at home on my birthday and had nobody to celebrate with." Nora told him.

"As a matter of fact, I would. You know I would."

He probably would, Nora thought.

"When is your birthday, anyway?"

"I'll give you plenty of warning" Nora told him.

She settled back into the flowered fabric of the banquette against the rose-colored wall of the busy room. Dan loved the oso bucco here and he loved to eat. He's just turned thirty-four, Nora thought, he's like a growing boy. Sometimes she forgot how young he was.

Dan managed a busy restaurant in Beverly Hills to pay the bills until he got work in the film industry. He didn't know many people in the city. He was hoping to sell the script they were working on, perhaps produce it. His best friend from film school had just produced and directed a low-budget horror film that had grossed six million dollars.

"We should plan on meeting as often as possible now that we're more than halfway finished." Dan said. He looked forward to the writing sessions with Nora.

"What's your schedule like next week?

Under the Martinelli's awning that stretched from the door to the street, Nora and Dan stood on the sidewalk and waited for her car.

"Thanks for driving. Sometimes I feel really crippled," Dan told Nora when her BMW pulled up to the curb and the attendant hopped out and handed her the keys.

"You can't go on like this much longer," Nora told him. Dan tipped the man and got in beside her.

"Don't ask me to give up hope."

Nora looked in the rear view mirror and saw an opening; she plunged into the stream of cars and turned off the radio.

"Dan," Nora told him, not without sympathy in her voice, "You have to face reality."

"It's hard. I loved that old Mustang. I drove that car all the way from Jackson Hole."

"It was stolen" Nora used an even patient tone such as a parent might use with a stubborn child. "Your car was stolen and now you have to get a new car."

"It won't be the same," Dan said.

"You'll have to work through your grief."

Nora drove slowly down Melrose Avenue past dark storefronts interspersed with one-story cafes and bars displaying jumpy neon signs. A few clumps of pedestrians walked in the dimly lit streets towards their parked cars.

"The insurance man said to wait three months. They might find it." Dan said.

"They never do. They don't ever find stolen cars. They don't even look. It's gone--your car is gone." Nora had never been so emphatic about the subject before, but she thought Dan was dangerously close to total denial.

Dan didn't reply. His pale face with the new short haircut tightened with regret and sadness. In the shifting light of the headlights and streetlights Nora thought she saw him brush away a tear.

"I should never have parked it on the street."

"Hey, come on, don't...don't blame yourself."

Nora was sometimes surprised at how close to the surface Dan's emotions were. It made her feel vaguely protective of him and, she thought, it made her mistrust him. She changed the subject.

"I worked on that hospital scene today. We'll go over that tonight."

"Great" Dan replied, "I hope we can get some of these questions settled. My week is really getting busy. You know they fired Ernie, so now I'm the only one there from Tuesday through Friday."

"But we'll still do three nights a week, right?" Asked Nora.

"Definitely." Dan's voice was positive again. Writing the script together had been his idea--he'd optioned a novel set in 1920 by a dead British writer.

Nora remembered how depressed she'd been last winter when a pilot she wrote and helped produce failed to get picked up by NBC. She had enrolled in a weekend screen-writing seminar and found herself sitting next to Dan, who had just come back from an extended stay in Nepal where he'd gone trekking. He was tan and his hair was longer then. He'd offered to lend her his notes. He seemed so full of enthusiasm and confidence. With him, it was easy to start something new and forget her disappointment. Now, after they had worked together for seven months, Nora had second thoughts. Still, she wasn't going to quit on the project until it was finished. She always finished what she started.

When Dan and Nora entered the house they found Jennifer and Michelle in the kitchen sitting at the round table drinking beer out of small juice glasses.

"Oh, Nora. Hi!" Jennifer greeted them with a note of surprise in her voice.

It was warm in the kitchen and Michelle was wearing the yellow satin nightgown. Jennifer wore what appeared to be an extra large man's T-shirt with nothing underneath. Michelle looked at Dan and then looked at Jennifer and began to giggle. She had a way of lowering her eyes and shaking quietly with mirth.

"Dan, I'd like you to meet Jennifer and Michelle," Nora's voice was polite, neutral, "they're staying with us for a while--for a little while."

Dan greeted the girls and they appraised him carefully. Michelle stopped giggling; she looked Dan in the eye but Jennifer didn't.

"What did you two do today?" Nora asked them as she reached for coffee filters and ran water into the glass coffee pot.

"Went to the clinic" Jennifer answered.

"We're okay," Michelle added. "We got our test results-- negative."

"We're celebrating!" Jennifer looked directly at Nora with a happy smile. Nora saw a quart bottle of beer on the table.

Michelle held up her glass. This is Japanese beer--Ginger said we could drink it."

"That's great" said Nora, then hesitated before she added. "Listen, Dan and I usually work here in the kitchen. Were you going to...?"

Jennifer looked up at Nora and Dan standing near the sink like they weren't sure where to sit. "What did you two do tonight ?" she asked. "Were you out on a date? Is this your date night? "

"Dan and I are writing partners," Nora said. "We work together."

"At night?'

"Sometimes," Dan answered, sitting down in a chair opposite Jennifer, meeting her curious stare. "I work at a day job."

Jennifer asked Dan "What are you two writing?"

"Jennifer, do you mind if we..." Nora began.

"A film script," Dan told her.

"What's it about?" Michelle wanted to know.

Dan answered, "It's a love story about a man and a woman in 1920."

Michelle and Jennifer exchanged a look; Jennifer's eyes rolled sideways. The idea seemed to amuse them.

"Listen Jennifer, Michelle, do you mind..." Nora's tone was considerate, respectful. "I'd really appreciate it if you two moved into the living room. You can watch TV while we work."

Jennifer took the beer bottle and her glass and started out of the kitchen. Michelle followed with her nightgown slipping down her arm; she stopped at the doorway, looked back over her shoulder, smiled a demure smile and said "Goodnight, Danny."

Nora watched Dan watch the two girls walk out of the room. He looked at their bare feet, their legs. She heard them whispering and giggling. Then the loud TV voice of someone asking a question and someone answering dissolved in television laughter abruptly muted by a closed door.

Dan arranged some papers on the kitchen table. "Can we read over this dialog again for the party scene?"

Nora read, "I thought you were like all the rest of those people."

"Couldn't you tell?" Dan took the other voice.

"That you were different? No, I was stupid."

"And I was young."

Dan tried to read Nora's expression. It wasn't easy to tell what she was thinking. Sometimes she went along with an idea for a while then abruptly rejected it. She was quick to jump ahead, to see where things would end up while Dan was still searching. But Dan understood the emotional arc of the story--a man loves a woman who is trying to destroy herself. She's proud, beautiful and damaged. He believes in the healing power of love. But that's not the whole story, Dan thought. He believes that the force of his love, the passion he feels, is the source of his own transformation.

Nora poured coffee and picked up a sheet of paper. Dan had just scribbled some long sentences across the margin. Nora appreciated Dan's dedication--he was never lazy, he never got depressed. He wasn't a very experienced writer, but he took writing seriously and he took her seriously. Nora remembered her last bout of depression--the gray, lifeless rock bottom of not caring, not wanting, not hoping. Dan never seemed to lose his basic good humor, his buoyancy--he'd learned to float. He didn't allow himself to be submerged, inundated, overwhelmed. She counted on him to remain steady while she circled and parried.

Nora talked about the Iris character--she wanted to work out a back-story describing her childhood. She thought she should research British women's education before World War One. Dan agreed but he didn't stay focused. He was restless and wanted to tell Nora about his boss, the restaurant owner, who was in Las Vegas gambling again.

"He was gone most of last week. His wife was in the restaurant today at lunch, she seemed worried. She told me he was due back tonight. I hope he made it. I think he's got a gambling problem. He may be losing more than he can afford."

"That's too bad." Nora had never met these people and didn't want to.

" Hey, I'm sorry. I know we agreed we wouldn't take work time to talk about personal stuff--I'm just venting."

Nora made it a point never to share personal information with Dan unless it directly related to the story they were writing. That's a word Ginger always uses, Nora recalled, "venting" like steam or exhaust fumes.

It was almost two a.m. when Dan left. Nora looked over what she'd written in the notebook she carried with her; she tried to keep a daily journal. She absently leafed through and saw a list she'd made over a month ago. Priorities: Find agent, finish script, expand circle of friends. Nora could hear the tittering of the TV coming from the living room though the door was closed. They might have gone to sleep and left the television on, she thought. Nora quietly opened the door to the living room where both girls were in bed on the turned-out sofa. The bluish light from the screen illuminated the motionless forms of two bodies.

Nora walked over and turned off the television and Jennifer sat up and turned on a table lamp. Michelle shifted, she was awake too.

"Nora? Did he go home?"

Both girls were sitting up in bed.

"Yes," Nora answered Jennifer, "Dan left.'

Jennifer asked "Don't you and Danny sleep together?"

"Goodnight." Said Nora, moving towards the door.

"You can tell us." Jennifer seemed genuinely disappointed not to be taken into Nora's confidence.

"What do you want to know?" Nora asked her. "About MY sex life?" She shrugged "What could I possibly tell you two about fucking?"

Giggling, both girls leaned forward, wide-awake.

Jennifer adopted a mocking childish voice. "Please Nora, tell us a bedtime story. I can't go to sleep this early, we're used to working nights."

"I can't go to sleep either." Michelle chimed in. "Tell us a story."

"Okay," Nora said. She sat near Michelle's knees on the edge of the thin mattress. "Once upon a time there was a girl who hoped and waited all night for her prince to come but he didn't."

"Maybe she didn't do what the prince liked" Jennifer chimed in, mock-babyish, "that's why he didn't come."

"Maybe the prince liked the princess to suck his cock," said Michelle. .

Both girls dissolved into high-pitched giggles. Nora kept her mouth from smiling. Her dark eyebrows rose higher as she questioned Jennifer.

"Do you ever have orgasms?"

"In my dreams," Michelle answered.

Jennifer said, "Wet dreams--yeah. Explosion in waterworld." They couldn't stop giggling.

Nora kept it up. "How late do you work, usually? Like an eight-hour night?"

"Depends on the customers" Jennifer answered, "When they're finished, we're finished. Pay day. "

You're real professionals," said Nora.

"Bona-fide hoes," Michelle, declared.

A sleepy voice came from the doorway: "You're keeping me awake. What's going on in here?" Ginger wore the long flannel nightgown with blue rosebuds that her mother had sent her.

There was a second of silence, then Jennifer said, "Nora was just teaching us how to masturbate."

"Are you interested in manual or automatic?" Nora turned and glanced at Ginger, then back to Jennifer, who met her eyes.

"It's kind of late. I was hoping to get a little sleep," Ginger's tone was almost apologetic.

"Okay." Nora stood up, "time for me to go to bed."

"Can I get a drink of water?" Michelle asked.

"Of course," Ginger said graciously.

Michelle walked into the bathroom. Jennifer slipped down under the covers, only her eyes moved above the sheet.

"Good night" Nora threw Jennifer a little wave before she walked out. Ginger closed the living room door and followed her into the kitchen.

"You know," Ginger said as Nora put coffee mugs in the sink, "self-esteem is the key. They're seeking an identity. I think we can help them find...I don't know...some answers."

"Right" said Nora.

"We don't even know for certain if they really...you know, maybe they're just imitating prostitute behavior, they're certainly not hardened criminals. They see themselves as sex objects but...well they feel safe here, I think," Ginger said. "At least they're off the streets and out of danger. There's a chance they can make some real changes if...Anyway, Nora, let's try to help them. It's worth a try, isn't it ?"

Nora shrugged. "I hope so. Goodnight, Ginger."

CHAPTER SEVEN

"Iris left the city, but at this point John doesn't know where she's gone."

Dan spoke to the ceiling as he paced the bare wood floor in front of the tiled fireplace which was one of the things about Dan's place that Nora especially liked. The rented one-story wooden bungalow was originally built as a summer cottage near the beach in Santa Monica. The 1930's fireplace tiles were glazed amber and green and the hinged wood-framed windows opened with old-style brass handles. A red and black Navajo blanket covered a sagging sofa in the crowded living room where Dan's bicycle leaned near the door.

A fresh breeze blew through the open windows. Nora sat and typed at the cluttered dining table where papers and dishes lay uncollected. On Saturday afternoons they usually worked on the screenplay from ten until five or so. It was cooler near the beach.

"Maybe he goes to visit a friend of hers, tries to find out..."

"They have no mutual friends" Nora replied, seated at the keyboard, fingers at rest.

"Her brother" Dan reminded her "remember? The alcoholic."

Dan liked to pace. He raised his arms in the air and stretched, almost touching the low ceiling.

"He's usually at home in his apartment-- his flat, drinking. That's where John first met Iris."

"That's right." Nora watched Dan pace. "John goes there and remembers their first night together. That unforgettable night of passionate love." Nora paused, thinking "What's the brother's name?"

"Let's call him Geoffrey."

"Is that Geoffrey with a G.?" Nora shifted restlessly in the stiff chair. "You want to type for a while?"

Dan and Nora traded places. She stood in front of the fireplace and stretched her arms.

"Geoffrey with a G." Dan sat down and read 'As he tried to rouse Geoffrey, John looked around the room and remembered the night he first met Iris.'"

"Yeah," Nora smiled. "She just happened by to see her brother and isn't expecting to meet anyone else and this man comes to the door—handsome, smoking, irresistible. And there's that business about how she's wearing this huge emerald and her hair and her hat."

"I mean he doesn't describe it but the idea is that they went to bed together, right?"

"Yeah, she seduced him there, in that room, while the brother..."

Dan abruptly got up and walked into his small but well-stocked kitchen.

"Want some chocolate cake?"

"No thanks." Nora never ate sweets.

Dan returned to his place in front of the screen holding a fork and a piece of cake on a plate. Greta, Dan's old boxer, waddled in from the kitchen where she'd been dozing.

"Hey girl." Dan patted Greta's head and vigorously rubbed her ears as she curled up near his feet "did I wake you up?"

Nora could smell the dog across the room.

"You need a bath." Dan bent down to rub Greta's belly and the dog rolled over on her back, paws in the air.

"Geoffrey never did show up, right?" Dan said as he typed "It was after midnight when... So, that first night...what?"

"We need the sex scene there," Nora said.

"So...?" Dan's fingers were poised to type; he looked at the screen then at Nora. "He undresses her ? First, the shoes, then...What's she wearing?"

"A three piece suit."

Dan looked at Nora's face to see if she was kidding, then he turned back to the computer and typed a few sentences.

"First the jacket?" Dan focused on the screen.

"Right, then the skirt."

"So, she's down to her slip?" Dan typed without turning.

"Wait," Nora said, " then the vest, then unbuttoning the blouse."

Dan typed, and then stopped. "Now is she?" Dan looked at Nora.

Nora met Dan's eyes "She's wearing only her slip now."

Dan turned back to the keyboard and screen. He sat motionless. Nora spoke.

"She's sitting on the bed. Then what? Does he get undressed?"

"No, I don't think we even see John—this is just a flashback" Dan said.

"You mean, this is all just what he's remembering—about her—about how she looked that night? We don't see him at all ? That's kind of interesting."

Dan picked up a worn hardcover edition of the novel and read, " 'Her dress was of green silk, a very lustrous satin.' --I love that," Dan said. He goes on about how all the women were wearing green that season—in the nineteen-twenties. Isn't that strange?"

"Yeah, that's kind of bizarre" Nora agreed.

"Okay, so she's practically undressed" Dan was staring at the screen again.

"Not quite" said Nora "stockings."

"Oh, okay, right. She removes her stockings" Dan typed, "slowly inching them down from her milky thighs to her ankles."

"You can skip milky," Nora told him.

"Okay...thighs," Dan focused intently on his typing. "Cut to...their two heads on one pillow."

"Wait" Nora walked over to look at the screen. "John's back in the scene now? What are they doing?"

"Talking" Dan said, "or maybe we should just have them in a long kiss and end the scene."

"Isn't that too predictable?"

Dan looked uncertain.

"I mean, can't we think of something with a little more edge to it?" Nora suggested.

"Okay, no kiss." Dan hit the delete button.

Nora could sense his disappointment. "Anal penetration?" She suggested, watching his face.

Dan shot Nora a look of exaggerated disgust.

"Stop!" he shouted sternly.

He kept his lips pressed tightly together and his eyebrows wrinkled as he read the remaining lines on the screen. Nora couldn't suppress her giggle and he turned and exhaled a faint but audible chuckle when he caught her eye.

"I'll make some coffee," he said. "Time for a break."

"Can't. I have to leave you early today, " Nora told Dan. "I should get on the freeway now before the traffic."

Dan tried but failed to hide the disappointment he felt. Nora was surprised, watching him, at how transparent his feelings were, how easy it was for her to know what he was thinking. Some people might have thought it was endearing, his lack of pretense, but it made her uncomfortable.

Tomorrow night, then," Dan said, not meeting Nora's eyes, straightening papers on the table.

CHAPTER EIGHT

"Ginger says a job would give us self-esteem."

Michelle and Jennifer sat on a blanket under the Magnolia tree in the backyard of the house on Westborne Street. Jennifer lit her cigarette, then leaned back against the smooth trunk and looked up. The tree had flowers the size of dinner plates, china white—their pungent perfume in the warm afternoon air reminded Jennifer of lemon soap.

"Like we're going to find a job without a car?" Jennifer asked rhetorically. "I mean, how far can we go?"

"We can't go anywhere" Michelle spoke as she looked around the narrow plot of yard with its dusty clumps of bushes and brown spotty grass. "This sucks...we can't walk anywhere from here. We're stuck without a car."

Jennifer held her toes up in the air and squinted to see if she liked the color.

"Get a job—sure—self-esteem. You know what Shell, I'd feel just fine if I had like five thousand dollars, a credit card and a car. I mean, it's bullshit, you know?"

"I know."

Michelle looked at her friend sprawled beside her. Jennifer had arranged her fine brown hair into little clumps held in place by rubber bands decorated with plastic bows. She was wearing her new lipstick that was Royal Purple. More like grape, Michelle thought, a grape Popsicle. Ginger had taken them to Buy-Rite Drugstore earlier in the day. They came home with clips and pins for their hair, magazines, lipstick, razors and cream for their legs and nail polish.

"I like this color." Michelle looked down at her bare feet. They had painted each other's toenails a pearly aqua—Tahitian lagoon.

Michelle paged through a new copy of People magazine Ginger had bought for them. She let them pick out what they wanted at the drug store. On the cover was Tiffany Manchester, a teenager who was the star of a popular TV series.

"Ginger said we need to respect ourselves," Michelle said, holding the magazine up to shade her eyes from the sun.

"Who's that?" Jennifer asked, pointing at the cover.

"Tiffany" Michelle said, "You know, on TV, 'Sophomores'."

"She looks like you," Jennifer told Michelle.

"No way." Michelle took a closer look at the photograph. Tiffany's hair was very straight and shiny. She was wearing a beaded halter top with fringe covering very little of her midriff.

"You think so? Really?" Michelle knew Jennifer wouldn't say it if she didn't mean it.

Jennifer took a long drag from her Camel. "I'd rather have money than esteem." She said esteem like a word in French or Latin.

"Actresses make like, a lot of money." Michelle said.

"All they do is pretend to be somebody else" Jennifer said. "How hard is that ? I could do that."

"Sure, me too." Michelle slid down to a prone position and looked up. She saw a flash of orange—a green and yellow and orange bird flew onto a branch above them.

"Look at that!" Michelle pointed, and then stood up to get a better look.

"What?" Jennifer stayed on the ground.

"Look!" Michelle said again, pointing, and Jennifer had to stand up and see what it was.

"A parrot" Jennifer said.

"How do you know?' Michelle asked Jennifer

"I know birds."

Almost immediately, a woman entered the yard through the tall row of oleanders that separated Ginger's backyard from her neighbor's. The visitor had a large head with long dark hair and a short broad body. She walked directly over to the tree and called up to the bird.

"Leo, Leo! What's got into you ? Did you fly over here to say hello to these friendly girls ? You come to Mama."

Michelle and Jennifer stood closer to each other and a few steps away from the woman, who kept her eyes on the parrot perched on a low branch of the Magnolia tree. When she held out her arm, the parrot flew fluttering to settle on her wrist.

"You girls aren't afraid of birds, are you?" The visitor turned to consider Jennifer and Michelle. "Gee, you have such pretty faces. Leo must like you—he came over to say hello."

"I'm not afraid," said Jennifer.

"My name's March," the woman told them, "like the month and the soldier's walk."

"Hi," said Michelle, "he's beautiful—this is Jennifer and I'm Michelle." She gestured to her friend who said nothing.

"Leo's been with me for quite a while." March told them.

Leo let Michelle gently pet his neck.

"You know how long parrots live?"

"A long time" said Jennifer.

"Are you girls living with Ginger now?" March asked, eyeing them both with careful consideration.

She looked directly into Michelle's eyes and then looked at Jennifer.

"You're separated from your families, aren't you?"

Jennifer answered, "We're on our own. We don't have families."

"Honey, we all got one to start with—just that we don't necessarily want to stick around with them."

Jennifer didn't pull back when March reached for her hand. She let the woman hold it, palm up. March examined Jennifer's palm intently and ran a rough finger over its ridges and mounds.

"You're a healthy girl—good eyesight, good digestion. Pretty soon, looks like you're gonna have some important news to tell people."

"Me?" said Jennifer.

March looked directly into Jennifer's gray eyes. "Many people will want to see you. You will have something very interesting to tell them."

Jennifer said "okay" in a flat joking voice like she didn't really believe it but Michelle knew her friend was pleased.

Michelle extended her hand, palm up, to March. "Read mine."

"I got to go back home and feed Leo. You two come over and visit me sometime."

March petted Leo's head with her index finger and brought his beak up to her mouth making clicking kissing sounds. She then returned the way she'd come—through a break in the tall oleanders that marked the division of the two properties. Michelle and Jennifer stood and watched the woman with the bright bird disappear behind the greenery.

"She's our next door neighbor," said Michelle.

Jennifer got comfortable on the blanket on the grass under the tree. She propped her head against the trunk, smiling, and lit a cigarette. Michelle lay down next to her and Jennifer felt Michelle's abundant curly hair rippling gently against her bare arm. She exhaled and smiled up at the sky, her eyelids closed against the glare of the warm sun.

...

Ginger arrived at Mandarette early enough to get a parking place just outside the restaurant which was on a corner facing busy Beverly Boulevard. She felt hot and clumsy as she followed the tiny Chinese girl to a table for two beside the red lacquered wall. It was cool under the powerful fans hung from the high ceiling in the quiet room where only a few tables were occupied so early in the evening. The last rays of the sun striped the east wall of the restaurant.

Ginger hoped Nora wouldn't be late. She herself always made a point of being on time and, in fact, Nora walked in the door just as she began to be concerned about it. Ginger knew that Nora was always punctual but she hated sitting alone in a restaurant, she wondered fleetingly why it bothered her. Probably because of Tim, Ginger thought, something about being alone.

"Did you take the freeway?"

"No, surface streets—better at this hour."

As always, Nora looked cool and collected. She settled into her chair and carefully removed the wrapping from her chopsticks and fiddled with the thin tissue.

"I think this room has good Feng Shui" Ginger told Nora. "Maybe it's the way the front door is cut into the corner instead of facing the traffic or maybe the extra-high ceiling, I don't know. But I always feel like this place is peaceful, don't you?"

"Oh, you mean that Chinese thing about buildings and directions?" Nora looked around for the waitress.

"Marcie had a Feng Shui expert come to her house and rearrange the furniture and he told her to put a red chair next to the back door and something metal on the west wall."

"But isn't that all based on religious superstitions" Nora said, "I mean, it doesn't really make any sense."

"Marcie said she noticed a big difference" Ginger continued, "I think there's something to it. I mean, some rooms, some places just feel, you know, more comfortable than others. It's not about decorating, it's something else."

"Maybe in some cases its just common sense like, I don't know, having a wide door." Nora conceded.

"Marcie took the big mirror out of her bedroom because the Feng Shui person told her it was bad—it causes nightmares or something." Ginger said.

"That's so ridiculous," Nora said, then noting Ginger's expression she added "who knows, though, maybe it makes a difference." Nora knew Ginger always took it personally if you didn't agree with her—she didn't really know how to have a disinterested debate, Ginger always wanted you to agree with her and if you didn't, she felt insulted, but she wouldn't admit it.

"So," Nora said, after they'd ordered pot stickers and green onion pancakes and glass noodles "did you check with social services?"

"Yes," Ginger told her. "I got online and looked through all the missing children data—nothing. I sent all the information to the Nebraska state bureau. I don't know if they're using their real names. They have I.D. that says they're eighteen—it looks legitimate."

"God, Jennifer seems so young" Nora said.

"So does Michelle," Ginger agreed, but they're not legally children—not after age eighteen. You'd be surprised how many parents—especially if they remarry and have other children-- just let their kids go. I mean as long as they aren't hanging around making trouble they just don't bother with them. There are thousands of kids like that on the streets—you should see the statistics."

"I can't believe it," said Nora.

"The family as we know it—as we knew it—is more or less in trouble." Ginger took on her academic voice. "Very young women get pregnant, can't support a child—her family can't or won't help—the father leaves town, then the woman meets another man. If she begins a new family often the husband doesn't feel a bond with the stepchild; often there's abuse of some kind; the stepchild doesn't fit into the new family. I see cases like that all the time--children without functional families. Or parents who really can't offer their children any kind of care because they're strung out with substance abuse and can't even care for themselves."

Nora's chicken with snow peas was steaming hot. She put some rice on her plate. It made her faintly nauseous, what Ginger was saying.

"For me" Ginger said as she chewed a forkful of tofu "the issue is compassion—or you could call it empathy."

I call it guilt, Nora thought. She said, "I think we were the last generation to be taught guilt. It's not so hard to learn to live without it. Guilt is a useless appendage—like an appendix. No one knows what it's good for; when it starts to hurt, if it gives you pain—take it out, remove it."

"Have we lost our capacity for..." Ginger began but Nora felt impatient to continue her thought.

"I haven't learned not to feel guilty but I've certainly overcome my fear of it. I mean, isn't that part of becoming an adult?"

"Nora," Ginger replied "what about personal responsibility? If you're not part of the solution, you're part of the problem."

"Oh please." Nora said.

Ginger poured two tiny cups of tea from the celadon teapot; spilling hers when she lifted it to her lips. "The thing is Nora, they're more or less stranded without a car. I've been encouraging them to re-evaluate their employability." Ginger's voice was earnest.

"You mean, get a job?" Nora tried not to sound sarcastic.

"Yes. But without transportation I don't know how they're going to enter the work force."

"Are you saying we should provide them with transportation?"

"If we don't, how can we expect them to become self-sufficient? Do you want them to go back to walking the street?" Ginger's voice rose.

"I used public transportation for years before I could afford to keep a car in the city."

"That was in New York Nora, you know L.A. is different." Ginger used an accusatory tone, like she was talking to a client who missed an appointment.

"But isn't there some kind of social service agency that can help them, I mean..." Nora wanted to change the subject.

"No, I can't figure out any way to get help for them—not from public sources." Ginger told her.

"It's not fair" Nora said. "Why us ? We can't afford this, why are we stuck with them?"

"Not stuck" Ginger's voice was conciliatory. "No, just think about what would have happened if we hadn't found them."

Nora thought about physical abuse, rape, and then stopped herself.

" You'd be surprised at how many lost children are out there. They turn eighteen, the law says they're free to leave home—then what? They have no protection. Nora, they will at least be safe. I feel really good about this." Ginger looked pleased with herself.

"At least they'll know somebody cares."

"I do care, but still..." Nora began.

"I can lend them my car tomorrow if you don't mind driving me to work.... and back." Ginger suggested.

CHAPTER NINE

Jennifer got out of bed before Ginger or anyone else was awake. When she opened the kitchen door she found a newspaper waiting on the porch. She picked up the neatly folded rectangle with a little thrill at the newness and neatness of it. Her mother and stepfather never had a daily newspaper delivered; nor did her father. Jennifer read the headline: New Delays in Rapid Transit Project.

Jennifer brought the newspaper inside with a pleasant sense of propriety. She walked into the kitchen and poured some orange juice and read her horoscope for Oct. 18: 'You are skillful at managing finances; a new enterprise will succeed if begun before the full moon.'

Ginger walked into the kitchen and opened the refrigerator.

"How are you this morning, Jennifer?"

Jennifer looked up. "I'm great."

By the time Michelle got out of the shower with her hair washed, Jennifer was dressed and ready to go. Ginger's clean blue Volvo was parked in the driveway.

"Don't you want some corn flakes?" Ginger asked Jennifer.

"No, I'm not that hungry."

Nora joined them in the kitchen. "So you're applying for full-time jobs, right?"

Nora seemed to be going somewhere in a hurry. She had all her makeup on.

"Right, full time," Jennifer told her.

Michelle sat down and Ginger poured milk on cornflakes for her. Nora took a long look at Jennifer.

"Is that what you're wearing?"

Jennifer looked down at her denim skirt. Nora probably thought it was too short or maybe the halter top...So there's some skin showing, Jennifer thought, big deal.

"I just mean," Nora said, as Jennifer walked to the sink "like maybe you should wear something a little more businesslike."

"Honey, this outfit does mean business," Jennifer said with her best Texas accent.

Michelle giggled, crunching her cereal.

"You look fine." Ginger said. Nora picked up the newspaper and began reading.

Jennifer couldn't wait to get out of the house.

"Are you absolutely sure you know which freeway to take ?" Ginger asked as she took a spiral-bound book of maps off the shelf. "You know where you're going?"

"We worked it all out last night." Michelle's long dark hair was still damp and she was barefoot.

"Hurry up and get ready, Michelle," Jennifer told her "We have to go."

Michelle ran into the bathroom again.

"Do you have an appointment?" Nora wanted to know.

"You can just walk in and fill out an application," Jennifer told her.

"Now remember" Ginger was Miss Helpful. "You have a lot to offer—you're bright and energetic and..."

"Willing to work hard," Jennifer completed Ginger's speech.

"That's right." Ginger looked pleased.

Jennifer hadn't driven a car since Michelle's stepfather had lent them his when they visited Oxnard where he was a mechanic so he had two cars. Michelle didn't know how to drive a stick, but Jennifer had learned from her boyfriend in Omaha the summer she

lived with her father and his new wife. If she made all the beds
and did the dishes they let her drive the car on Sunday afternoon.

Michelle strapped herself into the seat on the passenger side
and Ginger leaned her head into the window to talk to Jennifer.
"The brakes grab a little so don't jam on the brakes." Ginger told
her.

"Okay," Jennifer said, "no problem."

"I just fixed the air conditioning so don't run it full blast if you
don't have to."

"Okay." Jennifer nodded and tapped her fingers on the steering
wheel. They had painted their fingernails aqua pearl to match their
toes.

"Don't let anyone intimidate you, okay?" Ginger's face was
inches from Jennifer's.

"Remember, you're both very special and valuable individuals.
And please, bring the car back before dark."

"Don't worry."

Jennifer could still see Ginger standing in the driveway waving
as they drove down Westborne Street. Michelle opened the thick
map book and ran her finger down a list of streets.

"Here it is" Michelle said after a while "La Brea."

A tall even line of palm trees marked the block on Wilshire
Boulevard where huge elephants with curving tusks were stuck in
a black pool. Jennifer and Michelle stood next to the chain link
fence surrounding the large pond of black tar and looked at the
life-size mammoth elephant with huge white tusks and a smaller
one wading into the edge of the pool...into the black oily liquid.

"Smell that" Jennifer said, breathing deeply, "tar."

"It's tar? " Michelle wondered.

"I like the smell" Jennifer told her.

"Me too. These are like the real size?" Michelle asked.

"Yeah," Jennifer told her, "exact replicas of mammoths. I
came here once when I was little. My mom and dad brought me
here. I guess we were visiting her sister or something."

The two friends began to walk through the grassy grounds.
"See, they thought it was water." Jennifer explained.

"Who?"

"The animals. They like waded in, you know, to wash or drink
but...it just looks like water."

"Yeah" Michelle said, "but it's really, like, tar."

"Right, and they got stuck and couldn't get out."

"But they thought it was water" said Michelle.

"Yeah. They couldn't tell."

"They didn't know…"Michelle paused to lean on Jennifer and pull on the strap of her shoe "what they were getting into."

Jennifer had been eager to visit the La Brea tar pits for the two weeks since she and Michelle first arrived in L.A. on the bus from Oxnard. Jennifer felt a strange thrill knowing she had finally returned to this place that she remembered from her childhood. It had stayed in her memory for almost ten years. Her mother was living in Texas now with a new husband. They would never take a vacation together again, Jennifer knew that for sure. That one time, her mother and real father had driven with her to California -- the three of them together. She was never really married to Rick. He never wanted Jennifer to call him Dad—just Rick.

Michelle didn't like to walk. She was wearing those really high heels again. Jennifer thought it felt good to walk across the green park in the sunshine.

"What's that?"

Michelle pointed at a huge concrete wall covered with silhouettes of prehistoric animals.

"It's a museum where they keep all the bones they dig out of the tar pits. There are smaller pits all around here. People work all the time finding little bones and cleaning them; then they like fit them together and make whole skeletons."

"We could do that," Michelle said. "Maybe they'll hire us. Let's try to get a job here."

"I don't know." Jennifer tried to imagine the people who worked at cleaning bones.

"Let's try" Michelle said "why not?'

The entrance sign for the Museum of Natural History pointed down a sloping walkway not far from the largest tar pit. The sign inside the heavy doors said 6.00 entrance fee.

"That's like twelve dollars for the two of us." Michelle said.

"Hey, you can add."

Michelle stopped and whispered to Jennifer "Maybe we should just ask where the manager is."

"Manager?" Jennifer wasn't sure if that was right. She wasn't sure who to ask.

"Excuse me," Jennifer said to the old man at the cash register. "Where can we apply for jobs?"

"Apply for a job?" the man asked. "No, not here."

"Well then, like where should we go?" Jennifer spoke loudly and clearly.

"Not here" the man repeated, like he couldn't hear. "You want tickets or not?"

"No" said Jennifer and they moved out of the way as a family of four walked towards the cashier.

"Let's just go," said Michelle and Jennifer shrugged and headed for the door.

Michelle was navigating and Jennifer was driving the Volvo and looking out for the green and white freeway sign. They drove east on Wilshire Boulevard, block after block, driving miles past the Miracle Mile and into an area where all the signs were in Spanish and past blocks where everything was in a language like on the Japanese beer—letters like broken pretzels. Jennifer saw a sign on a bank: Korea Town.

"These signs are like all in Korean I think," she told Michelle.

Michelle looked at the twisted unreadable letters. "Are the traffic signs in Korean too?"

"No. How could they be?"

Jennifer couldn't believe how dense Michelle was sometimes. But Michelle never got angry, she never yelled at Jennifer, even when she told her what she really thought. Jennifer glanced over at Michelle who was trying very hard to read the map and look around and figure out where they were and where they were going.

She's my friend, thought Jennifer, and Michelle caught her eye and said "Don't worry Jen, we'll get there," and smiled a reassuring smile and Jennifer thought –there's no question.

If anybody asks, there's no question Michelle would say that I'm her best friend. We are best friends. The certainty of this relationship suddenly occupied all of Jennifer's awareness and she felt elated at the unassailable primary fact of it, which was as real as a trophy or a diamond ring. She realized that she didn't feel alone—even though they didn't know anybody else in the city besides Ginger and Nora. She and Michelle were more like sisters, except sisters sometimes didn't really like each other. But her friend really did like her and Michelle never gets mad at me, Jennifer thought, and she'll always be my friend.

Jennifer had never before driven on the wide eight-lane L.A. freeways. She had never driven in Indiana, where she was born and then when her mother moved her to Texas with her second husband she never got to drive there either; though ranch kids could drive in Texas at sixteen. Her father let her take a drivers ed class in high school when she lived with him in Omaha where finally, she was allowed to sit behind the wheel of a car, alone. Jennifer was a very good driver—her teacher gave her perfect grades. She reached over and turned the AC knob all the way to the edge of the blue arc and felt proud and glad that she had mastered the art of driving a car. The Volvo stayed cool as it purred along at 70 miles per hour in the second lane from the far left.

It's so easy, Jennifer thought, you just follow the other cars, pay attention to what they do. It's so easy. Just keep your eyes open. This was the safest lane; Michelle's stepfather had given them some pointers. The lane beside the fast lane is the safest one. Michelle switched on the radio—it was tuned to a classical station. She turned the dial past Spanish talk and wailing Mariachis to Prince singing "Little Red Corvette." Both girls knew the words and sang the chorus together.

"You know what Jen," Michelle said, "this is the first day we can go anywhere we want."

Jennifer smiled, watching the five lanes of traffic in front of her, she felt buoyant, as if she were almost weightless. She was driving with her best friend on an L.A. freeway.

"Yeah, we can. Anywhere we want."

Jennifer felt confidence in her control of the speeding car and in the knowledge that there was nothing they were likely to encounter today that she couldn't manage.

She assumed an easy confidence that she had always known was hers—but for the first time she felt it like power—her own. Her possibilities weren't limited by parents or teachers or money or distance or anything. She breathed in the pure oxygen of possibility. Her happiness extended to fill the entire car, then illuminated the freeway and passing cars with a misty golden glow.

There was music playing and sunshine and so much more to see of L.A.; it went on forever—anything could happen.

"Where the fuck are we?" Jennifer asked, in a cheerful satisfied voice.

Michelle looked at the map, then out the window. "We're heading west, I think. No wait—south. Is this the 180 ?"

"I don't know—maybe." Jennifer wasn't that worried.

Suddenly, Michelle sat forward in her seat and pointed.

"Look! Look Jen, there's the sign!"

"Yeah! Next exit ! All right ! We found it!"

Jennifer had been confident that they'd find Disneyland. I mean, how hard can it be, she thought. Like millions of people go there all the time. Still, they had driven there without getting lost, without having to ask anybody! Jennifer felt elated as she signaled right and looked into the rear view mirror and moved into the right lane. There were plenty more signs after they got off the freeway and it was easy to find the enormous parking lot.

It took ten minutes to walk from the car to the busy ticket booths at the entrance to the park where lines of people stood waiting. Small children darted in and out of adult hands.

"I've got, let's see..." Michelle dug into her purse and checked her pockets, "fourteen dollars."

"I've got twenty-three" Jennifer told her. "We need forty more dollars just to get inside."

"Maybe we should come back some other time," Michelle said.

"Are you kidding?" Jennifer knew she didn't mean it. "We can earn fifty bucks here."

"How?" asked Michelle.

"How do you think?"

As the two girls walked back to the parking lot, they stopped beside a clean white Oldsmobile parked in a blue handicapped zone near the busy entrance to the park. Jennifer and Michelle leaned against the trunk of the big car and watched clumps of adults with one or two or three children pass by. School was in session so most of the children were little kids under seven.

It made Jennifer happy to think that today was a school day— but not for her and Michelle. She thought of all the kids who were locked in classrooms this morning. She almost shivered thinking about how cold it was already in Omaha with summer over, freezing rain, dead leaves on the sidewalks.

Two guys who looked around thirty walked towards the Oldsmobile. The girls appraised the men without speaking. Michelle adjusted the neckline of her blouse; Jennifer took off her sunglasses, threw her shoulders back and licked her lips. The men were dressed for the heat in baseball caps and long baggy t-shirts.

"Hi there" Jennifer said as the two men got closer "How are you today?"

"Okay" said the fatter one, who slowed down and wiped sweat off his face with his hand; he looked at his friend who stopped and took a closer look at the girls. As the two men faced the Oldsmobile, Jennifer shifted her legs on the bumper.

"You guys having a good time?" Jennifer asked them.

The fat one nudged his friend "You tell 'em, Steve."

Steve looked at Michelle who smiled encouragingly, then he stared at the car and Jennifer. His friend looked behind him at the stream of people walking towards the ticket counters.

"Don't be shy" said Michelle.

"Are you looking for some companionship?" Jennifer asked them. "If you've got money, we've got some good ideas. Won't take long either."

"Why don't we go somewhere and talk?" Michelle suggested.

The two men seemed to be unsure as to how to proceed. Michelle stood up and beckoned, shyly, gently, with her right hand. Steve turned away as a sunburned woman in baggy shorts approached.

"Steve, we have to hurry, Kimberly has to go to the bathroom."

"Ma'am," Michelle approached the woman earnestly, making eye contact, "we don't have enough money for gas to get home—I was just asking your husband here—could you help us out? Even a dollar would help."

"No, we can't" the woman said, "ask someone else."

She put both her hands on the head of the small tow-headed girl who walked beside her, as if she didn't want her to get near Michelle or see or hear her.

"Well, god bless," Michelle spoke louder "have a nice day."

The two men, the mother and the daughter all turned and walked towards the ticket booths, blending in with other visitors who continued arriving in a steady stream.

"I'm hungry," Michelle said and they started off towards the far edge of the parking lot where they could see, through the shimmer of heat hovering over the black asphalt, a red and yellow sign that spelled HAMBURGERS in tall letters. Michelle had a way of leaning against Jennifer's shoulder as they walked, so she could adjust her shoe without stopping.

It was almost an hour before the two girls returned to the parking lot. Michelle proceeded unsteadily in her platform shoes, sipping iced root beer through a straw from a quart-sized paper cup. As they approached the parking area, Jennifer read a sign EMPLOYEES ENTRANCE above a double metal door. A man in a clean white short-sleeved shirt was walking in front of them, towards the door.

"Hey" she called "Hey you in the white shirt." The guy turned around. He was younger than Jennifer expected. "You work here?"

"That's right," he answered. He looked maybe nineteen. He wasn't in a hurry.

"Where can we apply for a job?" Jennifer asked him.

"You two? You want to apply here ? For Disneyland or Disney Hotel?"

"Disneyland," said Jennifer, "both."

"I'll show you where the office is."

The testing room walls were decorated with colorful cartoon characters. Michelle sat in a school-style desk directly in front of Jennifer. Her long clean hair flowed over her shoulders and onto Jennifer's desk like a black silk scarf—it smelled of jasmine-scented shampoo. There were about twenty other people seated at the small chair-desks filling out applications. The girls were tan and buff, the boys were scrubbed and muscular, like athletes— college students, Jennifer could tell.

Jennifer looked down at the application form on her desk. It was six pages long, like a magazine. Do you have dancing skills ? Yes, definitely. Last grade of school finished...that would be eleven, thought Jennifer; then thought how would they know, and circled one, after college. A smile began to form on her face.

Michelle turned around. "I'd say I have dancing skills, right?"

"Definitely," Jennifer whispered, "yes, you absolutely do."

Jennifer kept going. She circled singing and drama skills. She circled Spanish. She remembered the names of plays put on by the high school seniors at Glenwood High School in Omaha and she listed those.

The man behind the desk told Jennifer and Michelle to sit down while he looked over their applications. They were the last people to be interviewed. Don Bash over in personnel had send the two applicants to Chuck Mooney who supervised maintenance at one of the hotels at Disneyland. There were no jobs open at the park until next summer but the hotels needed workers. Michelle had been called in first but she asked if Jennifer could be interviewed at the same time so Chuck Mooney, associate director of personnel, said okay, bring your friend in.

Chuck had just come from a management lunch meeting and still wore his plastic name badge pinned to his short-sleeved shirt. He looked over the forms the girls had filled out.

"You can take a seat there, Janet" he motioned Jennifer to a tall backless stool next to the one where Michelle was seated. From his leather office chair, Chuck looked up at the two applicants. Michelle's knees were approximately at his desk level. Jennifer remained standing.

"I see you girls have some experience with hotel work." Chuck smiled at Michelle then looked at his watch. "Unfortunately," Chuck said, "it's a little late in the day to really complete this interview. My friends and I are meeting for a drink after work. It's something we do every evening. Maybe you two young ladies would like to be my guests ? We could all get to know each other better. We could sort of continue the interview there, if you know what I mean." Chuck smiled a confident, ingratiating smile.

Michelle said, "Sure, we can stop on our way home, okay Jen?"

"Where is this place ?" Jennifer asked.

She thought it was a good sign that Chuck wanted to talk to them. Obviously he liked Michelle and wanted to hire her to work at the hotel. They said there were ten applicants for every job at the amusement park; but they could probably work at the hotel until the better jobs opened up. Jennifer wouldn't mind working at the front desk of a hotel but she didn't want to make beds. But if there weren't any jobs at the front desk she could make beds until something better came along.

Chuck showed Jennifer on a map where to meet him after work. "You can't miss it, " he told them, "just take a right when you leave the parking lot, turn left at the first stop light and you'll see a gas station and a mini mall on the right. Go six blocks— you'll see a Buy Rite drugstore and across the street you'll see a neon sign that says Sportsmans Spot. There's free parking in the back.

Chuck spotted Jennifer and Michelle the minute they walked into the bar. He was sitting with his friend Jose at a table near the door. The cavernous room was filled with the big buzzy sounds of five television screens. They were all large and all tuned to the same channel—a basketball game was in progress. The chilly windowless room was filled with customers drinking and eating and exclaiming loudly at the developments of the game, which was the center of all noise and interest.

"That's them" Chuck nudged Jose as he got up and walked over to Jennifer and Michelle who followed him to the table where Jose stood up to be introduced and pulled a chair out next to him for Jennifer to be seated.

"What took you so long?" Chuck asked Michelle.

"We got lost" Michelle said, then looked at Jennifer. "I mean, we needed to get gas and stuff."

Bottles of beer were brought to the table, which was about ten feet from the largest TV screen Jennifer had ever seen. She found herself staring at the leaping players in purple and gold and green and white even though she couldn't hear anything very clearly.

"What?" Jose was asking her a question.

"I said, I'll bet you have a boyfriend, don't you Janet?"

"Huh? No...Not really "

"Jose here thinks you don't look old enough to drink," Chuck told Michelle.

"We're old enough to do anything we might want to do," Jennifer told him, "aren't we Shelly?"

"That's right," Michelle said, taking a long drink from the cold bottle.

The sound of the game was so loud, conversation required extra attention.

Jose leaned over to Jennifer and confided in her ear "I drive a 558 GFL Ultra with fuel injection."

Jennifer looked at Jose's smoothly handsome face in the dim greenish light and nodded encouragingly. His pungent aftershave mingled with the sour smell of stale beer in the chilly air-conditioned room.

"It's gunmetal gray" he told her proudly, "sort of silver—it's only got about six thousand miles on it."

"So you girls are looking for work?" Chuck said, loud enough so everyone at the table looked at him.

He leaned back in his chair and looked from one to the other. He met Jose's eyes and grinned, showing his crooked teeth. In the background, an explosion of thunderous grunts and boos greeted a referee's call.

"The job market is tough right now," Chuck continued, "Isn't that right, Jose?"

"Yeah, it is." Jose was distracted by the score of the game flashing on the TV screen. "The Lakers are in big trouble," he said.

Chuck's attention returned to the screen as a free throw shot up in an arc towards the basket then hit the rim and bounced off.

"Oww" he groaned, in precise unison with dozens of others in the bar.

Michelle shivered and Jennifer could see goose bumps on Michelle's soft plump arms which were, she thought, the color of cream mixed with coffee. They were absolutely without freckles or moles or marks of any kind, Michelle's arms. Her whole body is like that, Jennifer thought, flawless.

"You know, we promised Ginger we'd be back before dark," Michelle leaned towards Jennifer.

"I know that," Jennifer replied. She flinched as the entire room exploded with a high-decibel male exclamation followed by shrill hoots and warbling hollers. Jennifer looked around and noticed that there were only a few women in the Sportsmens Spot, and they were mostly old. She felt pleased that she and Michelle were among the invited ones, the chosen few.

CHAPTER TEN

I t was lavender-pink twilight when Jennifer steered the Volvo into Ginger's driveway in West Hollywood. Looking in the direction of, she knew now, Sunset Boulevard, Jennifer was satisfied that it was not yet completely dark. The two girls let themselves into the silent house and collapsed on chairs in the kitchen.

"We beat them home" Jennifer announced, "Ginger can't complain that we're late."

"My feet are so sore, " Michelle was rubbing her bare feet, now unencumbered by the high shoes with their painful straps. She was checking the refrigerator to see if there was anything to eat when the doorbell rang.

Jennifer hurried to the front door and was surprised when she opened it to see a tall blonde woman with very long legs wearing tall tight pants talking on a cell phone. The woman waved at Jennifer as they made eye contact.

"Just a sec," the visitor said into her phone. "Hi, I'm Nora's sister Pam," she said to Jennifer and walked past her into the house.

Michelle stared curiously as Pam entered the kitchen.

"She's not here," Jennifer told the visitor, closing the door and following Pam.

"I told her I'd be"...Pam began an explanation in reply; but something she heard on the phone diverted her attention.

Pam stood rigidly still and concentrated on speaking into the tiny chrome device. Her voice displayed an impressive tonal range, veering from low-pitched rasp to indignant screech.

"I didn't...No Silvie! I didn't say the color was bad...it just doesn't work with this haircut."

The visitor paused and smiled apologetically at Jennifer who stood a few feet away staring at her.

"I couldn't tell when I was in the salon...the lighting...Silvie doll, I know you have...of course you do...but..."

Pam rolled her eyes to the heavens and looked at Jennifer as if to acknowledge that she hoped and trusted that Jennifer understood how irritating it was to have to conduct this conversation in this room at this time. She also nodded in a friendly manner towards Michelle. The blonde visitor's behavior engaged Jennifer's full attention; she listened and watched every move Pam made.

Pam sat down at the kitchen table, phone to ear, her eyes focused intently somewhere outside the room.

"Silvie," she said, angling her head just slightly away from Jennifer, "I told you—I want the look that Sharon had in 'Armed to the Teeth'—remember that? ...Yeah, but sort of Texas teenager: sun-streaked but raw. Sweetie, this color is not it...No ! It's not. It's too gold!"

After this statement, Pam held the phone away from her ear and regarded the two young women in her sister's kitchen.

"Have we met?" She asked them, looking intently at Jennifer, then Michelle.

"We're staying here for a while," Michelle told her.

"Both of you?" Pam's voice squeaked with surprise. "Living here?"

"In there" Michelle pointed to the sofa bed in the living room.

"But..." Pam blinked with incomprehension but her attention was abruptly called back to the phone.

"Sylvie, don't be mad at me." Pam dragged out the vowel's long ee sound. "Remember, I was the one who raved about you to Kim. Please, do this for me. The hair's got to be right...tomorrow? Bingo ! After five, okay ? No, I'll be there on time, I promise. Fabulous. You're a giant. I owe you one, doll-face. See you."

Pam placed the cell phone on the kitchen table as Michelle and Jennifer watched her, alert and curious. The visitor had shoulder length golden hair and wore an almond-sized diamond on her right hand.

"So" Pam said, taking a deep breath and leaning back, "and you are...?"

Jennifer and Michelle told their names, nothing more.

But after a second, Jennifer added, "Nora and Ginger should be home soon."

"Okay fine" Pam said quickly, switching her attention to a new, more promising possibility. "Is there any wine in...? She jumped up and opened the refrigerator.

"Bingo!"

Pam poured white wine then distributed three glasses with quick efficient movements. She sat down again, took a sip and said, "There we are."

The little chrome telephone suddenly began to buzz and writhe upon the wooden tabletop. Pam picked up and stood up in the same smooth movement.

"Pamela Norris...yes...Dudley? Where are you ? Listen, what did you tell Berghoff I said...?"

There was a long pause during which Pam stared up at the ceiling.

"I don't care if you were kidding, I don't think it's funny. What were you thinking ? Don't you know Berghoff and Tyler are fucking cousins or something ? They're like related, Dudley. Yes, I'm sure. How could you be so clueless ? I can't believe how completely out of control this is. You are going to be so so sorry.... What?"

Pam listened, tense, not breathing. Jennifer could see her eyes narrow and ugly lines appear in Pam's smooth forehead.

Then a sudden exhalation: "No! Fuck you, Dudley ! You so lied to me. You are such a lying piece of shit... you...."

Pam angrily clicked off the phone and sat down again at the table and swallowed an inch or two of wine. Michelle stared at the visitor's face.

"You look familiar, sort of."

Pam relaxed her frown. "Ever watch 'Blood Ties' ? I have a recurring role as the Police Chief's wife."

"No way! That was you ?" Michelle eagerly studied Pam's face. Pam nodded then gave a modest shrug.

"You're like, an actress?" Michelle asked.

"That's right," said Pam.

Michelle nudged Jennifer. "She was on TV."

"I know," said Jennifer with a trace of impatience in her voice.

"What do you girls do?" Pam asked them.

"We're actresses too," Jennifer answered.

Michelle raised her eyebrows at Jennifer, sipped her wine.

"Just starting out, you know." Jennifer met Pam's large blue eyes.

"I see," said Pam "have you got an agent?"

"We're looking around," Jennifer told her.

Pam drained her glass and poured another. Her bright white sweater was decorated with beads at the low neckline. She must be famous, Jennifer thought, admiring the slim pants that fit Pam's long legs like shiny skin.

"Nora said she'd be home by seven."

Jennifer thought she detected a note of impatience in Pam's voice and was worried suddenly that Pam might leave.

"They should be here any minute," she reassured her. There was a pause as Pam seemed to lose focus and stare at the table. "Do you know of any acting jobs? We're like, you know, unemployed." Jennifer thought it wouldn't hurt to ask.

"You and eighty per cent of the actors in this town, honey." Pam chirped.

Jennifer looked at Michelle and Pam with the understanding that all of them, everyone at the table, belonged to a group of people who all had the same special needs, the same problems.

"I know, like that's just the way it is."

As Jennifer spoke she propped her bare feet on the chair next to her and held her wineglass with the stem dangling between her cupped fingers, like Pam did.

"You have gorgeous hair," Pam reached out to feel the texture of Michelle's hair and the younger woman smiled her shy smile.

Jennifer took out a pack of cigarettes, offered one to Pam who refused, then lit up. When she exhaled, Jennifer saw Michelle look at the smoke with a worried expression. Big deal, I'll put it out when they come home, Jennifer thought.

The little chrome phone pulsed and writhed again. Pam swept the phone to her ear with her right hand and held her wine glass in her left as she gracefully uncrossed her long legs and pointed her face toward the kitchen window.

"Pamela Norris. Barry ? Where have you been Sweetie ? I tried to...No. I thought...What? What did he say ? That's insane. That is so NOT what I said. Unbelievable! I absolutely never told him you...He's a fucking liar, Barry, I..."

Jennifer crossed her legs, inhaled deeply and leaned her chair back. Michelle then got up and looked out the window as Nora and Ginger walked in the back door carrying bags of groceries and dry cleaning. Jennifer saw Pam cover her left ear with the hand that was holding the drink and move over to a corner so she could hear the voice on the little telephone.

"Jennifer!" Ginger's voice was angry. This is a smoke-free household, you know that."

Jennifer quickly stood up and made fanning motions at the cigarette smoke. Michelle looked nervously at Nora then at Pam. Nora saw her sister.

"Oh Pam, we got held up, sorry I..."

Into the phone Pam said "Just a second, sweetheart..."

With her phone in one hand and glass in the other, Pam silently kissed Nora on each cheek; her expression now grave and fragile. "I've been waiting for you."

She spoke with her face close to her sister's face; her eyes clouded with the gravity of her need for refuge and understanding and special consideration. Then she went back to her cell phone.

"No, I swear to you I never said that. He's lying Barry—it's bullshit! That is just completely untrue."

Jennifer carefully stubbed out the burning end of her cigarette and pocketed the unsmoked part. Nora began to put away groceries. Ginger hung things in the hall closet then stood over the kitchen table with an expectant look on her face.

"How'd it go?" She looked at Jennifer, then Michelle. "The job search—any luck ?"

"Not really," said Jennifer. "But we tried. Let's go outside, okay Michelle?"

Jennifer took the cigarettes and lighter from her purse and walked out the back door with Michelle following. She sat in the old lawn chair and Michelle dragged a dusty folding chair over beside her. Jennifer re-lit her half-smoked Camel and took a long drag. Michelle didn't mind the smoke. It reminded her of her mother. She'd told Jen about it. She made a promise to her mother before she died that she would never smoke but she didn't mind if Jennifer did.

As Jennifer sat in the dark smoking, she noticed something flickering on the other side of the tall hedge, in March's yard.

"Look over there," she said to Michelle "is something burning?"

She pointed at an opening in the hedge. They could see orange flames and dancing shadows in the leafy darkness.

"What's burning?" Michelle and Jennifer stood up and walked toward the fire. "What is it?"

"Welcome neighbors." March greeted them with calm good humor.

Almost like she was expecting us, Jennifer thought. Michelle's dark eyes reflected the flame, like a cat.

"This is so cool," she said.

March sat on a three-legged campstool near a crackling campfire. Beside her was a pile of dry eucalyptus branches and split oak, which she fed into the blaze. After she added wood, March covered the rock-lined pit with a metal screen she kept for that purpose. The warm circle of fire was growing to just the size she wanted.

"Is that a tent?" Jennifer asked, walking beyond the fire towards a shadow-draped dome rounded like a tall igloo glowing purple and silver in the firelight. It was constructed of branches bent into a curved circular frame draped with layers of old rugs and heavy woven blankets.

"It's called a wikiup," March said as the girls were drawn to look more closely.

Jennifer had seen tents before, but they were made of canvas or nylon and had aluminum poles. This was different—it was both crude and luxurious. She imagined Bedouins on the desert had tents like this. A deep crimson Oriental rug carpeted the ground beneath the layered drapery of the arched walls. The inside of the tent glowed with the flame of a kerosene lantern set on a low table. Colorful pillows were placed beside the table to sit on.

"You made this?" Jennifer looked around as March stood at the door of the tent.

"Sure I did. Wasn't that hard. In my family, the boys used to make tents like this every summer. They're all gone now, except my brother Floyd. Our father was part Choctaw—he taught us. You have to get real springy willow branches and bend them over. See ?" March pointed at the rough frame, "You lash them together. My brother brought me some branches from up north— you need a special kind."

March bent to enter the tent, then lowered herself cross-legged onto a pillow.

She beckoned for Jennifer and Michelle to join her.

"Do you sleep out here?" Michelle wanted to know. Her hands felt the rough wool carpet as she sat down.

"This is sort of my living room—my night room," March told them. "I like to sit out here on warm nights. I keep it up until the rains start."

The girls sat on pillows admiring the pattern of the walls in the flickering light.

A collage of shimmering Indian silk mingled with Navaho weaving. The pillows were of cotton embroidered with the thick bright flowers of southern Mexico. In the yellow light of the kerosene lantern, March seemed younger and more animated. She took some cards out of her pocket and began to shuffle them on the purple silk covered table. Jennifer saw that they weren't regular playing cards with numbers or patterns; these were larger, had individual pictures on them—each one seemed to be different. March shuffled and reshuffled the cards.

"Can you read my fortune?" Michelle asked March, giving Jennifer a sudden hug with her right arm—a brief expression of her excitement, a very quick squeeze.

"It's nice and warm in here" said Jennifer.

"Not much wind tonight," March told them. "It's peaceful here. I like to stay up late, sometimes I even fall asleep in this wikiup."

"I could live here," Jennifer said admiringly.

"You want to go first?" March's small bright eyes searched Michelle's face.

"Here, shuffle the cards, take your time."

Through the triangular opening of the tent, Jennifer could make out the faces of Nora and Pam in the kitchen window next door. Nora was emptying out the last few grocery bags, finding a place for the extra loaf of bread and the large bag of granola.

Pam held a wine bottle upside down over her empty glass. "This one's finished," she said.

"I forgot to buy wine today," Nora said. "Sorry."

"Did Ginger go to bed?"

"No, I don't think so," Nora said. "Pam, about that money I owe you...you know I'll pay you back as soon as I can. I thought this project would be further along by now but it's taking longer than I thought."

"You never should have quit your producing job just when you were making some decent money. You know, it's not easy to get a feature film produced."

"I know what I'm doing Pam," Nora interrupted, trying to keep her voice at the intense dramatic pitch that would demonstrate to Pam that she was secure in her conviction. "I love what I'm doing" she added emphatically, "I'm just not sure when the script will be finished. We're working very hard. We're going to come up with something good. You can't force these things."

"Right," Pam said, checking the cupboards for liquor. "But you've been at this for almost a year. Nora, face it, like you need an income, babe." Pam found a bottle of warm white wine, decided to open it.

"Ginge?" Pam walked to the hallway and called "Ginge, want to have a glass of wine with us ?"

Pam always called Ginger Ginge, which made Nora cringe. "She can't hear you."

Pam shrugged and came back to the table.

"She has her door closed—she's doing yoga." Nora told her.

"Does that mean she can't drink?" Pam asked.

"No, Buddhists drink."

Nora picked up the plastic garbage bag from under the sink and carried it outside, leaving the door ajar.

The loud sound of the doorbell made Pam swivel in the direction of the front door. She heard a male voice call out "Janet ! Shelly !"

Pam pushed open the door and saw Chuck and Jose standing outside.

" You forgot something." Chuck said in his most ingratiating voice, holding up Jennifer's white sunglasses. Jose carried a brown paper bag.

"Where are your friends?" Chuck asked Pam in a friendly voice.

"Who are you looking for?" Pam eyed the two men; noticed the slim paper bag.

"What's this?"

"A bottle of Tequila" Jose told her. "How 'bout if we open it up? Why not? I brought limes and a bag of ice, too."

"Friends of Ginger's?" Pam asked them.

"Honey, we're everybody's friend." Chuck told her.

"Is that right?" Pam looked at the two men more carefully.

"What kind of work do you do?"

"Call me Chuck, I'm a talent agent."

"No kidding," Pam said. "Okay, let's have a drink."

Pam opened the door wider and the two men entered. As the three were getting settled in the kitchen, Nora came back with the empty garbage can.

"Look who's here," Pam told her, "Chuck and ..."

"Jose. How ya doin?" With a warm smile on his smoothly handsome face, Jose quickly stood up, introduced himself to Nora and shook her hand.

Nora was caught off guard. "Friends of yours?" she asked Pam.

"Listen" said Chuck amiably, "your girlfriends gave us this address—we met over in Anaheim."

"Anaheim?" repeated Pam, as though he'd said Tierra del Fuego or Indianapolis.

"Girlfriends?" Nora looked at Pam. "Anaheim?"

"Never mind." Pam relaxed into a kitchen chair. "We'll just have one drink while we sort this out, okay?"

In her dimly lit bedroom, Ginger sat on a sheepskin spread on the carpeted floor. Her long legs were crossed and her spine was erect as she took a deep breath and intoned "ONG NA NA VO, GURO DEV NA VO."

She felt the vibrations of each syllable deep in her solar plexus. Her navel chakra, Guru Singh called it. Ginger's arms and legs were long and shapely but her torso, her mid-section seemed to be gradually thickening, year by year. She had once been quite thin but now her breasts and stomach had grown heavier and fatter. Ginger tried not to think about her body. She wanted to meditate on acceptance. That was what they'd been working on in yoga class—acceptance and compassion.

The noises were getting louder. Men's voices, Ginger realized, as she gave up trying to meditate and listened closely. It sounded like one of the men was laughing very loudly and Pam was laughing. Then, as Ginger was bending forward from the waist with both legs stretched out in front of her, she heard the sound of breaking glass. It was a very disruptive sound and was followed by louder sounds, more laughter and then Nora's tense voice ordering someone to "watch out."

Barefoot, wearing her lycra yoga pants and a sweatshirt, Ginger went to see what was going on. At the kitchen doorway, Ginger saw a man in a suit sweeping something out of the way with a broom. Pam was seated at the table with a Hispanic-looking man.

"Hi Ginge," Pam called out as Ginger appeared.

Ginger had helped Pam years before with her substance abuse problems and they had remained friends.

The man next to Pam stood up and held out his hand and said "How ya doin?"

"I love what you're wearing," Pam said to Ginger "Have you lost weight?"

Ginger felt centered and clear after her yoga session. She smiled and nodded politely to the man.

"Isn't she adorable?" Pam said to Jose as Ginger surveyed the room calmly.

"Where is Nora?" Ginger asked.

"She went outside to find your little house guests," Pam told her. "This is Chuck," she added, indicating the man with the broom.

Chuck gave Ginger a wide friendly smile.

He picked up the half-empty bottle of Tequila and said, "let me pour you a drink."

"I don't think…" Ginger began, but Pam interrupted her.

"Buddhists drink."

"Hey, watch yourself" Chuck pointed at the floor and Ginger looked down to see a sharp chunk of broken glass inches from her bare foot.

With a deft little hop, Ginger landed on a kitchen chair, holding her feet in the air. Just then, Nora entered with Jennifer and Michelle.

"Janet! Shelly ! Jose greeted them, standing and opening both arms, as if he meant to embrace them.

"How'd you find us?" Jennifer demanded.

"Your address was on the application." Chuck explained. "You forgot your sunglasses." Chuck took the white sunglasses out of his pocket and offered them.

"You shouldn't have come here." Michelle burst out with a vehemence that surprised Jennifer as much as it did Michelle herself.

"You girls are a lot of fun," Chuck began in an ingratiating tone.

"Who…?" began Ginger.

She sat with both hands resting on her crossed thighs, soles facing up, palms open, thumb and forefinger pressed together in the vitality position. She took a deep breath and held it for a beat, then exhaled.

"Apparently Jennifer and Michelle met these men when they were applying for a job," explained Nora.

"We never invited them here." Jennifer's voice was tense as she advanced towards Chuck. "You better leave" she told him, pushing him towards the door.

"Wait just a second," said Pam. "Chuck and Jose here have been extremely friendly and considerate I think; and it's not up to these little…"

"Shut up Pam," said Nora.

"Why?" began Ginger.

"Go away!" Michelle shouted with a vehemence that made Ginger's spine stiffen.

"Both of you get out of here!" Jennifer yelled at the men who were now on their feet and edging towards the door.

Ginger wanted to leave the crowded noisy room and go back to her bedroom but she was afraid to walk across the floor in her bare feet.

"What's the matter with you people?" Pam asked in her husky squeak, "can't we be civil ?"

Ginger inhaled a deep breath and let it out slowly through her mouth before she spoke. "Pam, Jennifer and Michelle are very vulnerable around the issue of male authority. Please try to be sensitive to the fact that they have a history of sexual victimization."

"We never touched 'em, did we Chuck?" Jose was adamant. "I swear."

"I told you they were underage." Chuck had a sheepish Bill Clinton kind of expression on his face, but remained confident that he could handle the situation.

"Girls," he explained in a reasonable tone, "we're just looking for a good time."

He smiled and opened both hands when he said this like a magician waiting for his assistant to hand him his magic wand.

Jose appealed to Michelle. "We like you girls, we didn't mean anything."

Ginger realized that she actually believed him. This made her furious with herself—she could feel her body temperature rise. Her breathing became shallow and rapid. She carefully crossed the room and looked Chuck in the eye.

"Excuse me," Ginger said, "may I ask where you met these young women?"

"At my office" Chuck answered immediately "right girls?" He looked around for corroboration "they came in to apply for..."

"Are you aware of state and federal regulations governing sexual harassment?" Ginger spoke directly to Chuck.

"Hey man," Jose said, "we better get going. Time to go."

"But wait" Chuck said, in his most reasonable voice "they weren't employees and besides, we never touched 'em."

"Okay," Jose said, pushing Chuck as he edged towards the door. "Let's get going."

"Wait!" Pam was on her feet. "We're going dancing, right? You said you knew a new club on Hollywood Boulevard."

She reached for Jose's arm and looked around the room for likely club-goers.

Jose waved to Pam as he and Chuck opened the front door and disappeared.

Ginger said "Pam, why don't you let Nora drive you home?"

After Pam left with Nora, Jennifer and Michelle helped clean up the kitchen. Ginger carefully mopped the floor and the girls put bottles into the recycling bin and wiped the table and washed and dried the wine glasses.

"I'm tired" Michelle said and Jennifer followed her into the living room where they got ready for bed.

When Ginger opened the door to make sure the lights were out, Jennifer said "We never invited them here."

Michelle said, "we really didn't."

"I know you didn't," said Ginger "It wasn't your fault."

When Ginger finally got into bed and lay waiting for sleep to come, she felt pleased with the way the evening had been resolved. They're good kids, she felt sure, they just need a chance. We're making progress, Ginger thought.

CHAPTER ELEVEN

Dan paced from the fireplace to the table and back, reading aloud from a page he held in his right hand. "You have to allow me my excesses, Iris, because it is through excess that I contrive to express my emotional distress.   I feel an excess of desire, an excess of tenderness, an excess of anger because we remain apart. How to express this...this surplus, how ?"

Nora swiveled on the typing chair "excess that I contrive to express...Is that what you said?"

"They talked like that in the twenties," Dan said, "apparently — I mean, that's almost verbatim from the novel."

"It's hard to say. I mean hard for the actor." Nora objected.

Slobbery Greta waddled over from her filthy cushion and rubbed against Nora's leg.   Dan looked apologetic "I know she needs a bath. Greta, lie down," he commanded.

"Okay," Dan shuffled through some pages on the dining table "Here's where we left off...Iris has left the country house to go for a ride in her sports car."

"Her roadster," Nora said as she typed.

"Right, her white roadster — is that right?"

"No, it's yellow," Nora said, "remember the first scene? The yellow car under the street light ?"

"You're right—of course it's yellow," Dan agreed. "She's speeding in the dark on a treacherous curvy road."

"So why doesn't he follow her?" Nora picked up the thread.

"Didn't John swear he would never run after her--not after the last time?"

"But he's afraid she might hurt herself—get into an accident."

"Does he know where she's going?" Dan asked.

"Does she?" Nora looked at her watch. "It's already six o'clock. Ginger is supposed to meet me here in a half hour."

"The time goes so fast...it seems like we just started. We always seem to be hurrying."

"Ginger lent her car to Jennifer and Michelle. I told her she could get a ride home with me. She's at a yoga workshop on Third Street."

"Okay. Well, we covered most of that dinner party scene." Dan said. I'll finish typing that and you can polish the dialog on the hospital scene."

Nora got up and walked into the bathroom. As she searched in her pocket for a tampon she realized how slow-witted and tense she'd felt all day. Now she could feel the bloody flow beginning and she waited expectantly for her abdomen to relax. Her breasts and belly felt swollen and warm. Sometimes she welcomed her period because it gave her a respite from the demands of what she thought of as the daily push. The shoulder to the wheel energy it took to keep her life moving forward. Each month there was an excuse to let up on the pressure for a few days. Not an excuse but a biological command. Not a command but a request; a motion to adjourn.

Nora thought of what her friend Amy had told her about a woman she knew who had a sex change operation and became a man. The main difference the once-woman noted was that her moods, her personality, became constant. She didn't change from day to day; from morning to afternoon to evening. The male hormones held steady, didn't fluctuate. Nora thought it would be tiresome to never fluctuate, to stop ebbing and flowing. That would be stagnation. She had noticed that it was in the nature of males to resist change while women were physically and emotionally accustomed to it.

When Nora came out of the bathroom Dan was sitting at the dining table organizing the various piles of paper that represented completed scenes. " Look," he said pointing, we've done quite a bit of work here."

"Yes," Nora said, "It's starting to look like something." She absentmindedly let her hands fall onto Dan's shoulders as she stood behind him. She could feel the muscles in his wide shoulders stiffen. She quickly removed her hands.

He busied himself stacking all the papers into very neat piles and securing them with paper clips. "We can go over all this on Saturday," Dan said.

"Nora?" Dan got up from the table and faced her. "I know we agreed at the beginning of this project that we wouldn't waste our work time talking about personal problems and bullshitting. You know I respect that—our work comes first, but..."

"But what?"

"Well, you know, I live alone here—except for Greta of course, and sometimes, well, sometimes I just need..."

"A vacation?" Nora interrupted. "Please Dan, wait until we finish this –then you can take some time off."

"No, that's not it" he said. "I don't want a vacation—I'm happy to be writing this script with you. I look forward to seeing you—it's the high point of my day." Dan stood with his arms folded, he searched Nora's face with a questioning look.

Nora felt queasy and bloated. She sat down in the typing chair. She looked through some of the papers.

"Today I realized that it's been three years since I drove my old Mustang out here. Can you believe that ? Three years." His voice was distant, as though recalling the sequence of events that led to the present moment.

"You're still new to L.A.," Nora told him.

"It gets old fast though, doesn't it? I miss smells—the way things smell humid and green in the summer. Have you ever driven through the open sagebrush south of Yellowstone and smelled the air after a rain. ?"

"No," said Nora.

"It's like medicine," Dan told her "it cleanses your lungs and sharpens your senses."

Nora nodded patiently, she could tell Dan was in one of his nostalgic moods.

"I don't want to...I mean, this is none of my business, but if you were seeing someone—I mean dating—you'd tell me, wouldn't you?"

"We have a good working relationship, Dan. Let's not ruin it." Nora felt tired of her role as diplomat; she wanted to be simple and direct with Dan. "This project is really important to me."

"It's important to me too," Dan was adamant. "I know this is going to work, Nora, we really have something here."

"I think so too." Nora pushed for a brisk encouraging tone of voice, though she didn't feel it.

"You know I still remember the first time you sat down next to me in Donald Pratt's screenwriting seminar."

"Oh come on," Nora said with a little laugh, trying to lighten the mood.

"No really, I remember exactly what you were wearing and your hands..." Dan trailed off. "I just knew right away..." Dan didn't finish his sentence.

Nora felt her stomach cramping as she steadied her seat on the rolling chair. "Dan, we made a deal. We agreed to buy the rights to this obscure English novel that you're so crazy about..."

"Wait a minute," Dan protested. "You love it too. You said you loved it."

"I do. I think it's got huge potential but we're not there yet." Nora was tired of sitting, her lower back hurt. She considered reclining on the sofa but knew it would send the wrong message. She kept her voice calm and reasonable. "We've worked so hard on this; we've solved most of the plot problems—let's not rock the boat...we don't want to complicate things do we?"

"Nora," Dan tried to match her calm, polite tone "All I'm saying is that I feel like...I mean I think we understand each other...better than most...I mean, we have something special..."

"We see each other almost every day" Nora responded, so of course we're bound to feel...close."

"You feel it too?" asked Dan.

What Nora felt was tired. Tired of pushing. She wished she could lie on the sofa and unzip her jeans and ask Dan to rub her back. And then forget about it the next day like it never happened. What does he expect, she wondered.

"Let's just focus on the screenplay, Dan. I feel like that's the most important thing right now." Nora kept her voice cheery and agreeable. "We're comfortable together as things are—I don't want that to change, do you ?"

"No." Dan sounded uncertain. "No, you're right. Look, I know what we agreed when we started together and I don't want to make you uncomfortable. I'm just....I don't know. I guess I'm out of line....Sorry." Dan turned and fooled around with something on the computer.

"Dan, I just don't want to complicate things. You understand don't you ?"

Nora's voice was genuinely sympathetic. She liked Dan; he was just so immature and inexperienced.

"Okay," Dan said "back to the script." He motioned Nora to get up from the typing chair and he began reading from the screen. "John tries to follow Iris but her car is faster..."

Nora interrupted "I don't think she's going to visit anyone. She just wants to let off steam, to express her..."

"Passionate feelings." Dan offered.

"Okay, whatever...pent-up emotions" Nora paced towards the fireplace as she talked and Dan typed.

"Hey," Dan looked up "You hungry? Do you want a snack? I have some cold salmon."

"I'm not that hungry" Nora said. "I don't want to waste time..."

"There's fresh poached salmon in the refrigerator" Dan told her.

The doorbell rang then and Nora said, "That must be Ginger."

Dan cleared the papers off the big table and went into the kitchen. Ginger, it turned out, had not had dinner, so Dan took the salmon out of the refrigerator, made a salad and opened a bottle of wine.

"This place is nice Dan," Ginger said "You were lucky to find it. I love these old beach bungalows. "

"Try this, it's from Napa Valley," Dan said, pouring white wine into Ginger's glass. "A small winery."

"Umm, delicious." Ginger looked relaxed and energized after three hours of stretching and chanting. "Aren't you having any, Nora?"

"I have to drive."

After dinner, Dan served dessert and coffee. Ginger rubbed Greta vigorously behind her ears and, when the dog rolled over, she gently caressed her underside.

"You're a wonderful cook, Dan, this peach cobbler is delicious." Ginger always ate desert but Nora didn't.

"My family had a restaurant in Jackson Hole," Dan told her. "My mother was a great cook—taught me a lot."

"Oh, that's the famous ski resort, isn't it?" Ginger said. "Did you grow up there?"

"Yes, well, my family was there before it became fashionable," Dan explained. "They were loggers and mountaineers and prospectors, real pioneers."

"That's fascinating" Ginger said. "None of my relatives ever lived west of Pennsylvania. You must be a great skier, Dan" she added.

"I was considered pretty good at one time. I'm out of shape right now." Dan didn't look out of shape, he was obviously being modest.

"You're being modest" Ginger accused him, smiling. "This wine is so good." She drank the last drop in her glass then took a close look at the label.

Nora noticed that Dan was, in fact, somewhat thicker through the middle than when she'd first met him.

"What time do you have to be at the restaurant?" Nora asked him.

"I'm going in later tonight. I have to close up."

"Well, you might as well ride back across town with us" Ginger offered.

"No, I can take a cab" Dan said, " don't worry about me."

"Don't be silly" Ginger said, "that's a thirty dollar cab ride."

"Really, it's not a problem…" Dan protested.

"Dan's punishing himself because his car was stolen" Nora explained to Ginger. "It's part of an elaborate scheme of grief and denial."

Ginger saw that Dan wasn't laughing. Sometimes, Ginger thought, Nora thinks she can get away with being really insensitive. "Nora!" Ginger said.

"Sorry, only kidding" Nora quickly reacted to Ginger's accusatory tone.

"You're not in a big hurry are you?" Ginger asked her.

. . .

Dan insisted on sitting in the back seat, allowing Ginger the more comfortable passenger seat. The freeway was clogged, something had gone wrong somewhere up ahead; the traffic crawled. Nora stayed in the fast lane but it was no faster than any of the other four lanes.

"We need to express the implosion of passion, the overwhelming hunger for understanding. " Dan was reading from his notebook.

"The profound craving for intimacy coupled with the paralyzing fear of rejection."

Dan's pen on the paper made a sound like a tiny animal running. "Right," he said to Nora.

"Is it something they can create together or is it forever beyond their grasp?" Nora continued.

"He's motivated by an out-of-control appetite for tenderness," Dan looked up from his notebook and met Ginger's eyes after he said that; she turned away, faintly embarrassed.

Nora was looking in the rear view mirror at Dan. Ginger nervously calculated the number of feet between their bumper and the car traveling directly in front.

Ginger said, "I like the way you read it, Dan." She hoped she sounded encouraging but not judgmental. She didn't want to judge what they were writing; but she wanted Dan to know that she appreciated what he was doing. Ginger hoped Nora wouldn't think she was interfering. Maybe I shouldn't say anything, Ginger thought, as she turned and gave Dan an approving look; she noticed the long shadows his eyelashes cast upon his cheeks. Dan needs encouragement, she decided, when he met her eyes briefly. He has eyelashes like a girl, Ginger thought.

"We'll work on it next week," Nora said. "That hospital scene could be longer."

"Okay," Dan said, "here, this is good."

Nora stopped the car in front of a low beige building on a quiet commercial street in Beverly Hills. A line of perfectly cone-shaped evergreen trees in ceramic pots flanked the entrance. "Troppo" was spelled out in modern brass letters three feet high affixed to the polished stone facade.

Simple but luxurious, Ginger thought, as Dan disappeared inside. She'd had dinner here once with Tim when...she calculated how long it had been since she'd had dinner there or anywhere like it since Tim had...gone. But Tim's not gone, she reflected, as she watched a thin red-haired woman in high heels get into a white Mercedes in front of the restaurant. The attendant closed her door and her male companion drove the car towards Wilshire Boulevard. Tim hasn't gone away--he has a new address and a new wife and they live in her house in Pacific Palisades, not far from here. His new wife has two children—one in college and one teenaged boy at home. Ginger thought Tim probably liked the idea of a stepson--she suspected that he secretly felt disappointed that Jessica wasn't a boy. Ginger had been trying not to think about her daughter Jessica or the things she said the night she left for Toronto with her husband. Ginger tried to like Colin but he was a policeman. My daughter married a Canadian policeman. She had to say that occasionally, that phrase, when people asked.

CHAPTER TWELVE

"Are you going out?" Ginger was ready for bed when she saw Nora searching for something in the hall closet. The sound of muted explosions and machine gun fire came from the living room; Michelle and Jennifer were watching a movie.

"David Marsden's show is opening tonight," Nora explained, "I almost forgot."

Nora put on her indigo blue satin jacket in front of the hallway mirror. She used a touch of lavender shadow on her eyelids and covered her face and throat with a pearly lotion designed to reflect light. Her face looked smooth as porcelain, geisha-like; her eyebrows dark and even. Nora applied her favorite red lipstick, Yves San Laurent number 22 and she shook her hair in the mirror—it hung shiny and tousled—better not to comb it she thought. She quickly pocketed the invitation with the address as she went out the door. Ace Gallery-- Marilyn Monroe as photographed by David Marsden.

The long storefront gallery on Melrose Avenue was lit up like an airport with its glass doors open and guests spilling out onto the warm sidewalk, smoking and talking. Nora watched the people as she got out of her car and waited for the attendant to give her a claim ticket. Ace Gallery's patrons dressed more flamboyantly than usual for an opening—as if aware that they were also on view. Nora enjoyed the theatricality of it; the whole gallery was like a brightly lit stage.

Inside, the white walls were covered with brand new prints of photographs of Marilyn Monroe when she was at the peak of her career. The round cheeks, the dark lips, the pale curls, the innocent eyes, the curves. Nora had seen some of the pictures before, but never a whole room full. Voluptuous and flirtatious, Marilyn peeked out from under milky silk sheets, holding them just so; her round shoulders and slightly plump arms as soft and inviting as whipped cream, smiling. Nora didn't see David as she began looking carefully at the photographs—they were huge, some of them, four feet by three on matte paper. Marilyn's face close up, lips slightly parted, eyes vulnerable; wisps of tousled little-girl hair bathed in a frothy white overexposure which made the nostrils a casual tracery like a charcoal sketch.

"They say she is the most photographed subject in the world" Joe Sackman was at her left, looking at the same image.

"Really?" Nora tried to think of another possible candidate but could not. The Kennedys? The Beatles ? Princess Di ? Who else—the Queen, Madonna, Hitler, Michael Jackson ? No one woman ever belonged to so many, Nora found herself thinking. She realized how long she'd been looking at pictures of Marilyn— since she could remember, really.

Joe was a successful fashion photographer. He had once been married to Pam and so he was Nora's ex-brother-in-law but Nora seldom saw him after the wedding as she had lived in New York during the two years the marriage lasted. That was when Pam first moved to L.A. She'd left Joe for Alan but didn't marry him. Nora couldn't recall who came after that.

"I remember when I thought she was so old," Nora told Joe, who moved slowly from picture to picture, staring impassively through his heavy black-framed glasses.

Joe was well dressed and well read. He dated dozens of models and actresses but he had never married again. His overt self-absorption, his exaggerated self-regard, allowed Nora to feel comfortable with him. With Joe there was no question of involvement. He was interested exclusively in himself.

"But looking at her now she seems so young and ...happy." Nora concluded.

"Yes," Joe agreed, "David took these when he was just a kid, starting out with Life Magazine in the sixties. He discovered the negatives forgotten in a drawer, most of them were never published. The thing is, practically every shot was good—it's amazing."

"Yeah," Nora agreed, "incredible, they say she loved being photographed—it really looks like it."

"Wow," Joe said in the grave, matter-of-fact way people in L.A. used the word. They had come to a photograph of Marilyn standing, draped in a white sheet against a white wall; one hand held the sheet just high enough to cover her nipples and the right hand beckoned flirtatiously with crooked finger directly to the camera, to the photographer, to the viewer--come hither, come closer.

"This is gorgeous" Nora agreed with Joe. She appreciated having someone to exchange comments with in the crowded room. There was something about Joe, his disinterestedness, that made him easy to talk to. Nora looked around the room. She saw an actor she recognized; some older women dressed in suits and gold jewelry; some twenty-somethings in jeans and butchered hair with chains hanging from unexpected places. Moonlighting actors in uniform black carried trays of wine and bite-sized food to and fro, reciting descriptions of what they served: goat cheese with sundried tomato; stuffed Portobello mushrooms; smoked salmon with fresh dill. Nora took a glass of champagne and further along, grabbed a skewer of teriyaki chicken. She felt hungry suddenly, and glad she had come. The sunny face of Marilyn seemed to encourage celebration.

Joe moved into a knot of other men and Nora spotted tall smiling David surrounded by shorter people in a corner near the back of the gallery. She had seen him often in New York. He and his wife were old friends of Tony's. Although David looked tired, he greeted Nora warmly and introduced her to a couple on his right and offered her another glass of champagne. Nora felt a surge of admiration.

"Your work is amazing, David" she told him, "this show is fantastic—really unbelievable."

David's wife Laurette was dressed in a tight laced-up bustier in black brocade with a gray leather skirt. Nora told her " You look fantastic. I love your hair." Laurette always wore her hair long and loose and didn't mind baring her arms even though they weren't muscular and taut like a boy. Nora thought this was probably because she was French and she admired her for that. Laurette asked Nora "How is Tony?" and David had to interrupt and tell her that Nora and Tony had broken up.

"She didn't know" David apologized to Nora.

"But I am so sorry." Laurette's expressive face looked genuinely sorry.

"I haven't seen him in over a year" Nora told her. "Don't worry, he's okay and I'm okay, you know."

She almost said we're still friends but that would have been stupid. Laurette didn't care that much and besides, they weren't. Nora had never stayed friends with the men she had relationships with. It was either on or off. She knew that many women did— stay friends, but it seemed to her that the men she wanted as lovers were not people she wanted to be friends with. She had talked about this with Ginger who had warned her that such behavior indicated some kind of deep-seated pathology.

Maybe it did, Nora thought, examining a photograph that showed Marilyn from the back, her soft girlish face looking over her shoulder at the camera. She seemed to be looking at someone she loved or liked or wanted to…From Nora's point of view near the wall she caught a glimpse of the door and saw her sister Pam enter the gallery with her husband Van Aston who appeared slightly shorter since Pam was wearing very high heels. Nora could tell by the way her sister swayed and held Van's arm. Nora moved silently behind a partition to examine some smaller prints.

Pam and Van made their way directly to David, and Nora could see the kissing and round of compliments. Pam was in white silk Capri pants with some kind of fringed thing on top. Nora thought it was too late in the year for white but people in L.A. wore white all the time—white boots, white jackets—it was because of the heat, the tropical thing. Nora could never get used to it.

As Pam and Van made their way towards Nora, people in the crowd turned and stared at them because Van had been the star of a cable television show on Fox. Pam embraced her sister like they hadn't seen each other in years, kissing her very deliberately on both cheeks. Then all three looked at the nearest photograph.

"She actually looks kind of fat, don't you think?" Pam asked Nora.

"Our ideals of beauty change." Nora replied.

"It always blows my mind that you two are sisters" Van said in his lazy southern California drawl. He looked from Pam to Nora "I mean, like you're so, you know, different." Van so rarely voiced an opinion about anything that Pam and Nora gave him their full attention.

"But you know we're half-sisters, Van" Pam said patiently, as if talking to a child, as if possibly he had forgotten the fact that they had different fathers.

"Yeah, I know." He said, staring at a smaller print, then walking over to a very large Marilyn in bed with a sheet flowing between her legs and curving into a pleated fan over her famous breasts. He stood and looked, lost in thought.

Nora's father was a Greek-American who had been involved in shipping. He died of a heart attack when she was six. Her mother met Pam's father, a Florida real-estate developer, in Miami where they'd gone on vacation and stayed married to him for thirty years.

Tomorrow would have been Mom's birthday," Pam said to Nora who didn't answer. Pam loved to sentimentalize everything—like she's desperately looking for a reason to feel something, Nora thought, distracted by a handsome boy who came by with a tray full of glasses.

"Not for me," Pam said. Is she on the wagon again, Nora wondered, or dieting?

"You know what Kim told me," Pam said. "You can drink or you can eat—but you can't do both." Pam shared this gem of wisdom, these words to live by, like a divine revelation. Nora's red lips turned up in an involuntary smile as she remembered what Tony used to say about Pam—she may be annoying but at least she's not boring.

For a black second, Nora missed Tony desperately. It was a kind of falling, or fear of falling, vertigo, falling into the past. But the moment passed quickly and Nora asked Pam "Has Van found a script yet ?"

Pam shook her head and shrugged. It was an ongoing topic—a joke really--Van looking for a script to direct. He'd read, at latest count, one hundred and ninety film scripts but had not yet found one he liked. Nora thought it was because he was afraid to try; but Pam believed that one day Van would find the perfect script and become a successful feature director.

Nora suddenly felt tired. She looked around the room. The opening was over. The crowd was thinning out and the waiters were cleaning up. David and Laurette, still surrounded, looked like they were exhausted from repeating the same greetings and explanations and hearing the same compliments. Nora decided to slip away without saying goodbye. On the sidewalk outside the gallery, she ran into Joe.

"Why don't we stop by La Cava and have a drink," he suggested. "We should talk, I know a director who's looking for material."

In the dark living room of Ginger's house, Jennifer held up the plastic control and pushed a button repeatedly clicking from channel to channel to channel. Truncated arguments and gunshots with jazz; shiny hair and animals lapping up food snapped into the screen and were replaced again and again endlessly. Jennifer always had trouble falling asleep but Michelle could sleep through anything. The TV was turned to a very low drone and Michelle snored quietly beside her.

Jennifer held the plastic bar at arms length and decisively pushed the OFF button, watching the coughing housewife take her medicine and drain into a black hole.

"Michelle, wake up." Jennifer shook her friend's arm.

"What time is it?" Michelle always woke with difficulty, as if it was a great effort to travel from the dream state to wakefulness.

"I don't know. Come outside with me, okay ? I want a cigarette."

Jennifer got out of bed and pulled on the clothes she'd left on the floor.

"Can't you go by yourself?" Michelle asked, stirring slowly, her voice a soft moan.

Jennifer shook Michelle's upper arm gently. "Michelle, come on."

Michelle said nothing. She found her coat and followed Jennifer out the back door and the girls took their usual places under the Magnolia tree. The blanket they'd left outside was wet with dew. The penetrating white flower smell hung in the air.

"March must be asleep," Jennifer said, "I don't see any lights next door."

It's the middle of the night, Michelle thought, trying to pinpoint what time the middle of the night would be on the clock. Or it could be the very end of the night before sunrise. A thick cold stillness hung in the air. She looked at the sky—it was dark and clouded like black stone, empty of stars, moonless.

"You can hear the freeway," Jennifer said. In the stillness, the sound was magnified—a steady high-pitched hum. Closer in, something rustling the dry leaves under the shrubbery sounded like a large animal; but more likely a bird.

Michelle said nothing. She was half-asleep but not tired. In the darkness it was hard to know if she was really awake. When she was younger her mother never allowed her out at night, but sitting in the dark was exciting. With Jennifer, Michelle didn't worry about anything—she wasn't afraid. The same as being outside in the daytime but quieter, she thought, without sun but otherwise the same except you couldn't see that it was the same, so everything seemed different and strange.

Michelle had been dreaming about her brother. They were sleeping together in the same bed with her mother. But I don't have a brother, Michelle thought, vaguely questioning that fact, but she couldn't recollect the necessary evidence to verify it. She saw the brother of her dream, taller than her mother, with long hair. Not my brother, she thought, but a boy like him. Michelle wanted to untangle her thoughts, find where the end was and smooth out the knots. Get to the beginning of the dream. I have no brother. Michelle wasn't sure if her eyes were open or closed. She blinked slowly and recalled something about parrots as she watched the orange tip of Jennifer's cigarette rise and fall.

"I think the street lights must be out" Jennifer said," it's never been this dark before. Are you awake, Michelle?"

"I hear you." Michelle's voice was clear and close.

She smelled the cigarette smoke and white flowers and damp earth. Then Michelle felt the roots of the tree shift and shudder and she heard the strange noise — all the thick leathery leaves of the tree shaking and rustling crazy loud and a downward rush of wind from above which was high-pitched like a cat cry in the night. For a second, the back yard was frozen in a bright flash that captured a photograph — red and black and green, with outlines blurred. Then Michelle was on her knees, trying to steady herself.

"Jennifer?" When she saw her friend lying on the ground crooked, her arm at a weird angle, Michelle grabbed Jennifer's shoulders and shouted her name.   Jennifer sat back on her haunches and rubbed the side of her head.

"Did you see that?" she asked and then she heard singing rushing in her ears like water and she was gone again.   In the distance, Jennifer could faintly hear Michelle calling her name as she became weightless, a tiny body on the ground; and she looked down from above the flustered chattering tree and saw the striped blanket and Michelle shaking the limp white body that was Jennifer. The flash made the dark white and the white black, like a negative. She watched as the picture developed. Michelle was bent over her, yelling her name.

...

As Nora drove home she saw almost no sign of human movement on the Hollywood streets except for a few cars in the parking lot of the 24-hour supermarket on Sunset Blvd. After two o'clock, L.A. goes to sleep, Nora thought, remembering places in New York that came alive at three in the morning.   When she turned onto Westborne Street she was surprised to see all the lights shining brightly in Ginger's house.

Ginger met Nora at the door.   "Jennifer had some kind of seizure — she's got a head injury. I think I'll have to take her to the hospital."

Nora followed Ginger into the living room and saw Jennifer lying on the bed with a wet dishtowel on her head.

"Was it drugs ?"

Michelle, her face smeared with tears, stood beside Jennifer. "No, we didn't take anything — I swear ! We saw something. We both saw it !"

"Please try to tell us exactly what you saw, Michelle." Ginger asked, with the calm manner of one accustomed to dealing with crisis situations.

"It was like a bright light—I don't know." Michelle was crying and pacing.

Ginger was watching Jennifer, who appeared to be awake. Suddenly, she bent down and lifted the girl by her shoulders. "If you took something you have to tell me." Ginger demanded. Nora was shocked at her vehemence.

"No! No! We didn't take anything" Michelle insisted. Jennifer said nothing but her eyes were open and focused.

Ginger continued in the same tone. "And we need to have your parents' names—at least one—they'll ask at the hospital."

"She's eighteen" Michelle said, "her parents are dead."

"Why don't you stay here with Nora," Ginger suggested to Michelle.

"No—I'm going with Jennifer. You can't make me stay here."

Nora helped Jennifer into the back seat of the Volvo. She seemed subdued but alert. Michelle held ice wrapped in a towel against her friend's head. When Ginger started the engine, Nora leaned down to the passenger window. "Call me when..." but Nora didn't have any idea what was likely to happen.

Ginger said, "I don't know if they'll keep her overnight. I'll call you when we know something."

Nora watched them drive away. The streetlight must be out, she thought, it's darker than usual tonight.

At about five o'clock the phone rang beside Nora's bed. She had dozed off, fully dressed.

"We're all coming home," Ginger told her.

"Is she all right?"

"She's fine. She has a minor abrasion on her head, nothing serious." Ginger sounded tired.

Jennifer and Michelle entered the house first, Nora held the door open for them. "It's morning," said Jennifer slyly "time to wake up." She had a white horizontal band around her head like a war victim.

The two girls sat down at the table with their elbows touching, calm and satisfied. Ginger walked in and slumped into a chair.

"So, how did...what happened?" Nora asked.

"They think maybe it was a mild epileptic seizure" Ginger said in her therapist voice, "we'll find out later today--they did some tests."

"I don't think so," Jennifer said. Nora saw that Ginger looked annoyed, on edge; she had puffy gray circles under her eyes. The situation was out of her control. The girls were softly humming together—a slow lilting melody.

"Why don't you two try to get some sleep?" Ginger suggested to Michelle and Jennifer.

"I'm not tired" Jennifer said, "Are you, Michelle?"

"No. I feel fine," Michelle did look remarkably fresh, Nora thought.

"I'll try to sleep for a few hours—I have to see some clients later." Ginger made a motion towards Nora with both palms open like someone waiting to catch a basketball. Nora interpreted this to mean : I can't do any more, it's your turn. When Ginger left the room, Nora poured some coffee for herself, then wordlessly held the pot up, offering some to the girls—they shook their heads.

"Don't you want to lie down and rest, Jennifer?" Nora didn't relish the role of nurse but she didn't want to appear unsympathetic.

"I'm not tired" Jennifer repeated.

"What did the doctor say?"

"Nothing--there's nothing wrong with me," Jennifer said, "They didn't know."

"Then, why..."

"We saw something," Michelle told her. "It was...it..."

"It rocked me to the ground." Jennifer said "I was knocked out."

Michelle nodded. "But only for a second—she was like, stunned."

"You want some orange juice or something?"

"I'm not hungry" Jennifer said. She and Michelle hummed the same melody again. Michelle looked at her friend like she was admiring a new haircut.

"You know what I want to do Jen, I want to go visit March," Michelle said.

"Isn't it a little early? " Nora asked.

"Let's go talk to her, okay?" Michelle looked at Jennifer, who smiled and agreed.

Nora sat drinking coffee as the girls left through the back door.

CHAPTER THIRTEEN

Ginger was standing beside the sink in her flannel nightgown talking on the telephone when Nora entered the kitchen around noon. Ginger drank from a mug of coffee facing the window with the phone to her ear.

"No, she didn't... I'll call you if anything changes, Doctor, thank you."

Ginger hung up the telephone. "All the tests were negative," she told Nora. "Apparently Jennifer is fine. The doctor can't find any sign of injury to the brain or nervous system."

Ginger leaned over the sink to look out the kitchen window, searching the street in both directions; she seemed unusually alert, expectant.

"They're going to be here soon," Ginger said. "Let me know if you see a television news van outside...I have to get dressed."

"News van?"

Nora called after her as Ginger hurried out of the kitchen. Nora looked at the clock and figured she had slept maybe four hours. She followed Ginger to the closed door of her bedroom where she could hear the clinking sound of hangers moving on a metal rod in the closet.

"Did you say television news van?" Nora questioned through the door.

Ginger emerged wearing her striped Morrocan caftan and sandals. "They saw something in the back yard" she told Nora.

Ginger walked to the front of the house to look out the window again. Nora followed. "What ? What happened last night ?"

There was a knock at the back door. Ginger turned the bolt and opened the door to Jennifer, Michelle and March.

"Nora, I don't know if you've met March, our next door neighbor..." Ginger began.

Nora couldn't take her eyes off March's hair, which was braided in thick plaits entwined with purple satin ribbons. She had seen women in southern Mexico with braids like hers, but they didn't wear makeup like March who outlined her eyes with black and used powder blue eye shadow up to her eyebrows.

"Nice to meet you Nora." March seemed preoccupied, "Now listen, before the news team gets here I just want..."

"News team?" Nora echoed.

"They saw something in the back yard." Ginger told her again.

" Did you call the police?" Nora asked.

Michelle and Jennifer exchanged a smile as they sat down at the kitchen table. They looked serene and rested like they'd just had a good night's sleep and a healthy breakfast. Ginger stood watching at the window. With a little trill in her voice she said, "The Channel 8 news team just drove up."

"Now remember," March told the girls, "Don't get into any complicated explanations. They like it short and sweet. I told them about the spring and the lights."

Ginger hurried into the little bathroom off the kitchen and applied lipstick. March stood near the front door, smiling expectantly.

"Jennifer," Nora asked, "What did you see in the back yard?"

"We saw a being filled with light," Jennifer told Nora. "She told us to pray for the children of this city."

"Pray?" asked Nora, "Is that what...?"

"It was Mary, I think. You know, like a saint." Michelle seemed certain.

"How could you tell ?" Nora asked her.

"She was holy." Michelle replied.

The doorbell rang and a bearded man carrying a video camera entered the kitchen, followed by a younger assistant carrying a light which illuminated everything in the room with an unnatural white glare.

A woman with very shiny straight hair followed the cameraman into the kitchen. "Hi, I'm Candy Cummings" she shook hands with Nora, then looked around the room. She wore a tailored jacket and blouse with pearls.

"Which one of you saw it ?" Candy spoke in a firm clear voice. Michelle said "We both did. Me and Jennifer..."

"The being announced herself to both of us." Jennifer stared hard at Candy whose eyes kept moving around the room.

"Where did you see it ?"

"Right outside--in the back yard." Michelle pointed.

"Kevin ?" Candy spoke to the assistant "Can we get cable out back ? Let's shoot outside."

Ginger pointed in the direction of the back door. "You can go out this way."

Candy's assistant showed Jennifer and Michelle where to stand in front of the Magnolia tree.

"Let me know when you're you ready, Andy." The cameraman busied himself with his equipment and Candy turned to the girls. "Which one of you first saw the phenomenon ?" Candy asked, looking at Michelle, then at Jennifer.

"We both did," Michelle answered, her eyes on the microphone, "me and Jennifer."

"Your neighbor said something about a spring, or a pond."

Jennifer led Candy towards a pool of water that had formed near the Magnolia tree; the crew followed. The bearded man took a few steps back and adjusted the eye piece of his camera.

"Kevin, did you bring the paperwork ? We need to get everybody to sign a release form." Candy talked to her assistant over her shoulder as she hurried across the lawn.

March disappeared inside her back door for a minute and emerged with Leo on her shoulder. Kevin handed her a clipboard with a printed form and a pen. March signed her name to the form and handed it back without reading what was written on it. Ginger and Nora got forms too.

"What is this?" Ginger moved towards Candy.

"Just a formality—this gives us the right to use your image on television," Candy explained. " We don't have much time, so let's try to get started on the interviews. Kevin, you make sure everybody signs, okay ?"

"Am I gonna be on TV?" asked March. Candy looked at the bird and the braids like she didn't know.

"Were you the one who called ?" Candy asked her.

"I called the station last night when I saw some lights and heard a noise. Something happened here. When I saw the water, I knew you'd want to investigate."

"Did you see the...uh...vision?" Candy asked March, looking at the others, "Who actually saw the...?"

"Angel. It was a woman," said Michelle.

"The girls were on their knees when I got here," March explained to Candy. "This water came out of nowhere. It wasn't here before. I could tell something had happened. It was a visitation."

"A visitation ?" Candy repeated the word, looking over March's shoulder. "Andy, are we ready here ?"

Andy nodded, pointing his right thumb in the air.

"Rolling" the cameraman said.

Jennifer felt an electric surge of well being. She knew she would always remember this morning and how Candy's perfect hair caught the sunshine and how Michelle was smiling and the creamy peach color of Michelle's lipstick.

Jennifer watched Candy closely as she lifted her chin and looked into the dark glass barrel of the lens with a friendly, confident expression.

"We are standing in the backyard of a quiet neighborhood in West Hollywood where, as you can see, a small pond formed virtually overnight and two young women experienced what they describe as a supernatural visitation."

Candy held the microphone in front of Michelle's chin. "We're talking to..."

"Michelle Montano that's me" Michelle said, almost giggling, then after a quick look at Jennifer, who had a very serious expression on her face, she composed her mouth into a relaxed approximation of Candy's confident half-smile.

"And…"Candy then moved the microphone under Jennifer's face. Immediately, without hesitation, Jennifer said "Jennifer Reilly" in a serious but casual voice.

"These two…students?" Candy questioned with eyebrows raised just enough to express polite curiosity.

"Actually Candy we're out of school. We're both actresses." Jennifer explained in a cooperative tone, with a reassuring nod.

"Both of you ? Actresses ? Okay," Candy continued with a quick double bobbing of her shiny head. "These two young actresses looked up in the sky Tuesday night and saw something. You saw a woman ?" Candy wanted to clarify this for her viewers.

"She was floating," Michelle explained "She was kind of up in the air."

"Can you tell us what the… this being…What exactly did it look like ?" Candy asked Jennifer, pointing the microphone at her. She moved her face in close so they could both fit on the screen; Jennifer saw Candy's eyes calculate the distance from the lens.

"The being--she resembled a beam of light," Jennifer explained—no nonsense, matter-of-fact. Michelle nodded in agreement, blinking.

"Did she say anything ?" Candy held the microphone in readiness; waiting for the first word to drop from Jennifer or Michelle's lips.

Jennifer stood up straight and looked directly into the black barrel of polished reflections that the man was pointing at her. "She told us to pray for the children of the city."

"The children of Los Angeles" Candy repeated. "Can you give our viewers a little better picture of what you actually saw ?"

"She had wings," Michelle burst out.

Jennifer turned quickly and looked at Michelle's face, then swiftly faced the camera again. She had never seen her friend look so excited and happy. "She had a glow around her body…" Jennifer began.

"An aura ?" Candy sounded eager, helpful.

"Her aura glowed like sunlight," Jennifer said, "she held us in her embrace, without touching us, we felt her boundless love. She said she would help us all if we pray and…"

"Andy," Candy raised her hand in front of the lens and smiled apologetically at Jennifer as she spoke to the cameraman. "Sorry to interrupt; but we don't have much time. Can you begin with a wider shot ? The water, then the two girls, then the tree—maybe get that big white flower—good, then pan down to this one's face."

The camera moved, ending up on Michelle's face. "Could you just repeat that last line, Jennifer," Candy requested. "Exactly like before."

Michelle blinked her wide eyes and gave Jennifer a very quick fierce squeeze with her right hand. Jennifer said, "Her aura glowed like sunlight. She held us in her embrace, without touching us, we felt her boundless love. She said she would help us all if we pray."

Jennifer remembered then how it was to make herself weightless, to lose gravity, to float into...joy. That's what she knew; she was in control. She was in that place now where joy began. An opened open word: floating, buoyant, full joy, joyfull. She wondered if many other people had discovered what she knew. Possibly she alone felt this, gave it and received it, spoke to it, heard it. She couldn't have explained the idea to Michelle or anyone else. She must have been born with this talent; then forgotten it. And now she remembered it again--this talent for joy.

CHAPTER FOURTEEN

"Hurry up, Nora, it's on !" Ginger called into the kitchen from the living room where she and Dan were settled in front of the television. "Hurry!"

Nora walked into the room carrying three cups of after-dinner coffee. Dan and Ginger had their eyes focused on the television; they didn't turn to look as Nora set the cups down. On the screen was the face of a middle-aged man in a Roman collar who seemed to be emerging from the side door of a stone church.

Candy's voice could be heard asking "Bishop Flannery, what is the official position of the church on the incident in West Hollywood ?" The Bishop seemed calm, untroubled by the microphone close to his mouth.

"We will investigate if necessary," he answered, "but there is no evidence, so far, to credit this event as a miraculous visitation." The picture abruptly switched to a residential street.

"There's our house !" Ginger exclaimed, bobbing up and down on the sofa in her enthusiasm. Dan 's coffee sloshed into its saucer; he and Nora exchanged amused looks.

Candy's voice over the crowded frame explained "A steady stream of people continue to visit the West Hollywood home where two young women claim to have seen a celestial being with a message. "

On the screen, some old women carrying flowers, and some men, mostly in their 30's and 40's, could be seen gathered near the driveway of Ginger's house.

"Somebody broke the latch on the gate this afternoon," Ginger told Nora. "People think they can just walk in. It's kind of spooky." The two women sat with full attention to Candy's voice over the shaky hand-held camera view of their backyard.

"Burt, we're here at the actual location where the sighting took place. As you can see, a pond has formed in the exact spot where the two actresses saw what they refer to as the Angel Lady. Apparently, Burt, the water started flowing spontaneously a short time after the sighting occurred here."

On the screen, Candy approached two men standing near the oleander bushes; one carried white lilies in his hand. "Here are two of the dozens of people who have visited this spot since the story broke. Can I get your names ?"

A gaunt well-dressed man spoke into the microphone with a lisping voice. "Gary Kurtz. I live nearby and heard about what happened. Jeffrey and I both feel that the girls are telling the truth. I mean, I can sense that this place is special. Like, this spring didn't come from nowhere." Gary ended his comments with an emphatic shrug.

"How about you Jeffrey?" Candy asked his companion.

"I feel that this spring is genuinely spiritual, Candy." Jeffrey looked around with a reverent expression. "There's definitely a spiritual feeling here."

"Thank you," Candy moved her face closer to the camera and spoke more rapidly "From the modest backyard where a sighting of a celestial being has galvanized residents of a West Hollywood neighborhood, this is Candy Cummings. Back to you Burt."

The picture switched back to the newsroom desk and balding Burt in front of the Channel 8 News logo. Nora and Dan sipped coffee and Ginger leaned forward to catch his words. Burt said "Thank you Candy, We'll have an exclusive interview on the air tomorrow with the two young women who saw the Angel Lady."

"Angel Lady ? Angel Lady ?" Nora asked rhetorically "That is so lame. It's just inconceivable that they would actually put this on the air. It must have been a slow news night."

Ginger seemed to be in an indulgent, forgiving mood as she got up and turned off the TV. "March must have told everybody in the neighborhood. Well, it's harmless enough."

Nora was squirming with indignation. "We have people knocking on the door, looking over the fence. Angel lady ? Give me a break. They're exploiting people's ignorance--Candy knows this is irresponsible."

"Don't you remember when they had that picture of Jesus appearing spontaneously on the building downtown ? This isn't the first time they've covered this kind of thing. I'm sure it will all be forgotten in another day or so. What concerns me is that water in the back yard. I'm not sure what to do about it." Ginger looked worried.

"I have an idea one of the neighbors has a leak in their watering system and it's running over here. Maybe it's that duplex on the other side."

Ginger hated having to deal with emergency repairs. Something like new pipes or a sewer line could cost thousands of dollars. "I called Hans, he's coming tomorrow morning." Ginger was getting more confident about dealing with homeowner emergencies. Tim had always been the one who took care of plumbing and electrical problems. When she was alone in the house after the divorce, Ginger panicked the first time a pipe broke. But now she called Hans whenever anything went wrong.

"How can they get away with this ?"

Nora was really worked up. Ginger couldn't understand why she was so upset.

"In some ways," Ginger told her, "this represents a step forward for Michelle and Jennifer. Whatever it was that happened the other night—some kind of freak electrical surge or a stray police helicopter—whatever they saw, they made a personal interpretation that increased their sense of self-worth."

Nora rolled her eyes at Dan but he was nodding, agreeing with Ginger.

"The important thing," Ginger explained, "is that they are not victims in this situation. That's what makes it so positive."

"But they didn't do anything." Nora pointed out.

"Oh yes they did," Ginger said. "They managed to create a situation where they are in control—they've gained authority and respect. You could call that, in itself, a religious experience."

"What religion?" Nora's voice came out louder than she intended. She looked at Dan, then back to Ginger, "You don't believe they really…"

"That's not the issue," Ginger explained. " Something unusual and important happened to them and they interpreted it as they saw fit—now they own this experience, I think that's healthy.

"Ginger," Nora said, "has it not occurred to you that they could be making this all up?"

"What actually happened…who knows ?" Ginger shrugged. "Both of them shared the experience. They saw something. Neither of them is particularly religious, as far as I know. The important thing is, the experience was real to them in some powerful and life-affirming way."

"What is this about a spring ?" asked Dan.

"There's a puddle of water in the backyard for god's sake," Nora stood up impatiently, "It's probably a leaking lawn sprinkler."

Dan looked at her closely "You think they made it all up ?"

"What else can I believe?" Nora's voice was louder than before.

Ginger could tell that Nora didn't understand. She spoke slowly and carefully. "The way I see it is that if I want to show respect for Michelle and Jennifer, and the Angel Lady is real to them, I have to accept its reality in the framework of who they are and how they see the world."

"What ?" Nora sat down to meet Ginger eye to eye. "What are you saying, Ginger ? Excuse me, but can we get real here for just a second ?"

"You have to understand" Ginger continued, with a patient regard for her listeners' lack of expertise in such matters, "there are many varieties of religious experience. To acknowledge the divine is a first step. From there, all systems of worship and morality and prohibition follow."

"So," Nora remained face to face with Ginger "we've got celestial beings unconnected to any specific…"

"Identity. Yes. It's a very pure concept." Ginger explained. "Very primal."

Nora shook her head.

"Ginger's right, Nora," Dan said. "The beautiful thing is that this Angel Lady is nondenominational—she doesn't represent any belief system. There's nothing to answer to because you don't have to believe in any specific set of rules or conditions. There's no guilt, no sin, no requirements of any kind."

Ginger went into the kitchen and came back with two porcelain bowls containing the crème caramel that Dan had prepared.

"Am I the only one who has a problem with this ?" Nora asked.

"What Dan said is true," Ginger leaned back and spooned some dessert into her mouth. "This is a non-threatening belief."

"But we have disembodied beings here, traveling around talking to people."

"Are you threatened by that, Nora ?" Dan asked with a little laugh. Ginger giggled, she looked approvingly at Dan, at his eyelashes.

"Maybe I am" Nora answered. " You don't think it's weird that people take this story seriously ?"

"This crème caramel is delicious, Dan," Ginger told him "I have to remember how you did this." Ginger could see that Nora was genuinely irritated. "But I do think it's a step forward for them, Nora, I really do" she said in a soothing voice. The phone rang and Ginger crossed the room to pick it up.

"It's Michelle," she told the others as she listened. "Yes, we saw the TV," she said into the phone. "Where are you ?"

Ginger covered the mouthpiece and told Dan and Nora "They're next door with March." Ginger smiled as she listened. "That's great Michelle." It was clear that Ginger was hearing good news. "You are ? Jennifer too ? That's wonderful. We love you too. Oh, thank you...thanks very much..."

Ginger hung up the telephone and looked at Dan and Nora with a pause before she spoke.

"They're going to pray for us."

"Great," said Nora.

The next morning Ginger was up early to check on things. The water standing in the back yard seemed to be a little deeper than before. In the front lawn she could see footprints and some litter. The old metal latch on the gate leading to the back yard was broken, it had come loose and was hanging by one screw. She decided to move her car out of the driveway so Hans could park his truck close to the house.

An old man in bedroom slippers and a stained zipper jacket shouted 'good morning' from the sidewalk. "Is this what they showed on TV last night ?" he called to Ginger.

"Yes it is," Ginger told him.

"I live across the street," the man said. "Tebby's the name."

Ginger went over and shook the man's hand and introduced herself.

"Where's your husband ?" Mr. Tebby asked.

"He's gone," Ginger told him.

"That's too bad," the old neighbor remarked, "They're tearing up your lawn, you know that ?"

Ginger nodded and the old man did too; then he shuffled back across the street.

"You're meeting the neighbors." Nora stepped out the front door.

"I've been here sixteen years and I only know the woman next door by name, I've never been inside her house." Ginger told Nora.

"Did you call somebody about the water ?" Nora asked.

"Yes, Hans should be here soon. He can fix anything."

Soon after Nora left, Ginger was relieved to see Hans' white pickup truck drive into the driveway. There was something about the man that made Ginger feel she could rely on him. Hans was a problem solver; he liked to fix things. Today he was wearing a clean white cotton T-shirt covered by a beige cotton cardigan with coordinated khaki pants and immaculate white tennis shoes. She watched him get out of his new Japanese pickup truck and survey the property. Hans was disturbed by the damage to the lawn.

"Terrible, terrible" he muttered as Ginger led him towards the gate.

Ginger saw how distressed Hans looked when he came upon the large pool of water standing in the grass.

"Is it the irrigation system ?" he said aloud almost as if he were talking to himself, hurrying to open the plastic control box at the side of the garage. When she was left with the house, Ginger didn't realize at first how important it was to water the lawn in California. As a child she remembered lawn sprinklers as something used only when the weather was exceptionally hot and dry. But in L.A., every lawn and garden had to be regularly watered all year—except for six weeks or so in winter when the rains were steady. Hans had saved the landscaping by explaining all this to Ginger. He had supervised the installation of the automatic watering system as well as many other repairs over the past few years.

As he intently studied the water gauge, Ginger thought Hans looked like the actor Montgomery Clift with his square jaw and piercing blue eyes. He stood close to six foot four inches tall with broad shoulders and a trim waistline. He always tanned his face, but not too much. Like all tall women, Ginger enjoyed being near a man so much taller and stronger than she. Hans had worked for years as a male model before he became a handyman. As a child in Northern Germany he was orphaned in World War II and adopted by an American woman in Philadelphia who he still referred to as his American mother. When Ginger and Hans discovered that they had grown up in the same city they both recognized a significant bond. Sometimes Hans stayed for lunch with Ginger; he liked to talk about politics and they agreed on most issues—especially the more controversial ones. He had a stiff formal way of speaking but did not mind sharing the most private details of his life.

"I was very handsome when I was young" he once told Ginger. Hans' w's veered slightly toward v's and vice versa. "Do you remember the director George Kostas ? No matter, he was very successful in England in the early sixties. One night, at a dinner party, he said to the guests 'Hans is more handsome than any actor I've ever worked with.' He wanted to give me a role—the lead, in one of his films, but I said no."

"Why Hans?" Ginger asked him.

"I was young," he explained. "I didn't know anything." Hans was puzzled by the puddle of water. This made him anxious.

When Hans couldn't figure something out right away; or if he couldn't fix it, he became anxious.

Ginger wanted to reassure him. "Maybe a pipe broke under the ground where we can't see it," she offered.

"If that was the case," Hans pointed out "one would see the water meter moving—you would notice that there was a large increase in your water bill." Hans checked all the places where there could be a leak. "Vhat is possible is that there is an underground spring here. This has never happened before ?"

"Not since I've lived here." Ginger was sure she would have noticed.

"We have to get an expert to check this." If he was at all uncertain as to how to fix something, Hans always advised that work be delegated to a well-qualified expert, whom he often supervised. Following his recommendations made Ginger feel competent and secure.

Ginger was very glad that Hans always came when she called him. In their conversations, Ginger had learned things about Hans' private life that weren't so reassuring. He once told her that he'd just broken up with a man who had stolen his watch and lied to his friends about him. Ginger saw that Hans compensated for his lack of control in his emotional life by an exaggerated need for control in other realms. That this particular state of affairs was a source of anxiety for him was a fact that he never seemed to acknowledge. Though he had a sophisticated vocabulary, his English was not entirely fluid.

Often Hans neglected to send a bill for his services and Ginger was certain this happened because Hans had low self-esteem. Finally, she spoke to him about it and urged him to bill her as soon as he finished working. Hans took his work and the people he met very seriously. He rarely laughed unless it was indicated specifically that something was funny and intended to be a joke. Then he laughed gratefully and heartily, but politely.

CHAPTER FIFTEEN

Nora saw the TV news crew's van parked in front of the house and hurried inside to find out what they were doing.

"You missed most of it" Ginger said when Nora found her standing in the back yard. "They interviewed Jennifer and Michelle earlier, now they're ..."

"Quiet please."

A slim woman in a baseball cap and khaki shorts held a finger to her lips. She seemed to be in charge of telling people where to stand and carrying out the instructions Candy gave her.

"Are we ready, Andy ?" She asked the cameraman, who had set up a tripod with his camera pointed at March.

Under the baseball cap, the assistant moved quickly and spoke in a self-important voice. "Dorey" she said to a petite woman in tight jeans seated on a wooden crate "She's a bit shiny." Dorey sorted through a large metal case full of powders, lipsticks, brushes.

They have a makeup person, Nora thought, they must be really serious about this story.

Candy walked towards the tree, adjusting her microphone while March faced the camera with a solemn expression--cooperative but not eager. The assistants and Candy stood by while Dorey powdered March's nose and forehead and arranged her braids so they hung symmetrically in front of each ear

"What is your feeling about the significance of this mysterious message March ?" Candy asked, poised, alert and interested; holding the microphone tilted under March's chin.

"Well, Candy, this was very out of the ordinary—the lights, the strange musical sounds. There's no question in my mind that the girls were chosen to be ...to channel..."

"To channel a message from another dimension ?" Candy tried to helpfully clarify what March was saying.

"That's right, Candy. They were the ones chosen. They were somehow ready. I don't know-- they were the right people at the right time, let's put it that way."

"Okay," said Candy. "Do you think we'll hear more information from this...this source ? Will she make another appearance ?"

"With this kind of..." March began but Candy indicated to the cameraman that she wanted to stop.

"Just a second. Cut. Dorey, will you do something with this ?" Candy pulled on a lock of hair hanging in front of her left eye, obscuring her vision.

Looking important and determined, Dorey approached with hairspray and comb.

She fiddled with Candy's hair for a minute, patted it into place, sprayed it and said "Is that better?"

"I think it's okay now." Candy told her. "Okay Andy?"

"Rolling," the cameraman answered.

"Thank you for sharing your impressions of this significant and increasingly mysterious event, March."

"You're welcome, Candy." March nodded in a sincere, friendly way. "Thank you."

"March Redhill, speaking to us about the mysterious sighting in West Hollywood, a Channel 8 exclusive," Candy concluded. "Back to you Burt."

"Okay," Candy nodded at Andy, "let's cut it there."

Ginger and Nora watched the crew begin to pack up their gear and prepare to leave. Ginger caught Candy's eye. "Hi Candy, continuing coverage, huh ?"

Candy seemed to be in a hurry; she kept on walking. "That's right," she said.

"Will this be on television ?" Ginger asked.

"Probably. Unless a bigger story comes in."

"Candy," Nora moved in closer, " Do you honestly think this simple-minded nonsense is really news ?"

Ginger backed away, she looked embarrassed.

"Our viewers are interested in this, I'm reporting a legitimate news event. If you have a problem you can call the station." Candy continued walking towards the van.

"This is private property—look what's happening here." Nora gestured to include the water and the damaged grass.

"I gave them permission to film here." Ginger stepped forward.

Candy stopped and spoke to Ginger with a friendly smile. "We may want to interview you if the station decides to go another day with this story, Ginger."

"Me?" Ginger said, "Well, if you really ..."

"I understand you rescued the girls from the streets when they were homeless," Candy said. "You're part of this story."

Ginger smiled modestly. "What did they say about me?"

"This story could get bigger," Candy told her. "I just want you to be prepared. I'll be in touch."

When Nora went back into the house, Ginger lingered outdoors, chatting with the assistant director and the woman who did makeup.

...

Later in the evening Nora was working in the kitchen when she heard a knock at the back door. She saw Jennifer through the square glass panes smoking in the dark. When she opened the door Jennifer tossed the cigarette, crushed it with her foot and walked in.

"What's going on ?" she greeted Nora. "Where's Ginger?"

"She's at yoga class."

"I came over to get some shampoo and stuff that we left in the bathroom," Jennifer told Nora. "Don't forget, we're on at eleven. Channel Eight."

"Jennifer, can I ask you a question ? Did March coach you or anything ? I mean, did she tell you what to say to Candy ?"

"No, of course not. She wants to keep this as low key as possible." Jennifer seemed protective of March. "We think, I mean, I think that it's a mistake to let too many people go near the water."

"Right." said Nora. "Listen Jennifer, do me a favor ? Tell me what really happened the other night. What did you see, really ?"

"We had a religious vision." Jennifer told her. "We received important information."

Nora looked curiously at the younger woman's face. She seemed different—more confident and alive. That was the only way to describe it—she looked more alive.

"What kind of information ?"

"Watch the news. I kind of explained it on camera."

"What ?" Nora's voice was combative, "You can't tell me in person ?"

Nora saw something in Jennifer's eyes that she had never seen before—it looked like pity but might have been impatience.

Jennifer turned to look up at the wall clock. "The thing is, we're expecting a phone call from an agent. I'm supposed to be available so we can talk—it's like a conference call. You know-- with more than two people"

"What agency ?" asked Nora.

"Influential Artists." Jennifer told her. "It's one of the newer talent agencies but they have some very experienced people."

"Who...?" Nora began but Jennifer interrupted impatiently.

"Candy knows some people there. She recommended us to them." Jennifer looked at the door, Nora saw how eager she was to leave.

"Maybe we can talk tomorrow sometime," Nora suggested.

Jennifer was opening the back door. "Yeah, I'll call you."

Nora watched Jennifer walk through the dark shrubbery to March's house. Just before eleven Ginger came in and joined Nora in front of the television.

"Apparently KQOR is getting a big response to Jennifer and Michelle," Ginger said. They told me all kinds of people are calling in asking about Our Lady of West Hollywood. I think the story strikes a chord with people."

"It strikes a chord with fanatics and loonies," Nora said. "You know, if the girls are runaways and if their parents are looking for them, this would certainly blow their cover."

"If" emphasized Ginger, "anyone is actually looking for them—which I doubt."

"It looks like Jen and Michelle are getting along fine," she continued. "March has more room than we do and they seem happy there. By the way, is Dan coming over tonight?" Ginger asked casually.

"Why?"

"Turn it up!" Ginger suddenly sat up straight as she saw Candy's face on the screen. Candy was standing beside Michelle and Jennifer giving a capsule review of past events.

"Is that Michelle?" Nora asked, "She looks different."

"She had her hair styled" Ginger pointed out. "I think she borrowed one of March's dresses."

Michelle looked composed (yes, that's the word, Nora thought) composed and serene. Her naturally curly hair had been professionally straightened to a uniform sheen. Nora thought Michelle looked better on television with less makeup; she looked younger but somehow more sophisticated.

As the camera moved over the water and the magnolia tree, Candy turned to Jennifer. "Why do you think the Angel Lady appeared to you and your friend—was there something specific that she wanted to tell you about—warn people about? Was this a prophecy?"

The TV framed Jennifer's small young face. She looked alert but not nervous; confident but not arrogant.

"Candy, I really don't know why—why the Angel Lady chose us; why she decided to appear at this particular time and place." The camera closed in on the leaves of the tree—a sunbeam played on one of the huge white flowers, the size of a cabbage or a baby's head.

"I understand," Candy continued "that you received some information regarding a future event—is that correct?"

"You could call it a prediction," Jennifer said, "but Michelle and I aren't sure if we should, you know, announce what she said because people might get the wrong idea, they might be..."

"Frightened?" Candy offered.

Michelle broke in firmly "We don't want to cause, you know, worrying."

"Can you tell us anything about the prediction ?"

"We're praying night and day to the Angel Lady to tell us the right thing to do." Jennifer said.

Candy held the microphone in front of Michelle. "Did she predict something that will happen in the near future ?" Candy was careful, not too pushy.

Jennifer and Michelle looked at each other. Jennifer nodded to Michelle, who answered. "We don't think it would be right to issue a warning; but she did tell us that we can expect a natural event of some magnitude."

"A natural disaster?" Candy asked, "is that what you mean?" Michelle nodded.

"Did she give you a specific time or place ?" Candy persisted. Jennifer looked calm and cooperative but she just shook her head slightly. "Do you think she was referring to an earthquake?" Candy wanted to know.

"All I can say is—she doesn't want people to suffer. That's all. We're praying to...to do the right thing." Jennifer said.

"Jennifer, if it is an earthquake that she was referring to, do you think it will happen soon, let's say, within a week ? Also, was there any indication of how severe it might be, did she mention a Richter scale number; will it be over a six point oh?"

Candy was trying to be more specific.

"Candy, when it's the right time, the message will be, like, revealed." Michelle added.

"Unbelievable !" Nora shouted at the screen. "Can you believe this ?"

"Shhh," Ginger put a finger to her lips, "Watch."

"There you have it Burt." Candy's face full screen. "The angel lady in West Hollywood apparently warned them about a future event and these two young women are struggling to decide how much they should share with the public."

Burt's voice then face appeared behind a desk in front of the station's orange and brown logo. "Our phones have been ringing with viewer's questions, Candy.

Does it look like there might be an announcement later?"

"We'll have to wait and see, Burt. Both of these young women are trying very hard to do the right thing."

"Yes they are." Burt, in his deep paternal voice, approved. "And it can't be easy. Thank you, Candy Cummings in West Hollywood."

At Troppo on Beverly Boulevard, a television set was mounted above the deep stainless steel sinks where busboys and kitchen helpers washed dishes in a low-lying cloud of steam. Dan walked into the kitchen to check the refrigerator and looked up to see Jennifer's face on the screen. Chuy, a short man with a large head, was grinning up at the television.

"We gonna have a big one, man," he said.

"Yeah, terremoto, si." Said Jaime, who was holding a very tall pile of dinner plates. He swayed back and forth, causing the plates to lean precariously.

"Terremoto!" he shouted. The other dishwashers watched and laughed.

"When she say it will be happ'ning man ?" asked Miguel, taking off his apron and getting ready to leave.

"Nobody knows that." Dan said, "nobody can predict an earthquake."

"He knows," Chuy said, pointing up at the sky. "He knows. Up there man, El Senor."

"Yeah, it's coming" said Miguel, nodding his head as he left the restaurant.

When Nora pulled up in front of Troppo, Dan was locking the front door and checking the trash bin in the alley. The street was deserted. The Gomez brothers who ran the restaurant parking concession were folding up the orange VALET PARKING sign and loading it in the back of their dented Chevrolet pick-up truck.

Dan got into Nora's BMW trailing a faint aroma of garlic and coffee. "Its amazing what those cable news channels will cover, isn't it ? They're really milking this Angel Lady thing."

"I thought they would have dropped it after one shot" Nora said. "But, apparently the station had a big response to this--Our lady of West Hollywood."

"I heard that," Dan said.

"I wish it would rain," Nora said as they stopped at a red light and watched a stream of young men with tight pants and bare biceps walk from one side of Santa Monica Boulevard to the other.

"We may not see any rain before the end of November," Dan said.

From the street, Nora could see inside the glass walls of an all-night gym where rows of buff boys stared up at television screens as they doggedly pedaled stationary bicycles under fluorescent lights. Nora drove on into West Hollywood's flat tree-lined residential blocks. When she turned onto Westborne she saw faint lights which got brighter as she drove towards Ginger's house.

A clump of people stood on the sidewalk. Some carried candles in glass cups. They seemed peaceful, hovering near the edge of the front lawn. Nora was glad of Dan's presence in the front seat. She wondered if the visitors were people from the neighborhood or if they came from other parts of the city. Nora parked at the curb, got out and slammed the door. She wanted to shout 'go away !' at the quiet people. The silent watchers stayed on the sidewalk as Nora and Dan entered the front door.

Nora took a bottle of wine out of the refrigerator and Dan dropped a couple of books and his notebook onto the kitchen table.

"They seem harmless. Maybe they come at night because that's when they think they might see something." Dan's voice was calm and even.

"I don't know what they're looking for." Nora sounded annoyed. " It's just crazy. What do they think they'll see?"

"Well, you know, people need to feel there's something more; something other than, you know, the daily world. They need to think there's something more than this."

"But what ?" Nora asked. "What could they possibly hope to find here ?"

"At least they're peaceful" Dan said.

"Yeah, but people like that—people who would do this; they might do anything."

"Who's to say ?" Dan asked. "Who has the right to judge?"

Nora shrugged. "I just hope they lose interest. I mean, how much longer can this be news ? Unless we have the second coming next week, people will forget about this.

"Have you considered calling the police ?"

"If we do, we'd have to file charges. Ginger doesn't want to charge someone with trespassing…it's complicated." Nora was seated now, looking at her notes.

"Yeah, it is," Dan opened his notebook. "What about this scene with Iris in France? "

Nora opened her notebook, and positioned her pen. She really felt she could think better with pen in hand. She was glad to have Dan in the house. Not that he would be required to fend off crazed interlopers, but just his presence, his male presence, was for some reason reassuring.

"Okay, so Iris' friend Constance wants to go visit her in France but there's a problem—some of Iris' guests are divorced, and Constance, her closest friend, can't be seen in a house where divorced people are staying."

"That's going to be hard to adapt. I'm not saying we can't use it but I think we somehow have to translate the core experience, let's call it the emotional reality, into the equivalent contemporary experience." Nora and Dan had solved similar problems in the story before, but this was tough.

"We have to show that she really wants to visit but she'd risk her reputation if she goes to this place where she'd meet people who might represent, like, social contamination."

Dan shook his head "Right—this is tricky."

He opened the book, a 1923 edition bound in faded blue and filled with yellow squares marking pages. He read: "He was like a ship forever tossed on the seas of his own sensibilities."

They both smiled. Dan waited for Nora's quick snort of a laugh that seemed to come from somewhere deep inside her. Her quick convulsive chuckle pleased him. They both loved this novel. The last gasp of pre-world-war romanticism undiluted by irony. Dan remembered Nora saying that when she first read it.

He opened to another page and read: "One notes, with a degree of satisfaction, that it was often the most sincere men and women of each generation who were the most rapidly infected by the particular affectation of their time."

"Wow" said Nora thoughtfully, "I think that might be true, don't you ?"

"He goes on to talk about affectation—here take a look." Dan handed the book to Nora.

After a few minutes, Nora read aloud from the novel: "Hopeful, helpless—I'm at your mercy. Without you I feel weak, empty. You give me strength, direction, faith. Iris, you are my source of devotion and its object. You are my religion."

"She's become indifferent to him by this time."

"You could say he's trying to get her attention."

"We have to figure out this ending" Nora said. She wanted to go look out the window. She couldn't see any lights. Maybe they went away. Or, she thought, maybe they opened the gate and went into the back yard.

"I think we agree on the last scene" Dan said. "Iris recovers from the suicide attempt and marries John." Dan looked impatient, like he didn't want to discuss it any more.

"Somehow, I don't know if Iris—you really think they should get married in the end ?"

"What else are they gonna do ?" Dan's voice sounded tired. "They love each other, he's lonely and she needs him."

"Yeah, but she has these suicidal tendencies," Nora reminded him. "Maybe she should just go over the cliff."

"What, like Thelma and Louise ? But then what does he do ?" Dan asked.

"He cries. He weeps convulsive choking sobs."

Dan looked deflated. "I'm not saying the ending should be saccharine or contrived but there is such a thing as uncontrived happy—easy happy. You know what I mean—Iris might, in the end, let her guard down. She could just, I don't know, give in."

"Iris is essentially a tragic character" Nora was adamant. "She was born in the wrong century. She feels trapped because she's at odds with the prevailing morality. You could say, the prevailing sensibility."

"Morality and sensibility aren't the same thing," Dan said, "are they ?"

"One certainly influences the other." Nora seemed to have given the question some thought.

"But that doesn't mean she can't find happiness," Dan searched Nora's face for agreement. He sensed that she opposed him but with only a fraction of her strength—he understood that if he threw more weight behind his argument she would reveal reserves of even deeper conviction. Nora was careful never to squash Dan completely—she allowed him to state his case, then usually blew holes in it. Dan won some of their disagreements and she won others. She played the diplomat and tried to keep a sense of balance and fairness. Dan was the hot-headed artist. He approached writing with a sense of danger, discovery. To Nora, it was a magic trick—more like an elaborate deception involving seamless technique.

"Look, we'll just let it develop; the characters will grow into what they're meant to be; Iris herself will determine her fate." Dan said.

"I don't want to disturb you but I'm just going to make some hot cocoa." Ginger entered the kitchen wearing the Moroccan caftan. Also eye makeup, noted Nora.

"That sounds good," Dan said.

"You're up late," Nora said to Ginger as she took milk out of the refrigerator.

"Did you see out front?" Ginger asked. "I can't sleep. How many were out there?"

"Not many. Maybe six or eight." Dan told her. "They seem peaceful enough."

"How long do you think they'll stay out there ?" Nora wanted to know.

"Until 2:30; that's when the ....the sighting took place."

"Then they all go home and watch TV ?" Dan seemed to be more amused than concerned.

"I don't know, Dan. I hope so." Ginger's voice took on a slightly victimized tone.

"They looked harmless, right Nora ?" Dan seemed to want to reassure Ginger.

"I don't know," Nora said, "I really don't know."

CHAPTER SIXTEEN

Jennifer opened her eyes but she had no idea where she was-- what bed, what house, what city. Gradually she became aware of her back, her hands, her feet, her mouth floating unanchored in a constant warmth, neither hot nor cold. Jennifer savored this moment of awareness without memory or location. It lasted such a short time, she could feel it ending as soon as it began. The experience of not-knowing that was like an iridescent bubble bursting as soon as it formed a perfect, floating circle.

Her eyes saw a wide sun-filled white square with lacy curtains: an open window. A breeze stirred the fabric, gentle, light, the ceiling white. As soon as Jennifer saw the other bed, Michelle, the name, the knowledge of the other girl, her friend, made itself known. Memory awakening just that much later than her eyes, she thought: March, her house. Before the words formed, there was the presence of the woman March in the restless curtains and the smell of Michelle's jasmine perfume and the tug, the pull and finally the gravity of memory, which drew all the clues towards Jennifer -- a magnet shaped like herself that attracted these facts like metal shavings. Jennifer lay in the clean bed and felt the precise weight of the sheet and blankets against her skin. She knew March and Michelle were in the house with her, though she couldn't see them or hear them.

Candy had arranged for them to meet two agents. That was today, tonight--for drinks. Jennifer smiled up at the ceiling and thought: We're meeting agents tonight for drinks. This knowledge altered her point of view, her gravity, her force field. A picture formed, unbidden, of a suit, a man, a haircut, a necktie, a smell like chrome and stale perfume—money. A gent, not a gentleman-- a certain age, aged aunt, aged gent. She saw an ant in a tuxedo, she saw a kind old woman, a stout man in a black suit.

She looked out the window and could see a tall bush blooming with pink flowers. She knew the pretty flowers' name--camellias. She could feel it coming over her, the joy; it sometimes happened without warning, when she wasn't prepared, wasn't expecting it. The joy she never mentioned to anyone-- the joy that filled her so full she had to move or make noise so she wouldn't be overwhelmed by the pink of the perfect camellias, the lacy dance of the curtains. She felt buoyant with ideas, luck and purpose. Jennifer counted all her future activities as possibility, as potential. She silently spoke: "thank you, I'm grateful, not worthy but full of bountiful thanks." Suddenly, the possible was gravity for her, was determined, weighty and real. Her room, her window, her friends and helpful elders waiting; she got out of bed.

Michelle and March were watching TV on a small set perched on the kitchen counter that separated the sink and stove and refrigerator from the yellow Formica table in the dining area. The only sound in the small room was the audience applauding and the dry seedy rustle of Leo on his perch in his wire cage. Flowered drapes were drawn against the late afternoon light. March and Michelle kept their eyes on the screen as Jennifer entered. A middle-aged woman with short hair and red lips was talking to a thin man in a leather jacket, chains hanging from his belt.

"Tell us about your experience, Larry."

Larry spoke in a relaxed, intimate tone to the woman. "Well Rita, I was riding home from the desert on my Harley when I got clipped by a big semi. Knocked me off my bike and broke my leg in three places. I lost a lot of blood. While I was laying there, in a puddle of blood, it happened."

Rita looked at the studio audience and back at Larry "Tell us what you saw."

"It was like a tunnel" Larry said. I saw a long dark tunnel and at the end of the tunnel I could see myself lying there on the ground."

"An out-of-body experience" Rita spoke to the audience.

"Yeah, and then I saw a light, a very bright light, and I thought, now I've seen god."

"You saw god ?" Rita asked him. Larry shrugged "I thought I was dead for a second or two, then I saw something that was like a light and I came back to life."

"And then what happened ?"

"I woke up in the hospital. Somebody found me by the side of the road and saved my life."

There was a half of a lemon meringue pie left out on the counter near the TV; March saw Jennifer eyeing it.

"Help yourself honey," she said.

"And you belong to a group, don't you Larry ?"

"That's right—Night Riders. It's a support group for people who ride motorcycles who have had near-death experiences."

"Thanks Larry," Rita said. "We're running out of time."

Jennifer found a fork and a plate and sank down beside Michelle on the soft cushioned sofa. The edge of the fork cut easily through the white froth and tart lemon.

"Just check out our website at seedark dotcom," Larry said.

March turned off the TV and moved into the kitchen. "Don't forget, you have to be at Cabernet by seven," she told Jennifer.

"I know," Jennifer smiled.

"Can you drive us, March ?" Michelle asked.

"Is that on Sunset Boulevard ?" March was busy putting dishes away.

"Let's see." Jennifer found the card in her purse. "Yeah, Sunset Boulevard."

"You girls better start getting ready." March told them.

Jennifer and Michelle got to Cabernet early. From the sidewalk there was a long yellow and white striped awning covering the spacious restaurant's entry.

"How will we know what they look like ?" Michelle asked.

"They'll know us." Jennifer told her "they've seen us on TV, remember ?"

"Oh, right, okay."

Michelle sometimes had a problem connecting the dots, Jennifer thought, without rancor. Jennifer never minded Michelle's lack of sharpness, it was part of her overall mildness. It was Michelle's nature to yield, to agree. Jennifer hated to argue; she was intimidated by anger. She was grateful that Michelle never got angry but sometimes she had to let her know when she said something stupid.

Jennifer wore her new blue leather skirt and a transparent nylon T-shirt studded with rhinestones. Michelle began walking towards the entry doors but she stopped to look behind her, causing Jennifer to narrowly miss bumping into her back.

"You go first," Michelle told Jennifer, hanging back a little. The V-necked dress she wore was tied very tightly around her small waist.

Jennifer said nothing and walked briskly up to a tall blonde woman standing behind a high desk. The tall woman had a phone to her ear and was writing something with a pencil so she was too busy for a moment to look up, but finally she greeted the two young women.

"Good evening, welcome to Cabernet."

Jennifer smiled and said "Good evening" in a loud clear voice and Michelle stood very close to her and watched.

"Do you have reservations ?"

"No," said Jennifer, "we're meeting some people."

"Do you want to wait in the bar ?" asked the friendly blonde, pointing to a room on her right.

Jennifer and Michelle walked into a carpeted room with a circular glass bar upon which was the largest bouquet of flowers Michelle had ever seen. The flower arrangement was the size of a small tree towering over them. It's as tall as me, Michelle thought.

Michelle nudged Jennifer and pointed at the flowers and said "Hey Jennifer, look at the size of that..." but Jennifer turned away, pretending not to hear.

She was trying to decide whether to sit at the bar, where there were only a few seats, or at a table—they were tiny and round and also scarce. The circular glass bar was illuminated from within, giving the impression of lights shining through water. Everything reflected the shimmering watery light: the smooth walls, the tabletops, the undulating shelves full of bottles.

As they walked toward an empty table, someone tapped Jennifer's shoulder and Scott in a dark suit introduced himself and pointed to his identically dressed companion and said "This is Josh."

In a way, Jennifer thought, they almost looked alike except that Josh had more hair and looked much younger than Scott who had cut his dark hair very short and wore a beard that just covered his chin. A goatee, she thought, like a goat. Josh, very thin and only a little taller than Michelle, had unusually narrow shoulders, which made him look younger than he actually was.

"This is Michelle" Jennifer was completing the instructions.

"I know" said Scott.

"You saw us on TV, right ?" Michelle said with a pleased look at Jennifer, who felt a sense of belonging, of being significant and lovable.

"We certainly did see you" Josh said, but I have to tell you girls, you're even better looking in person. Isn't that right, Scott ?"

"Absolutely," Scott said, as his eyes swept the room. Scott didn't seem to have time to look directly at anyone's face, he seemed to be expecting someone or something else that might require his attention; his eyes constantly looked over shoulders, up stairs, through windows.

"Are you looking for somebody?" Jennifer asked.

"Somebody else ?" Scott said, very briefly checking Jennifer's eyes. "No, why ?"

Josh managed to grab a chair (very quickly, Jennifer noticed admiringly) and the four found themselves sharing a glass-topped chrome table about the diameter of a tree stump.

"What do you girls like to drink ?" Josh asked.

Then Scott said "Hey Dude, why don't we order some martinis? You girls like martinis ?"

"Sure. I do. Don't you Michelle ?"

Jennifer nodded and smiled and Michelle nodded vigorously, like she was enjoying herself with friends, Jennifer thought.

The noise level in the room rapidly increased as more people crowded into the bar area. The stone floor and open ceiling seemed to create a sort of echo chamber which rang with the throb of recorded techno. The music was a wall that people had to speak over, or not at all. Conversation required breath and force.

"How long have you lived in L.A.?" Josh looked directly at Michelle. She paid close attention to his lip movements.

"When did we move to L.A. ?" Michelle leaned towards Jennifer.

Jennifer moved in closer to Josh "We've been living up north for the past year but L.A. is our home."

Michelle carefully held the steep cone of the slippery martini glass with two hands and raised it slowly to her lips as she watched the conversation continue. She liked the vaporous chill of the alcohol on her tongue. It was like you didn't swallow it, it just seemed to evaporate in your mouth, she thought, and hoped there'd be time to have more than one.

Scott asked Josh where he parked and Josh asked Michelle if she'd ever done any commercials. Josh said on the street but it was impossible to hear what Michelle said because she was sitting near Josh across the little table and she cupped her hand to his ear and answered him as though she were telling him a secret.

"We really liked what we saw of you on Candy's show," Scott told Jennifer. "This story could have legs. I mean, you two are very photogenic and the concept is sexy. Nobody like you has ever come forward with something like this. It's fresh, it's hot, it's young. The recognition factor is huge. We wanted to meet you two immediately, as soon as we saw that first segment, right Josh ?"

Josh put his hand to his ear to indicate that he couldn't hear what Scott had said.

"I said, Michelle and Jennifer are hot, " Scott repeated loudly in Josh's face.

Josh smiled and nodded his head up and down several times. He seemed to be fascinated by Michelle. He watched her every move, Jennifer noticed.

"I'm thinking maybe talk show appearances, Dancing with the Stars, that kind of thing. We want you to know that we love your work."

Scott completed his sentence looking directly into Jennifer's eyes with a sincere smile. "You two are so absolutely fresh."

"You girls are hot."

Josh spoke loudly enough that all of them could hear but he was really staring at Michelle. Michelle looked at him with her eyes sparkling and her lips open, but she said nothing. She couldn't think of anything to say; it took so much energy to shout above the music and she felt so relaxed it didn't seem necessary or worth the effort.

Jennifer caught Michelle's eye then and smiled; she was happy and she wanted to let Michelle know how good she felt. She saw that things had "come together" and she had a new, more complete, more colorful, almost musical sense now of what that phrase might mean. The crowd, the room and the alcohol all seemed to be part of this new construct, this coming together that Jennifer saw as beginning and end, like a prophecy.

Jennifer jumped in. "We're committed to finding the best representation we possibly can. Candy told us good things about your agency."

"We are so solid. Especially now, right Josh ?"

"You know who we signed last week ?" Josh asked the assembled. "It hasn't been announced yet, so please keep this quiet, okay ?"

"Who ?" Michelle asked, responding to Josh's enthusiasm with genuine curiosity.

"Melissa !" Josh smiled and made a motion with his fist and forearm like he was repeatedly punching the air in front of him.

Michelle didn't know who Melissa was. She wondered if she just used her first name or if they were expected to know the last name. Doesn't matter, she thought. They think we know.

"I was part of that deal," Scott said.

"You were ?" Jennifer asked, with a smile of admiration. Scott looked pleased with himself.

Josh was signaling the waitress for another round of drinks. Michelle finished hers quickly, Jennifer noticed. The bar had become so packed with people it was almost impossible to hear anything but the noise of the crowd and the throbbing repetitive churn of intensely piquant recorded music.

Later, Scott suggested they all go to his apartment. He wanted to show them a video of a pilot which meant a TV show that they were starting.

"Where did you girls park ?" Scott asked when they walked outside. He handed his ticket to the parking attendant under a yellow umbrella

"We got a ride with some friends," Jennifer said.

"I'll make sure you get home" Josh said. "ride with me.

The TV pilot was about a policewoman who finds out her husband has been killed by a hit and run driver. The show started with the accident, then the dead body, then the police car drove up with the siren noise. Jennifer heard Michelle's loud yawn.

Scott's big bright television took up almost the entire wall of his small living room. Jennifer reclined on the gray carpeted floor and watched. Michelle and Josh were on the black leather sofa behind her.

Scott came in from the kitchen holding a bottle and said "Want to drink this vodka straight ?"

He picked up the remote switch and froze the television picture in a frame of the policewoman bending over the dead body in the street.

"Sure" said Josh. "Put some ice in mine. Michelle ?"

"Sure" she said.

"Ice ?"

"Okay." Michelle looked so pretty in white against the black leather, Jennifer thought. She wondered if she liked Josh as much as he...

While Scott was in the kitchen, Jennifer pressed Play and the policewoman stood up and started screaming. Jennifer kicked off her shoes and stretched her bare legs on the floor. Then she pressed Rewind and the policewoman knelt down in the street again. She heard Michelle giggle but she didn't turn to look. Jennifer pressed Play, then Rewind again, quickly, watching the policewoman jump up and down. There was a soft scuffling sound in the room like bare legs rubbing on leather.

Scott came in with drinks and set them on the glass table in front of the sofa; then he sat down on a chair. He eagerly pushed Play again and they watched the show continue. At the end, white names slid across the black screen and Scott pointed out his.

"You were in this ? " Jennifer asked.

"No. I got an associate producer credit." Scott said.

Scott put another movie on and turned out all the lights in the room. He moved down onto the floor next to Jennifer and put a pillow under his head. The movie, called "Party Pooper" was about a guy who was about to get married and his friends throw a bachelor party and invite girls who are professional strippers.

About fifteen minutes into the movie, Michelle and Josh slid off the sofa very quietly and went into a room next to the kitchen that must have been the bedroom. Neither Jennifer nor Scott turned around to acknowledge their exit. Scott laughed out loud at things people said in the movie; but Jennifer didn't think it was that funny.

Scott had a shallow forced laugh; Jennifer thought he laughed like someone was watching him. She got up and walked to the window and looked down four stories at the busy street below. Just a block away she could see the giant billboards and street lights of Sunset Boulevard and the long lines of red taillights crawling slowly between buildings.

Jennifer propped her head on a pillow and watched the screen; Scott made himself comfortable beside her. Sometime after the video ended, Scott put on an old movie with the sound very low. Scott made no conversation, he seemed to assume she had nothing to say. Her bare legs looked blue in the TV light, as though they were very far away and when she felt Scott's hand above her knee, moving up to the soft part of her thigh, it was as though she were watching someone else. Scott, his hand, her leg, were of small concern. Though she was repelled by Scott's very real differences from herself--his dull insensitivity, his single-minded, thick skinned aggressiveness-- Jennifer felt sympathy for his undisguised human desire for connection. Scott, she knew, was no different from hundreds of other men and she knew that nothing special was expected of her—nothing difficult or different.

Then the television went black and the wide windows in the living room began to rattle and the floor swayed. Jennifer heard a sound like a freight train traveling too close to the room—like it jumped off the rails and was racing downhill, picking up speed, shuddering and rattling out of control. The lightweight sofa and glass table in the room slid and jumped.

Jennifer watched as the furniture moved. She did not move. Scott, however, jumped up and fell backwards, disoriented. He panicked, flailed, got into a crawling position on all fours and yelled "Josh ? Josh !"

Jennifer said nothing. The floor shuddered again, perilously. She knew she had to find Michelle. When the movement stopped, she stood up. Scott seemed to have forgotten about her. He was wedged against the sofa with his head in his arms. Jennifer rushed into the bedroom. Michelle was alone among the tangled sheets. Her wrists were tied to the metal post of the bed with a necktie. Someone was pounding on the adjoining bathroom door. The frame of the door was crooked; the door looked twisted on its hinges.

Josh's voice could be heard: "Let me out ! The door won't open."

Jennifer wordlessly helped Michelle finish untying the knot which connected her to the bed frame. "Better get dressed" Jennifer said, and in the dim light, Michelle began to retrieve articles of her clothing from the floor.

Scott ran in and tried to open the bathroom door but it was stuck. "Fuck," Scott yelled. "Are you okay ?"

"Get me out of here!" Josh's voice was panicky.

Scott pulled on the doorknob but it was stuck and wouldn't budge.

Michelle got dressed quickly and the two girls went into the living room. All the lights shining in the city and the street had gone out. Only a pale glow in the dawn sky illuminated the room. Jennifer found her shoes, then stood with Michelle at the window.

"Wow, look."

She could see all the long avenues that stretched to the south and west without one electric light. She held Michelle's hand and wondered if this was "the big one" and if there were thousands of people buried in rubble. Michelle thought how afraid she'd be if Jennifer weren't with her. The two friends stood and gazed at the long avenues with their square buildings unplugged and silent in the morning's silver pink haze. Jennifer had never seen anything so peaceful and majestic. It was like looking at a remote mountain range. She thought: We were in a major earthquake but we weren't hurt. Then she felt the joy again; it came over her like a blush, unbidden. And the words, unrehearsed, came out of the silence within her, said without sound: Please help us, we are helpless before your mighty upheavals. Glorious that we are safe, she added, pleased with the unexpected words that occurred to her and pleased with the way they made her feel, glorious, grateful to be alive.

Scott and Josh could be heard pounding and shouting at the bathroom door. Jennifer walked into the bedroom and saw Josh's pants on the floor, she searched each pocket thoroughly and in the hip pocket found his billfold. Jennifer slid a credit card out of its leather slot and approached the door. She told Scott to stand back and carefully slipped the plastic card into the space between the door jam and the latch. She jerked the knob and the door swung open.

In the small windowless bathroom Josh stood naked, his face twisted and wet with tears. He pushed past Jennifer and Scott and walked towards the undraped window of the bedroom. He found his pants and put them on in the gray semi-darkness. He blew his nose loudly. Nobody said anything for a minute.

"Fuck !" Scott said, "Did you feel that ? That must have been a five point oh at least."

"No glass broke" Jennifer told him. "I mean the windows are all okay."

Scott and Josh went around the apartment checking on things. "The kitchen's a mess" Josh called out to Scott who was looking for a flashlight.

Scott shined a big flashlight at the window which flared bright silver like an oversized mirror. Jennifer became aware of a buzzing sound coming from the floor. It rang and rang until she realized it was a telephone. Scott pointed the flashlight at the floor and picked up the receiver.

"Scott Kleefeld's office. Who ? Oh yeah, put her on." He told Jennifer: "It's Candy at Channel 8."

"How ya doin Candy ? Yeah, woke us up for sure. Where are you ?" Scott smiled into the phone.

Jennifer, standing beside him, could hear the excited buzz of Candy's voice coming over the receiver.

"Yes we are representing Jennifer and Michelle at this time." Scott spoke in a crisp businesslike voice. "Yes, I can definitely put you in touch with them.   When ?   Yes, I definitely think that's possible. We are definitely interested.   We need to sit down and talk.   I don't know what kind of numbers we're looking at. I don't know yet, Candy, but I think we can make this happen. When ? Let's see."

Scott held his watch up to the flashlight and Jennifer held the beam steady on the dial. "What time ?   Okay, I don't have a problem with that."

"It's Candy,"   Jennifer told Michelle.

"How much are they prepared to ...?" Scott slipped his loafers onto his bare feet as he spoke into the phone.   "Yes, we'll be there.   I guarantee it, don't worry, Jennifer and Michelle will be there."

CHAPTER SEVENTEEN

Nora hurried into Troppo around five o'clock the next afternoon. Dan was in the back of the restaurant talking to Chuy when he saw her walk in the front door. She was wearing her red jacket. There was something about the color red on Nora, with her dark eyes and hair, that made her seem more alive when she wore it, more dramatic. She rarely wore red but Dan couldn't take his eyes off her when she did.

"Sorry it took forever to get here-they closed off La Cienega." Nora sank back into the soft gray upholstery of a booth in the back near the kitchen.

Dan wanted to tell her how pretty she looked but he stopped himself because he worried that she might interpret a compliment as flirtation. But we are friends, he thought; Nora wouldn't be annoyed at a compliment from a friend. But then he thought: better to keep things simple.

"The restaurant was dead at lunchtime. It's been really quiet all day." Dan sat down beside Nora with a sense of anticipation because he could tell she was in a good mood. She always enjoyed storms and natural disasters.

She said "People want to stay home today. They're nervous. What if there was a big one right at rush hour ? It's strange that most earthquakes happen in the early morning, isn't it ?"

"Not always. The last San Francisco quake was in the afternoon."

"I think I prefer to be in bed." Nora looked around the room at the serene gray and white linens, the pale blond wood, the paintings framed in black at regular intervals on the white walls. "Did you have any damage here ?"

"This building seems to be very solid. In Santa Monica I didn't feel much-just a rolling shake. Greta was acting really strange though. I kind of hated to leave her alone today."

"Our place really shook." Nora said. "We lost most of our glassware in the kitchen. Of course it was a lot worse in Studio City."

Chuy brought two bowls of linguini with clams from the kitchen and set them in front of Dan and Nora.

"I'm starving. This was a good idea." Nora dug into the hot food with a keen appetite. The linguini was firm and buttery and there was just enough garlic. The little clams were flown in from Canada. Dan liked to watch Nora eat but he didn't want her to know that. She had a finicky appetite.

"Did you get any work done ?" he asked her.

"Not really. We were watching television all day with the earthquake pictures. Of course, you saw Jennifer and Michelle, right ? We must have seen that interview six times. Channel Eight is showing it all the time. 'We're praying to do the right thing'...Nora spoke in a squeaky voice, imitating Michelle. 'We don't really want to predict'... Some of the other stations picked it up, too. Ginger said she saw them for a few seconds on CNN. They're going to be on Larry King next."

"Really ?" Dan was surprised.

"No, but I wouldn't be surprised if they were. This is so out of control. They have people actually believing that they predicted the earthquake."

Dan had seen the interview with Jennifer and Michelle on the news that morning interspersed with the video footage of collapsed parking structures, freeways twisted and warped, piles of broken glass.

"We've had so much going on at the house. Ginger is upset about the water in the backyard. It got worse. This morning it looked wider and deeper. She was waiting for the guy from the city to show up. I don't know what they can do."

"Is there any way I can help ?" Dan asked, feeling the velocity of Nora's thoughts; she was obviously energized by the sense of emergency that permeated the city. His words came more quickly as he spoke with her.

"I don't think so." Nora shook her head. "I'm eager to go over that London hospital scene tonight. I have a new idea for that."

But before Nora could tell Dan about her idea he pointed over her right shoulder and said "Look who just walked in--near the window. Isn't that Jennifer and the little one, what's her name ?"

"Jennifer and Michelle--here ?" Nora turned in the direction indicated. She saw the girls sitting down at a corner table with two men in suits. They all seemed to be laughing and talking. They didn't see her.

"Unbelievable, it is them" Nora twisted for a full five seconds then turned back to face Dan. "What are they doing here ?"

Dan shrugged and began to stand up. "Let's go find out."

"No," Nora hissed, putting her hand on his shoulder "don't."

"Why not ?" Dan looked puzzled.

"They might be, you know, what do you call it--turning a trick." Nora told him, her eyebrows high, her voice low.

Dan stared past Nora's head at the foursome across the room. Jennifer was talking to a guy with a thin stripe of beard on his chin. The bearded one's friend, who looked very young, had his arm over the back of the seat where Michelle was sitting. His hand dangled down onto her bare shoulder.

"In the afternoon ?" Dan was dubious.

But Nora knew them better. "Maybe they started early today. Maybe they don't want March to know."

"But Nora, those guys don't look like-- they look very ordinary--the men I mean." Dan took a second look at the beard, it was barely two inches wide, it didn't even cover the guy's chin.

"Dan, all those perverts look just like the boy next door--suit, tie, underarm deodorant. Next thing you know, body parts in the freezer, right next to the vanilla ice cream." Nora laughed quietly, like a conspirator.

Dan watched as a waiter carried a bottle of champagne to the corner booth. He saw Michelle jump and exclaim when the cork popped. They seemed to be celebrating something.

"Do you think they see us ?" Nora continued eating, she didn't want to turn and look.

"I don't think so," Dan looked over at the table. "Hey, Michelle is getting up. Looks like they're both...Jennifer and Michelle, are getting up and they're...the guys are staying. The girls must be going to the bathroom."

"I'm following them," Nora said. "I'll find out what's really happening."

Dan watched Nora as she walked across the room and disappeared behind a tall row of miniature bamboo in a stone container at the edge of the dining room.

Both stalls in Troppo's spacious toilets were occupied when Nora walked in. The polished granite walls and wash basins were lit with warm indirect lighting and the mirrors were large and framed in stainless steel. Nora wiped oil and garlic off her lips and applied her darkest lipstick. Michelle opened a metal door and saw Nora.

"Nora ! Hi !" Michelle embraced her and Nora felt she was genuinely glad to see her. "I talked to Ginger, thank god you're both okay."

Then Jennifer came out of the second stall and voiced her surprise at seeing Nora. As they hugged, Nora felt a rush of feeling and camaraderie and at the same moment, awkwardness, as if their association were intimate but somehow, undefined.

"So what are you girls doing here ?" Nora asked them. "Got a date ?"

"Yeah," Michelle began, "I mean no, we met these dudes who are agents and they want us to work for...I mean, they want to work ..."

"They're going to represent us," Jennifer said. "They saw us on TV."

"They're both really nice," Michelle said, "We're celebrating."

"We signed a contract today," Jennifer explained.

"That's great," Nora told them, "So you four are.."

"We're going to grab a bite to eat, then go to a concert. Melissa is appearing at the Coliseum tonight. We have backstage tickets. They know her." Michelle's voice was excited.

Nora wanted to ask Melissa who, but she didn't. "That's great," she said "but don't you have to be home at night ? What if the angel lady makes an appearance and you're not there ?"

"I don't think that will happen, Nora. Our feeling is that she can see us and knows where we are at all times." Jennifer explained.

"Well, that's very convenient" Nora said. "She just waits until you have time for her, then she swoops down ?"

Michelle's wide eyes looked distressed. "No," she said, "that's not the way it is."

"What about all those faithful followers who are looking to you to deliver some kind of important message about love and divine intercession. What about that ? And what about warning people about the next disaster ?"

Jennifer looked at Nora with a calm untroubled smile. She couldn't tell if Nora was serious or not. "It's not really in our hands, we're not the ones in control; we just have to be present, to be listening."

"Well, congratulations" Nora raised her hand in a kind of waving gesture and the two younger women said quick goodbyes and left the bathroom.

Nora and Dan took Third Street towards West Hollywood, where traffic seemed to be less hectic than usual, as if people were staying home to recover from the shock of the previous night.

"You know, I thought I saw my car today. I still look for it. I keep thinking I'll find it somewhere." Dan spoke as Nora made a left turn. She looked in the rear view mirror and hurried through the intersection as the light changed to red.

"Dan," Nora said, rapidly changing lanes to avoid a bus, "you will never again see your car. It was stolen over a month ago. The chances of it being recovered are zero, zilch."

"I know someone who had his car stolen and a month later it was found and..."

"That was in Wyoming ! This is L.A. ! I know it meant a lot to you, Dan, but close the case, stop suffering. Get a new car." Nora sounded impatient.

"Okay, I know you're right. I looked at some cars the other day. You know they don't use chrome any more. Why is that? What's wrong with chrome?"

"Just get a car, any car."

"I can't do it yet. I'm not ready. I know you're right. Please, Nora, it was like a member of my family."

"Okay," Nora sighed, waiting in a long line of cars to turn right, "I know."

When Nora and Dan approached Ginger's house, she saw an L.A. Dept. of Water and Power truck in the driveway. The circumference of the pool of water had increased, they saw when they walked into the back yard, it was deeper now, engulfing the grass and some of the smaller shrubs. Wooden barricades and yellow police tape had been placed near the edge of the water where two other city employees stood with shovels.

Ginger was listening to a man in rubber boots and orange coveralls explain the situation.

"We've got a residual pocket of volatile gas under the topsoil here. The ground water has started moving--that's not a good sign. Could be more material under the house. It's not safe."

"You mean," Dan asked "it could blow up?"

"There could be a volatile type of situation here. This whole area north of the La Brea tar pits is potentially combustible. We know the stuff is bubbling up out of the ground--has been for thousands of years. Remember what happened back in '87 down on Fairfax and Third? The explosion at K-mart? It's all part of the same methane deposits under ground."

"I remember that," Ginger spoke up, "some shoppers were injured. So, what are you telling us?"

"We're going to have to work on this. We'll ask you to vacate the premises for a few days while we do some drilling. Usually we can manage to release some of the pressure so there's no danger of explosions. See, when they built up these neighborhoods back in the forties, nobody knew how close to the surface these methane deposits were. It's a very unusual geological stratification."

"Are you saying we have to move out of our home?" Nora asked.

"'Fraid so, Ma'am. Just for a while until we get this thing under control."

"What if we decide not to go ?" Nora asked.

"Ma'am, this is for your own safety. The earthquake shifted the subsoil in this area; we can't be responsible."

"But can't we wait and see ?" Nora asked.

Ginger looked pained. "Nora, I don't think we have a choice."

"I'm just following the rules, ma'am." The LADWP man motioned his co-workers to help him measure the diameter of the pond. Dan was surprised at how large it looked now—the surface of the water had almost doubled in size since it first appeared.

Dan turned to Nora and Ginger, "You know you're both welcome to stay at my place. I have an extra bedroom and somebody can sleep on my couch. It's really no problem at all."

"That's really generous of you Dan," Ginger said. "Are you sure we wouldn't be in the way ? This is kind of short notice."

"You won't be in the way," Dan said "I enjoy having friends around. Also, Nora and I can fit in some extra writing time."

"I guess we'd better start packing." Ginger had a way of standing up straight and breathing deeply when she was under duress that reminded Dan of his mother, who was the most hard-working woman he'd ever known.

"What about the neighbors ?" Nora asked the DWP man.

"They'll be okay. See, this is the lowest elevation on the block. If we do the drilling here, nobody else will be affected."

Dan went into the kitchen with Nora while Ginger went into her bedroom to pack a bag.

"Are you okay ?" he asked her. He was surprised at how disturbed she appeared to be at the thought of leaving home for a few days.

"I feel like this is all wrong. I can't explain why." Nora looked at Dan with a questioning expression; as if she wanted him to explain it.

"Don't worry; we'll get along fine," Dan said. He was surprised when she leaned in for a quick embrace. He could smell the rose petal odor of her lipstick when she brushed his cheek. He thought the meaning of the embrace was a thank you; or possibly a request for sympathy. It was impulsive and sincere; he knew that. His skin felt scorched in all the places she touched him; the front of his chest and neck and cheek. He sat down and waited for the warmth to dissipate as Nora went into her bedroom to pack.

CHAPTER EIGHTEEN

Jennifer walked into Scott's small grey and white kitchen and looked around. Chrome appliances crowded the counter, and cups and glasses and plates were stacked in the cupboard, but there was no food anywhere in sight. She opened the refrigerator and saw a jar of mustard, a six-pack of beer, some bottled water, nothing to eat. Jennifer sometimes felt tempted to eat when she was bored so it was a good thing there were no snacks in Scott's kitchen because she felt bored now. Scott had asked her to wait for him while he finished talking on the phone and he'd been talking for fifteen minutes with no sign of finishing the conversation.

Jennifer walked into the bathroom again to look at her hair. Earlier in the day, she had spent two hours with Martin on Rodeo Drive. Candy had recommended the well-known hair salon and offered to pay the bill. Martin was friendly and helpful and made some suggestions about hair color as he was cutting her hair. It was darker now, a deep eggplant shade that made her skin seem even paler than usual.

The bathroom was a tiny room off the hallway. The only light came from a bulb shaded by a rectangle of frosted plastic on the right side of the mirror. The left side of the mirror was dark where the bulb had burned out; leaving a blotched gray shadow. Jennifer thought her left side was her best side. She turned and faced in the opposite direction, holding up a small compact to see the angle of the new haircut. She took dark purple lipstick out of her pocket and touched up her lips. Jennifer knew Michelle and Josh were waiting downstairs in his Mercedes parked on the street. They'll call if they get too impatient, she thought. They were all supposed to meet Ethan and his partner at six to get to the screening on time.

Jennifer walked down the hall to Scott's office. He was sitting at his desk overlooking the window with his back to the door. His computer screen and printer and other machines were black silhouettes against the fading light. Scott was listening to a man's voice coming from the phone he held against his ear as he sat hunched in his large desk chair which rolled freely around the polished wood floor of the tidy room. He looked around when Jennifer walked into the room but didn't otherwise acknowledge her presence. In the small room, she could faintly hear the loud demanding male voice coming through the receiver. She liked to listen to Scott talk business —especially when he was negotiating a deal, it was exciting to be in the room. Jennifer enjoyed the way these conversations aroused Scott to a heightened color—his face grew pink and he breathed noisily through his nostrils as he listened; earnestly and avidly fighting to interrupt the person on the other end. When he was breathing heavily and shouting into the phone, Jennifer wanted to lean in and smell behind Scott's ear. At those moments, when his cranial artery was almost visibly throbbing, she could detect an odor which she believed was testosterone—a raw exciting scent not unlike the airport smell of jet fuel. Maybe a little like brandy or matches, Jennifer thought.

Scott ignored Jennifer when she stood behind him and put her hands on his shoulders. She could feel the tense, tight muscles between his neck and arms; she attempted a gentle massage but he shrugged impatiently and moved away. She knew that no matter what she did or where she touched him while he was on the telephone, Scott would not acknowledge her presence. She respected him for this and liked to test him. Jennifer leaned against the door and watched Scott talk. His eyes rested briefly on her but his full attention was on the phone call.

To tease him she lifted her short skirt above her waist and watched his face when he looked. She was wearing her new white lace thong. She wanted him to at least smile. He stared but made no sign of appreciation, humor, desire. She turned her back to him and wiggled out of the skirt, then she walked towards him and sat on his lap.

"I'm not sure Corey is convinced of that," Scott said into the phone. He lifted Jennifer with one hand and slid her off his lap as he stood up smoothly, holding the phone in his right. "I'll run it by him, Kev, but you know yourself it's a done deal" he said, "there's not much wiggle room."

Jennifer stepped back into her skirt and stood in Scott's line of sight. When he met her eyes she held up ten fingers and whispered urgently. "Ten minutes—we have to leave !"

Scott nodded once at Jennifer, indicating that he heard her; then sat down again in his seat, hunching his shoulders and bending towards the floor to stretch his back.

"Okay," Scott said as he inhaled a huge gulp of air and resumed an upright position, "Give it a shot, but if Corey has a problem with the language, trust me, it's not going to happen."

Jennifer could sense that Scott's conversation was nearing an end—though sometimes a new, unexpected piece of information could introduce a fresh loop of exchanges that prolonged the negotiation past the predictable time frame. She hoped that wouldn't happen because she really wanted to go to the screening. It was a new movie with Nick Reddy and she heard he was going to be there. Scott's name was on the invitation so there was no way they were going without him.

Jennifer stood in front of Scott's face and leaned in closely. "I'm going downstairs—Josh and Michelle are waiting. If you're not in the car in five minutes we'll leave without you."

Scott pressed the receiver against the palm of his hand with an impatient angry gesture "I've got the invitation" he told her. Then he quickly put the receiver up to his ear again without missing a beat. "I don't believe that," he said into the phone.

Jennifer felt bored and frustrated. There was nothing to do in the apartment; she didn't want to stay another minute. She walked out the front door without saying goodbye and waited in the stuffy hallway of the narrow apartment building for the elevator to take her downstairs. The elevator was always slow and was out of order yesterday. She considered walking down the four flights of stairs but she was wearing high platform sandals and negotiating stairs was troublesome. Jennifer stared at her reflection in the corroded wall of mirrored tile next to the elevator. Her legs were long and as pale as her face with the same pink porcelain skin that she knew was her most beautiful feature. Her legs looked like a child's legs elongated with a minimum of muscle development. She had small round knees and flat ankles and straight soft calves perfectly smooth and unmarked from ankle to thigh. But her legs were exceptionally long and looked even longer when she wore her short blue leather skirt and the high heels. Sometimes, when she was depressed, Jennifer contemplated her body and was encouraged by the small perfections she alone possessed. She often felt that she owned nothing but her body with all its vulnerability and impermanence. She had no home, no car, no property but she controlled a tangible asset-- herself. When the elevator finally arrived, Jennifer walked in and pressed the lobby button marked with a star.

The lower portion of the elevator's walls were scraped and smudged with black and the interior reeked of insecticide. When Jennifer pushed the button the doors closed and the floor bumped and stopped. She pushed the button again and the doors opened halfway, then shuddered closed. The sheet metal walls of the elevator shimmied as the elevator began to move. The doors opened at the next floor but no one got on. When she pushed the lobby button impatiently the doors closed then opened then closed again and the elevator began to move but then stopped, then moved erratically, stopping then starting abruptly. Jennifer then felt hot panic coil in her chest and under her arms as the floor seemed to drop -- faster and faster until the sensation of falling caught her and held her pinned down, wincing and afraid to breathe.

The elevator was falling ! She knew she had to save herself. She remembered and instinctively felt at that instant that if she jumped up when the elevator hit bottom she would be airborne and not feel the impact of the car when it hit the ground. Jennifer counted the third, then the second floor whizz by and then, when it felt right, she held onto the steel railing near the buttons, gathered all her strength and jumped high into the air. Her arms felt the shuddering impact of the metal cube hitting the bottom of the elevator shaft, but she wasn't hurt. A loud screeching alarm was activated and she could hear someone shouting. But she wasn't hurt. She sank to the floor of the elevator and took a deep breath and out loud said 'Thank you, thank you, thank you. She struggled to remember a worthy phrase.

I'm so grateful. She sat and ran her hands over her tender bare legs. Thank you, she prayed.

A voice outside the doors called "Is anybody in there ?" and Jennifer called out.

Later when she was back in March's living room, lying on the sofa with a blanket over her, Jennifer saw what it all meant. She felt shaken by what had happened but secretly elated, also. She realized that she and Michelle had many new possibilities and they could look forward to expanding their audience. Jennifer saw that they would need new agents for the next phase of their careers. Scott and Josh simply didn't appreciate what they were trying to do-- the potential.

The elevator incident showed her that this was her moment and Jennifer knew that when the other networks recognized her and connected the dots they'd be calling. Just as the thought occurred to her, the telephone rang and March answered.

"It's Ginger " March let her know in a quiet respectful voice like a nurse.

"What does she want?"

"She saw on TV that you were in an elevator accident."

"Which station ?"

Jennifer sat up, threw off the cover and held her hand out for the phone, which March quickly gave to her.

"She said it's on now."

Jennifer pointed urgently at the television as she spoke into the phone.

"Ginger, hi! What channel is it on ? ...twelve ? Okay," Jennifer pointed at the television and motioned with her head to March "Channel twelve."

Jennifer had not yet seen the footage of the local news team arriving with the ambulance. As the doctor was checking her for damage after the crash, reporters had thrown questions out of the blue and she couldn't remember—maybe she'd been in shock—what she had answered or what station the people were from. On the screen she saw herself sitting on the floor of what looked like a very dirty and dark elevator.   Someone helped her step out through the twisted doors into florescent lights and asked her if she was hurt.

Her hair looked great and the dark lipstick she wore made her face look very pale. Her long bare arms and legs looked white in the glaring light.   I'm so glad I wore the black sleeveless blouse, Jennifer thought. Michelle hurried into the room and turned up the sound on the TV.

The face of an anchorwoman Jennifer had never seen before filled the screen.   "A freak elevator accident in an upscale neighborhood near the Sunset Strip proved to be no problem for Jennifer Reilly, the young woman who predicted the recent Arroyo Seco earthquake. Here's what happened around six o'clock this evening, Lloyd."

Jennifer almost forgot Ginger.   "Are you all right ?" Ginger's voice on the phone asked, but Jennifer just said, "yeah, no problem" as she watched the television.

She didn't really want to talk to Ginger but she didn't want to hang up on her, so she held the phone to her ear, not saying anything, watching herself on the screen.   She could hear the sounds of the same program on the other end of the receiver, and Ginger breathing.   The camera was showing the broken cable above the elevator car and how it had somehow rusted and broken; then the reporter held a microphone in front of Jennifer's face. The fluorescent light in the basement hallway couldn't have been more unflattering. My eyes look all dark and my neck looks too skinny, Jennifer thought to herself; but Michelle and March murmured their sympathy and admiration.   Then, on screen, Jennifer began explaining what had happened.

"You jumped in the air when the elevator landed ?' The reporter was a thin woman with shoulder length dark hair. She had a harsh, worried face with dark liner around her eyes.   She held the microphone in front of Jennifer and asked "How long were you in the air ?"

"There was no way I could know for sure when it was going to hit", Jennifer explained, I just had to think fast. I'd heard somewhere that if you jump just before…just before it hits the ground…So I just took a guess and leaped."

"You're a lucky girl" the worried reporter said. "Back to you Lloyd."

Jennifer heard the beeping signal on the phone that meant there was another call coming in. "Ginger, are you still there ?"

"Oh, Jennifer, I didn't know if you were still..." Ginger's voice was sympathetic and apologetic.

"I need to take this call that's coming in now, okay Ginger ?" Jennifer asked, "I'm sorry but I just..."

"Fine, no problem. Bye. " Jennifer hit the button and heard Candy's voice.

"Why didn't you call me ?"

"Candy, I had no time, it happened so fast. You know I would have called you if I could."

"Where was Scott ?" Candy wanted to know. "That was his building, wasn't it ? Why didn't he call me ?"

"He was upstairs," Jennifer told her. "He didn't want to leave and I did, so..."

"I can't believe we missed this," Candy sounded irritated.

Candy's irritation signaled a reaction in Jennifer that she'd never experienced before--she thought it was responsibility, that was the word. She had never really felt responsible before and now she had to be, because of the fame, because people expected her to be something special. "I didn't have time to call anyone, the rescue team took me to the hospital in an ambulance."

"Okay, whatever, but we need to schedule an interview a.s.a.p. I can see a way to tie this in to the earthquake prediction footage — we can show some of that. I can probably do three minutes on this for tomorrow."

"Fine," said Jennifer. "You want me in the studio or do you want to come out here ? Wait," she said to Candy, "March, could we do an interview in your tent ?..."

"March says we can" Jennifer told Candy, as she caught Michelle's eye. She was bouncing up and down with excitement.

...

When Jennifer in the elevator came on the screen, Dan hurried to turn up the sound on his TV and Ginger immediately telephoned Jennifer. Nora moved her chair closer to the small screen and watched the entire thing without saying a word.

"She obviously has a pathological need for attention." Ginger said when the three of them were talking about it later, sitting in Dan's living room.

"The elevator cable broke" Nora said. "How does that...what do her needs (Nora prolonged the long ee sound so that the word sounded almost foreign) have to do with what happened ? It was an accident."

"Aren't there people who really are accident-prone ?" Dan asked the question to Ginger. Nora got up and went into the kitchen.

"Yes, it's documented. Certain individuals have sometimes a sixty or seventy percent higher likelihood of being victims of accidents than the average. Of course, in this case we don't know if this wasn't something they staged to look like an accident. Jennifer and Michelle certainly benefit by any kind of exposure— no matter what it is. I believe some of these news stories are partially staged."

Nora came back from the kitchen. "What? Ginger, do you think they staged this? You must be kidding. That's very unlikely. I mean it would be almost impossible."

"Isn't it strange though that after all the publicity they got with the earthquake, this happens just as things were quieting down? I mean, I can't help but think they somehow manufactured this little piece of 'news'." Ginger did that motion in the air with both hands that indicated quotation marks around news. "I'm not saying Jennifer thought of it herself. Those agents she's involved with now—you know who I mean—they might have engineered the whole thing somehow."

"Ginger, you saw the wreckage of that elevator car. A television news station doesn't have the budget to go out and fake something like this. It's not a movie." Nora felt annoyed at Ginger's ignorance. "Jennifer was in an accident. There's really no reason to interpret it any other way."

"It does seem incredible that it would happen now, so soon after..." Dan shook his head. "Have you seen the girls lately ?" he looked at Ginger.

"I'm going to check on the house this afternoon after work; maybe I'll stop in and see them." Ginger said. "Do you need anything from your closet, Nora ?"

Ginger noticed that Nora was wearing the same cotton sweater she had worn yesterday and the day before.

"No," Nora said, "I don't need anything."

Ginger parked near the corner of Westborne and Melrose and approached her house on foot. The yellow plastic tape was still draped around her driveway and doorway but she ignored it and opened her mailbox where the mailman continued to deliver bills and junk mail. When Ginger walked into the kitchen, it seemed unusually dark. She wondered if the city had forgotten about her, if the mysterious problems would ever be fixed. Ginger turned on the lights and considered having a cup of coffee before she went out back to check the water; then she remembered there was no coffee in the house so she sat and went through the mail, throwing away the thick envelopes that held requests for money from the institute for the blind, the national organization of women, mothers against drunk drivers, veterans of foreign wars, and the civil liberties union. When she was married to Tim, Ginger had frequently made small contributions in response to these direct mail requests, but she knew she couldn't afford to now. She felt guilty when these groups sent something to her, like personalized address labels, and she sent nothing in return. She knew it was a fund-raising strategy that didn't require a response but still, she felt faintly but personally neglectful.

Ginger put the veterans return envelope and a dentist bill into her bulging leather handbag and went outside.

The pool of water had come to a stop very near the Magnolia tree and seemed to be holding steady. Some metal poles and more of the plastic tape marked the circumference of the puddle which had become a pond. Ginger had never noticed so many of the fragrant white flowers on the tree before. Probably because of the plentiful water, she thought. Then her attention was diverted by the sound of several voices just beyond the oleander bushes in March's backyard.

Ginger saw Candy's bright blonde head walk from the street to the back of the house. Ginger noticed then that a video camera was set up on a tripod next to March's squat patchwork tent, which was open wide to reveal the framework of branches and poles holding the structure upright. Jennifer and Michelle were busy talking to a makeup girl who held a mirror for Michelle who had her hair styled straight and shorter than before. Jennifer looked very pale, but Ginger knew that was the new style.

"Are they filming here today ?" Ginger asked March when she came out of her house . Her black hair was braided and she had a bright expectant look on her face.

"They told me Candy is putting together some interview footage," March told Ginger. "How are things over at your place ? Did they say when they'll be finished drilling ?"

"No," Ginger shrugged, "they can't tell me anything for sure." March nodded politely and waved at the girls. "I'll be there in a minute" she called to them.

Ginger waited for March to invite her over, but her neighbor seemed preoccupied with all the activity so Ginger retreated to her own yard. Through the shrubbery she could see most of what was going on; she brought one of the old lawn chairs over and sat down to watch.

As Ginger watched, she saw Candy holding her microphone and talking to the girls. Jennifer wore white—a loose gown with long sleeves. Michelle sat gracefully on a hand woven cushion wearing a dress covered with embroidered flowers. Ginger moved closer and tried to hear what Candy was saying.

"Does the fact that you are hearing these "voices" as you call them, suggest to you that you have a special purpose in life, Jennifer?" Candy asked. Jennifer didn't answer immediately, so Candy specified "Some specific mission to accomplish ?"

"Yes Candy," Jennifer's voice was quiet and calm. "But I think it's important to remember that we all have a special purpose in life—you have yours and I have mine, and..." Jennifer looked directly at the camera, "the same goes for everyone watching."

"It appears that you have information about events before they happen-- would that be a fair description ?" Candy asked.

"Candy, I think we all have the power to sense what the future holds—most people don't develop that power but it still exists within everyone. This is not something supernatural but actually completely natural. The fact that we are so cut off from our true nature, our god-given open and complete selves, is what creates the illusion of past, present and future. In meditation and prayer we realize that we exist in a continuum of what I call layers—

layers of time consciousness, layers of sensitivity, knowledge, understanding."

"But how does that explain your ability to predict disasters ?" Candy wanted to know. "Could the average person learn to do this ?"

"I can't answer that." Jennifer shook her head slowly.

Candy turned to Michelle, who was sitting near Jennifer. "Michelle, you've shared these experiences, what can you tell us?"

"I can tell you that the best things happen when you're not afraid, Candy. I think if people wouldn't worry so much, you know, get stressed about what might happen, or feel bad about what already happened, then good things will happen. Like if you're mentally in a good place—like Jennifer in the elevator—then bad things won't happen to you."

"That sounds like good advice, Michelle" Candy said.

"Jennifer, do you have any advice for our viewers?"

"Stay in the moment" Jennifer said. "Celebrate the open moment."

"Thank you," Candy said. "That's a beautiful thought."

Candy motioned to the sound man to move in more closely with his microphone as she moved out of the way and Ginger could hear Jennifer and Michelle humming in a kind of harmony without melody or rhythm. They reached an impressive volume that swayed and merged and became one tone.

Ginger wanted to go and talk to the girls personally after the crew left. She particularly wished she could sit inside the tent and...well, she didn't want to do anything inside the tent, she just wanted to sit inside it. She knew she couldn't just go sit inside March's tent without a reason so she went back to her house and called the Pacific Gas and Electric Company. She asked for Luis and when they were finally connected he said that he was still waiting for the results of some tests they'd made and he would let her know as soon as possible.

"But how long do you expect us to wait, Luis ?" Ginger was on a first-name basis with Luis, she talked to him every day, though she had never met him. He told her he appreciated her difficulty and would do everything in his power to make sure the problem was cleared up as soon as possible. "We're doing everything we can." he assured her.

Ginger hung up the telephone and realized that she felt a deep sense of loneliness and insecurity. She decided that her feelings were related to a loss of control and fear of the unknown. She thought this might be a good time to re-fill the prescription for Silexin she had been taking during the period of her break-up with Tim. She dialed the number of the Buy-rite pharmacy on Sunset Boulevard.

CHAPTER NINETEEN

Dan was rubbing the cold white carcass of a six pound duck with a clove of garlic. "You don't have to do anything, really," he explained to Ginger, "they have so much fat on them that you can just put this bird in the oven for two hours or so and it won't dry out. It just gets crispy and delicious."

Ginger looked over at Dan from the counter near the sink where she was peeling apples. The two had found themselves in his small but well-stocked kitchen cooking dinner on Monday evening when she came back to Santa Monica from her office and Dan had the day off.

"You'd better put it in the oven soon," Ginger said to him, looking at the clock.

"Are you giving me orders in my own kitchen ?" Dan joked with Ginger who apologized, laughing.

He enjoyed having Nora and Ginger in the house. The arrangement had worked out smoothly for over a week. Ginger felt uneasy at first but when she analyzed her feelings she realized that she was simply uncertain as to how she should conduct herself when staying in the home of a friend's friend in an emergency situation.

The unplanned, unstructured arrangement put her off balance but she was gradually feeling more relaxed about it.

She felt that she should try to give Dan as much privacy as possible so Ginger spent more time at her office in West Hollywood doing the paperwork she had formerly done at home. Usually Dan was at work in the evenings when Ginger returned from her office and she went to sleep before he came back late at night. But this evening it happened that it was just the two of them at home together for the first time since they'd begun living under the same roof.

After Dan put the duck into a shallow roasting pan in the oven, Ginger chopped red cabbage. She was following a recipe that called for onion and apples.

"This is going to take at least an hour," she told Dan.

Dan was happily munching on celery sticks and reading the movie reviews in the Los Angeles Times ("the film is nervy enough to create anticipation about where things are headed which makes it all the more surprising and disappointing when that destination turns out to be nowhere at all.")

"Try some of this Zinfandel," he offered to Ginger as he sat at the small table in the corner of the kitchen.

Ginger stood holding a glass and he poured. She wore a maroon corduroy skirt and a gray turtleneck. An oval slice of pale green agate hung on a silver chain from around her neck. In the heat of the kitchen her cheeks were pink which made her eyes seem very green surrounded by the reddish gold of her hair. Dan looked up at her from his chair as she threw her head back and took a long thirsty drink of the wine. It was a wine he especially liked. Ginger had a long graceful neck and hands.

"This is good" she said with a heartiness at once feminine and sincere.

"Let's finish this and I'll open another bottle," Dan said, pouring an inch into his glass and the remainder of the wine into Ginger's glass.

When he stood up in the narrow kitchen and moved to open the cupboard, he was obliged to brush against Ginger as he turned sideways to pass her.

Her loose wavy hair brushed his face; it smelled like oranges and honey and fresh bread. He was aware of her proximity as if for the first time.

He was standing on the floor in his socks. With her shoes on, Ginger was the same height as Dan. She sat down and made herself comfortable on the bench against the wall beside the small table.

Dan told Ginger about the owner of Troppo who liked to go to Vegas and gamble and how he rarely took care of business, leaving all the details of running the restaurant to Dan.

"I should fire one of the waiters and hire somebody else but since he's never around to oversee these things, we have a problem."

Ginger listened with careful interest as Dan told her about some of the other problems that had come up over the weekend. On Friday, the cheese had been delivered late and when portions of it were found to be moldy, they had to throw it away, leaving them short and unable to fill a number of orders late Saturday when they were very crowded. Ginger saw that Dan needed to talk to someone. She asked him questions about his work and he told her how eager he was to leave the restaurant business and concentrate on film-making. Dan was someone who took his obligations very seriously, Ginger could see that.

"You are so conscientious, Dan," Ginger lifted her long legs up onto the cushioned bench and settled her back against the wall as she nibbled some bread. "I admire how dedicated you are to doing your work and making sure it's done well."

"Thanks, Ginger," Dan felt slightly embarrassed about talking about himself for such a long time, as though he needed …Something in Ginger's tone of voice made him feel transparent and exposed, as though Ginger was trying her best to be supportive because she thought he was insecure. He hoped she didn't think he was a loser, everyone felt insecure at times. Dan knew he was no worse nor better than other single men he knew. Though, because Dan knew so few people in Los Angeles, he found he couldn't really compare his situation, his lifestyle, to anyone he knew personally. Dan's close friends from school were all married with small children and lived in suburbs far from Los Angeles. Which left, as possible comparisons, the men he worked with at the restaurant and his next door neighbor, a surfer who repaired skateboards in his garage. Dan had always thought of himself as a normal person, but at some point he felt he might have lost track of how to judge normalcy, how to gauge it in himself or in others. He wouldn't have admitted to Nora how much he really enjoyed the unplanned visit of the two women; maybe because he had grown up with two sisters. It had changed the atmosphere in his place. They had been so careful not to inconvenience him, especially Ginger. The show of consideration touched him.

"You know it's a nice change for me to have roommates. I've lived alone for such a long time," Dan told her.

It helped that Ginger loved Greta and didn't mind walking her and feeding her. Sometimes Dan was tired when he came home at night; while Ginger was usually back earlier in the day and able to go for long walks in the neighborhood with the aging, overweight boxer who would return home panting and happy. The small warm kitchen was filling with the savory odor of roasting duck and Dan thought about making a salad but he decided to pour himself and Ginger another glass of wine first. Greta got up and put her head in Ginger's lap.

"How long ?" Ginger asked him, "how long have you been living alone ?"

Dan watched how gently and softly Ginger rubbed Greta around the ears, where she loved to be petted.

"Three years," he said. It didn't sound like a long time.

Ginger told Dan that she had been divorced three years, apropos of nothing, she reflected, after she said it. She certainly didn't want to behave as though she were on a date when it was more appropriate that she should behave like a guest who was grateful for the hospitality Dan extended.

Ginger sat up straight and took a deep breath.

The small table pushed into a corner of the kitchen left just enough room for Dan to lean back in a wooden chair opposite Ginger. He wore what she knew was called a rugby shirt, with a stiff white collar and dark blue and red stripes, agreeably faded. The shirt was clean but threadbare, torn in spots. Dan got up and rummaged in a drawer, then draped a clean white tablecloth across the battered wooden table as Ginger sat and watched, scratching Greta, silent. When she realized that they had reached, she and

Dan, the comfortable point in an acquaintanceship at which constant conversation was not necessary, Ginger felt an enormous sense of pleasure and relief.

"Let me set the table" she said. "I know where everything is."

The duck was dark brown and tender and the red cabbage savory and fragrant with caraway seeds. They had set a plate for Nora but she didn't come.

Dan had second helpings of the cabbage. Ginger spread butter on a chunk of dense bread. She kicked off her shoes and drew her feet up under her long skirt on the cushioned bench. Dan had lit a candle and turned off the overhead kitchen light. The room seemed very warm.

"Let's see what we have for desert" Dan said "maybe some ice cream."

He got up from his chair just as Ginger simultaneously stood up in the narrow aisle. This time, when they brushed against each other, face to face, Dan realized the breadth and softness of Ginger's body, which, he sensed, was almost the same weight as his own. In fact, in this brief second Dan knew the width of Ginger's shoulders and the smooth curve of her upper arms, the warm flesh draped copiously through her soft middle section and her long thighs. To steady himself he put his hands on her waist, gently, without purpose. He heard her sharp intake of breath, involuntary.

Ginger squeezed past Dan and walked out of the kitchen. It was much cooler, almost chilly, in the unheated living room. The lights were dim.

She put her hands to her face which felt warm, as though she had a fever; she turned and looked back into the kitchen.

"There's coffee ice cream," Dan said, as he searched through the small freezer at the top of the refrigerator. Ginger watched him from the doorway, giving Dan room to move and find what he wanted, then she walked back into the kitchen and he moved aside to make room for her.

...

Nora had accepted her sister Pam's invitation to a dinner party on Monday night with some misgivings. She was unsure about the level of marital harmony in the Aston household. Nora knew Pam had a spare bedroom but she wanted to see how she and Van were getting along before she told them about needing a place to stay.

There was no way of predicting how long Ginger's house might be uninhabitable and Nora liked to be prepared for the worst. She had carefully considered other people she might ask to stay with, but couldn't think of anyone else she knew in Los Angeles who qualified as more than an acquaintance.

Nora drove up Mulholland Drive to her sister's house just after sunset. Since she was early she parked her car herself, though she saw women in pink jackets decorated with the logo "Party Parkettes," setting up a sign "Valette Parking." This indicated a large party; more than 25, Nora guessed. As she walked inside the gate, she stopped to admire the lights of the San Fernando valley which provided a sparkling backdrop to the long oval swimming pool built to the edge of the hillside. In the distance, the sprawling residential areas of the valley stretched to the horizon.

There were gimmicky floating toys in the bright aqua pool: an inflatable green turtle with a round indentation on its back to carry a glass; a clear plastic mattress with red handles bumping softly against the side. These made Nora think of Florida for some reason. She remembered that Pam always wanted to be tan and still sunned herself, despite repeated warnings from her dermatologist and her sister. As she entered, she saw that the caterers had unloaded some of their equipment near the garage and uniformed staff people were hurrying in and out of the kitchen carrying boxes and trays.

"What's going on ?" Nora greeted her sister. "Looks like a big party."

"We invited about 40 people for dinner."

Pam was dressed in tight silk Capri pants, pink beaded sandals and a polka-dot blouse that seemed to be shredded at the seams in the latest unstructured style. Nora followed her through the large black and white and chrome kitchen and into their living room, which was anchored by a wide fireplace of beige stone and looked out on the valley through a wall of sliding glass doors.

"You haven't seen this yet, have you ?' Pam asked.

Nora saw that the entire room was now colored white and beige. All the exposed wooden beams of the ceiling and the paneling around the fireplace had been painted white and the wooden floors were bleached beige-white. Nora knew what to say.

"This looks great, Pam, when did you do all this ?"

"I just finished it last week," Pam said, "what do you think ?"

Pam showed Nora the overstuffed white sofas and white coffee table and the white lamps and the white chairs. Nora made approving sounds and nods but she had the unpleasant sensation that she had wandered into a strange house that belonged to someone she didn't know. Everything looked new and smelled new, an odor like plastic and paint.

"It really is..." Nora groped for adjectives "brighter, I mean, it's a real change."

"It's cleaner, you know," Pam explained. "I like it better—I was sick of that old dark furniture."

Van Aston entered the living room and gave his sister-in-law two friendly kisses acknowledging both cheeks. He had a perfect golden tan and his hair was cut so that it looked both severe and becoming. Van's hair was always impeccable.

"Van likes it much better, don't you sweetie ?" Pam said to her husband.

Nora observed how Pam tried so dutifully to include Van in conversation but it was always futile. The man rarely had anything to say.

"What ?' he asked.

"The living room." Pam explained.

Someone from the catering crew came into the room asking Pam where to set up tables, so Nora was left with Van.

"Read any good scripts, Van ?"

Nora knew this was a safe question because it acknowledged her brother-in-law to be a man who was involved in important work.

"No," he said. "Not really. Gus keeps sending them. Sometimes two or three a week."

"Uh huh." Nora had this conversation with Van almost every time she saw him. Neither was particularly interested in the subject.

As far as Nora knew, Van never read anything but scripts. And he found fault with every one. Except for some coffee table books and some celebrity biographies, Nora had never seen a novel or a magazine or anything resembling literature in the Aston house. Nora suspected that Van was terrified at the idea of directing so he was keeping the fear at arm's length by saying no to the first step of the process.   It was so obvious that it seemed almost embarrassing to call attention to Van's behavior so she never discussed it with Pam.   Van offered to get Nora a drink and followed his wife into the kitchen.

Nora wondered if they were both on the wagon. Usually they stopped drinking together and Pam had seemed relentlessly sober lately.

"Who's coming ?" Nora asked her sister as she helped Pam count napkins and arrange platters in the huge kitchen.

"Steve Garritson said he'd be here-- you know, the director of 'Over Easy'? He just got a big movie over at Paramount that they'll be shooting in Africa. It would be so fabulous to go to Kenya on location. Steve's girlfriend is in my acting class. She's a model and really sweet. You know Van had a starring role in Steve's first film ?"

"Really ?" Nora had seen "Over Easy," it wasn't bad.

"And Ed Hackamore said he'd come but you never know," Pam shrugged her shoulders.

"Ed Hackamore the writer ?" Nora asked.

"Yes. Have you seen 'Dark Purpose' ? It's really brilliant. They're pushing it for a possible Oscar nomination. He could win again this year."

Nora was now certain that Pam and Van were on the wagon because her sister was drinking a glass of Pellegrino and Van had walked away from the bar empty-handed. This seemed to bode well in terms of domestic harmony. Pam had married a man who loved drama as much as she did and when she felt the need for histrionics, he gave as good as he got. Nora had stayed with the Astons when she first moved to Los Angeles and found them in the middle of a drinking season. She moved out as soon as possible. But, apart from a binge here and there; they didn't seem to be going at it like they had in years past. Neither had a fixed work schedule but both needed to be available to go to auditions when called. Van was officially trying to make a career change from acting to directing; but he'd made so much money doing the cable sitcom he had no immediate need to earn income. He'd fallen into acting because he was good looking and was cast in a successful film his first time out; but he seemed to have no real love for the craft. Pam, on the other hand, devoted herself to weekly sessions with a high-powered acting coach who worked only with select students. She and her classmates regarded the teacher as a kind of guru who gave them advice about every aspect of life.

"It's about not striving" she was telling Nora, as they moved folding chairs and decided where to put vases of fresh flowers. "If you let it flow through you, the creative stuff, you know, the juice; rather than trying to direct it, just let it go ? Then you are in the zone. What Chad calls 'the juicy zone'."

"Chad ? Is that his name ?"

"He's so amazing," Pam told her sister. "You should come to one of our classes or 'sessions' as he calls them. You could observe. It's like learning life lessons-I think it would help your writing. He like has insights ?"

Nora wondered why Pam was making questions out of statements. It always made Nora uneasy when people expressed certainty with a question. She also wondered how Pam could believe that some self-important acting coach's 'life lessons' might provide creative insight into anything more complex than a weekly soap opera; but Nora held her tongue. She was aware that the half hour before guests arrive is a delicate and difficult time for a hostess and Nora decided to be supportive.

"I saw Peter Sackman at David's show," she told Pam. We had a drink together. He seems depressed."

"He was always depressed," Pam said. "That's one of the reasons we split up."

Nora knew what some of the other reasons were but she didn't mention them. Pam had begun moving lamps from one place to another and plumping sofa pillows with short quick slaps. Her movements had become somewhat distracted and obsessive. She pushed a large potted palm outside to the flagstone pavement, then moved it again to a spot near the French doors. Nora knew that Pam normally would have a drink in hand by now. Sober, Nora saw, Pam was overwhelmed by the myriad of details, uncertain of herself and her ability to feel festive and celebratory. Pam always needed to be the life of the party.

"You know what Nora, I have a little headache, I'll just go upstairs and take a pain killer. I'll be right back. If anyone comes, I'll be right down."

Nora leaned back in an overstuffed white armchair and looked out the sliding glass doors at the lights of a million houses on thousands of streets in the immense San Fernando valley below. The grid of residential streets was bound by criss-crossed ropes of freeways with lights moving white in one direction and red in the other, like a bloodstream in a cheap aspirin commercial. She realized what a broad meaning the innocuous phrase "pain killer" might have; how many pain killers there are in the world and how many people need them. She thought of several celebrities she'd read about recently who'd been hospitalized because of an "addiction to painkillers." Some of them had illegal access to the powerful drugs given to cancer patients in the final stages of excruciating pain. Nora considered the idea that civilization itself was based on pain killers; it was all a question of degree. Houses could be construed as pain killers because they alleviated the discomfort of living outdoors; shoes made walking on stones less painful, religion made death more bearable, etc. Nora was about to go into the kitchen for another glass of pain-killing wine when the first guests arrived and Van hurried into the room to greet his agent, Gus Reidel with his partner Devon. After Van introduced Nora he disappeared, so Nora asked Gus how long he'd been at William Morris and he told her, then said nothing more as he poured himself some wine.

His young companion sat down in a white chair and stared out the window without greeting Nora. He wore an un-ironed white shirt and black jeans and loafers without socks.

Pam had set two long white tables near the pool beside the open doors into the dining room. The night remained warm and windless. Groups of candles illuminated the tables and strings of tiny white lights lit up the doorways and were draped over the trees outdoors. Nora was seated next to Nigel Twick, a short, balding man who came to the party with Steve, the director. He had known Steve for a long time, since their days at a London advertising agency, Nigel told Nora, in his melodious Welsh accent. Nigel was a writer who had collaborated on the three music videos that Steve Garritson had directed with Black Soup, a hugely successful rock group. Nora knew that the unusual imagery and unique style of these widely-copied MTV spots had not only focused attention on Black Soup, but had established Steve Garritson's reputation as a hot new director.

Nigel, with a modest air, confided to Nora that he had provided the "concept" for all of Steve's music videos—the neo-Gothic style, the mirror effects, the famous séance scene where Cass Moffat, Black Soup's lead singer, levitated over the head of a man in a top hat until his face disappeared under her skirt. Though not a Black Soup fan, Nora had seen the video a number of times, it was almost as famous as the Michael Jackson or Madonna classics.

Nigel was obviously not from Los Angeles. He was polite and sociable and wore a bow tie with a crisply pressed shirt. He apparently didn't know anyone at the party except Steve, who was busy talking to Ed Hackamore, the writer who had won an Academy award for his last script and had a long track record of successful films. Steve's next project was a script Ed had written. Nora admired Nigel's shirt, a tan woven stripe, very thin, on crisp white cotton. Across the table sat Maya Frost who was around forty and dressed in a vintage chiffon dress from the twenties that revealed her perfectly toned upper arms and slim hips. She was an old friend of Pam's who collected antique clothing, and as far as Nora knew, spent most of her time traveling; though she called herself a jewelry designer. Bret, a lanky blond who was Maya's boyfriend, sat to Nora's left.

He looked like he might be an actor and Nora found talking to actors in general very difficult, and males under 30 particularly. Most were painfully self-conscious or adhered to dubious spiritual practices or tried to appear well-read. Bret looked to be under thirty and he professed to be a filmmaker with a project he wanted to direct. He told Nora he'd done some work as a cinematographer but he preferred video to film because, he explained, it's much faster and actors can give better performances when there are fewer lights. Nora was going to interrupt him and mention some great performances achieved on old slow black and white film, when she realized that Bret might be unfamiliar with the films that were her personal touchstones. Bret told Nora his film school affiliation and mentioned an independent documentary that he'd done some work on. He also said that "Blade Runner" was his all-time favorite film and he was very sorry he was missing "X Files," which he watched faithfully on Monday nights.

Maya was saying to someone across the table that she and Luke, the tall sandy-haired man to her right, both had apartments in the same building in New York. Luke came to life and began to praise the stealth and cunning of the building's superintendent, a man named Lopez; his admirable personality, his family and number of children, Lopez' skill at fixing plumbing and cable television problems, and his dependence upon Christmas bonuses to keep his considerable holdings afloat. Luke then praised the view from Maya's apartment and Maya said Luke's roof garden was one of the best she'd seen in Manhattan. Bret then asked Luke if it was his Ferrari that he had seen parked outside. Luke acknowledged that it was, then described how much he enjoyed driving the car, it's precision of steering and quickness of acceleration; its innovative engine design and his willingness to undertake any errand, no matter how small, for the pleasure of driving said car which he had recently purchased, brand new.

"How much does a car like that cost ?" Bret asked, a casual intimate tone. Luke gave the younger man a disgusted look and told him. Then neither said anything more to the other.

Nora asked Bret what he particularly liked about "X-files" and Maya looked over at her with a disapproving look on her face, so Nora continued..."I think people are fascinated because it's about death."

Nora saw that she had awakened a spark in the eye of Bret. He was titillated by the idea of violence in general and death in particular. He said "It's way more intense and dark than any other series." Nora knew that dark meant profound to Bret.

"But why do you think it's so popular ?" Nora pursued.
Maya looked over at her boyfriend and said "Isn't Luke's roof garden just the best place in our building in New York ?" and Bret immediately agreed.

Nora then turned and continued her conversation with the Welshman, Nigel Twick. "So you're a writer," she said to him. "What do you like to write about ?"

Nigel's voice, which had been light and bantering all evening, took on a sonorous Richard Burton kind of tone. "I write about children who are in danger or have lost something; or are themselves dying or lost," he explained to Nora with a meaningful gaze, level and full of conviction.

"I explore tenderness, pathos and unrequited love and I always like to put animals in it; preferably horses or birds."

Nora was struck momentarily speechless with admiration. She had never before heard such an answer and she realized then that Nigel was probably brilliant and the hottest creative spark that had ever come near Steven Garritson.

"You don't find your subject a little depressing ?" Nora slowly and respectfully turned the warm gaze of her Maria Callas eyes on Nigel and smiled an endearing smile, but he wasn't fazed.

"Not at all. Those are simply the subjects that interest me." Nigel said with quiet dignity as he looked down the table at Steven Garritson, who was laughing heartily at something that insufferably pompous Ed Hackamore was saying.

His old friend Steve had begun to ignore him on the fifth day of his visit to Los Angeles; he hadn't spoken to him all evening, nor had he bothered to introduce him to anyone at the party. Perhaps he should have stayed in a hotel instead of at Steve's house, Nigel considered, but there was the driving problem. He had never before visited California and he thought the people spoke too loudly and spent too much time driving. He had been obliged to go everywhere with Steve and Becka or stay at home alone, and it was beginning to be a bit exhausting—not to mention the jet lag. He thought of telling Nora all this, a kind of light-hearted but sincere confession; but he could tell she wasn't the sympathetic type. She was the type who wanted to be impressed.

Nora looked down the table at Steven Garritson, who was explaining that he never ate meat because he'd worked for a while at a meat-packing plant in southern Australia. Pam and Van both seemed to find this bit of information extraordinarily significant.

They were nodding frequently and sympathetically. Steven's girlfriend, Becka, a very tall girl with a perfect head of shiny red hair, was saying that her parents were Amish people who lived on a farm in Ohio and her mother had spent her entire life in a wheelchair. Obviously, Nora thought, the dinner party was proving to be an opportunity for Pam and Van to bond more intimately with the director. They might both end up with roles in his film.

Later in the evening, as the guests began to leave the table and cluster on the patio in small groups, Pam and Becka became deeply involved in a discussion of their acting teacher's ideas about dramatic movement as a way of inhabiting multi-generational gender history. Nora poured herself some coffee and slowly made her way towards a small group she saw clustered around Ed Hackamore, the writer, who was talking to Van and Steve and Luke, the dominant males at the party. Angular and tan in a well-tailored linen shirt, Ed had a somewhat bored expression in his eyes.

"A character has to earn the audience's love," Nora overhead him saying.

Maya Frost joined the cluster at the same moment as Nora did. Ed smiled indulgently as the two women sat down in adjoining chairs. "Are you two sisters ?" he asked.

"No," both said in unison, to Nora's intense irritation.

She wondered if Maya heard the patronizing note in Hackamore's voice. Both women wore sleeveless dresses with high-heeled sandals and, Nora realized, had similar haircuts.

"Tell me about yourself" the writer asked Maya in his commanding voice "where did you come from ?"

She explained that she'd grown up in Bel Air where her parents met L. Ron Hubbard and were among the first to join the Scientologists. Maya had been raised as a Scientologist and said there were many misconceptions about the group, though she herself was no longer a member. Nora realized that she had become not an object but a subject. The other men watched.

When Hackmore turned to her and asked the same question Nora said her father was a Greek ship owner who, after his business had been ruined by Aristotle Onassis, ended up marrying an American and living in New York.

"After he died, my mother moved to Florida because she loved the beach" Nora heard herself saying, with the uncomfortable feeling that she was revealing too much and too little that was completely true.

The manner in which Hackamore asked the questions indicated that his curiosity about the women was sparked not by any personal interest but by a desire to know and understand human beings in general. The man was removed from the common levels of social intercourse, that was clear. Nora imagined that before she and Maya arrived the men had been involved in discussing new developments in filmmaking or avant-garde writers but they had interrupted that talk when "the girls" arrived for a bit of frivolous chitchat.

Nora tried to think of a remark she could direct to Hackmore that would indicate her seriousness; her interest in the arts, writing in particular; and specific personal uniqueness. She couldn't immediately think of an appropriate way to begin.

Maya, however, jumped in. "I was in Sri Lanka last week," she began "the police have begun persecuting the Buddhist minority. I'm part of a committee to restore human rights to Sri Lanka." Ed Hackmore responded that he also belonged to a Buddhist group in New York that was working with refugees from Burma. Maya darted a triumphant look at Nora and immediately began exchanging cards and information with Ed, having achieved first-name familiarity in a few minutes.

Nora noticed that Luke was looking at her with interest.

"Didn't I meet you at David Marsden's show at Ace?" Luke asked. He had very light blue eyes that, though not large, seemed permanently amused. His disheveled sand-colored hair framed a face lined and worn in a way that Nora interpreted as slightly self-indulgent but intelligent.

As they watched Ed Hackamore walking into the house with Maya, Luke shook his head. "Precious Mr. Ed, the talking horse."

"Is he a friend of yours?" Nora asked.

"Not really, but we go way back. I knew his first wife." Nora saw that Luke had a quick smile and a way of looking at her that seemed fully engaged. She suspected that he had a sense of humor and this suspicion made her heart beat faster. She met his eyes in the semi-darkness and she saw it again, the light of humor, a pale fugitive spark.

"May I bring you a drink?" Luke asked Nora with a hint of exaggeration in his politeness.

Nora hesitated then agreed. She watched Luke's long legs walk into the house with a relaxed loping gait. Most of the other guests had moved inside; the party was breaking up. She felt at peace sitting outside in the warm night with the underwater pool lights casting a dappled aquatic glow which rippled over the walls and shrubbery.

She smelled chlorine and the greasy metallic smell of Los Angeles smog mixed with the voluptuous perfume of night-blooming jasmine. She felt she was floating without a fixed point of departure or destination, untethered and buoyant.

...

When Ginger walked back into the kitchen Dan said, "I wonder where Nora is?"

"She was going to a party at Pam's tonight," Ginger said, "She'll probably spend the night there." Ginger looked at the clock. It was past one o'clock. "I should..." she looked at Dan and paused.

Dan leaned across the aisle of the kitchen and pressed his hand against the cupboard. Ginger's face was at his inner elbow. "We could watch a movie on television," he said.

"I think I should ..." she began and Dan shifted his weight towards her. Ginger's full hips pressed against the counter and the back of her head against the cupboard. His right arm encircled her waist and his upper hand lifted her face to his. Later, Ginger remembered only the eager heat of Dan's face, the sweet grape taste of his mouth, the odor of his unmade bed, like yeast or clay.

Nora returned to Santa Monica around nine thirty the next morning to the noise of Dan running hot water into a sink full of pots and pans and the loud splashing whine of the shower going full force in the back. The water pipes hissed and roared in the thin walls of the old bungalow.

"Good morning," Dan greeted Nora in a loud hearty voice as she put some orange juice and milk into the refrigerator. In the steam-filled kitchen it sounded like they were standing under a waterfall.

"I stopped at the market," she said.

"Great" Dan answered, nodding energetically as he lifted a clean cast-iron pot onto the counter. Nora wanted to take a shower but there was only one bathroom. I have to find another place to stay, she thought, soon.

"Good party?" Dan asked, busy with his kitchen tasks, not looking at Nora.

"It was okay," she answered, waiting for him to move so she could fill the coffee maker. "What time do you want to work tonight?"

"I made some plans for tonight" Dan told Nora, "do you mind if we work in the afternoon instead?"

CHAPTER TWENTY

Josh Samuels was singing along to the lyrics of Prince's "Sign O' the Times" as he drove south on Highway 210 on Friday afternoon. Josh had been looking forward to this day with eager anticipation ever since Michelle had agreed to go with him to Whispering Palms for the weekend.

On his last trip to the desert resort in June, he'd taken Amy Kittman, who worked in the agency mail room. Today, however, Josh felt much more eagerness than he'd ever felt with Amy or, for that matter, Monica Lewis, with whom he had shared a weekend at Whispering Palms last Thanksgiving. Turning to look at Michelle leaning back drowsily in the beige leather passenger seat of his Mercedes 450 SL, Josh felt a rush of excitement that seemed to him of a different order than the mere desire, lust really, he had felt for Amy or Monica. As he followed the creeping line of cars which merged to the right onto four lanes marked Palm Springs, Josh's imagination leapt ahead to Whispering Palms.

He imagined Michelle, undressed, sitting beside him in the steaming hot spring-fed pool that was the raison d'etre of the rustic desert resort. He saw Michelle as a kind of Polynesian goddess rising naked from the water; her brown nipples eagerly erect in the path of rivulets of warm water rushing down her firm...Josh's mental images flitted in and out like quickly shuffled cards; he didn't dare focus too long on any specific... Long wet black hair dripping onto.... A back view of Michelle naked, bending down to test the water's temperature. Josh exhaled audibly and looked at Michelle who met his eyes and smiled her shy inscrutable smile. Josh loved her silence, her uncritical acceptance of him. She never complained or seemed impatient, nor did she talk about herself or ask him questions about his past.

Michelle had surprised Josh by immediately agreeing to go to Whispering Palms with him when he first asked her; she made no stipulations or contingencies. Josh imagined that Michelle must have a deeply religious or spiritual view of life. A way of thinking that was mysterious to him. She was entirely unlike anyone else he knew. As it happened, Josh's parents, Roz and Gary Samuels, had a house in Palm Springs, just a short distance from Whispering Palms, where, this Friday, they were celebrating their 30th wedding anniversary. Josh had almost forgotten about the event until reminded by his older sister Ruth, who lived in Beverly Hills in the same neighborhood as his parents. Ruth always called to remind him when he was expected for some family event. He took the opportunity to ask for Friday off work at Aspiring Artists, explaining that he was obliged to attend the celebration. Since his uncle David, his father's brother, was the head of Josh's department, he knew this excuse would carry some weight. Josh promised his sister he would come but didn't mention Michelle because he was afraid Ruth might tell him not to bring her.

The Mercedes was traveling away from the suburban sprawl now and there were empty patches of clean sand on either side of the freeway. Josh was planning how he could stop by his parents place, give them the gift he'd brought for them, stay an hour or so and immediately head for Whispering Palms. He hoped his brother Neal wouldn't be there—he wanted everything to go smoothly. Josh began to think about the deluxe suite and the king sized bed he'd reserved; about the bed containing Michelle and her warm, freshly-bathed body. As he looked over at Michelle he breathed a deep steadying breath. He felt perspiration on his upper lip and his armpits were damp as he turned the air conditioning a few notches lower. He knew he shouldn't get impatient, not now. He had to get through the next five hours, then the weekend was his. Josh felt in his pocket for the pills. What harm could one little valium do, he thought. He punched two small sky-blue pills out of their foil circles and swallowed one.

Michelle, pointing out the window, asked with lazy curiosity "What are those things ?"

"Those are windmills", Josh explained, as they drove by a field of sand sprouting an orchard of posts topped by metal propellers revolving in aimless circles.

"What are they doing here ?"

"They've been there for a long time," Josh said, "I think they're supposed to make electricity or something."

"Electricity ?" Michelle was puzzled, she didn't see any cables or wires.

"Want some ?" Josh offered the small blue tablet to Michelle. She shrugged.

"I took one" he told her. "You know, just to chill out."

"Okay" she said, accepting the tiny tablet and tossing it back in her mouth, then drinking from a plastic bottle of water she found on the floor of the car.

A green sign popped up on the highway: Palm Springs 50 miles.

"That's where we're going, right ?" Michelle said to Josh.

"We're just going to stop by and say hello to my parents; then we'll continue on to Whispering Palms" Josh explained, "the resort is 25 miles from town, surrounded by desert, you'll like it, it's great"

Michelle stared out at the landscape—a hand-painted wooden sign advertised Date Shakes. She thought of ice cream and a boy and girl holding hands and shaking. Her eyes registered the widening expanses of parched sandy earth dotted with palm trees, but her thoughts kept returning to Jennifer. In the days since the elevator accident her friend had often argued with Scott on the telephone and said she wanted to leave him and his agency.

Michelle didn't want to change anything. She felt satisfied with the way their lives were going but Jennifer was always thinking and planning the next thing. Michelle wondered where or how they would meet other men like Josh and Scott. She supposed an agency was an office where people had computers and files and telephones but she wasn't sure exactly how agents did what they did. She was continually surprised at all the things Josh knew, the complicated plans he made. Michelle sighed and closed her eyes; she felt Josh put his hand on her thigh and she reached down and squeezed it and opened her eyes and smiled at him. He knows where we're going and how to get there and what we're expected to do, she thought. A deeply pleasurable feeling of having nothing to worry about engulfed Michelle and she reached over and gently rubbed Josh's thigh with her open palm.

When Michelle and Josh drove up the long driveway of the Samuels house the sun had sunk low on the horizon, casting a reddish glow over the pale yellow exterior of the sprawling modern structure.

"We're just going to stop in and say hello, then we're out of here," Josh explained to Michelle.

He opened the trunk and took out a neatly wrapped present that his assistant had bought and delivered—some kind of bowl or something that Ruth told him his mother would love. Josh felt he should try to please his mother because he knew he was her favorite. His sister and brother always accused her of favoring him, but it wasn't his fault, Josh told himself, he didn't ask for any special treatment. His older brother was such a fuck-up, such a big disappointment, that all of his mother's ambitions and expectations had settled on him.

Roz Samuels greeted them at the door and embraced her son enthusiastically.

"I brought Michelle with me, Mom, we're on our way to Whispering Palms." Josh told his mother as Michelle stood by, smiling her shy smile. His mother looked fondly upon her narrow-shouldered son and the petite curly-haired brunette at his side.

"Gary!" Mrs. Samuels called loudly to her husband so as to be heard in the far reaches of the house, "Josh is here—he brought a girlfriend."

Michelle stood in the entrance to the house noticing how large and empty it seemed. The floor looked like concrete and the few furnishings seemed over-sized. A huge vase made of reddish clay leaned against the wall beside the front door. It seemed to Michelle that it would be almost impossible to pick it up, much less fill it with water. But Michelle's observations were interrupted by Mrs. Samuels' questions.

"Where did you meet Josh ? Are you an actress ?"

"Michelle is getting started on a television career." Josh told her. "She's incredibly talented."

"How exciting !" Roz said, putting her arm around Michelle protectively, "Now you just make yourself at home, okay ?"

Michelle nodded and smiled, she wasn't sure what to say to this wiry older woman with her very black hair and large jewelry. Josh's mother seemed to be in a hurry for some reason and Michelle wanted to sit down or possibly lie down, if the opportunity presented itself. Michelle thought about Roz saying "girlfriend." She was Josh's girlfriend now, tonight. She tried to determine whether she was always, in every situation, Josh's girlfriend or if that was a description valid only here on this particular happy occasion.

"Show Michelle around, I'll find your father."

Roz hurried into another room, leaving Josh to lead Michelle through a room painted orange with a huge yellow and blue painting on the wall through sliding glass doors that opened onto a long L-shaped swimming pool enclosed within the landscaped patio in the center of the large house.

Michelle breathed in the dry hush of the desert air and sank down onto a stone bench near the edge of the pool. She felt limp, as if her legs had become spongy.

"We're not going to stay long," Josh reiterated, as he sat down beside Michelle and embraced her.

Her jasmine perfume filled his nose as he put his hands on her breasts and she giggled in her quiet, content way. He loved that she had nothing to say. She rarely volunteered a comment. "Want to jump in the pool ?" he whispered.

"Get in here, Josh !" He stood up when he heard his father's commanding voice calling from the doorway. "So you managed to make it, after all !"

Josh immediately walked inside to greet his father, but Michelle wanted to stay seated, she didn't feel like getting up. She could faintly hear other voices and a loud dingdong doorbell and Roz greeting guests. Michelle stretched out on the concrete bench and looked up at the night blue sky, deep and dark and studded with stars.

Josh was pressed into duty by his mother to sort out the parking problems complicated by a half dozen cars driving up at the same time. His sister Ruth arrived in a bad mood because her husband cancelled at the last minute which made her late. Uncle David came with his wife, Donna, whose face was a bright pink resulting from a special chemical peel that hadn't quite healed yet. His Aunt Sofie, who was in a wheel chair, insisted that he push her into the kitchen so she could check on the caterers.

"Where's Neal ?" Ruth asked her brother as he walked out of the kitchen. "Dad told me he was here."

"Neal ? I haven't seen him."

Josh wondered if his brother was deliberately avoiding him because he owed him money or if he was avoiding everyone. He decided to move his car into the street so that in another half hour or so he could duck out and make his escape without anyone noticing.

Michelle found herself yawning. She knew Josh had to talk to his relatives but she didn't think he would mind if she took a little nap. She saw a long wooden bench near a wall at the far end of the pool where a small waterfall tumbled among copper dolphins. Lights were positioned on the ground pointing up at the spiny trees with nodding trunks which cast dancing shadows on the high angular walls of the house. When Michelle stretched out on the slatted wooden bench, she felt as comfortable as if she had found a feather bed. She felt warm and out of the way and drowsy.

In the dining room, which was filling rapidly with the assembled guests, Gary Samuels, a compact man in a pink shirt, greeted his family and friends, urged people to eat, comforted his daughter, complimented his wife, bear-hugged his brother and searched the room for his older son.

Neal Samuels finished checking the extra-sensitive alarm system on his Land Rover with a special tool he carried for that purpose. He decided it was safe to leave it parked overnight in the back of his parents' garage, though he would have preferred a better lock on the door. His ears were buzzing and his body felt wired from being on the road for so long and he smelled bad. With the help of some Mexican methedrina and a little cocaine, Neal had just driven alone for three days on the road from Acapulco to Tijuana, without stopping to sleep. Once he'd made it across the border he decided to drive the extra miles and spend the night at his parents' house instead of dealing with the hassle of finding a hotel room, hiding the two kilos of cocaine he had in his car, and worrying about whether someone might find it. This way felt much safer. He could rest up and leave for L.A. in the morning. Neal had not been aware of his parents' celebration when he arrived at the house, so he had received a much warmer welcome than he'd really expected. He allowed them to think that he intended to surprise them on their anniversary and they were obviously touched at his thoughtfulness.

Neal walked out the side door of the garage into the quiet courtyard where he bent down to dip his hand in the warm water of the L-shaped swimming pool glowing aquamarine among the carefully landscaped desert plants. He could smell the accumulated sweat from all those hours on the Mexican highway permeating his jeans and t-shirt. He decided to undress and go for a quick swim while the party guests swarmed and bumbled over the buffet table.

Michelle dreamed she was on a raft rushing down a fast moving river. She saw Jennifer on the bank and waved to her but Jennifer couldn't see her. Michelle was unable to get her attention. She needed to call to Jennifer to ask her to help, but she couldn't make a sound. Michelle could hear the roar of the waterfall rapidly approaching; she had to yell at the top of her lungs to get Jennifer's attention before it was too late. She gathered energy in her throat to call out but the sound stayed stuck there, mute. Michelle was afraid, she knew she was going over the falls unless someone heard her, saved her. In her panic, she opened her mouth to shout but, again, nothing came out.

Finally she stiffened, strained, and shouted "Hel....!" A blast of inarticulate sound abruptly penetrated the curtain from sleep to waking. The effort woke Michelle, sweating on the bench in the dark, and the sound attracted the attention of Neal.

Neal heard a brief panicked syllable then saw a girl sit up on the bench near the wall. He stood up to his neck in shimmering spirals of water-- not moving, silently listening and watching. He could see the girl clearly, and knew she wasn't a relative or friend of his parents. He tried to imagine what she was doing there. He wondered if she might be an older daughter of the Samuels' housekeeper, Yolanda, whose children were sometimes seen in the kitchen or utility room. Neal watched as the girl rubbed her arms and ran her fingers through her long thick hair. He could clearly see her face—untroubled and sweet, soft with sleep. Something about her expression touched Neal, so he called to her.

"Hey, come on in, the water will wake you up."

He then dove deep to the bottom of the dark pool, to allow her a moment of privacy. A moment in which Michelle, stiff and drowsy, shed her wraparound dress in one quick motion, her bra and thong in another, and dove into the pool.

The water was the temperature of stone, cool enough to be refreshing but warmer than the night air. Underwater lights along the blue tiled walls of the pool cast their pale gleam illuminating the shimmering blue-green broth. As Michelle dove towards the lights, she felt the water caress her heavy breasts which became blissfully weightless and buoyant. She hoped Josh's parents wouldn't mind them swimming without bathing suits but apparently Josh thought it was okay. The water felt so good she surfaced and dove deep again and again, enjoying the sensation of water flowing against her warm face and long hair, through her armpits, her pubic hair, rippling her vagina's sensitive fins. She paddled underwater with her eyes open, enclosed in the safety of the water's soundless hush, until her breath ran out and she surfaced to look for Josh in the other end of the L-shaped pool.

Ruth sat near the fireplace inside the dining room eating a large serving of noodle pudding; a dish she never cooked at home but which her parents always served. Her brother Josh came in carrying a dinner plate piled high with food, and sat down beside her.

"Where's your girlfriend ?" Ruth asked him.

"She was taking a nap when I checked so I just let her sleep."

"A nap ?" Ruth's question contained a hint of both disbelief and disapproval.

Josh hated having to explain everything to his older sister who always wanted to know his personal business. He hoped his parents didn't ask where his girlfriend was—luckily they were busy talking with their friends. He tried to hit on a plausible excuse for Michelle falling asleep and regretted giving her the valium. She probably has a different metabolism than I do, he reflected.

"I think she's just been working too hard lately," Josh explained, chewing a large chunk of grilled salmon.

"What does Michelle do ?" Ruth wanted to know.

Josh regarded his older sister with her no-nonsense haircut and inquisitive face. Both he and his brother were small men, barely weighing in at 130 pounds, but Ruth was heavy and wide on her short frame.

"How much do you weigh, Ruth ?" Josh sounded like he really wanted to know.

"Fuck you," his sister answered good-naturedly. "Come on, what does she do — is she an actress ?"

"You could say that," Josh answered, preparing for the next question.

"What's she done ? Anything I've heard of ?"

"Not really. She's just getting started, you know. She was on TV not long ago."

Josh didn't want to alienate Ruth, he needed her on his side.

"A series ?" Ruth asked. She was involved with mortgage banking and didn't know much about the industry.

"No, just some guest appearances. Believe me, she's amazing. She's a terrific talent."

Josh wanted Ruth to be in favor of Michelle in case his parents...But Josh couldn't bring himself to imagine the complexities of introducing Michelle as a potential...Josh ate his food quickly, barely tasting it. After dinner, he'd go and wake Michelle and prepare for their rapid departure at the first possible moment.

...

Neal didn't want to scare the girl. He retreated to the other end of the pool and let her swim. Maybe she was the daughter of one of his parents' guests — or a distant cousin recently grown into nubile womanhood. He wanted to keep a low profile. But she obviously recognized him, maybe they had met as children at some family gatherings, she wasn't shy. Neal dove deep into the bottom of the pool, grateful for the respite, the silence, the freshness of cool water. He was an expert swimmer and often went scuba diving in Zihuatenejo with Jorge, his Colombian friend. The events of the past week were still fresh but unrecollected in Neal's mind. Things had gone much more smoothly than last year. It was too bad Nicole had decided to fly back instead of driving with him but that was probably safer. He didn't expect her to take any risks, he'd made that clear from the beginning. Neal surfaced and studied the glowing expanse of the pool. He couldn't see the girl, she probably hurried back inside. He dove deep underwater again and swam towards the other end of the pool, eyes closed.

Michelle came up gasping for air after counting to see how long she could hold her breath. She was wide awake now and was looking forward to the rest of the weekend with Josh. She felt a wave of gratitude to him for bringing her to this beautiful place. He was swimming towards her now, deep under the water, so she dove down and wrapped her arms gently around his waist from behind. Josh twisted sharply and turned to look at her, but the chlorine in the pool stung her eyes so she kept them shut as she pulled him close, pressing her body against his back. She held on to him as he swam through the water, a game she had played as a child with her stepfather. He continued swimming with long strong strokes and she held on to him.

When he got to the far end of the pool, Neal wiggled out of her grasp and came up under Michelle's legs, boosting her up on his shoulders as she surfaced and steadied herself on the edge of the pool, giggling and dripping. He ducked his head from between her legs and dove quickly back underwater and swam to the opposite end. Michelle sat for a brief moment on the concrete in the night air which now felt cold against her skin. She noticed a slight abrasion where his thick hair had rubbed against tender skin when he lifted her legs over his shoulders.

She slipped under the water again and let her hands feel her nipples which were like hard berries. Michelle stretched an arm along each angle of the corner of the shallow end of the pool; she closed her eyes and pretended she was lying in a bed with the lip of the pool as a pillow. Her body floated easily if she didn't stiffen or try to move. She contemplated her feet and her thighs and the black mound of curly hair between them as she bobbed gently on the surface of the water. As she lay there, she felt a disturbance underwater as two hands gently slid up her legs to the underside of her thighs. Then Josh moved his hands to squeeze the soft flesh of her back side and tilted her pelvis up out of the water.

"Oh," she said, resting her head back on the lip of the pool, and closing her eyes "oh."

He stood between her floating legs and moved them open gently but firmly, holding her thighs with both hands as his tongue found the hard spot in the center and she moaned again softly, oh, allowing her whole body to accept this unexpected sensation. He knew how to tease her gently with the tip of his muscular tongue and then slowly taste her opening from the center to the edge. He knew how to speed up and apply pressure without being rough. Josh has never done this before, Michelle thought, as she felt her breasts stiffen and her face grow hot. He abruptly pulled her unresisting body to a standing position facing the side of the pool and pressed himself against her from behind. His hands found her breasts and rubbed her nipples until she cried out, faintly, a muffled exclamation that became a sigh as he continued, his penis pressing urgently behind her into a cleft of soft flesh. Michelle found herself entering a state of pleasure that transformed her into a weightless slippery being who moved in graceful rhythmic movements.

She was no longer Michelle but something of a different order –a water nymph, an open lotus flower; and he wasn't Josh, but a wily underwater sprite, born in the dark pool under the jeweled sky. He lifted her from behind with thick forearms under her thighs and penetrated her in a decisive movement that both surprised and delighted her. She marveled that the heated consistency of her liquid center, more viscous than the water in which they were submerged, allowed him to do what he did. She held on to the side of the pool and he buried his face in her hair and neck, covering it with kisses and gentle bites.

When he let go of her she floated for a while, weightless, no longer aware of holding on or letting go. But when she turned her head to look for him, she lost her buoyancy, and stood on her feet in the shallow end. She peered into the depths of the pool for his gliding body but saw it was empty and still. She swam around the corner of the L and searched underwater and around the dark shadows of the courtyard but found no one.

"Josh ?" she called out softly, thinking he was close by, but there was no answer.

Neal ducked into a back door and found the bathroom in the guest room. Not long afterwards, his mother opened the bedroom door and called his name. "I'm in here, Mom," he said, over the roar of the shower.

"Don't you want to come out and see your brother and sister?" his mother's voice was coaxing, as if talking to a small child. "Uncle David is here too."

"I'll be out in a minute" Neal called, and his mother shut the door.

When Josh finished eating dinner and went back outside, Michelle was putting on her clothes in the dark corner near the bench.

"You're all wet" he said when he found her and Michelle smiled, reached up and touched his hair and found it dry.

"You went swimming ?" he asked. She smiled and nodded. "Are you ready to go ?" He asked her and she nodded and took his hand and they walked through a side door into a dark garage then out another door onto the street where his car was parked, waiting. Josh opened the car and prepared to drive away.

"Wait," Michelle said, "I forgot something," and half-running, she returned to the pool area through the garage. She found her purse under the bench and hurried back the way she came. When she stepped into the garage, Michelle thought she heard a splash in the pool. She turned around and looked, but saw no one. In the dark she tripped over some tennis rackets and fell against a Land Rover that was parked there. A loud car alarm erupted in a high decibel bleat, startling her. She ran outside to the sidewalk where Josh was waiting.

"I set off a car alarm in the garage" she told him and they both grimaced for a split second at the terrible noise shattering the desert night. Josh held the door open for her and she sank into his passenger seat, frowning, holding her ears. "I'm sorry."

"We can't turn it off now," Josh said, starting his car. He thought about going back inside and making explanations, but immediately rejected the idea.

"My father will go out and turn it off; he'll think the cat did it." Michelle looked so shaken he felt he should reassure her further.

"Don't worry about it," he told her as they drove away into the dark suburban streets, "accidents happen."

The two-lane highway from Palm Springs to Whispering Palms was almost deserted at night. Josh drove rapidly and Michelle was silent, gazing at the stars crowding the dark dome of the desert. The resort was small but well-marked, with lighted signs on the highway directing visitors down a winding driveway to the entrance. When they reached the small reception area, the white-haired man on duty at Whispering Palms found Josh's reservation and prepared to lead them to their rooms.

"Oh, wait a minute," the old desk manager said. "I got a message for you-- it came in late this afternoon." Josh thought a frantic call had probably come in from one of his clients. How do they find me ? he thought.

"It's for Michelle Montano," the manager said, handing him a piece of paper with a name and number. Josh took the yellow slip of paper and gave it to Michelle who looked puzzled. She had told Jennifer where she was going but why would she want...A cold bolt of fear struck Michelle between her ribs, she felt it palpably like a blow. She knew, without question, this was bad news. She followed Josh to their suite, two spacious rooms furnished with comfortable chairs and pastel rugs and a big bed. She felt numb and terrified and far from home.

Michelle sat down on the bed and looked at the message: Call Jennifer as soon as possible—then March's home number. She dialed the telephone beside the bed and sat on the edge of the mattress and listened to it ringing. For a minute she thought no one was home but then Jennifer picked up.

"Jen, is that you ? I got your message" Michelle began, then she heard Jennifer's little sob and she felt the pain again, like a warning, as she listened. "No ! When ?" Josh looked up from unpacking his bag, Michelle's voice was unnaturally shrill. "No !"

Michelle didn't keep the receiver against her ear, she let it go to her shoulder, like it was too heavy to hold up. Josh saw her face dissolve into tears. He walked over to her but she didn't look up at him.

"What happened ?" He saw the tears drenching her face, and he was afraid to touch her.

"Where is she ?' Michelle asked into the telephone, ignoring Josh. "Okay, we'll meet you there." She hung up the telephone and buried her face in the pillow of the bed, sobbing.

"What is it ?" Josh said, "Tell me what happened."

"It's March," Michelle sobbed, "she got in an accident with a truck." She sat up and took Josh's hands, "She's hurt really bad. She's in the hospital, her head is...like, crushed or something."

Josh knew he should say something comforting. "Crushed ?" he said, "Can they...I mean, what's the prognosis."

"I don't know" Michelle's voice sounded angry suddenly, like she felt impatient with Josh. "Her head was..." but she couldn't say it or think it, the picture was too horrible to bring into focus. "We have to go to the hospital."

"Where is she ?" Josh asked.

"Cedars Sinai Hospital--Jennifer said she's in intensive care."

"We can visit her Sunday if you want," Josh said, "we can leave early."

Michelle stared at Josh with a deeply questioning expression as if she had never looked at his face before. "We have to go back first thing in the morning," she said. " Jennifer doesn't think she'll ... Josh, she could die."

"You don't know that," he said, "maybe it's not as bad as Jennifer thinks."

"Josh," Michelle met his eyes directly and spoke with unwavering conviction, "we have to leave for the hospital first thing in the morning."

CHAPTER TWENTY - ONE

Jennifer thought it had been a long time since a nurse or a doctor had looked into the room-- number 6560, March's room. The wide corridors of Cedars Sinai hospital were crowded with patients walking painfully in wrinkled bathrobes and employees chatting among themselves and visitors walking uncertainly in and out of doors, but there was no nurse sitting at the desk outside March's hospital room. Jennifer looked at the empty nurse station and realized she was not really sure what should be happening. She had visited a hospital only once before at the age of thirteen when her mother gave birth to her half-brother. This time, she was alone, she didn't know anyone in the huge building except March, who was unconscious. The doctor who had bandaged March's head and neck was supposed to come and examine her some time today. Jennifer had seen March's eyes open for a few seconds when she greeted her this morning. March saw Jennifer and recognized her; that was all, then the eyes were gone.

Jennifer couldn't find out anything from the hospital people. After breakfast, a nurse had come in to check the transparent plastic bag full of liquid flowing into March's arm, but she left in a hurry. No one seemed to be helping March, no one was taking responsibility for her recovery, but the nurse said they would call her next of kin. Jennifer knew that meant March's brother but didn't know where he might be found. If she hadn't answered the telephone call on Friday night, who knows, March might have been left here, alone in the hospital, without anybody.

Scott had been calling her every day since she'd been on television with the elevator incident, but she wouldn't meet with him. This morning though, when she needed a ride to the hospital, he was the only person she could think of to ask...Jennifer wasn't worried about Scott. He's history, she thought, but at least he was useful today--he knew where the hospital was and drove her here. Scott did possess one admirable quality: if he said he would do something he usually did it. This was a quality Jennifer valued highly but had learned not to expect in a man. Still, she thought, it's not enough. Jennifer knew, after just a few weeks with Scott, that he was the type of man who was always thinking about what might happen or how things could be better or worse. He just wasn't able to be present and he never really enjoyed anything. March had taught her that, how important it is to be present.

Jennifer stood in the doorway of Room 6560 watching all the gray-faced sick people, the slow-walking recuperating people and the cheerful gossiping hospital workers and the sullen angry hospital workers. She stopped and let herself be there, fully alive. It was a moment she really wanted to escape from, but instead she willed herself to be present, to look out of herself. She saw confusion, apathy, concern and fear in the faces passing by, but Jennifer herself felt prepared for anything.

As Jennifer stood in the doorway inhabiting the moment, Floyd Redhill walked slowly down the hospital corridor and stopped when he read the number above the door. He was a broad man, perhaps five foot ten inches tall with a square chest and round belly under his wide leather belt. He had a ruddy tan complexion and a tilted-back walk which was accentuated by the cuffs of his denim jeans rolled up high above scuffed cowboy boots. Jennifer knew he must be March's brother, and she was expecting him.

"I guess they called you." she greeted Floyd. She felt she already knew him. March had told her some things about him. Something about his mouth was like hers, the set of the jaw.

"How is she ?" Floyd said first. Then, "you must be Jennifer."

They moved respectfully over to March's bed and stared at her closed eyes, her head swathed in bandages. Only her regular breathing indicated life, she was so still. Floyd took off the sand-colored cowboy hat he was wearing. It curved downward in the front and back and turned up tightly at each side, forming a narrow crescent shape. As he stood holding his hat looking at March, Jennifer looked Floyd over. He had a broad nose and his eyes were heavy-lidded and wide-set under shiny black hair combed in thick straight lines. His clothes were faded but not dirty. He brought a damp earthy smell into the pastel hospital room, as though he had been walking through deep grass.

What is there to say, Jennifer wondered. They both took the measure of the patient. She didn't move, except for the steady rhythm of her breath. "What did the doctors tell you ?" Floyd asked.

"A head wound, crushed her skull." Jennifer spoke softly, as if she didn't want to be overheard.

"That's what they told me," Floyd nodded. "Her lungs are strong," he added.

Jennifer nodded her head for longer than necessary. March was breathing--that gave her a reason to be in the room. She was glad to have Floyd there with her.

"I drove all night from Portland," he told Jennifer.

"They just let me in to see her this morning. She was in intensive care all night." Jennifer kept her voice low, almost whispering. "The accident happened yesterday."

"Full moon" Floyd said with a short nod of his head.

Jennifer felt a little shiver when he said that because she had never heard a grown man say those words before. Standing closer to him, Jennifer noticed the odor of apples—Floyd smelled exactly like a bushel of apples stored for a while.

"Has she...?" Floyd began, indicating March.

"Said anything ?" Jennifer knew what he meant. "No, nothing, she can't really..."

Tears came to her eyes then, and because Floyd was there she finally let herself cry and he saw it but didn't get worried or impatient. Jennifer sat down in the chair and held her hand in front of her eyes and cried. She cried because she didn't want to lose March, and for Scott not loving her and for all the times she hadn't had time to cry or couldn't for some other reason. She didn't mind crying in front of Floyd. He took a clean handkerchief out of his pocket and gave it to her. She wiped her eyes and blew her nose. Afterwards she felt both exhausted and exhilarated as though she'd run a race.

Jennifer wondered how long they'd have to wait before someone came in and told them what to expect or what to do or what could be done. Floyd stood with his arms folded over his chest at the foot of the bed looking intently at March. He reached under the sheet and lifted March's ankle and traced a pattern on the sole of her bare foot with his thick index finger. Her breathing altered very slightly but otherwise there was no response.

"We should take her home," he said.

Michelle hurried into the room then and saw Jennifer and looked at March. She touched March's shoulder hesitantly and stared at her face, then began to cry. Jennifer embraced her friend as though it had been months instead of twenty-four hours since they'd last seen each other. When Josh entered the hospital room behind Michelle, Floyd studied him curiously. Josh avoided looking directly at March or at Floyd; he kept his eyes on Michelle.

Jennifer walked out of the room with Michelle and Josh and explained everything she knew about the accident and what the doctors said.

"But she'll be okay won't she?" Michelle asked. Jennifer looked at Josh because she didn't want to answer that question; she was hoping he might help. Josh was tired, he shifted from foot to foot nervously like a bantamweight boxer looking to see which way to duck.

He said "Head injuries are the worst kind because...Look, Michelle, you'd better be prepared for the worst."

"It's not... It's not hopeful." Jennifer took her friend's hand. "We can't expect..." Michelle stood looking at the floor, her eyes swollen and pink.

A nurse hurried past them into the room and pulled the curtain on a metal track that blocked March's bed from the wide door. "I'm her brother," they heard Floyd say, behind the thin curtain. They heard the nurse talking to Floyd and words like "coma" and "crushed" and "brain-dead."

Josh drove Michelle and Jennifer back to March's house and said goodbye to Michelle on the street after he lifted her small overnight bag out of his trunk. Jennifer stood in the doorway watching her friend kiss Josh goodbye waiting for Michelle to walk inside the house with her. She hated the way it felt to go inside the empty house without March being there. Leonardo the parrot needed fresh water. Above the sink Jennifer found the jar of cashews March fed the bird as a special treat. She opened his cage and Leo flew onto the top of a lamp.

"Open" said the bird. Open was one of his words. Jennifer said "cashew" and held it out.

"Catch you" said Leo in his screechy bird voice that somehow reminded Jennifer of March. "Gonna cat chew."

Jennifer tried to pretend she felt okay but Michelle didn't try, she sat down and stared at the kitchen table. Jennifer opened the refrigerator and closed it, she hesitated to turn on the television but she knew that if she sat down and started to think she'd lose it, she'd be sad again and March wasn't coming back. She knew that now. She felt her departure as though it had been written like a ticket, something planned-- March was leaving. Michelle's shoulders shook and she put her head down on the kitchen table and cried as Jennifer had earlier, but louder, with Jennifer bending over her and patting her head.

"Don't worry, it'll be okay. We can go see her again tonight."

Floyd rang the doorbell a little later. He wore his hat and looked the same, not tired or depressed. Nobody spoke at first. "I stopped and picked up some chicken for us," he said, walking into the kitchen. Floyd said he was hungry and asked the girls if they wanted to eat something but they didn't move. He opened the refrigerator and then there was the sound of a knife chopping beside the sink as he cut up some tomatoes and onions. They shared a meal of chicken and leftover beans at the yellow table. Floyd didn't talk much while he was eating. He had two helpings of everything and belched loudly.

The sound made Michelle giggle and Floyd said "My belly says thank you."

He belched again and Jennifer said "You're welcome." Jennifer felt better after the meal, when all three sat lingering. The girls noticed the visitor's every move but he didn't seem self-conscious.

"I guess I'll take a nap now," Floyd got up from the table, slipped his boots off and stretched out on the couch. Michelle brought him a pillow from her bed and he said, "Thanks, sis."

"Leo, come." Jennifer held out her arm for the parrot to hop on, "let's go outside."

Michelle and Jennifer walked slowly with Leo to March's tent which stood near the fire pit in the dry grass. The bird flew to the top of the tent and perched, looking to left and right in the afternoon sunshine. Jennifer hesitated before she lifted up the entry flap and looked inside. Everything was just as she'd left it. The blackened kerosene lamp was still sitting on the little table and the cushions were in place. It was warm in the tent, and the thick woolen carpet on the ground was soft and dry. A faint smell of incense clung to the heavy blankets covering the bent wood frame. Jennifer and Michelle made themselves comfortable, lying on their backs on the carpet. Michelle stared up at the top of the tent and spoke in a quiet, resigned voice.

"She's going to die isn't she ?"

"You never know," Jennifer told her friend "but you have to be prepared."

"How do you...how can you be ?" Michelle asked Jennifer with real curiousity, as though she felt sure Jennifer had the answer.

Jennifer wanted Michelle to feel better. "We all know we won't be here forever," she began but her voice shook and her throat tightened. "We know death will come for everybody sooner or later because there are no exceptions. Everybody dies."

Jennifer, for a brief second, contemplated her own mortality, then for a few seconds longer, tried to imagine Michelle dead, but could not. She knew they had other things to worry about; she became impatient with the subject— it was dull and frozen and too heavy for her. She felt hot with anger that this putrid ugly death had intruded into their lives, it wasn't fair, it would slow them down. March no longer claimed a place in the world; the busy noisy place she had once occupied was now vacant. It happened so quickly, Jennifer thought, how could she. How could she not be. March had retreated into the black and white of memory and abstraction; she'd left this fragrant warm world.

Jennifer lay on her back on the carpeted ground and allowed her thoughts to come and go at their own pace without ordering them or straining to come to any conclusions. She heard quiet snoring next to her and she inched closer to her friend so she could position herself against the soft warmth of Michelle's back; the comforting curves of her shoulders and hips. She closed her eyes and moved Michelle's perfumed hair so it wasn't tickling her nose. It was quiet and peaceful inside the tent.

CHAPTER TWENTY - TWO

Nora lifted her suitcase out of the trunk of the BMW. Her car was parked next to Pam's white Mercedes in the three-car garage next to the swimming pool. Her sister was waiting in the garden and helped Nora carry her belongings to the bedroom down the hall from the kitchen.

"I appreciate this, Pam" Nora began "I didn't expect..."

"Don't worry about it." Pam waved away her gratitude. She was wearing new purple and white nylon workout gear with a double digit twelve stretched taut across her expansive breasts, as if Pam were a well-developed player on a sports team. "You can have this room as long as you need it. It used to be the maid's room but we don't have a live-in now."

In the kitchen Pam began pushing carrots into a hole in a round machine that made a loud grinding noise. "Want some carrot juice?" she asked Nora.

"No thanks" Nora said. "Do you have any coffee ?"

"We can make some." Pam moved quickly around the black and white kitchen. It was huge, twice the size of Ginger's, Nora estimated, with dozens of cupboards, yards of granite countertop, a restaurant-size stove and a gleaming stainless steel refrigerator the size of a bank vault.

Nora realized that Pam was happy to have her in the house. Maybe she felt bored with no work and only fitness classes and auditions and shopping to fill her days but, on the other hand, it was more likely that Pam was going through something difficult with Van and needed emotional support. Nora didn't really think of herself as close to Pam, they were so different in every way. But, her sister often loaned her money, recently some fairly large amounts, so Nora felt she should do whatever she could to be supportive when Pam was in trouble.

She reminded herself that the screenplay was very close to being finished. If Dan would agree on a way to solve the problem of the ending, they could begin to shop the script around and possibly earn some option money before the end of the year. Nora realized that she always had a problem with endings. By January of next year, she told herself, she would find an apartment--no matter what. She kicked off her shoes and picked up a Vogue magazine to leaf through; she gave it her total attention though she wasn't particularly interested. There was an article on a party that involved young socialites dressing up as gauzy sprites and fairies to attend a Mid-summer Night's Dream party based on an exhibition of Victorian fairy painting at a famous museum in Manhattan. Nora examined the details of the dresses the women wore and their hairstyles. She remembered her childhood when she'd often spent hours in her room lying on her bed, engrossed in a magazine. Being in the same house as her sister intensified the memory.

Nora realized that she was experiencing, for the first time in over 15 years, the stifling angst she associated with her family. How could she have forgotten the deep estrangement she invariably suffered when she...But Nora stopped herself from opening that particular demon-stuffed box. She was a practical woman and knew that this was the best, most advantageous place for her to be at the moment. Her other housing options were less convenient or much more expensive. The script was close to being finished. When it was sold she would be solvent again. She affirmed that to herself, shook off the interruption and continued reading an article on new sunscreens for aging skin.

It was the time of day that Pam's Chinese herbalist told her was the time of the liver, which is after four and before seven in the evening. Because her liver needed to be cleansed of toxins and Pam hadn't yet managed to do so; she noticed that she was in an angry and venomous mood almost every day at this time. Each organ of the body corresponded to a specific emotion and to a time of day; the Chinese woman had given her a chart explaining it. Pam planned to do the liver cure as soon as she completed the intestinal cleanse which she'd begun six weeks before. The intestinal cleanse would kill all the mold or yeast which was currently clogging up her body. Pam was eating only raw vegetables and brown rice and a little yogurt. She poured herself another glass of water from the pitcher she had carefully purified. Cheryl recommended drinking eight liters a day of distilled water, rather than the bottled mineral waters because they were often full of salts, which, Pam knew, made you gain weight and the plastic bottles were full of carcinogens or something similar.

Van Aston walked into his home carrying two large bags of groceries and found his wife sitting in the kitchen drinking water. He placed the bags on the granite counter top and began taking out food items and putting them away.

"Salami ?" Pam said, looking at what he'd brought. Van didn't answer, taking some donuts and several packages of cheese out of the bag and opening the refrigerator.

He placed one item on a shelf carefully, then, with butter in hand, he asked his wife "where does the butter go ?" staring intently at the door of the refrigerator, the yellow rectangular box poised in his hand like a missile.

"In the plastic box in the top corner." Pam answered him, though he had not greeted her when he entered the room and this was the first comment out of his mouth. In fact, he hadn't even looked at her, she realized, as far as he was concerned she was wallpaper. Pam was a woman who had been in marital counseling more than once and knew that marriage had its rough spots and that one's partner could not always be expected to display sensitivity or understanding. Still, she felt suddenly outraged.

"Can't you see ?" she ended on a shrill high-note of rampant aggression, emphasizing the last word. Van pretended to ignore her and knocked over a bottle of catsup onto the glass shelf of the spotless refrigerator.

"I thought I'd go and buy some food since there was nothing to eat in the house." he said. "Somebody has to do it," he muttered. Pam stood up from the black leather seat of the chrome chair. She was wearing her old leopard-skin sandals with high wooden heels which made a sharp staccato sound as she walked across the stone tiles of the kitchen. Van was standing beside the refrigerator slicing thick slices of salami from the large roll that he'd bought and eating them off his Swiss Army knife.

"What are you eating ?" Pam's voice was gentle, her inquisitive tone perhaps a bit ingenuous.

Van then looked up at her and for the first time, met her eyes, "Salami" he said, in a way which suggested surprise at her inability to identify common edible meats.

"That looks disgusting" she said.

"Well, what do you expect me to eat ?" he replied.

Pam sighed, they were both so familiar with this material. It had worked once or twice, but Van always overplayed the victim role.

"Don't go into the victim thing" she warned, feeling even more enraged at his laziness, his limited sense of timing, his general lack of fire or wit or originality.

Everything he did she had seen before. She resented his neediness, his inability to understand that she was not his mother, but his wife. She had once loved him so much that she thought she could fulfill all of his needs; but their therapist had helped her see how mistaken she was about that. Pam believed that if she were to leave Van he would collapse into a helpless drugged existence, prey to who knew what agonies. It was this fact that allowed her to stay with him. Also, she knew that without his income she couldn't afford to live in a house of this size. She wouldn't have enough to live on if she divorced him, at least if she left now. Pam was waiting to get a role in a movie that would pay her enough that she could buy a house of her own similar to this one, which Van had owned prior to their marriage.

Van got up and walked to the refrigerator and took out a beer and opened it and took a swig from the bottle and left the room. She was up for the lead in a small film that her agent said could pay three hundred thousand dollars. That would be a welcome influx of cash but Pam wasn't sure if it would be enough to actually walk away.

"You're drinking?" She managed to deliver the line with an understated note of curiousity which kept him off-balance, wary.

"So what." Van replied.

"So what ?" she asked.

"Don't start on that !" he finally found the energy to be nasty. It was almost his default mode, Pam thought.

They both knew what came next. "I thought you promised !" She tried to infuse some genuine surprise or regret into the familiar line, but it came out flat.

"It's not a big deal." He was still refusing to look at her. Pam admired how he delivered the line as if he believed what he was saying. Van had a handsome profile, his face was silhouetted against the purpley brown sunset sky of the smog-choked valley below as he stood in front of the living room's sliding glass doors tipping the cold bottle of beer down his throat.

Pam thought about the expectations she had "brought into the marriage" as the therapist put it, when she'd first married Van and they began living together in the Mulholland Drive house. They were so happy together in the beginning; it seemed they had so much in common; they both loved to swim and it was sunny almost every day, winter and summer. Pam no longer thought it was Van who had changed. At first she blamed everything on changes in him, but gradually, with her therapist's help, she came to see that his basic character was consistent, she had simply failed to recognize the kind of man he was. She had mistaken his moodiness for sensitivity; his carelessness with money for generosity; his eagerness for sex as love for her. Pam knew she only had herself to blame for these miscalculations. She should have known better, should have identified his obvious shallowness and immaturity immediately, but she didn't.

"You never learn," she told him. "You lie, you ignore what's happening to you, you don't care about anyone but yourself."

"Maybe so," he agreed, leaving her out entirely.

"You are truly insensitive," she told him, "and pathetic. I feel sorry for you."

"That's too bad." he retorted.

God, he is infantile, she thought, he curls up like one of those little bugs that roll into a ball if you touch them. A ball of protection. But what is he protecting, she wondered. What is he protecting himself from? "You act like you're afraid of me" she charged him, her voice accusing him. Her inability to influence him was so obvious that she injected a genuinely disbelieving note in the line, an emphasis on the word afraid that was new. It wasn't in the original script.

"Oh, go to hell." Van countered, with an attempt at masculine aggression which petered out into childish nastiness again.

Pam felt bored, the whole exercise had become stale, he wasn't really trying. He had no real talent.

"Are you telling me to leave ?"

"You can go any time you want" Van answered, downing the last of the beer.

"I thought we were going to spend some time together today," Pam picked up the thread of her original complaint, she wasn't finished with him.

Van still felt hungry so he walked back into the kitchen to cut some more chunks of salami and put them on a paper towel to carry in to eat while watching television. He ignored Pam who had taken a seat in the living room . Van was surprised to see his sister-in-law Nora in the kitchen.

"Hi Van" Nora said, running some water into a cup at the sink. Van looked so exceptionally blank that Nora added "did Pam tell you I'm staying here for few days?"

"No." Van shook his head. Maybe she did and he'd forgotten. He opened the refrigerator and put the salami inside. Pam heard the sound of the refrigerator door and hurried into the kitchen. "Don't tell me you're having another beer," she said to Van with venomous sarcasm in her voice.

Pam saw immediately that she should have waited to verify the accusation because Van was now the falsely accused one and she was the lying accuser. She then noticed Nora standing in the kitchen. Pam said nothing and Nora hurried out of the kitchen and locked the door of her room. It was a silent lock which would not give a signal to anyone paying attention on the other side; only Nora knew the door was locked, and no one would try to touch the knob, she knew that too.

As Nora sat on the bed reading she could hear Pam's voice in the kitchen. It was uncannily similar to their mother's voice, and similar also in text. Pam had managed, with two very different men, to re-create her mother and father's marriage. My sister is a woman of deceptive cunning and strength, Nora thought. What is it she wants, she wondered, does she want him to be stronger or possibly, just give in entirely?

Nora feared and loathed marriage; yet she feared being a woman who never married. It seemed like failure, she thought, and believed it might be less shameful for a man; less a failure. Nora felt herself falling into the kind of vertigo she dreaded. She couldn't help feeling that she was not vitally connected to anyone or any place or any important activity. The screenplay project, which she hoped would result in financial independence and personal satisfaction, was taking twice as long as she expected. She feared she would never succeed at a career or at marriage, which would be a double failure. She didn't want to calculate how much money she'd borrowed from Pam in the past year. Nora tried to think of someone to call, another voice she could talk to, a small comfort to lift her out of this despondent mood. She couldn't face being the unmarried older sister isolated in a spare room in an air-conditioned house surrounded by smog. This wasn't her. It was unbearable, this feeling of being in the wrong place with the wrong people; yet she had no idea where she did belong. Nora knew herself to be someone who wasn't daunted by genuine disaster, it was emptiness that terrified her. She picked up the telephone and dialed the one person she thought could rescue her from this dark mood, Dan Downing.

. . . . .

From his perch atop March's tent, Leo surveyed the swaying oleander branches, olive-like in their shape and color, and he admired the rough music made by the wind rustling the heavy leaves of the neighboring Magnolia which was loaded now with the big white flowers. He flew across the hedge to rest on a branch of the sturdy old tree. The water on the ground underneath sparkled in the sun but he didn't want to land on the grass, there were dangerous cats in the neighborhood.

Leo knew the girls were asleep inside the tent but he had been in the sun too long, he needed water and shade. He needed to go back inside. March never left him outdoors alone so long. Leo flew to the window of the house and landed on the flimsy branch of the pink camellia bush, which was too slight to hold his weight steady. From the low branch he could see into the living room where his cage stood open with food and water in it and the man with shiny black head feathers lay sleeping beside the window. Leo squawked a short inquiring squawk to see if the man was really asleep, but the sound didn't stir him. He squawked again, louder, and then a prolonged kaweeee. The man turned over and almost rolled onto the floor. Leo shouted a two-syllable squaa-walk, twice, very loud and close to the window. The man opened his eyes and looked at the ceiling, awakened. Another squaa-walk and Leo had his attention.

"What chew want, old parrot bird ?" the man Floyd pushed up the window and spoke to him. Leo considered whether to move to the sill; he tilted his head to the left, then to the right, trying to gauge the angle. "What ? You want back in the house? Back in your cage ?"

Leo wanted the man to open the window wider, it was only halfway open. Leo hopped over to the wooden windowsill and squawked impatiently. He wasn't a small bird. Floyd heard him and opened the window as high as it would go.

Jennifer walked into the room then and asked Floyd "Is Leo here ? I can't find him outside."

"He's right here at the window, girl. He needs to come inside. Why didn't you keep an eye on him ?"

"I meant to," Jennifer said, "I'm sorry !" Then she began crying again and Leo flew into the living room and perched on the lamp near her, wondering and sympathetic in the way he cocked his head and blinked his eye.

"Now, come on sis, don't cry."

Jennifer had never been called sis before. Did he mean sissy or sister, she wondered. Floyd got up and steered Jennifer by the shoulders to the sofa so she could cry sitting down. She had never cried so much in her life. Leo quietly went to his cage and pecked at a cashew but couldn't eat.

Floyd just sat beside Jennifer while she wept. "It's tough for you gals, I know" Floyd said, after a while, "A raw deal." He patted her head in a smooth motion front to back, very steady, like petting a cat. He asked her how they'd come to meet March and how long they'd been living with her. He didn't seem surprised at anything Jennifer told him.

"What do you girls do for a living?" he asked her.

"We make our money on the street" she told him.

"How long you been doin' that kind of work?" Floyd wanted to know.

"A year or so," Jennifer told him. After crying so much, she felt lighter, as if she'd been emptied out and scoured clean. "I really liked some things about being a whore and some things I didn't like. But we're planning to be actresses now, though" she explained to Floyd. "It's just a matter of time before we'll have name recognition and then we'll get one of the top agents. March always said 'get the best agent and you'll get the best jobs.'"

"Did she?" Floyd said with a thoughtful laugh. Then he asked "what did you like about... your work ?"

"The street work?' Jennifer paused to think. "What I really liked was the moment when men exposed their private parts to me for the first time. I always felt a thrill when that happened because suddenly I was in charge, you know, there's nothing else like it –it was always exciting, that first exposure, like a wall coming down-- even if I didn't know the guy's name."

"Yeah," Floyd nodded, "I guess it would be. And my sister was helping you get to be actresses?"

"That's right," Jennifer said, "You know she was in a movie?"

"Yeah, that was quite a while back" Floyd said. "When she was still driving a cab."

"She told us how she got discovered by that director, what's–his-name, anyway, he was famous and he got into her cab one night and they talked and then he ended up giving her a role in his movie."

"I saw it," Floyd said. "In the seventies. The movie was called 'Concrete Details' and the lead actor was that singer who..."

"He got an academy award for it," Jennifer said. "March told us she could have gone on to other roles but her boyfriend didn't want her to. He didn't want her to be an actress. If she'd had a good agent she could have had a movie career, I'm sure. She knew so much." Jennifer paused and her face reddened. "I mean, she knows." Jennifer felt deeply ashamed to have put March in the past tense when they really didn't know if...

"Now don't start cryin' again." Floyd patted Jennifer's head as she buried her face in his shoulder. He had a pliant muscular shoulder that smelled like wood smoke and closer in, leather. Floyd wasn't like any of the men Jennifer had known before. He didn't seem impatient or worried about anything. She could tell he never judged people—March was like that too. They just accepted you the way you were, without expecting you to be like them. Floyd patted her back, then stroked her slowly and firmly from her neck to her tailbone with his large right hand. His palm and fingers spanned the entire space from her spine to the rounded edges of her ribs and he continued stroking her back gently as she buried her face in his shoulder.

When Jennifer began unbuttoning Floyd's shirt he asked softly "What about your friend?"

"She's asleep in the tent outside" Jennifer told him. She was grateful when she saw by the look on his face that he wasn't afraid. He stood up to take off his jeans; his pubic hair was silky and sparse around his thick penis. He had almost no hair on his muscular thighs or on his chest, his burnished skin was unmarked with moles or freckles. Floyd stretched out on a blanket on the floor of March's living room and Jennifer, admiring his body in the daylight, undressed herself, standing over him, as he watched from below. She felt his eyes on her then, her own thick pubic hair curly and reddish-gold in the afternoon light. It excited her to feel him looking at her, to know that she could give him something he wanted. When she took off everything, she squatted over him and ran her hands up his body from his belly to his shoulders, then from his thighs upwards, very slowly and gently, enjoying the buttery feel of his skin and his smoky fruit smell. Floyd was smiling and relaxed, as if he expected this and was accustomed to her and knew her well.

"You and me were married once," he said.

"In another life?" Jennifer asked, assuming he and March shared the same religious beliefs.

"I don't know when," he said, reaching for her, "doesn't matter."

Jennifer licked Floyd's neck from collarbone to ear lobe just to taste the salty sweetness of his cinnamon skin. He wiggled a little like he was tickled and buried his nose in her armpit and Jennifer laughed out loud. She pulled him close to her to make him stop. She could see and feel how excited he was but she wanted to prolong this play because she knew he was good at it. He was more relaxed and playful than any of the men she'd known before and she was in no hurry. She ran her fingers through Floyd's thick oily hair, which was as shiny as black glass or polished stone. Obsidian, she remembered the name, closing her eyes as he stroked her belly and nipples with his leathery hands.

"You're just a young girl," he said, touching her small barely developed breasts. "How old are you?"

"Doesn't matter" Jennifer said, looking straight into his eyes "does it?"

"No," he said, "not to me." And he leaned over her and kissed her throat and neck and shoulders.

CHAPTER TWENTY - THREE

Dan Downing had just come out of the shower when the phone rang. He picked up the receiver in the kitchen with a towel wrapped around his waist.

"You sound a little depressed" he said to Nora, whose voice seemed strained. "Are you sure you want to stay with your sister? Maybe that wasn't a good idea."

"No, it's fine," Nora told him, "it's just for a few days anyway. I'm okay, really, just feeling, you know, a little unsettled. I was hoping maybe we could get together tonight instead of tomorrow. We're so close to working out the ending."

"I don't know about tonight, Nora. We're under-staffed at the restaurant, I sometimes end up working really late and I'm not so sharp after midnight."

Nora had never heard this from Dan before. He had always been more than eager for their late-night sessions. "Don't worry," she said, "I'll drive. Pam's place isn't that far from the restaurant. Just call me when you're ready to go, doesn't matter what time it is. I'll come and pick you up."

As Nora listened for his response, Dan hesitated longer than she expected and a red flag floated into the silence. She felt something in her chest contract and her throat constricted.

Finally Dan said, "Okay, I'll call you when I'm finished—it might be very late though."

"No problem" Nora said.

When she hung up she realized how tense she was. Maybe Dan met someone, she thought--it wasn't impossible. He was actually a very attractive man who enjoyed the company of women. That in itself made him desirable to any one of thousands of women in L.A. Out of the city's population of nine million, there were thousands, maybe tens of thousands of exceptionally beautiful talented girls who had come to Los Angeles from all over the world to be actresses and singers and models and...who knew what else. It was Nora's firm belief that there were fifty attractive sane capable females in the world for every one male with similar qualities, especially in New York and L.A.

Men, in general, were simply not as capable of adapting to urban social realities as women, Nora thought. The males who were left to live alone after leaving their families and school often turned anti-social or, as Nora remembered her friend Melanie always said, feral. Melanie's theory was that some men (the feral ones) grew to resent women because males weren't taught to nurture themselves or others and didn't have the skills necessary to create meaningful relationships, so their frustration and self-hatred became directed against women. Nora knew some feral men who became defensive loners, hostile to women because they resented their own need of them. Still, maybe it wasn't their fault; maybe women weren't willing to...To what? Nora wondered, what do men really want ?

Nora wondered when she would hear from Luke. He seemed so confident and bright and successful and he said he lived alone. He had promised to call as soon as he got back from New York, apparently he was a music producer. Nora wasn't sure what he produced but she was curious and looking forward to finding out more about him. He's probably delayed in New York, she thought.

Nora felt restless and cooped up; she had to get out of the house. She had an invitation to a seven o'clock screening of a low-budget documentary film directed by a friend from New York. She had plenty of time before her meeting with Dan. She decided to leave early to find a good parking place.

The documentary was showing at a theater in Westwood, an area of the city Nora usually avoided. The neighborhood adjoining the University of California at Los Angeles was once known as a "village" but there were only a few remnants of the old Craftsman style architecture on the busy streets now shadowed by recently-built apartment buildings. Westwood "village" was crammed with new cheaply-built retail stores selling jeans and t-shirts and sports shoes side by side with fast-food and coffee franchises. Where there were once used bookstores, there were now slick corporate megastores. But Westwood still had some of the largest and most attractive movie theaters in the city. Nora drove her BMW into a block-wide parking structure which towered over the Spanish colonial movie house next to it. She drove up and around six levels without seeing an empty spot and finally found a parking place on the rooftop level.

After she locked her car, Nora stood for a second to look down at the crowded streets bordering the green UCLA campus. Tall bobbing palm trees lent a tropical ambiance to the clusters of garish mini-malls and rows of storefronts with electric signs advertising falafels and pizza and ice cream to the students crowding the sidewalks. Only the pastel sky was easy on the eyes, delicate, unblemished and serene. The magic hour, Nora had heard it called in film production, the brief transition between day and night when light lingered but shadows disappeared. She felt a sharp sense of nostalgia, standing on the stained raw concrete roof under that lovely sky, as if she were missing someone or something—but she couldn't name what it was, or who.

Nora spotted the director of the film, Larry Karper, in the lobby of the old theater. A small man, he was surrounded by people and seemed to be intently explaining something to a woman in a black pantsuit who was taking notes. They wouldn't have much money for advertising this film so attracting any kind of attention from the press would be crucial, Nora knew. She stood and examined the film poster: "Boots Baylor and his Band" the title was printed in a sort of 1930's type face above a picture of a man's hands playing a banjo. She could sense the tension around Larry, the pre-show jitters that were part of the event. If the critics praised the documentary, it might be distributed for showing in select theaters in major cities; if not, the film would be shown only at festivals, then shelved, with no way to recoup the financial investment.

"It's hopeless" Larry told her when he finally saw Nora and had a moment to talk. "I know they'll hate it. A forgotten Southern Black banjo player popular before World War two—who cares." Larry had large sad brown eyes behind thick glasses; he was about the same height as Nora and probably weighed less, she thought. He spoke in a perpetually dejected tone in lamentations that invariably ended in a flat whine of defeat.

"It took me three years to shoot the footage thanks to that incompetent amateur production manager I hired. My editor got retinitis and I had to wait for him to recover before we could do the final transfer. It looks too grainy to me, but what do I know. Boots was supposed to be here tonight but he's in a hospital in Baton Rouge, he'll probably die there. I think the guy's a genius but what do they care. This female journalist over here (Larry said the word journalist like pederast) didn't know who Thelonius Monk was." Larry shook his head and sighed. "What's the use?"

Though he always expected the worst, Larry somehow had a knack for eliciting a steady stream of financial support and favors from the people he knew. He constantly complained about his health, the incompetence of people on his crew and his bad luck with women, yet he always did what he wanted and got films made. There was something about his relentless negativity, his frail unhealthy physique, his stubbornness in the face of overwhelming obstacles, that induced people to help him. Larry always dressed in old but distinctive clothing and he decorated his West Village apartment in dark depression-era furnishings, including antique kitchen appliances. He was implacable on matters of taste and style. What he embraced, he loved whole-heartedly and exclusively. What he dismissed (which was almost everything popular and commercially successful) he hated with an unyielding rancor. As Larry seldom displayed even the slightest concern for anyone but himself and his own projects and he never, as far as she knew, encouraged or helped other filmmakers, Nora believed his stalwart position on matters of taste was what ultimately gained Larry respect among his peers. He only liked a narrow range of music, art and film, he read almost nothing and wasn't particularly well-informed, but what he loved, he really loved, and Nora thought that must be the reason for his success.

The theater was almost full for the screening but Nora didn't see anyone she knew as she walked in and selected a seat. When the film ended and people began filing out, she saw, across the rows of seating , a tall sandy-haired man who looked familiar. She realized it was Luke and got up to hurry through the narrow row of seats and follow his back merging with the crowd in the aisle emptying into the lobby. She caught up with him near the popcorn counter.

"Hello Luke," she greeted him with a casual kiss on the cheek, "when did you get back?"

"Oh, hi" he said a bit absently. "What did you think? I liked it, did you?"

"Yes. The music was terrific" Nora said. "Do you know Larry?"

"No, actually..." Luke glanced quickly to his left and right, "a friend of mine invited me to come ..." He then caught the eye of his friend, who returned at that moment from the bathroom. She was quite tall and very slim, with close-cropped platinum hair, probably a model, Nora thought at first glance.

"Trina, this is Nora Gregorian."

Nora found her head crooked at an uncomfortable angle staring up at Trina and Luke, who were both around six feet tall. She felt short and insignificant. The women exchanged greetings and Nora made an excuse to hurry away. She saw Larry surrounded by people waiting to talk to him. They were practically lined up, Nora thought, it looked like the film was a success. Larry looked pleased as one person after another patted him on the back and praised his work. Nora decided she could congratulate Larry another time and she hurried outside. She stood for a moment under the elaborate marquee of the old theater, watching the audience file out, hoping she wouldn't bump into Luke again. Everyone who emerged seemed to be in a group or a couple.

Nora began to look forward to seeing Dan. She thought it would be a good idea to drink some coffee and look over her notes. Down the block, she found a small table in a new but dirty café, with careless litter on the smartly tiled floor and at least three or four unwashed street people silently occupying the colorful plastic tables. The rich smell of greasy donuts and all-night coffee filled the place which was lit as brightly as a supermarket. Nora took out the notebook she always carried. She loved the atmosphere in the place. It was completely free of comfort, charm or history. She wrote the date at the top of a blank page and then she wrote, "free of hope, history, humanity." Then, on another line she wrote Priorities: "finish script with Dan; find good agent; find new living space; re-connect with New York friends; meet new men."

Writing these few phrases made her feel centered, empowered. There was nothing like holding a pen in hand, Nora thought. As long as she could hold a pen and write she could order her universe. Nora drank a double latte and began to consider dialog for the final scene between Iris and John. She: "I loved you in ways you never discovered because I never wanted you to." "The nights were so memorable, why should we add a long tedious string of afternoons?" She then wrote: "Why should we dilute the vintage wine of our memorable nights with the tepid tea of afternoons?" He: "I ask so little, just that you must stay, you must. I ask only for your proximity, nothing more."

Another line occurred to her and she wrote: "marriage snaps the elastic of love."

Leaning back in her chair, Nora squinted her eyes in the blue-white fluorescent glare which seemed almost painfully bright after the darkness of the theater. She imagined Iris, as she often did--a slender woman wearing a chic hat and perfectly tailored tweeds, circa 1920, with a frown on her exquisitely beautiful face, unable to find a man who quite pleases her. Nora wondered if she had really deeply investigated the character in the ways her writing teacher had recommended. She wondered if any writer did and thought the good ones probably just saw the character whole, without sewing on attributes like so many buttons. She liked writing in public places occasionally, sometimes it freed up the imagination, took you out of yourself. "What does Iris really want?" she jotted down. The character of John was easier. He simply wanted Iris, loved her above everything. His motivation was never in question. But Iris, she seemed to want to escape from-- what? The circumstances of her own life?

Nora sipped her coffee and stared out the window at the girls in jeans and t-shirts and the boys in jeans and t-shirts hurrying by.

The uniform sameness of people depressed Nora. She appreciated individual style and uniqueness. She wondered why she had bothered to dress for the screening in her favorite red silk blouse and black velvet jacket. In the glare of the florescent light, Nora noticed that the jacket was beginning to fray at the cuffs; there was a threadbare line at the wrist. It distressed her to think that her beautiful jacket was getting old and would sooner or later look shabby. Iris doesn't want to marry John because she wants to remain in charge of her own life, Nora noted. She wants to be free. Free to do what? To be alone? Maybe marriage represents getting old. Maybe she can't think of herself as a wife because her only power rests in her ability to seduce men. Nora wrote: "seduction equals power equals freedom."

Because Iris is beautiful. "What good is beauty to a wife?" Nora wrote. She felt a solid sense of satisfaction with that. She read it over and amended the line to "What use is beauty to a wife?" She thought of Madame Bovary and Anna Karenina. Once married, no wonder so many women become frumps—beauty invites desire, a frightening liability. Nora thought of her beautiful friend Sarah who had married a stockbroker and moved to New Jersey. She had gained weight and cut her hair short and after her first child was born she looked almost like a different person, she had lost all of her appeal, her style. Nora knew Dan wouldn't be free until sometime around midnight but she didn't want to be late. It was now almost eleven o'clock. By the time she walked to the parking garage and made her way to the top floor, Nora had decided to stop by the house on Westborne Street and see if she had any mail. She had plenty of time to do that, then pick up Dan at the restaurant.

Ginger's house was dark and didn't look any different except for the yellow plastic tape around the circumference of the front yard. Next door, all the lights were on at March's house. Soon after Nora had collected her mail and some other items she needed, the doorbell rang.

"You're up late Michelle," Nora said as she swung the door open.

"Hi Nora," Michelle's voice was strained and subdued. "Is Ginger around ?"

"No, want to come in?"

Michelle walked in and went into the kitchen and sat at the table, her shoulders slumped.

"What's wrong ?" Nora asked her.

"It's March," Michelle's voice cracked, "she was in an accident. It's really bad."

Michelle covered her face and sniffed back tears.

Nora didn't know what to say. She glanced at the clock. It was getting close to midnight.

"Will you help me ?" Michelle asked her. "I want to do something that March taught us—we have to make a fire in the fire pit out back. Please, Nora ?"

"Michelle," Nora tried to be soothing, "I know you're worried…"

"We have to do something !" Michelle paced around the kitchen.

"I'm sorry Michelle, I'm going to have to leave in a few minutes," Nora told her.

But Michelle was so upset and insistent that Nora followed her outside. Michelle lit a kerosene lantern and began to gather some small branches and twigs from the ground. She placed them in a loose pile in the center of a circular pit in the grass.

"March has a permit from the city for this" Michelle told Nora. "Because she's a native American. Did you know that ?"

"No," Nora didn't know. She saw that March had a pile of firewood stacked nearby. Nora was concerned about Michelle, she seemed so distraught. "Jennifer will be back soon, won't she?"

"I'll be okay," Michelle said. "I'll just wait here by the fire."

"Okay." Nora felt somewhat reluctant to leave. "Don't worry, I'm sure things will work out." She awkwardly patted Michelle's shoulder.

Michelle lit some newspaper and brought it to the dry wood. The flames licking at the twigs and small branches made a hungry smacking sound. The two women stood still and stared as the flame crackled into fire; orange sparks flying above ragged shards of wood.

"Every fire is different, no two are alike," Michelle stared into the flames as she spoke. "That's what March told me once--every movement of the flames is a dance, never repeated."

Nora looked at her watch. The orange firelight reflected off the glass face. She had to call Dan and make sure he knew she was coming. "You gonna be okay ?" Nora asked Michelle, who nodded but didn't look up from the fire. Nora left her sitting on a small stool near the tent in the flickering orange firelight.

CHAPTER TWENTY - FOUR

Nora hurried into Troppo expecting the restaurant to be empty, but one large table was occupied by a group of noisy people who seemed to be drinking copiously. She took a seat at the small bar and asked for Dan. "He's busy in back" the bartender told her.

She'd never seen this one before. The bartender's hair was cut short and stood on end in stylish waxed spikes. He was around twenty-five and had the square-jawed, bright-eyed face of an actor.

"Hi, I'm Seth," the young man said in the slow ingenuous manner of southern California "I just started working here three days ago. "

Nora sipped a glass of wine and wondered how long she'd have to wait. She avoided meeting Seth's eye so he wouldn't think she wanted to chat with him. Dan walked out of the kitchen looking harried and told her that a large party had arrived after ten o'clock and he wasn't sure when he could close the restaurant. After Dan hurried back to attend to business, Nora took the red notebook out of her bag. The light at the bar was so dim she could barely read what she'd written earlier. She took out a pen and drew arrows and stars and spider webs in the margins of a page. "Explain restraint," she wrote, then "desire coupled with revulsion."

After a while, Dan came out and sat down beside Nora. He seemed pale and looked thinner in his charcoal gray shirt and tie.

"Have you lost weight ?" Nora asked him.

"I just had a phone call from Ginger." Dan told her. "March, your neighbor next door, died tonight." Dan looked closely at Nora's face to gauge her reaction. "I'm sorry."

Nora assumed he meant he was sorry to be the one to tell her, not that he was sorry for her because she hardly knew March. Nora immediately thought of Michelle. Nora saw the girl sitting by the fire, the dancing shadows on the grass. She saw her face clearly as in a photograph.

"Ginger said we should go over there and, I don't know, make sure they're all right is what she said," Dan told Nora. "Michelle and Jennifer probably don't have any idea what to do—it was very sudden."

Nora's first reaction was surprise that Ginger expected Dan to get involved in what was really not his concern. How do you make sure someone is all right, she wondered. Maybe Ginger thinks she knows the proper procedure for situations like this, Nora thought, but how can...

"We can swing by and just...I don't know, see if there's anything we can do," Dan suggested.

"I hardly knew her." Nora had to say that. It didn't matter now. She remembered the exact color of the purple satin ribbons March wore in her hair.

Dan and Nora pulled over to the curb behind an old Chevrolet pickup truck with Oregon plates. March's house was dark except for one small light in the back and no one came to the door when they rang. They could hear people talking in the backyard so Dan followed Nora as she squeezed through the bushes beside the narrow overgrown path around the side of the silent house. Nora stopped abruptly when she heard a series of rhythmic sounds, like a hand hitting a drum or pounding. Dan, behind her, put his hands gently on her shoulders.

"Do you hear that?" He asked, close to her ear. "What is it ?"

"I don't know, maybe we shouldn't go back there," Nora kept her voice low.

A steady unvaried pounding began to get louder; just one-two, one-two, one-two, like knocking on a door.

"Don't you want to let them know we're here ?" Dan asked.

In the darkness near the ground, he and Nora saw three figures seated around a crackling fire in a circular pit. The knocking sounds seemed louder. "They're busy with something," Nora said. "It's late, I think we should just leave."

"We might as well say hello since we're here." Dan walked purposefully towards the fire and Nora reluctantly followed him. When they got closer she saw a man in a plaid shirt seated beside the fire with a heavy wooden box overturned in front of him like a table. He kept on steadily drumming with his hands on the wooden surface. Jennifer and Michelle sat on either side of the man facing the fire.

Without looking up, the drumming man called out. "Come and join us by the fire, you two, you're welcome here."

Michelle and Jennifer turned and looked as Nora and Dan walked into the flickering circle of light. Nora tried to think of something to say—sorry to hear about...But before she could say it, the man said "help me Jen" and Jennifer began beating on the box in the same one-two rhythm. As the man continued pounding with his left hand he threw some small white objects onto the wooden surface. They clattered like pebbles thrown against a window.

Nora and Dan seated themselves close to the fire and watched. Both the girls seemed to be so engrossed in what the man was doing, they hardly noticed the visitors.

"It's a twelve" Michelle spoke in a loud voice.

The man scooped up three small white pieces in his hand and tossed them again. As they tumbled onto the surface and came to rest, Nora could see that he was throwing bones, tubular and ridged like sections of a small animal's spine. In the dim light she could see that there were black circles painted on the bones, each one slightly different.

"Eight" called out Michelle as she glanced briefly at Nora and Dan.

Jennifer and the man both continued the simple rhythmic pounding as he swept up the bones and threw them onto the board again. The game, if that's what it was, required rapt concentration on the part of the players. Neither Jennifer nor the man throwing the bones looked at the visitors after they sat down. It was as if they were expected, Nora thought, as she made herself comfortable beside Dan in the circle of heat and light from the fire.

"Time to ask questions" the dark-haired man with the bones said. He seemed to speak in time to the steady pounding on the wood. He threw the pieces, they clattered, he scooped them up and threw them again. "Call the months" he requested.

In a tense but steady voice Jennifer spoke up "January." Then, when the bones stopped rolling and stood still again she said "February."

After the next throw, she called "March" and the spilled bones leapt high in the air, and for three or four beats seemed to move in the same rhythm as the pounding.

Jennifer said "Yes !" like an answer and an exclamation, then she darted a look at the black-haired man whose eyes were almost closed. Nora saw Jennifer's face transformed in the firelight. She looked expectant, as though she were confident that something wonderful would happen very soon. Nora leaned forward to look at Dan's face; he sat very still, absorbed in watching.

Nora tugged on Dan's arm and whispered "It's late, we can't stay." But Dan shook his head stubbornly, he wanted to see what would happen next. Nora found a blanket on the ground near the tent. She wrapped it around her as she sat watching and listening to the steady rhythms. For long stretches of time, no one said anything as the bones rattled on the board and Michelle called out numbers. Occasionally, the man would say one word: sometimes a day of the week, sometimes a year, sometimes a place and then the litany of numbers would resume. Nora found herself getting tired but Dan didn't seem to want to leave and she felt it would be wrong to interrupt the game or whatever it was they were doing.

Dan wondered what tribe the man came from. This was obviously some kind of native American gambling ritual. Ginger had mentioned something about March's brother being at the house so he knew the man with the bones must be the brother, but how had Jennifer become so adept... When he was a teenager in Wyoming, Dan knew some boys who grew up on an Indian reservation nearby. He remembered them talking about gambling in the same way he and his brothers talked about basketball or baseball. Gambling was a skill and an art to Indians—they admired good gamblers like the other boys looked up to athletes.

Dan saw that there was a stack of wood not far from where he was sitting. When he got up and placed a log on the fire, both Jennifer and the drumming man looked up briefly and nodded, encouraging his participation. Dan noticed that Nora had dozed off, she was curled up in a blanket on the ground.

Jennifer had to concentrate all of her attention on the game. You had to be completely in the moment or it wasn't possible to do it—to keep the rhythm and the counting. She wanted Floyd to know he could count on her. March once told her that he was the best gambler in the family. Floyd didn't spend much time explaining anything; he just did what he thought should be done, without asking for permission. Jennifer had never before been invited to join in a man's activities; it was different than working with a girlfriend. She felt as if she and Floyd shared the same pulse, the same heartbeat. When he caught her eye as the bones stopped on the wood she exhaled an audible trill of exhilaration, as if she were out of breath from dancing. Floyd didn't smile as he was throwing the bones, he concentrated with his head and neck and hands. Without watching him, Jennifer could feel his movements like a dance.

They said at the hospital that the body would be ready to be picked up in the morning. Floyd wanted to bring her home immediately but they said no. There was no way. March would never come home again. This knowledge made Jennifer want to pound and count and not let her mind wander. She thought Floyd must know the right way to get through the night. Jennifer distanced herself from her memories and losses—all the past confusion-- with measured drumming and flawless counting. She felt wide awake and determined to clear a path through the maze of dark shadows. They would make no mistakes in counting. Once the path was established, Jennifer had faith that the morning would bring answers to the night's questions. Answers, one-two, she pounded, by morning, one-two, by sunrise.

Floyd threw the bones and Michelle counted the dots: "nine."

Then nine came up a second time. "Nine again," Floyd called before he threw a third time and the three bones rested as they counted their black spots.

"Nine three times" Michelle counting, called out, and Floyd caught Jennifer's exhilarated smile.

He saw she was pleased by this improbable concurrence, this exception to the random. Floyd courted the exception and challenged the haphazard. From where he sat, there were no stars to be seen, nor moon, but Floyd knew exactly where he was and what had to be done and he knew the moonrise would be visible two hours after midnight. Jennifer worked with him; he could count on her. Floyd maneuvered against the ragged swagger of Chance, the bully who wore big gold chains and cheap shoes. Chance came accompanied by his careless slut of a daughter, Accident. In the firelight, the bones grew more and more animated and Floyd's technique and stamina prevailed. He did not waver or rest; he knew how to let the rhythm carry him forward as the fire inspired the tumbling dance of the bones and illuminated the staggering questions in the shadows.

"Mother mountain and Sister star, come sit at my fire." Did he actually hear that, Dan wondered, as he opened his eyes. How long had he been dozing ? Nora remained curled up on the ground next to him, asleep. Dan saw that the man with black hair was still at it, throwing the bone pieces onto the board with Jennifer and Michelle engrossed in their counting. The pace, the drumming rhythm, seemed somewhat slower now and Dan realized that he'd completely lost track of how long they'd been sitting in the dark. Ginger would be expecting to hear from him. He felt self-conscious about checking his watch as he had to tip his wrist towards the fire to read the time. The man throwing the bones noticed everything. His bright heavy-lidded eyes fastened for a second on Dan, who felt vaguely impolite.

Dan got stiffly to his feet and walked to the wood pile, bringing back several logs for the fire. He squatted near Michelle and whispered, "We have to go."

Michelle nodded understanding without taking her eyes off the bones. Dan touched Nora's cheek gently and she woke up with a start, shaking her head and looking at each face in the circle quickly and intently.

"I think we should go now" Dan whispered in a low voice to Nora as if they were in a church or a theater.

Nora nodded agreement and got to her feet with the blanket still wrapped around her shoulders. She looked down at the three players as the drumming and counting continued. She couldn't gauge the boundaries of waking and dreaming, but she knew she was walking into the dark, away from the fire, with Dan.

Jennifer was sorry to see their circle become smaller because, even though Dan and Nora didn't do much, their presence added something to the night's occasion. Floyd and Michelle and Jennifer repositioned themselves around the capricious heat and smoke of the little fire in the chill of the windy October night.

Jennifer responded as Floyd introduced a small fluctuation into the game. He left the bones on the board for an extra beat after their number was counted. Instead of toss, pound, settle, pound, call; the rhythm was altered to toss, pound, settle, pound, call, pound pound. Then gradually, at his discretion, the settled bones sat for three, then four beats after their count was called. Jennifer's eyes were fixed on the tubular white bones, their shadows like spilled ink on the board. She imagined the size of the spine they had once been part of. A small animal, she figured, one-two, bigger than a house cat. Her eyes stayed on the bones as Michelle called three, then watched the white shapes as they wavered on the board; the firelight causing all shadows to quiver and stretch.

Suddenly, a wide furry animal about a foot long with a thin tail like a rat and a pointed brown head nosed out of the center of the fire, paused and waddled with small hairless paws into the darkness beyond the circle. Jennifer almost screamed when she saw it; the animal frightened her with its abrupt movement, but the others didn't seem to notice. She didn't dare interrupt the intricate new rhythm. She wondered if the animal was a possum or a mole. She was pretty sure moles were smaller and not as blimp-shaped as this creature seemed to be. A possum then, opossum she thought, trying to remember what she knew about the animal that made her feel something like sympathy or recognition mixed with fear. Seeing it so closely was different than seeing it on TV or in a picture because she knew the animal was looking at her; the awareness was reciprocal. The wild speechless possum saw her.

Jennifer wanted to call the animal but then Floyd looked at her, keeping the rhythm steady and she met his eyes and knew that she had to let the animal go, she had to focus on what they were doing, she couldn't let anything distract her.

"Three" Michelle called out, then "three" again, the bones in their little puddles of inky shadow were running in a series.

The two girls watched Floyd call "three" before he threw again; and after three came up for the third time he called it again, knowing he had to go for five because three four times was no good. Had to hit three five times. Floyd knew this but the girls didn't know it. He knew he was taking a chance. Sometimes he pushed his luck. You had to sometimes, because then your luck knew you had faith in it. You had to demonstrate how much you trusted your luck or else it might desert you. Floyd threw the bones without pausing or deviating in any way from the established rhythm. He could barely see in the flickering light. Michelle was paying close attention and counted quickly.

"Three." she said with a girlish thrill in her voice.

Floyd didn't smile but he felt Jennifer looking at him. "Three five times," he said, as the waning orange moon made its appearance in the dark sky.

CHAPTER TWENTY - FIVE

In the moonlight, Dan and Nora made their way along the narrow path and back to the street. When they reached Nora's car, Dan offered to drive and because she felt so sleepy Nora handed him the keys. Dan adjusted the seat for his longer legs and turned the ignition. The motor sputtered and coughed but did not start. Nora then thought she should try it, so Dan got out and she walked around and took the driver's seat, rubbing her eyes. When Nora turned the key, a metallic whining sound came from the engine and she knew the battery was dead. The two looked out at the empty street as if they might find assistance, but no cars moved and the dark houses on both sides slept in their shadows.

Nora swore under her breath and Dan felt somehow responsible. "We could call triple A roadside assistance."

"It's so late, we might have to wait a long time. I'm really tired, let's sleep here. We can wake up early tomorrow and deal with it." Nora's voice was heavy with fatigue.

"You think it's safe to stay in the house ?" Dan sounded mildly apprehensive."What about the underground gas or whatever it is ?"

"Nothing has happened in over a week, it must be okay by now. The city should have cleared this up last Friday. I think the paperwork is lost and they're just stalling."

Dan lifted the yellow warning tape and Nora unlocked the front door. When they walked into the unheated kitchen and turned on the light, Nora was shivering with cold but she hesitated to turn the switch on the thermostat because she wasn't completely sure the furnace was safe. She feared a spark gone awry; a small explosion spreading fire under the house.

"Let's have a drink," Dan said, opening the cupboard where bottles were kept. He found a half-empty bottle of brandy and two glasses. His hand shook slightly as he poured. "A little nightcap," he said, imitating a jovial old man's voice.

"What do you think is going on next door? Nora asked him. "That was strange, wasn't it?"

"Strange to us," Dan said, "but March's brother seemed to know what he was doing; apparently it's some kind of Native American ritual associated with a death in the family. I thought it was fascinating, didn't you?"

"Where did this Floyd character come from? Did he know the girls before—they seemed to know how to...I mean, how did they...?"

Dan shrugged. "Ginger said he was March's only relative." Dan felt a slight twinge of regret or guilt when he said Ginger's name. He should have called her earlier, it was too late now. He wanted to tell Nora about the Indians he knew when he was a boy in Wyoming but he wasn't sure of the name of their tribe (were they Pawnees or Crows?). He realized that he didn't know what had happened to them when they got older and he thought Nora probably wouldn't be interested anyway.

"I have some ideas about how to end the script," Nora said after they'd sat for a few minutes. She felt suddenly awake, lucid and clear-headed. "You know, Dan, we could finish it off tonight if we really focused. We only need a short ending scene."

She swallowed a mouthful of brandy and said in an affected clipped accent "How wretchedly cold it is tonight, John."

"Indeed," Dan responded, looking directly into Nora's eyes. "I would have thought you impervious to such considerations, Iris."

Nora had her notebook ready. She picked up her pen. "Nights capture us," Nora continued, in a voice Dan hardly recognized, "We, who go out into the night, can be caught, can become night's prisoners."

"You, of all people, should know that. In view of..."

"In view of the circumstances of my recent betrayal ?" Nora raised her eyebrows like question marks and met Dan's eyes.

"Unlike you, I'm a very cautious person, Iris, and I never repeat gossip."

"I know so little about you John, but so much about nights. You could say I'm an expert on nocturnal subjects. Night and its stratagems; night's shallows and depths, its rewards, its punishments."

"Always punishment, Iris ? Can there be no end to it ? When will you have your fill of pain and punishment ?"

"John lights her cigarette. You know so little about pain, John, you have so much to learn."

"I can't pretend to be eager." Dan blinked rapidly and suppressed a smile as he poured more brandy. He felt a rush of excitement so intense it approached the edge of fear.

"I suppose you think," Dan began, then thought for a second. "I suppose you think you'll receive some final reward or punishment in the end ?"

She answered with quiet vehemence. "No, not for me. Sometimes I imagine something like vindication but I've yet to experience it. I should have to say that I doubt whether there will be anything for me in the end. I expect no redemption, no reward for my virtues; no punishment for my vices."

"Vice, a sharp, pointed word."

"But don't you see how a woman's character is revealed in her vices much more clearly than in her virtues."

"I see only fire and ice when I look at you, Iris, not vice."

"She laughs coldly and turns away, dismissing him."

"Iris, tell me what you really want, he demands. What do you expect ?"

"Nothing. I expect nothing... John grabs her shoulders, fragile in their chiffon gown. He shakes her more violently than he intended, shouting. Why must you be so cold, so full of doubt ? Why ?"

"Oh John...you're hurting me...and she collapses against his chest sobbing." Nora was enthusiastic now, writing quickly.

"Iris, please stop doubting." Dan dictated, as he stood watching Nora write. Then he added. "You must believe me, I love you more than anything in the world." Nora glanced up at him and wrote the line as he said it.

"Let's read over this" Dan said, pleased and excited. "This might be it—this might be the way to tie everything together."

`Nora read aloud what she'd written. She took the Iris role, standing for the final speech. "I doubt whether there will be anything for me in the end. I doubt if..." and she trailed off.

Dan grasped Nora's delicate shoulders firmly in his hands "Why ?" He shook her with the rough vehemence of his question. "Why must you always be so full of doubt ?"

"Oh Dan," Nora said, and collapsed against his chest, sobbing. "Oh Dan, I'm so tired, I'm sorry. "

Did she collapse against his chest ? Later, the next morning, Nora found herself wondering. They slept in her bed. It was the only possible place. She woke up with Dan sleeping beside her, soundly motionless. She didn't try to remember what happened the previous night; but she recalled how Dan accompanied her into the darkness of her cold bedroom. She was afraid to strike a match; feared an open flame. The darkness remained unbroken until Dan switched on the small bedside lamp and draped her red silk blouse over the too-bright light, making the bed wine-dark and the walls rose-colored. Now, in the lull of daybreak, Nora's blouse still hung disheveled over the top of the lampshade, its buttons all undone and sleeves flung open.

Nora carefully shifted her position and reached over and touched Dan's fine chestnut hair which had grown long enough to curl slightly, tenderly. What had happened the night before had happened to her skin. Nora considered the line as it occurred to her. Would Iris say it ? She wouldn't, not Nora. No, she wouldn't speak or move or think, she would remain mute. Still, the events of last night replayed themselves unbidden. She would not reach for them, refused to recollect.

Her eyes measured the dawn light accruing moment by moment in the wide window facing the bed. The white curtained rectangle gradually changed from dove gray to cloud gray to pearl—an overcast morning. Nora watched but shunned words, rejected sentences. She took in the cooing cloudy morning only with her eyes, her ears, without fully waking her brain and tongue. His body asleep, sound asleep, and the room, asleep. Her eyes saw all the dim colors of the abandoned room dotted with discarded clothing, while she kept still in the shared heated nest where he slept. Wordless, she weighed the silence, while the white-gloved morning stood waiting.

He turned over, and rolled over again, uncovering his bare mountain shoulders and when she arranged a blanket over them, he turned again, facing her, eyes open. Nora thought his face became beautiful then, as his incomprehension awoke to self possession.

"You" he said, and he was quick to grasp the situation; much faster than she, avid and purposeful, his hands and arms immediately engaged. She remained submerged in her skin, avoiding all discourse, all extraneous quibbles. He only named her, did not ask; only recognized what was offered, made no declarations.

She felt completely at home now. The boundaries were clearly drawn around the bed, which was their own private refuge and comfort. A wan bleached sunlight visited the bedroom but remained shyly diffident; did not intrude. Nora wondered if there might be a way to remain in the bed for a while; perhaps a few days. There was no truly pressing reason to leave the house as it stood now, off limits. No one would think to look for them there.

Nora liked the sound of that, the rhythm. She repeated it word for word, aloud, "No one would think to look for them there."

"Who ?" he said half-dozing, kissing her arm with eyes closed as he asked.

"Where ?"

She gathered his warm faintly damp and fragrant body to her, pressed herself against him from breasts to toes and said "I don't want to get out of bed."

"Please don't," Dan said. "What's the hurry?"

...

From inside the tent, Jennifer looked out the wedge-shaped opening at the gray morning sky and tried to guess the time. Floyd woke at the exact same time she did and was, like her, immediately alert, fully aware. Michelle remained sleeping soundly when Jennifer turned towards Floyd. The three of them had fallen asleep side by side last night in the small tent. Jennifer wanted to undress Floyd again but she knew there was no time. They both knew how much there was to do this morning. They crawled out the narrow opening on their knees and stood near the circle of ashes left in the fire pit. Floyd found his boots where he left them on the grass. He held on to Jennifer's shoulder as he pushed his feet deep into the well-worn leather. Floyd liked the way his boots held his toes firmly and set his knees at a certain angle. He stood and took a deep breath of the morning air of Los Angeles which smelled like stale grease and gasoline fumes.

They left Michelle sleeping in the tent and walked into the house. Floyd made coffee, filling the whole house with a busy morning fragrance. They both knew what time they had to meet with the hospital people. Floyd wanted to get there early; he didn't want to keep March waiting any longer than he had to. He probably has to sign some papers, Jennifer thought. They didn't talk about it. It was enough to be up early and prepared; though Jennifer wasn't sure what to be prepared for. She felt confident that Floyd could handle whatever needed to be done.

Jennifer knew that what Floyd had done the night before had prepared them for this ordeal. They were obliged to enter enemy territory where men in ties and suits and women in white uniforms would question them. They would ask for information and money. Jennifer knew that Floyd would not have enough information or money to satisfy the uniforms; they both knew that. But, prepared as they were, she wasn't afraid; she felt confident and strong. She admired how Floyd rarely looked at her or touched her. He moved steadily and consistently to complete whatever task was at hand — organizing, preparing, cooking, eating, washing. He didn't use the telephone or turn on the television. He searched through March's drawers and cabinets for important papers and put them in a brown paper bag to carry with him. Jennifer wanted to be useful and she wanted Floyd to trust her. She hoped Floyd would see that even though she was young and new to the city she could be a valuable ally.

Floyd Redhill and Jennifer Reilly set out for Cedar Sinai Hospital in his pick-up truck around six o'clock in the morning. The rush hour had already begun and Jennifer was able to show Floyd a shortcut to Beverly Boulevard that took them to the hospital in a matter of minutes. They followed the PARKING signs and found themselves at the end of a long line of cars waiting to take a ticket for the automatic gate that rose and fell like a scissors, cutting cars one by one into the dark cement layers of the parking tower.

In the taller building beyond the parking garage, in a room somewhere, the body of March lay waiting. Jennifer sat beside Floyd in a procession of cars that stretched uphill and behind them, waiting for their turn to enter the building. Something was delaying a Buick at the entrance to the parking tower. The driver of the big car was a tiny old man who had to open his car door and get out to reach the ticket dispenser with his arthritic arm. With difficulty, he pushed the large button on the machine which looked like an oversized parking meter, but nothing happened. The little numbered piece of paper he needed did not slide out of the metal slit and the horizontal barrier in front of his car remained closed.

The driver again pushed the green plastic button on the meter but nothing moved so he pushed it again, harder, still with no success. Five or six more cars accumulated in the line waiting to enter the garage. With as much force as he could muster, the old man hit the button with the heel of his right hand, but the gate remained down. Someone in a car directly behind Floyd and Jennifer honked a loud horn.

Floyd counted the number of cars between his pickup truck and the green Buick-- five. He shook his head when he saw the old man attempt to shake the heavy steel ticket dispenser. He looked over at Jennifer. She saw what had to be done without being asked and she got out of the car and walked quickly up the ramp towards the old man. She counted the cars as she went. She needed to be sure.

Floyd watched Jennifer walk along the narrow concrete edge of the ramp that held the line of cars. Jennifer looked beautiful from the back, she had a long torso and long legs and that feathery hair that never stayed in place. She is beautiful, Floyd thought, and healthy as a horse. He rolled down the window of the pickup truck so he could hear what was being said.

"You having a problem here ?" Jennifer asked the man in the Buick.

Floyd couldn't understand the man's reply. Possibly he didn't speak English. He saw Jennifer hit the ticket button a few times then walk to where the barrier gate was welded to a heavy metal apparatus for raising and lowering. She pushed against it. She was stronger than she looked, but she couldn't budge it. A car horn sounded an impatient yap up ahead of Floyd. He tried to determine which car it was, who was driving. He wondered if Jennifer could tell. Then he saw her disappear inside the dark mouth of the parking garage, looking for a gatekeeper. There was a flurry of horn honking when she disappeared inside. Floyd couldn't tell if the drivers waiting in line wanted to voice their impatience or express support for Jennifer's efforts; he wasn't sure what kind of people were in the cars, or what they might do.

Jennifer didn't return to the barrier gate for what seemed a very long time. Floyd began to wonder if he should get out and look for her when Jennifer appeared at the entrance with a fat man in a brown uniform. The man looked Mexican to Floyd, but he wouldn't have been able to tell if he came from some other country. The man in uniform had a large bunch of keys on a chain that rattled at his waist as he walked up to the machine that refused to function and confidently inserted a key into a hole in back. He twisted and turned the key and tried again but the gate remained closed. He tried another key. Jennifer stood beside the Mexican and the old man got back into his Buick. Nobody in line was honking now, all eyes were on the man in uniform. He tried another key and that one didn't work either. Even from so far away, Floyd could tell that Jen was getting angry. She had a way of tossing her head quickly away from what irritated her, like a horse with a bit. After a while she started walking back down the ramp towards Floyd and when he could see her face he was surprised at how peaceful and confident she looked.

"You got a crow bar ?" Jennifer asked Floyd when she reached his window. Her voice was exasperated, but not angry.

"Go ahead, get in the truck, I'll take care of it," Floyd said and Jennifer climbed into the cab of the pickup as she was told and Floyd got out, lifting his hat from the seat to his head in one smooth motion.

Floyd had a determined high-heeled walk and wore his hat tipped forward as he headed up the ramp holding a crow bar in his right hand. Jennifer leaned forward in the front seat watching him. Floyd didn't waste any time chatting with the uniformed Mexican, he went directly to the automatic metal gate and hit it with a loud clang of the heavy metal rod just as Jennifer expected him to.

Floyd saw where the main bolt holding the horizontal arm met the side joist and he hit that as hard as he could. He knew the blow was successful when he heard metal clang against cement. A portion of the gate had broken off. Carefully, Floyd aimed his next blow at the weakest section of the welded frame. He knew Jennifer was watching him; he turned to glance in the direction of the faded green pickup, sixth in line to get in.

The guard moved towards the gate, glancing nervously back inside the garage. He wanted to get a better look at what Floyd was doing but he seemed reluctant to get near him. A thin Black man with gray hair and glasses appeared at the entrance to the parking garage and shouted something at the guard that Jennifer couldn't hear. Both of them approached Floyd, who was demolishing the last of the gate with careful well-placed blows.

There was a conversation among the men which was drowned out by a chorus of car horns. Jennifer interpreted the honking horns to mean that the drivers of the waiting cars were impatient. There was now nothing to keep them from entering the garage and they saw no reason to wait while the details of transgression and retribution were discussed. They wanted to park their cars and enter the hospital where loved ones, sick and damaged, were waiting. But Floyd, holding the crowbar, and the two men in uniform went on talking, ignoring the waiting cars and the din of horns.

Jennifer got out of the pickup and walked slowly up the side of the ramp. The two uniformed men were speaking loudly to Floyd, keeping their distance, out of reach of the crowbar. Jennifer heard the words 'damage' and 'pay.' Floyd wasn't talking but he didn't take his eyes off the men, he saw Jennifer and gave her a nod. She poked her head into the Buick and spoke with the old man; then she walked back to the pickup. As she got into the driver's seat, it struck her once again just how lucky it was that she'd learned to drive a stick shift back in Omaha. She felt genuinely grateful about that. Once the Buick started moving, the honking stopped. The old man drove very slowly but as soon as he passed the gate, Jennifer shifted Floyd's old pickup into first gear. The cars ahead filed slowly past the three men arguing over the remains of the gate.

When Jennifer drove up to the entrance and stopped, Floyd quickly ran and jumped into the passenger seat and locked the door. The two men in uniform were caught off guard. They yelled and pounded on the window, but Jennifer stepped on the gas and swerved into the dark parking garage, taking a hard right turn against the arrows and signs, speeding towards the elevators, going the wrong way.

She slowed down when she saw a door marked STAIRS, checking the rear view mirror to see if the uniformed men had caught up, but she couldn't see them. Floyd knew he didn't have time to wait for an elevator. He grabbed the bag full of March's papers, jumped out of the truck, opened the metal door and headed up a flight of cement stairs. Jennifer managed to make a U turn just as the line of cars blocked the narrow corridor heading towards her. She knew she had to get out of the building before the parking attendants spotted her. Around the next corner, there was a sign pointing to EXIT and she made a quick turn and headed towards the booth where a man collected money and opened the exit gate.

Jennifer rolled down the window and said "Hi. I didn't get a ticket because the machine was broken. What should I do ?" She said it with a polite helpless tone, as if worried that she might have inadvertently made a mistake, but an honest, easily remedied one.

The man in the booth, without deliberation, immediately replied "fi dolla" in an almost incomprehensible accent that made the two words into one. Jennifer didn't argue, though five dollars seemed like too much. She took a bill out of her pocket and paid the man, a digital screen instantly flashed the amount, the gate rose and she was out; heading back to the street where the rooftops of Hollywood gleamed in the distance.

Jennifer drove around the block and up Beverly Boulevard where she found a place to park in front of Super Kleen Laundry. She put some quarters in the meter and set out to walk back to the hospital. She knew where Floyd was meeting the doctor but it was hard to locate the floor because there were a number of different buildings and elevators. But, when Jennifer got off on the sixth floor of the Gleason building she found Floyd waiting in the hallway.

They found room 6560 empty and stared at the bed, now stripped bare, where March had died. They worked quickly. Jennifer closed the door and Floyd took out a small pouch of loose tobacco which he poured in a circle about the size of a mixing bowl on the floor beside the bed. Once the tobacco circle was formed, he bisected it with another line of the loose tobacco and then another. The circle was divided into four quarters. North, Floyd said, facing towards Sunset Blvd; South, he said, turning the other way; then East, towards the La Brea tar pits; then West. Floyd bowed in each of the four directions, then Jennifer took three oranges from her pocket and placed them on the floor near the circle and a small bunch of the pink camellias from March's garden and some of Leo's green feathers tied with a purple satin ribbon. Floyd took Jennifer's hand and they both stood in silence for a minute.

"Okay, let's go" Floyd said, and they hurried out of the room where March had died towards the row of elevator doors on the sixth floor of the huge hospital.

CHAPTER TWENTY - SIX

Ginger awoke at seven as usual. She didn't mind the hard single bed in Dan's extra room which wasn't really a bedroom but a kind of office where he kept a desk and books. She remembered, as she sat up and turned off the clock radio, that she hadn't heard Dan come in. After Michelle called about March she had considered driving over to the house but it was so far and...Dan must have come in very late. She had gone to sleep waiting for him.

As soon as Ginger looked around the living room, she knew for certain that Dan had not returned because there was no sign of his jacket or the canvas bag he always carried. She carefully opened the door to his bedroom, turning the knob as quietly as possible, and saw that his bed had not been slept in. As she moved around the small kitchen going through the automatic motions of breakfast, Ginger felt unsettled and uncertain. She thought about March and her sudden death and speculated about possible reasons for Dan's unexplained absence. She tried to imagine how the two events might be related, but nothing made sense. It wasn't like him to stay out all night, she found herself thinking; then realized she wasn't really certain about Dan's habits. Ginger knew that she couldn't presume to have a complete knowledge of what Dan might do or where he might spend the night.   She had made certain assumptions, but she had never asked Dan if... Ginger thought probably she would have heard something if...But of course, she wouldn't, because how would anyone know that she...Ginger felt a wave of panic coming on so she sat down and focused on her breathing. She inhaled and slowly exhaled. Any number of things could have happened.   She tried to think of a likely explanation but there were so many unknown quantities, so many possible places and people. By the time she had finished off two slices of buttered toast and a second cup of coffee, Ginger decided to call Michelle, but she didn't want to call too early.

Michelle woke up naked with a stiff neck inside the damp tent. As soon as she saw that Floyd and Jennifer were gone, she wrapped a blanket around herself and crawled out of the tent. She could smell the perfume of the heavy white flowers which were beginning to fall off the big tree next door and into the muddy pond. Michelle hurried inside the house to get warm. In front of the wide picture window in the living room, the domed cage where Leo slept was still covered with a towel for the night.   When Michelle removed the cover, Leo squawked loudly and rattled up and down on his perch.

"It's me, Leo," Michelle said quietly. The parrot cocked his head and looked at her sideways like he was trying to figure out a complicated problem. When Michelle took some cashews and water to the cage she looked out the window and was surprised to see Nora's car parked in the street outside.

"I wonder what's going on next door?" Michelle said to Leo in the high strained voice people use when talking to birds.

A large orange truck with City of Los Angeles written on the door pulled into Ginger's driveway as Michelle stood watching. The phone rang then and Michelle heard Josh's voice on the line. "Where have you been, Michelle ? I've missed you." Josh sounded stern, somewhat peevish. His tone seemed to suggest that Michelle had deliberately ignored him.

"I miss you too." Michelle knew Josh's feelings would be hurt if she didn't say that.

"You could have called; didn't you get my messages ?" Michelle realized that they'd forgotten to check the answering machine that March kept on the kitchen counter. She could see, as she stood talking, that the message light was blinking. She told Josh about March and tried to describe how much had changed and how she felt like everything was suddenly different. Josh said he was sorry to hear about March but Michelle heard the impatience in his hurried words.

"Michelle, there's a screening tonight--it's the premiere of Brad Wicker's new movie. You have to come with me. There are some people I want you to meet at the party afterwards."

"I don't know," Michelle began. She felt sad and quiet inside, almost solemn.

"Look, this is really important," Josh told her. "These are people who might be able to do something for you."

"But I should stay and help Jennifer..."

"Jennifer can get along for one night without you," Josh interrupted impatiently. "This is more important."

"I don't know, Josh."

"Michelle, trust me, these are people you need to meet. I know you've had a rough time these past couple of days but we can't let this slide--this is a real opportunity. I'll pick you up at seven, we can't be late. Promise me you'll be ready, okay?"

"Okay," Michelle said, feeling certain that Jennifer would understand why she needed to meet people who could help them get jobs. March would have wanted me to go, she thought. Michelle saw that another city utility truck had pulled up in front of Ginger's house. Two men carrying heavy equipment walked into the back yard and within minutes, the shattering noise of a loud jackhammer echoed around the neighborhood.

Soon after that, Michelle watched Ginger's Volvo pull up behind the city truck and park right in front of Nora's white BMW. Then Ginger got out and pressed her face against the window of Nora's car like she was looking inside. Ginger sort of lingered on the sidewalk looking around, so Michelle ran out and greeted her with a hug.

Ginger said, "Michelle, it is just so unbelievable what happened. I feel terrible about March."

"It's been really hard, Ginger." Michelle looked up at the older woman with tear-filled eyes. Ginger followed Michelle into March's living room.

"Was Dan here last night?" Ginger asked her.

"Yes, he came with Nora." Michelle told her. "Her car is still parked out front so they must have spent the night next door. "

"Both of them ?" Ginger asked.

Michelle nodded. "I guess so." Ginger looked towards her house with a worried expression on her face and Michelle thought she must be upset about the men digging in her back yard.

"Hans said he would come by before noon," Ginger said. "He wants to try putting in a drain."

Michelle didn't want to be alone while she waited for Jennifer and Floyd to come back. "Stay for a while, okay Ginger ?"

Ginger sat down in March's living room and considered the situation. She knew how emotionally insecure Michelle was, and now a woman who had become, in a sense, her surrogate mother, had died in a tragic accident. Clearly, Michelle needed help.

"How old were you when your mother died ? Ginger asked Michelle. "Were you close to her ?"

Michelle didn't know why Ginger wanted to talk about her mother. "She died when I was fourteen," she told her. "She had lung cancer."

"Were you close ?" Ginger asked. Michelle didn't know how you could not be close to your own mother.

"Uh huh," Michelle said.

"Most probably" Ginger explained, getting up and looking out the window, "you transferred many of your feelings about your own mother to March and now you may be feeling some grief that is actually connected with the first maternal loss. It might help to talk about it."

Michelle wondered why Ginger didn't sit down, she kept fidgeting and pacing around the room. "But March was different, she..." Michelle stopped when suddenly Ginger walked into the kitchen to check the clock.

"It's almost ten o'clock" Ginger said, clenching her fists. Without saying goodbye, Ginger abruptly left. Michelle couldn't imagine what had upset Ginger so suddenly. She decided to follow her in case something was wrong.

When Michelle entered Ginger's house she heard a door slam in the upstairs bedroom and some voices shouting. Michelle couldn't hear what was being said but she could tell Nora and Ginger were arguing. Then Ginger came running down the stairs, collapsed into a chair at the kitchen table and buried her face in her arms. Michelle saw that she was crying.

A few seconds after that, Dan Downing hurried downstairs wearing Nora's lavender bathrobe. He seemed surprised to see Michelle and horrified to see Ginger crying. He looked from one to the other as if he was trying to decide who to talk to. Just then the front doorbell rang. Ginger hurried out of the room, ignoring Dan.

"Hi Dan," Michelle said, as they found themselves opposite each other at Ginger's kitchen table.

"You okay ?" he asked.

Hans was at Ginger's front door holding a long extension cord. "Do you have an outlet where I can plug this in ?" he asked when she swung the door open.

Ginger showed Hans a plug next to the back door. When she walked back into the kitchen Dan stood up and lifted his arms in the air, like he was trying to find words to explain something.

"Nora's car wouldn't start..." Dan began.

Ginger seemed to notice Michelle for the first time. "Go home, Michelle," she said. Michelle stood up, she wasn't sure what to do. "I'm sorry." Ginger said to Michelle. "I have to...there are some things I have to discuss with Dan."

Michelle felt sorry for Ginger, who, she noticed, was always getting upset about things that happened to other people. Michelle made herself comfortable in the corner chair near Leo's cage where she liked to sit and watch TV. She turned on Entertainment Empire Interviews, one of her favorite shows. Today, the man with the microphone introduced Brad Wicker. Michelle thought the name sounded familiar, then she remembered that it was the same name Josh had mentioned. Michelle turned up the sound on the TV.

"Can you tell us a little bit about your latest film, Brad ?"

"Yes Kip, it's called Bound to Deliver and it's about a man who commits a crime to rescue the woman he loves." Brad was a pale-faced man with a spiked hairdo and thin square glasses.

"Would you call this a teen flic, Brad ?"

"Not really Kip, there's something for everyone in this picture-- Suspense, action, mystery, comedy, romance, and I believe, a message about self-acceptance that is very timely and important for audiences of all ages."

"Is this something you relate to personally?"

"In many ways yes, Kip, it came out of a difficult time in my life when I was feeling pressured to fit in. Tom, who as you know is a great star and a wonderful human being, plays the hero of my story who has to come to terms with what's really important to him. And Kim Barrington is wonderful as the woman he loves. What I tried to say in this film is that we have to appreciate ourselves and others for who we are; and not live our lives according to what other people expect us to be."

"How true is that ?" Kip exclaimed enthusiastically, raising his eyebrows and grinning at the audience. "Thank you Brad Wicker, for being here with us today--I just want to say that I think your new movie is 'bound to deliver' big box office this weekend!"

The doorbell rang and Michelle opened the front door expecting Jennifer and instead found Nora, who looked almost like a different person without makeup. Nora immediately dialed a phone number and explained to Michelle, as she waited with the phone to her ear, that her battery was dead and she was waiting for triple A to come and deal with it.

"How long will it take?" Nora spoke into the phone as Michelle switched off the TV. Nora repeated the address. "It's parked on the street," she said, and hung up.

"I'm going to wait here if that's okay with you, Michelle." Nora slumped into a kitchen chair. A companionable quiet filled the room. Nora apparently didn't feel like talking. Michelle didn't see any need to ask questions, she was happy to have company. Leo hopped up and down on his perch, shaking the seeds in the bottom of his cage, making a musical rustling sound like rain.

Michelle opened the refrigerator and found some orange juice. She poured two glasses and put one in front of Nora, who thanked her. The sounds of workmen and loud motorized tools came from Ginger's back yard. Through the window, Michelle could see Ginger talking to a man in orange overalls. As Michelle stood and watched, a green and white taxi drove slowly up Westborne Street. It stopped in front of Ginger's house but did not pull over because two cars and three trucks crowded the curb. The taxi's horn honked twice.

Nora stood up and joined Michelle at the window in time to see Dan hurry out of Ginger's house and get into the taxi. She stood and watched as it pulled away and disappeared down the street. Michelle heard Nora make a sound through her nose like air escaping from a balloon and she thought she heard her mutter the word "coward."

But Nora wasn't in the mood to explain and Michelle didn't feel like talking either. She was grateful that Nora didn't try to act sympathetic and ask her how she was feeling about March.

CHAPTER TWENTY - SEVEN

Ginger was making coffee and putting away groceries. She was happy to be back in her own place but she wasn't happy about the way the backyard looked. Hans was unscrewing the tip of the water faucet in the kitchen sink and separating the small metal parts that were threaded into the spout; he held up a round screen about the size of a dime to show Ginger.

"Look how much sediment is caught in here--this is affecting your water pressure." Ginger nodded and feigned interest just to humor Hans. She knew he had a deep-seated need for approval and since he was always doing little favors for her she wanted to appear grateful. But Ginger was preoccupied with the events of the morning which had left her feeling hurt and confused. Hans replaced the newly cleaned filter and turned the faucet on.

When the aerated water flowed vigorously from the spout he was pleased. "Look, the pressure is much better now."

"That's great" Ginger said, forcing some enthusiasm into her voice.

It was growing dark and she had invited Hans to have coffee with her. The city work crew had finally left after digging a long trench to remove the tree roots which they said were clogging a storm drain running through her property. The work had taken all day and left her back yard in a muddy mess. Finally, the supervisor had inspected everything and said there was no longer any danger from underground gas leakage.

Ginger couldn't stop thinking about how Dan had left without saying anything--without explaining. She didn't expect an apology; but Ginger felt he owed her an explanation, some acknowledgement of her feelings. And Nora had refused to speak to her at all. Ginger felt a little guilty about walking into Nora's bedroom, but she had no way of knowing...

"How are you feeling ?" Hans sat down opposite Ginger and looked directly into her eyes with his wide pale blue eyes. Ginger was always taken by surprise at her friend's odd mixture of pragmatism and empathy. He took others' problems as seriously, perhaps even more seriously, than his own. When he first spoke to Ginger in the morning, he could sense something was wrong and he encouraged her to sit down and tell him the whole story. He seemed so genuinely concerned that Ginger had described in detail her feelings for Dan and his perplexing relationship with Nora and all the resulting confusion she felt. Hans, so knowledgeable when it came to fixing what was broken in the material world, seemed defenseless in the face of emotional turmoil. He felt, as she did, that what Dan had done was cruel and inexcusable. He shook his large well-shaped head in sad commiseration about the ways of men.

"I just don't want her to live here any more, is that unreasonable ?" Ginger said to Hans. "I feel that she violated my trust."

Hans' handsome face reflected the strain he felt, as if talking about such behavior was excruciatingly difficult; so difficult that he could only shake his head and keep his lips pressed tightly together in an expression of pained distress.

After Hans left, Ginger wanted to look in on Michelle and Jennifer to make sure they were okay. She felt vaguely guilty that she'd done nothing to help the girls deal with the shock of March's death. She knew how important it would be for the girls to work through their feelings of abandonment and loss.

Ginger was surprised, when Michelle answered the door, to see that she was dressed to go out for the evening. The girl's hair was pulled back in a smooth sophisticated style and she was wearing a short white low-cut dress with a pleated skirt that looked like a tennis outfit. Ginger was even more surprised to find Nora sitting at the kitchen table.

Nora did not get up or greet Ginger when she entered. "Did you get your battery fixed ?" Ginger asked her.

"Yes, I had to buy a new one." Nora avoided eye contact with Ginger.

"I'm going to a movie premiere with Josh" Michelle told Ginger, excited anticipation in her voice, "Nora took me shopping and helped me do my hair. How do I look ?"

"You look beautiful, Michelle." Ginger knew how crucial it was to build the girl's self-esteem.

"Want some orange juice, Ginger ?" Michelle seemed eager to make Ginger feel welcome.

Ginger wasn't sure what to do; she had expected to find Michelle in need of consolation. She sat down opposite Nora at the table. Nora met Ginger's eyes with a neutral expression, neither hostile nor friendly, as if they didn't know each other. Ginger wanted to clear the air. She knew she wouldn't be able to sleep tonight unless she reached some kind of closure with Nora.

When Michelle disappeared into the bathroom, Ginger began "Nora, I didn't know you were…I mean, I thought maybe something was wrong in the house, I only wanted to check to see if you were okay."

"You could have knocked, Ginger, you deliberately barged into my bedroom."

"I'm sorry, I thought you were alone, I thought maybe something was wrong."

"Something was wrong ? Yes, you were wrong. I pay rent you know, I have a right to my space."

"Why did you lie to me ? You told me there was nothing between you and Dan, that he was just a writing partner--why didn't you tell me ?"

Nora stood up. "Ginger, I'm not required to keep you informed about my private life. If you feel that Dan has some sort of obligation to you, then that's something for you and him to work out. I'm not going to say I'm sorry that Dan didn't live up to your expectations. That's your problem, not mine."

Ginger took a deep breath and tried to keep her voice steady "I'm not saying that I have an exclusive relationship with Dan; I just know I'm not going to be comfortable about you and I living together after what happened today."

"In that case," Nora replied, "I'll move out as soon as possible."

"I think that would probably be best."

Ginger tried to keep her voice as cool and even as Nora's, but mid-sentence she broke down and lost it. Ginger was furious at herself but she couldn't help it, tears rolled down her cheeks.

Nora left the table and noticed an open pack of Marlboros that someone had left on the kitchen counter. She lit one, inhaling deeply, and opened the kitchen window as she stood with her back to Ginger, smoking.

Michelle returned from the bathroom, having completed the final touches on her makeup. Ginger couldn't help but notice that her eyes looked exceptionally dramatic; she wondered if Nora had given her some tips. Makeup secrets, Ginger thought. The phrase, a cliché of fashion magazines, suddenly struck her as idiotic, hilarious. What is the secret, she wondered, what is the secret makeup ? Ginger laughed and sobbed at the same time; it came out as a kind of snorting choking sound.

Michelle hurried to Ginger and put her hands on her shoulders. She saw how upset Ginger was. "Don't worry Ginger, you'll feel better in the morning--you've had a hard day." Michelle's voice was soothing and sympathetic.

"I'm sorry," Ginger sobbed, and Michelle tried to hug her but the taller woman pulled away and blew her nose loudly. "Goodbye Michelle," Ginger said, not looking at Nora, "I'm going home now."

"We'll pray for you," Michelle told Ginger who nodded her head several times and hurried out the door.

"I didn't know you smoked." Michelle said to Nora.

"Is there anything to drink around here by any chance ?" Nora asked.

Michelle pointed to a low cupboard and Nora lifted a bottle of vodka onto the counter. She poured some of the clear alcohol into her orange juice and held the bottle aloft. "Anyone else ?" she asked.

"I'll try some" Michelle said.

Nora mixed Michelle a drink. "It's called a screwdriver," she told her. Michelle giggled at the silly name and the two women clinked glasses. Just then, the door opened and Floyd and Jennifer entered the room.

Nora saw at once that they were high on some kind of drug. Jennifer was smiling for no reason and her eyes glittered as if dilated. Floyd's face was flushed a deep red. Michelle rushed to embrace Jennifer, as if she'd been gone for a long time. "What happened?" she asked her friend, "I haven't heard from you all day, I was worried."

"Sorry," Jennifer told her, "I didn't have time to call. After we dealt with the hospital people we had to drive over to a bank in Santa Clarita where March had a safe deposit box. Floyd found the key but we didn't know what was in it."

"It took a while to make all the arrangements for the cremation," Floyd explained to Michelle. He kissed her forehead and squeezed her shoulders as he said it-- a gesture that Nora thought looked intimate and soothing.

"Are you planning a memorial service ?" Nora asked.

Jennifer said "Floyd thought we should take March's ashes and go out to the desert and scatter them. I think March would have liked that. We probably won't be able to do it until a few months from now. We can all go, if you want," she added, including Nora.

The room was quiet for a moment as everyone stopped to think about the woman who was no longer there. Nora became aware of the parrot in his cage, a gentle rattle, a murmuring sound inside his beak as he rocked on his perch, watching them.

"I have something important to tell you," Jennifer said to Michelle who looked at her friend curiously. She had never heard her speak in this new tone of voice sounding dazed and confident at the same time. Michelle edged near enough to touch Jennifer's arm.

"What ?" Michelle felt Jennifer's happiness like electricity or alcohol, something that ran through her blood and made her heart beat faster.

Jennifer looked at Floyd "Is it okay if I tell them ?"

"If you want," Floyd said.

"Floyd's going to sign March's house over to me" Jennifer said. "He doesn't want to live in L.A. and..."

"He's going to give you this house ?" Nora didn't believe it.

Floyd spoke quietly "I'm March's legal heir, and the house is almost paid for. In fact, since she bought it in the sixties, this place is worth a lot more than the current mortgage."

"Floyd doesn't want to live in L.A. and he doesn't want to sell the house so he wants us to have it," Jennifer said to Michelle. Michelle hugged Floyd and kissed him and then she hugged Jennifer.

"That's certainly very generous of you Floyd," Nora said.

"But Floyd will always have a place to call home," Jennifer explained to the other women. "That's part of our deal. He can always come and stay, whenever he needs to."

Nora appraised Floyd carefully, as if she could judge his character and his veracity by the shape of his head or the condition of his boots. Floyd stood still and held his hat in his hands. "I came to make sure my sister was well-treated" Floyd said. "I did what I thought she would have wanted. I have a place to live up north in the warm months; I move to the desert in the rainy season. Don't need a house in the city; too much to worry about."

Michelle pressed close to Jennifer. She could feel her friend's happiness in her arms and face--her whole body was taut and eager. Jennifer whispered in a voice that promised secret confidences: "Michelle, you won't believe what happened today, I have to tell you."

Jennifer led Michelle into their bedroom and they hugged each other in front of the mirror beside two unmade twin beds. This is our home, Jennifer thought to herself, looking around the room as if seeing it for the first time. "Is he really going to give us this house ?" Michelle asked her.

"Yes," Jennifer shrugged as if to explain that she couldn't explain, "he wants to."

"Josh is taking me to a premiere tonight," Michelle told Jennifer. "Nora helped me find this dress--it's vintage."

"Vintage ?" Jennifer wasn't sure what that meant. Michelle vogued in the mirror, making a little curtsy.

"You know, like it's old but...in perfect condition and better than new. Nora said it's a vintage tennis dress from the fifties. She said I had a fifties figure."

Jennifer couldn't help but feel faintly covetous of Michelle's body and the way the dress hugged her tiny waist and dipped just low enough in front to expose the perfect cleavage of her high round breasts--but the feeling lasted only for a fraction of a second as Jennifer reminded herself that she now owned a house.

Michelle was aware that she looked prettier than she had ever looked in her life. The certainty of her beauty made her feel generous and calm as she applied some fresh lipstick.

Jennifer ran her hand over Michelle's hair which hung like black satin over her mocha cream shoulders. "You look great Michelle, you're perfect" and something inside Jennifer was almost sad at Michelle's perfection because she doubted that anyone could appreciate the vivid radiance of Michelle as fully as she did. She feared, standing beside her friend looking into the mirror, that Michelle was destined to be admired and envied but not truly appreciated. She saw how easily Michelle's beauty would attract and excite men but how unlikely it was that any man would ever really try to understand her. Only Jennifer truly understood Michelle and therefore, she thought, deserved her loyalty and love.

Jennifer stood behind Michelle and wrapped her arms around the soft front of her. They stared at themselves posed in the mirror like a framed portrait--Jennifer angular and fair with her candid gray eyes and thin arms behind curvaceous Michelle whose soft face always looked so child-like. Jennifer felt a pang of regret that she would be staying home while her friend went out.

"We'll always stick together, won't we ?" Jennifer asked, leaning down to breathe in the jasmine of Michelle's hair.

"Always," Michelle said as she patted both of Jennifer's arms, then added "I wish you were coming with me tonight." Michelle's confidence in her own beauty made her magnanimous.

When Josh Samuels pulled his car up to the curb on Westborne Street he looked at the time--it was six-thirty on the dot. He hoped that Michelle wouldn't make him wait. The drive into Hollywood could take fifteen minutes at this time of night and parking could take between five and fifteen minutes. Josh knew Michelle was probably still upset about her friend's death but he hoped she was sufficiently over it so it wouldn't affect her behavior this evening. Josh had called Cal Portnoy over at Warners and talked for ten minutes about Michelle. Cal was an old friend of Josh's uncle David and he was going to be sitting with them at dinner. If Cal liked what he saw, Josh was sure he could make things happen for her. Josh knew how important it was to find young actresses. There were so many women who came to Hollywood after college or after several years of experience in off-Broadway or regional theater or modeling but not that many who were actually teen-agers, and that's what was so perfect about Michelle--she was so young. Josh had learned about the tremendous value of youth as a commodity. From his point of view, experience in acting was of no practical value. Michelle had huge potential because she had no protective family to hold her back, no artistic pretensions, nothing to fall back on, nowhere to retreat. She had time to learn and could afford to make mistakes. She would be in no hurry to marry or have children. She was perfect. She could be molded into whatever was necessary. Josh straightened his tie and rang the bell.

When Josh walked in, Nora stood up so she could get a good look at him. He was barely five foot six and had very narrow shoulders but he didn't seem at all intimidated at being the object of scrutiny. Josh was poised and businesslike and his jacket was tailored in the latest style. He held out his hand to Floyd and said "Hi, I'm Josh Samuels" and repeated the greeting to Nora.

Floyd hung back after he opened the door, as if he wanted to put some distance between himself and the younger man in the suit. He remembered seeing Josh at the hospital.

"We have to run, don't want to be late," Josh told them, "you know how it is, if you're late you don't get a good seat."

Nora walked towards the back bedroom. She could hear a steady humming sound, a prolonged note that climbed and dipped. Michelle and Jennifer were harmonizing in front of the mirror.

"Josh is here," she told Michelle.

"You look fabulous" Josh said when Michelle walked into the living room. "The dress is great."

"Where are you taking Michelle ?" Floyd asked Josh, who looked at Michelle to determine whether he was expected to respond.

"We're going to a movie premiere," Michelle explained. Josh started to open the door.

"Not so fast," Floyd said, holding the door half-closed. "What time are you coming back ?"

"Don't worry, Floyd," Jennifer told him. "It's okay."

Floyd stood in front of the door and looked Josh straight in the eyes. "If you so much as lay a hand on this girl, you'll have me to reckon with."

Josh grinned and nodded like Floyd was kidding. "Don't worry about it," he said, not meeting Floyd's eyes, looking nervously around the room for support.

"Don't think you can stay out all night without us knowing it."

Josh kept smiling but he was afraid of Floyd who had a broad barrel-shaped chest and his arms, visible below the rolled up sleeves of his plaid shirt, were thick as logs from elbow to wrist.

"I'll make sure she's home right after the party," he said, simulating obedience and humility with an ingratiating smile.

Floyd moved away from the door because Michelle looked so eager to go. Josh continued smiling at him and the rest of the people in the room.

"Have a nice evening," he waved, resting his left hand on Michelle's soft shoulder as they walked to his car.

CHAPTER TWENTY - EIGHT

Michelle was surprised, when she and Josh stepped out of his car, to see an actual red carpet laid directly on the sidewalk of Hollywood Boulevard from the parking lot to the Pyramid Theater almost a block away. Thick ropes strung waist-high on both sides of the carpet separated the invitees from the gawking crowds who lined up to watch them enter the ornate doors of the old Egyptian-style movie palace. Uniformed security guards with leather gun holsters stood under the brightly-lit marquee and the street was blocked with police barricades.

"Tom is going to be here tonight," Josh told her, "and maybe Kim too."

Every few minutes flash bulbs erupted when the contingent of paparazzi spotted someone of sufficient fame to provoke their enthusiasm. The line into the theater moved slowly as new arrivals on the red carpet were obliged to wait while the more famous among them deemed it prudent to stop and smile and pose for the cameras before entering the building.

As Josh and Michelle began to approach the entrance a sudden explosion of flash bulbs illuminated a blonde woman in a tight blue dress. Michelle wasn't sure who she was but she looked familiar. The blonde paused for a second and smiled to the right as lights from several cameras flashed at once, illuminating her hair and skin so intensely that for a split second she glowed white, like a ghost or a marble statue. A voice in the crowd yelled "over here Kim" and the woman turned left towards the voice and smiled the same pleased smile, briefly stationary in the face of more white flashes, then continued on her way.

Michelle felt herself growing more nervous and excited as she realized that people on the sidewalk, on the other side of the roped-off carpet, were watching her, even though she was only walking in to see a movie. When Josh and Michelle reached the cluster of photographers near the entrance, a flashbulb went off, momentarily blinding Michelle and then another photographer knelt to get a shot and Josh suddenly stopped walking and Michelle realized they were taking pictures of her.

"The paparazzi think you're an actress" Josh whispered to her, and Michelle smiled a pleased warm smile and faced the exploding lights, seeing a tangle of agitated men with cameras and white spots in front of her eyes.

The renovated lobby of one of the oldest theaters in Hollywood was preserved exactly as it had been in the twenties, with glittering mosaics and gold leaf in an Egyptian motif covering sconces and nooks inhabited by pharaohs and queens. A purple carpet patterned with peacock feathers was illuminated by dramatic chandeliers the size of bicycles blazing from the high domed ceiling. Josh hurried to secure seats in an area that was marked reserved, though his tickets said general admission.

Michelle sat and watched as the audience entered in clumps and couples, searching for seats, calling to friends, waving across the aisles. Most of the men were paunchy and balding and many of the women wore tailored black suits so they tended to all look alike. In fact, most of the men were really old, Michelle noticed; though they were usually with younger women. Josh was among the youngest men in the room and she knew he was almost 27. Just before the film was about to begin, a group of scantily dressed women with shiny hair and a handsome black man with neat dreadlocks and several tall younger men with broad shoulders were led to a row of seats that had been roped off and reserved. Without being told, Michelle knew they were actors. The movie was about a man who robbed a bank by posing as a millionaire; his girlfriend was a recovering drug addict and he wanted to rescue her from some dealers in Honolulu who said she owed them money. The last scene was a rapid-fire chase in speed boats where, at the end, one of the boats rammed into a pier and burst into flames.

When the lights went up after the credits and applause from the audience, Josh wasted no time in steering Michelle through the thick crush of people heading for the exits. He didn't want to risk ending up at the wrong table at the party. Even though his uncle David had arranged things, he knew many other people would be trying to get close to Cal Portnoy and it was crucial that he meet Michelle tonight.

The party was held in a huge white tent that had been erected in the parking lot behind the theater. Since the movie was set in Hawaii, the decorators had provided sand for the floor and large potted palm trees wired with tiny white lights had been placed inside, suggesting a dim tropical island ambiance. As the guests entered the tent, girls dressed in grass skirts offered leis made of fragrant flowers. Josh saw that there were probably thirty tables in the tent; some of them reserved for the producers and stars of the film. He left Michelle near the tent entrance and made his way to the center of the room, placed his jacket on the back of a chair at one of the reserved tables, and began to elbow his way back through the jostling crowd. Josh knew it would take Cal some time to get seated as there would be many people who wanted to talk to him, schmooze, and congratulate him. He figured it might be 45 minutes to an hour before Cal actually sat down. Josh was pleased to see some actors in the room who were clients of Cinecast Enterprises, an agency he knew was on the verge of bankruptcy because the head of the company was about to be indicted for embezzlement.

"You want something to drink?" Josh took Michelle's hand and led her through the crowd towards a narrow bar where a couple of bartenders in white jackets worked feverishly. Michelle asked for a screwdriver and Josh sipped a diet Pepsi as he looked over her shoulder at people in the crowd.

"Stay here for a minute, okay?" Josh left her standing alone and walked over to a couple and said "Patricia, I heard you were getting married. You look fabulous, by the way. Is this the lucky guy?"

Michelle couldn't hear what was said after that. She watched Josh follow the couple as they made their way through the crowd, then she lost sight of him. The tent was filling up rapidly with men and women in black suits.

"Debbie ?" someone touched Michelle's shoulder, but when she turned she saw an apologetic look on the man's face.

"Oh sorry, thought you were Debbie Stevens," the man said. He wasn't too old, about Josh's age and he had a foreign accent.

"Where are you from ?" Michelle asked him.

"London," the man said. "And you ? Are you an Angelino ?

Or is it Angelina ?" he added. He was blond and wore thin square-framed glasses.

Michelle didn't answer immediately. His pale gray tie patterned with tiny green jugglers caught her eye. "What's your name ?" she asked him, "I'm Michelle, not Debbie."

"Well, Miz Notdebbie, I'm pleased to make your acquaintance. I'm Peter Revel."

Michelle looked around, Josh had disappeared. She smiled at Peter and said "Are you an Englishman ?"

"Not exactly," Peter said, "I'm Russian actually, but at the moment, London is my home."

"At the moment" Michelle told him, swallowing a large gulp of her drink, "you're in Hollywood."

Peter laughed and looked carefully at Michelle. "Thank you for reminding me of that," he told her. "You must be an actress."

Michelle saw that Peter liked her and she liked him. She wanted to explain things to him honestly and directly so that they could be friends. She finished her drink and set the plastic cup in the sand at her feet.

"I've been on TV" she explained, "but I'm not exactly an actress yet because I was just myself on TV, you know, not a made-up person."

"That's fascinating," Peter told her. "You look so exotic. I thought you must be Hawaiian. In this room full of women in black, here you are, in white, pristine and lovely as a flower."

Peter's words began to get lost in the general noise of the tent, which now included background music, the theme from the film, throbbing techno-jazz with a hip hop beat. Michelle looked up at Peter and he fingered her lei, as if curious about the shape of the flowers. She caught sight of Josh talking to a muscular man with a ponytail. She wondered when they were going to sit down and eat.

"Want another drink?" Peter asked Michelle and she said yes.

Michelle lost sight of Josh but she knew he wanted her to be ready to sit down when it was time but she needed to go to the bathroom but couldn't figure out where it might be. Peter moved towards the crowd near the bar and began talking to a red-haired woman in a sarong.

Michelle wished Jennifer was with her because she'd know where to find a bathroom in a tent. A sign behind the bar caught her attention--Ladies Room was lettered on a piece of cardboard, with an arrow pointing through an opening in the heavy cloth. The sign directed guests to a door in the back of the theater so she got in line with several other women.

"Heidi, I can't believe I've been gone for an hour, Old Knobs is probably wondering where in the hell I am," a woman standing in front of Michelle spoke looking up at her friend, who wore very high heels. Both were dressed in black suits. The speaker, who had short silver-white hair, carried a voluminous handbag in which she was searching for something buried.

Heidi looked down and up at Michelle and said "you must be freezing in that dress."

"No," said Michelle. "I'm okay."

The smaller woman stopped digging in her purse and stared at Michelle for a moment.

"You look familiar, were you in the movie?"

"I just..."

"You were in that tennis scene, weren't you?" The woman nudged Heidi. "Didn't I tell you? I never forget a face. You remember, where the bank robber pretends to be a member of the country club and sneaks onto the tennis court?" Both women now looked at Michelle with interest.

"Doesn't she have a beautiful tan?" Heidi said. Her friend agreed. Michelle smiled at them and said nothing because she couldn't decide what to say.

Someone came out of a door then Heidi went in. The silver-haired woman gave Michelle a card and said "I'm a talent agent, if you ever want to talk about getting new representation, call me. I like your look and having sports skills is a plus."

Michelle looked at the card. "Thanks Dawn," she said.

When Dawn entered the cubicle and Heidi emerged she stopped and said in a low voice to Michelle "Dawn is one of the best--she handles half of the cast of Emergency Police Action." Heidi watched Michelle's face to see how she would react to this information but Michelle shrugged and smiled, did not reply.

"Really, she's hot right now," Heidi said, nodding affirmation of her own statement.

"Thank you," said Michelle as the woman gave her a little wave and went back into the party. When Michelle finally found Josh he was upset because he'd been looking everywhere to find her, he said it was time to sit down for dinner with his uncle and Cal Portnoy.

"You don't have to be nervous," Josh told Michelle, but she could feel how clammy Josh's hands were and how quickly his eyes darted here and there, as if he was looking out for something unexpected to pop up. Josh was disappointed when he saw that Cal was not seated at the table yet--he was still talking to Brad Wicker at his table nearby. He and Michelle sat down at the large round table set for ten. It was unoccupied except for one other couple, a middle-aged bald man and his wife, yellow-blonde with a bored look on her face. A waiter came and poured wine. Michelle felt a little on edge just because Josh was nervous.

A man with smooth hair all combed back from his forehead bent down and whispered in Josh's ear. "I need your help for a minute Josh."

"Have you met my uncle David ?" Josh asked Michelle and she shook her head no. Josh stood up to face his uncle and so did Michelle. She thought his hair looked like he was facing a strong wind.

"Michelle, this is my uncle, David Samuels. I know you remember me telling you what a wonderful guy he is, super brilliant agent and all round mensch." Josh smiled broadly and spoke in a tone that combined overt insincerity with an obvious effort to please.

Michelle was puzzled at first. She couldn't remember what a mensch was and wasn't sure Josh had really told her anything about this uncle. She smiled the same pleased warm smile she had smiled at the photographers and shook the man's soft hand.

"I've seen you on television," Josh's uncle said, leaning towards her face and looking her over from head to toe. "But you're even better-looking in person."

"Oh." Michelle wanted to get to know this man but he made her feel bashful. She could sense that Josh was a little afraid of him. She had a sudden impulse to break the ice.

"Why don't you sit here beside me ?" she suggested.

An avuncular smile briefly creased David Samuel's well-groomed face. "Thank you Michelle, I will plan on it."

But instead of sitting down beside her, David scanned the room intently, his attention fixed on a spot towards the back. He wasn't tall but he looked important, Michelle thought; he had good posture and thick heels on his shoes.

"But first, I need to borrow Josh here for just a minute to help me clear something up, okay sweetheart?"

"Okay," said Michelle.

"Don't worry, I'll bring him back very soon," David added, putting his hand on Josh's shoulder and steering him into the crowd.

No one else sat down at the large table and there were several empty chairs on either side of Michelle. The tent seemed to be filled with people talking and jostling shoulder to shoulder on the sandy floor. Michelle smiled awkwardly at the couple across from her. The older woman with yellow hair said "I'm Sarah Hilyard and this is my husband Bob." She had to shout a little. Her husband, in a gray suit, nodded at Michelle in a bored but polite way.

Michelle told them her name and Sarah nodded and began to say something but the table was so wide and the noise level so high they couldn't actually engage in conversation. As Michelle was looking around trying to see Josh in the crowd the chair on her right was suddenly occupied by Peter Revel who had a glass in each hand.

"I've been looking everywhere for you," he told her, handing her a drink.

"You can't sit there" Michelle told him.

"Why not ?" Peter asked, leaning back and swallowing several inches of his drink as if he'd just finished a taxing bout of work and needed to quench his thirst and make himself comfortable.

"Because it's taken," Michelle told him.

"I don't see anyone," Peter counted four people at the table, including himself.

Josh wasn't sure what his uncle was up to but he knew it probably had something to do with Stacey Wilder. David had been going out with her for so long that some of his acquaintances assumed he was already divorced from his wife; but that was not the case.

Stacey was a costume designer who worked on big-budget movies. She was rarely in L.A. because she spent most of the year filming in distant locations. This was convenient for David because he could hook up with Stacey when she was out of town working. Stacey had designed the costumes for tonight's film, so David knew she would be in attendance but he had no choice--he had to bring his wife Donna because she was a huge Kim Barrington fan.

Josh had met Stacey many times at parties and clubs with his uncle David. She was a lot of fun but she had a tendency to overdue it with drugs, especially cocaine. Not that she was an addict or anything like that, but she sometimes did a little too much. Stacey had never married; she was an L.A. girl who had friends in the industry so she started young, working as an assistant to one of the top costume designers. Because she was ambitious and talented, Stacy became successful in her career at a young age; but the long hours and demanding travel schedules had begun to tell on her. She sometimes needed a little cocaine to keep alert, to stay on top of things, but she hated to stay home, she was always ready to go on to the next party--a girl you would call fun to be with. And she'd had a little too much tonight. David was explaining to Josh that Stacey had already made a scene earlier when he and Donna were entering the theater. She was loud and sloppy and showed David some snapshots of the weekend they spent together at an exclusive resort in Hawaii during the filming.

"She's going around showing those pictures to everybody," David said. "She's completely out of control tonight. What we need to do is make sure she gets a ride home before she really embarrasses herself, and me."

Josh admired the way his uncle confronted problems head on and didn't waste time pretending his nephew didn't know about

Stacey. David was a man who never hesitated to cut to the chase, Josh thought. He sized up a problem, figured out a solution and acted. His uncle David had been a mentor to Josh since he'd left U.C.L.A. As it happened, Josh was several credits short of getting his B.A. degree but that didn't stop his uncle from hiring him at Influential Artists and giving him a responsible position in his own department. Josh wanted David to know he could be trusted and he was willing to do anything to prove himself worthy of the older man's confidence.

In the large crowd, it took the two men several minutes to find the girl. Stacey was tall with broad shoulders; stacks of bangle bracelets encircled her long bare arms. Her thick curly hair was tied up in an elaborate style that included braids and velvet bands. She was standing outside the tent with several other women, smoking and talking. When David and Josh approached, Stacey's friend said to her "Here he comes."

Stacey sniffed loudly and patted her hair. She wore a floor-length yellow Chinese silk dress slit up the side to mid-thigh with lace underneath. Heavy hoop earrings hung at the sides of her square-jawed pink face which was enlivened by a tiny diamond stuck decorously in the flare of one delicate nostril. The dress was cut low enough to reveal the small tattoo of a dagger over her right breast. Dressed as she was, she resembled a Turkish harem girl in a Victorian painting. Josh was intimidated by her but his uncle David found her irresistible.

Two of Stacey's girl friends left when David walked up and greeted her. "Where you going ?" she shouted after them in a throaty low-pitched voice that carried for yards, "you don't have to leave."

One friend stayed beside her though and boldly faced David, who indicated that he preferred to speak to Stacey alone. Josh hung back discretely, intently studying the crowd in an off-the-cuff imitation of Clint Eastwood playing a secret service agent guarding the president.

David spoke first, laying his hand gently on Stacey's bare shoulder "How are you feeling, Stace ?" His voice was intimate and concerned.

"I feel fine, thank you very much," the young woman replied, removing the man's hand from her shoulder and flinging it back at him with considerable force. "You want to talk about feelings ?" Here Stacey sniffed the night air with explosive force and vehemence. "Well how do you feel and what do you think I feel and fuck you fuck you fuck you, David."

Josh admired two things above all about his uncle. One was that he always looked great-- his hair was impeccable, perfectly groomed and never out of place; and he never ever lost his temper. No matter how angry he got, David never shouted or blew up at anyone. He had explained once to Josh how important it was to act, rather than react-- something he'd learned in a Japanese martial arts class.

Josh saw that Stacey was in even worse shape than he'd expected. Her eyes were red, and black mascara trickled down her cheeks. Her remaining friend melted into the crowd as several nearby guests began to point and stare.

"What do you want me to do, David ?" she shouted, "pretend I don't see you ? Pretend you're not here ?" Stacey sniffed again, a loud deliberate hiss like a bicycle tire taking in air.

Josh realized that this might take a little longer than he'd planned. His uncle betrayed not the slightest impatience or discomfort. His demeanor was that of a concerned friend who wanted to spend quality time with Stacey.

"Listen," David said to Stacey, not touching her but straining to make eye contact, "look at me--I'm here for you."

"You asshole," the woman shouted, "you lying asshole."

Josh looked at the crowd with what he hoped was a steely unperturbed gaze. Several people had stopped talking and were overtly staring but they weren't people of any importance, as far as he could tell. They were mostly younger guys who had stepped outside the tent to smoke in the chilly alley near the parking lot. It was important that no one from the agency or anyone of real consequence, like David's clients or business partners, would see him in this situation.

"I was so impressed with the work you did on this film. It was magnificent, really. This is academy award material, Stace, you are going to get a nomination this year. I'm so proud of you--you are the best, you know that ?"

David tried to pat Stacey on the shoulder but she again pushed him away.

She looked around for her friends but they'd all gone back inside. "Leave me alone" she warned, "You have no right to touch me."

"Stacey," David said, "Do me a favor and give me those photographs from Hawaii."

"They're mine, you can't have them !" She clutched a brocade evening bag to her chest.

David glanced at Josh and motioned him to help. Josh surprised Stacey from behind and threw his arms around her, pinning her arms to her sides. She struggled but Josh put his full strength into it and David pulled Stacey's purse out of her hand.

"You're in no condition to drive" he told her.

Josh held on as tight as he could but Stacey Wilder was a strong girl and outweighed him by fifteen or twenty pounds. She struggled free and tried to snatch her purse back from David but he slipped the purse to Josh who ran back into the crowded tent with it. David handed a hundred dollar bill to the parking attendant near the tent entrance and said: "I want you to get a taxi for the lady, she's in no condition to drive."

Josh thought he could faintly hear Stacey yelling at David in the parking lot as he hurried through the crowd under the tent. He concealed the purse in the pocket of his jacket and estimated that he hadn't been gone more than fifteen minutes.

When he reached the table, Josh saw that Donna Samuels, his uncle's wife, was sitting beside Michelle. They seemed to be engrossed in conversation. Josh had known Donna since he was a little boy.

"Aunt Donna" Josh said, bending down and kissing her on the cheek. "You look great. How have you been?"

"Where's David?" Donna asked.

"He went to find the men's room," Josh told her.

"Well, do you notice anything different about me ?" Donna looked expectantly at her nephew. Josh took a few seconds to examine his aunt. Her hair was still the short dark brown he remembered, her face looked the same but, yes, she did look thinner.

"You've lost weight," he said, adding with forceful enthusiasm, "you look terrific."

`"Yes, I lost twenty-eight pounds," Donna confided, looking first to Michelle then to Josh. "I went on the knife diet, you know what I mean ?" Michelle shook her head, looking puzzled.

"They cut the fat off me," Donna explained. "I went down two sizes, it's like liposuction but different."

Josh wondered how long it would take for David to get rid of Stacey and join them at the table. As he sat down next to Michelle who was seated beside the open seat where he expected Cal Portnoy to sit, Josh looked around the table and saw the usual faces: Cal's partner Bob Hilyard and his wife; Dan Morton and his wife Heidi who was a casting agent; and Donna Samuels beside the empty seat waiting for her husband. There should have been three seats left but Josh counted only two. It was then he noticed a man with a handsome face and square glasses sitting next to Don Morton's wife. The guy was in close conversation with her. He knew it wasn't the Morton's son; maybe he was an actor friend of Cal's who had a small role in the movie. Josh thought he looked vaguely foreign and he wondered who invited him; he had heard that sometimes Cal went out with male 'friends' to events such as this. Josh had heard talk that sometimes...Not that Cal himself was gay but he had gay friends. In fact, just the other day, Josh had heard that Cal financed his new picture in Rumania with money from the Russian gay mafia.

Donna was telling Michelle and Heidi about an experience she'd had in Mexico when a local shaman in Zihuatenejo had cured her kidney stones. "It was completely painless" he heard her say; "he came right to my hotel room."

Heidi told Donna "Michelle reminds me of a young Natalie Wood; she's so petite but I understand she's a championship tennis player."

"She's adorable and incredibly talented," Donna said, instinctively feeling a maternal pride in her nephew's girlfriend.

Josh saw that Cal Portnoy was on his way to the table now. He was a large man who had become pale and hairless with age; a pair of thick black-rimmed glasses defined his face. Several of the men stood when he came to the table and Cal greeted his friends in his gravely voice. In response to Donna Samuels' inquiry he explained "Judy couldn't come with me tonight, she did something to her back."

"Oh, the poor thing," Donna said. "I'm going to give her the number of this wonderful Sikh chiropractor I know, I'm sure he could fix it. He does aura cleansing and believe me, it really helps. I had my aura cleansed yesterday, can you tell ? "

Cal was introduced to Michelle by Josh who said "This is the girl I told you about, isn't she beautiful ?"

Cal said "Hi Michelle," but he barely looked at her. Momentarily mute, she nodded at the old man and smiled her shy smile.

"Maybe you'd better go see what's become of David," Donna said to Josh. Doesn't he know we're all having dinner ? What's taking him so long ?"

Josh thought it might be a good idea to see what he could do about that. He excused himself and hurried away. Once Cal was seated, the waiters brought more wine and people began to eat. Michelle regarded the old producer with special attention. He sat to her left and she could hear his labored breathing in between conversation with various people at the table. Josh said he was somebody who could help her but Michelle wasn't sure what that meant.

Cal took some pills out of his pocket, swallowed them, and drank several gulps of water as Michelle watched, trying to think of something to say. She was annoyed at Josh for leaving her alone. Peter Revel moved over and took the seat that had been intended for Mrs. Portnoy.

"How are you Cal ?" Peter greeted him. As Cal didn't respond, Peter told him his name and said "We met in Bucharest last summer."

Cal looked at the young man with an expression of blank indifference. Michelle noticed that he didn't bother to answer Peter, the old producer just nodded acknowledgement that he'd heard him speak and went on eating his salad, staring down at his plate.

"You may remember my father, Ivan Revelinsky Benivetscu?" Peter continued.

"Ivan ?" Cal Portnoy repeated, abruptly putting his fork down and facing Peter. "From Bucharest ?"

"That's right," Peter replied.

"You're his son ?"

"Right."

"What are you doing here ?" Cal asked the well-dressed young man, with an emphasis on the last word.

Michelle thought Cal seemed a little bit annoyed to find a stranger at his table. Her sympathies went out to Peter who had been very nice to her, she thought, when Josh had practically abandoned her. There was something in Michelle's personality that required a partner. She had never been really comfortable operating on her own. She was beginning to think that Josh didn't really understand her but she sensed that Peter was very smart and obviously very helpful.

"I came here because my father told me you were an honorable man" Peter told Cal, looking him straight in the eye.

Michelle put her hand on Cal's arm and he turned his dim eyes behind the thick lenses towards her. "Peter is a very good judge of character and if he says you're honorable I believe he's right." Michelle spoke in a playful tone but she could see a spark in Cal's eye.

"Did you know Peter gave up a lucrative cabinet position with the new government to pursue a film career ? They're talking about making him Minister of Culture" Michelle continued. She didn't feel shy when she knew Peter was backing her up.

The old producer peered curiously at Michelle. "You were on Channel 8 with that earthquake business, weren't you ?" he asked. Michelle nodded.

"David told me about you." Cal leaned forward and looked more closely at Michelle.

Peter smiled at her over Cal's shoulder and blew a quick kiss with his full lips. Michelle felt encouraged suddenly, and a little giddy. She smiled at Cal and asked "Does your wife know you're sitting next to a girl who thinks you're very sexy ?"

Peter smiled broadly. Cal glanced around the table to see if anyone else had heard but apparently they had not. The wives talked to the wives and Dan and Bob compared notes on last week's box office receipts.

Heidi wanted to join in the conversation. "Michelle, you looked so great in that tennis court scene."

"Fantastic," Peter agreed, giving Heidi a warm smile. "Michelle here is a world class tennis player." Peter said loudly.

"You play tennis ?" Cal said. He pictured Michelle on the tennis court, serving. "You should join us at my place some Sunday," Cal offered.

His knee had been acting up lately, but he still played sometimes. Looking at Michelle, he felt like playing a few sets.

Michelle smiled and said, "I'd love to, Cal," then "will you call me ?"

Peter gazed at her with an expression she recognized as admiration. Michelle asked Cal for his pen and she wrote her phone number for him. He pocketed it with a sly smile.

...

Josh walked out of the tent to the place where he'd last seen his uncle with Stacey Wilder but there was no sign of them. He couldn't see the attendant or any people in the huge parking lot. Josh began to walk past rows of cars towards the far end of the lot, wondering if David had gone home with Stacey, when he heard his name being called.

David came running towards Josh. "You still have her purse ?" he asked, out of breath. As Josh handed the small brocade purse to David, he spotted Stacey leaning against the wall of the old theater. As the two men hurried towards her, Josh could see Stacey was struggling for breath, a wheezing rattling sound came from her throat.

"I need... my inhaler," Stacey spoke in a broken wheeze. Her face was white and streaked with tears and smeared make-up. David opened the purse and took out a small canister with an aerosol dispenser attached. Stacey held the thing in front of her mouth and squirted it, inhaling the medicine.

"Asthma ?" Josh asked David. He nodded and spoke in a low voice though there was no one else around.

"I didn't know it was this bad."

Stacey sniffed loudly and breathed in and out carefully. She leaned against the concrete wall of the old theater and looked up at the narrow strip of night sky visible between the buildings. Neon signs on Hollywood Boulevard splashed color into the darkness. She wished suddenly that she were somewhere else, anywhere that she could lie down, preferably on soft grass. Stacey knew how perfect it would be to lie down on some fresh green grass. How tired she felt and choked with too many people and too much talk and too much to drink. If she could just lie down and have a glass of water and sleep, she thought. Then she dreamed she was lying beside a stream wearing a flowing dress like a Greek toga, white and soft. David was with her but he wasn't talking or asking for anything. He was just relaxing and playing music on a wooden flute. Above the flute, she saw a formation of sparkling silver fish swimming through the air as smoothly as if they were in water but they swam against the sky. She was amazed at their beauty and she then saw more fish-- yellow, silver and pink with lovely symmetrical markings like butterflies cavorting in unison, reflecting light, iridescent and buoyant, swimming in the air as if it were liquid.

"Try to hold her will you !" Josh put Stacey's arm around his neck and shouldered her weight to keep her from falling. She was slowly sinking to the ground.

David grabbed her other arm and managed to hold her upright. "Let's get her to your car," he told Josh. " I came in Donna's car tonight so you'll have to drive."

"Where does she live ?" Josh asked. The two men were just able to keep Stacey stumbling forward.

"Not far," David said, "a few blocks above Sunset."

"Come swimming with me, David," Stacey said. Her eyes were closed and her head wobbled on her neck. "Let's go for a swim, okay ?"

"Just keep walking, Stace, we'll get there," David spoke to her as if to a child or an animal. Josh began to feel sorry--for Stacey and David, but mostly for himself.

Meanwhile, Michelle was telling Donna about what happened to March and how sad she felt about her passing. "You poor thing" Donna felt very protective of Michelle. Her own daughter, Monica, had found a job and moved to Washington D. C. two years before, so Donna knew something about the hazards a girl could face when she was single and far from home.

Peter was telling Cal about an idea he had for a television show that involved families who trade their children. "Like we find an adolescent who can't stand his parents, right, then we find another family to adopt him. He says goodbye to his birth parents, and hello to his new parents who maybe have a different lifestyle that suits him better. The audience votes on what family he goes to.

"Not bad," Cal said, "might hit the right demographic. What else have you got ?"

"Mother Knows Best." Peter spoke rapidly to Cal, "that's the title. Every week we find a son or daughter whose mother has never revealed the name of their father."

"What's the payoff ?" Cal asked.

"We pay the mother fifty thousand to bring in the actual father, we administer DNA tests, and he meets his son or daughter for the first time on the show, with live audience of course."

"That could work," Cal seemed interested. "We'd need to develop it."

"How about Father Knows Better ?" Peter flashed a smile at Michelle and added "Or...who's your daddy?"

Cal had recently produced his first reality show and it was doing much better than he'd expected on a budget less than half what he paid the writers on "Slight Problem" a weekly sit com that was probably going to be dumped next season.

"And Michelle here would make a perfect hostess," Peter continued, his delivery fast and sincere. "With Michelle appearing every week, the demographic would skew younger and we could involve rap and hip hop artists." Michelle met Cal's eyes and searched for the spark she knew was there.

"I know I'd love to see this happen, Cal." She opened her eyes wider, questioning.

"We could have a pilot for you by next month," Peter told the producer.

"What kind of budget are we talking about ?" Cal asked Peter, and Michelle, knowing she was no longer needed, looked around to see if Josh might be returning, but there was no sign of him.

Peter and Cal were talking numbers and Donna was talking to Heidi and seemed to have forgotten about her husband so Michelle understood that no one was concerned about Josh and David's absence. It must be part of the job, she thought, maybe Josh had to help his uncle with a client or something. She didn't feel lonely anymore because Donna was so nice and Peter had become her close friend in the course of the evening. Michelle drank another glass of wine, feeling drowsy and content.

Cal was the first to get up from the table and the others followed. "I'm going to call you," the producer said in Michelle's ear as he kissed her goodbye.

Michelle smiled warmly and said nothing. After she kissed Bob and his wife and promised Dan and Heidi she'd stay in touch and turned to say goodbye to Donna, Michelle realized she had no way to get home.

"Do you need a ride, honey ?" Donna seemed to read her mind, but Peter spoke up immediately.

"No problem, I'll take her, we live just a few blocks from each other."

"Are you sure? Why don't you come with me ?" Donna said, she didn't know this boy Peter, he seemed to be drinking heavily and she wanted to make sure Michelle got home safely.

"Thanks anyway Donna, but Peter lives practically next door to me, it's not out of the way at all."

"Are you sure ?"

"No problem." Michelle told Donna again how glad she was that they'd met and they made a plan to have lunch together soon.

Walking out into the parking lot, Peter took Michelle's hand and said "Of all the women I've met in Hollywood, you are the most fabulous." He led her to his car, a rented BMW convertible, and, even though the night was chilly, he left the top down and they drove up towards the Hollywood hills where he was house-sitting in his aunt's house while she was away in London.

CHAPTER TWENTY - NINE

Nora stayed up late drinking and talking with Jennifer and Floyd around the yellow Formica table. Jennifer was in a celebratory mood and Nora was in no hurry. Though it was close to midnight, Nora didn't want to think about her next move; she was tired of planning and worrying. Sometimes it's better to let things float, she thought; take the path of least resistance.

"When did you move in next door here, Nora?" Floyd's slow deep voice was somehow reassuring. He had a way of really looking at you when he talked. He drank only water.

"Almost two years ago." Nora usually hated answering personal questions but Floyd seemed genuinely interested.

After two tall glasses of vodka-laced orange juice, Nora felt relaxed and talkative. She noticed that when she drank she always became much friendlier. Luckily, Nora reflected, I'm not a habit-forming kind of person or addictive personality; I'm not compulsive like Pam.

Jennifer discovered a second full bottle of vodka in March's freezer and she poured some more of the clear syrupy liquid into Nora's glass.

Jennifer told Floyd "Nora helped us when we first came here."

"I didn't do anything," Nora protested modestly.

"You made a difference," Floyd said in his quiet emphatic way. He looked directly at Nora for several seconds like he was thinking and considering.

As Nora eyed Floyd's wide-cuffed blue jeans and his worn silver and turquoise belt buckle she tried to remember if she'd ever actually talked with a Native American before. There was something about Floyd--his deliberate way of listening and watching and moving -- that inspired confidence. He stays real, Nora thought, he keeps things real.

"Where did you grow up, Floyd?" Nora wondered if he lived on a reservation but it seemed somehow rude to ask that specifically. She couldn't tell how old Floyd was; his tan face was smooth and his hair was black but he had a thick weathered body. She noticed deep scars on his hands and forehead. Maybe he's not a Christian Indian, she thought, maybe he worships coyotes or peyote or something.

"I was born in Montana but my dad died when we were young so my mother moved us to New Mexico," Floyd answered. "We used to go back in the summer and stay with my grandmother and ride ponies. That's beautiful country up in the north," he added.

When Floyd said Montana, Nora immediately thought of Dan. We finished the script, she reminded herself, allowing a palpable wave of satisfaction and relief to settle into her shoulders and arms and neck. After so much time spent working on it, the completed screenplay was a fact she had not yet had time to consider, to absorb. The characters in the screenplay populated her memory like people she had known in the past. Dan was mixed into the story too, like a character; but when she thought of Dan she remembered his taut shoulders, his earnest voice.

"Why don't you sleep here tonight Nora?" Jennifer asked. "I know you want to move out of Ginger's house as soon as possible. You could start moving your things in the morning when she goes to work. The living room is all yours."

Jennifer pointed at March's wide overstuffed couch which, to Nora, who had slept but a few hours the night before, looked very inviting. She was beginning to have second thoughts about driving all the way to Pam's house in the dark. She knew people who had been arrested and jailed for drunk driving. Before Nora made up her mind to accept Jennifer's invitation, the telephone rang.

Jennifer answered the phone, then listened for a minute or two before she told the others. "Michelle wants to know if we can come up to her friend's place in the Hollywood hills."

"You mean Josh?"

"No, she's not with Josh," Jennifer explained to Floyd. "She's with someone else--Josh left her at the party. She says we should definitely come."

"Josh went off and left Michelle ?" Floyd sounded disgusted, "We'd better go get her."

Nora said they should take her car. They couldn't take Floyd's pickup because they wouldn't all fit in the cab, so Jennifer drove because she had the directions in her head and Nora didn't want to. It wasn't long before the car turned off Highland Boulevard above Hollywood and headed uphill on a very narrow winding street crowded with parked cars.

"Is this Alta View Terrace?" Nora wasn't familiar with the neighborhood but Jennifer was an excellent driver and seemed to know where she was going. Floyd sat in the back seat, relaxed and silent. The BMW pulled up in front of a long stucco house with a tiled roof that had no windows facing the street. A hanging lamp illuminated tall carved doors in an arched entry.

Jennifer pounded on the door and called "Michelle!" but then Nora pushed a doorbell and they could hear an electric chime sound inside the house.

As Nora, Floyd and Jennifer stood waiting in front of the tall double doors they saw no sign of movement on the narrow street nor did they hear any sound except for the wind rustling the tall eucalyptus and cypress trees that swayed between the dark houses. When the door opened, Jennifer saw at once that Michelle was having a good time.

"Come in everybody." Michelle's voice was excited. "Nora, you came too --that's great!" Jennifer could tell that Michelle was happy to see her friends, and her mood was contagious. When Michelle led the visitors into a large living room, Jennifer couldn't help but stop and stare out the wide arched windows that framed a night-time view of Los Angeles. The city unfolded below like a black velvet cape woven with ribbons of multi-colored lights from the foothills of Hollywood to the edge of the vast sparkling horizon.

Peter Revel reminded Jennifer of someone, maybe an actor, she thought. He was so pale and smooth and stiff, like he was molded of chocolate, she thought, white chocolate. He greeted each of Michelle's friends with a polite welcoming smile.

Floyd told him "Thanks for watching out for Michelle here."

Peter and Michelle exchanged a quick glance and with a little bow Peter replied, "It's my pleasure, Floyd."

Though it was well after midnight, it seemed to Jennifer that the evening was just beginning. They made themselves comfortable near a large stone fireplace and Peter asked them if they wanted to try some ecstasy he had brought from London.

"It's absolutely pure; the best there is," he said, "Brand X."

"I didn't want to take it without you guys" Michelle said, looking at Floyd and Jennifer, who personally felt gratified at the invitation .

Michelle thought Nora would say no but she just shrugged and said "why not?"

Peter handed small orange pills to each of his guests. It took just a second to swallow them.

"Why do the lights blink on and off" Jennifer was standing in front of the windows looking out at the city. Peter explained that it was an optical illusion caused by waves of hot air rising from the ground over long distances. He stood beside her and pointed out the lights of Hollywood Boulevard extending from east to the left and west to the right as far as they could see.

Michelle and Peter opened a bottle of champagne because they said they were celebrating. Peter said something about a pilot project and Jennifer heard Nora asking him questions about it. Then Nora said she was celebrating something too.

Floyd followed Jennifer through French doors onto a balcony that opened to a sloping hillside dotted with tall trees. In the dark distance below, an immense city blinked and buzzed, tied with moving ribbons of lights. She slipped her arm around Floyd's waist and pressed against him as they gazed at the lights of Los Angeles and smelled the pungent resin of Eucalyptus trees in the night air. Laughter echoing inside the house wafted through the open doors.

"Look at all those lights," Floyd said. They stood together looking, not talking for a while. "When was the last time we got any sleep?" he asked Jennifer in his matter-of-fact voice.

"I don't know but I don't feel tired at all, do you?"

"I wouldn't mind getting some sleep," Floyd said.

Jennifer leaned against the side of the balcony as she felt something like a wave of seasickness that stopped short of nausea and went straight to the brain. Her equilibrium was affected, her knees went wobbly and her stomach tightened. She felt a lump in her throat like excitement and anticipation that rose on its own, unbidden by events. Jennifer wanted to find a place to sit down, or better, a soft place to recline.

"Let's go back inside," Floyd said, his hands on her shoulders.

In the semi-darkness of the living room they found their friends absorbed in an animated discussion. Jennifer gathered pillows and placed them in front of the fireplace. Floyd sat on the floor with his knees open and his ankles crossed as he stared at the flames burning in the wide hearth.

Michelle had become unusually talkative. From across the wide room, Jennifer heard her friend's rising and falling voice as pure sound without parsing the individual word meanings. Michelle laughed frequently and was telling Nora and Peter about something someone said to her. Jennifer could almost hum the tune of her friend's description. It began with a confiding introduction, built to an emphatic revelation and culminated in an invitation to share Michelle's point of view. Jennifer stretched out on the carpet in the large living room and considered her surroundings. She observed how the flames of the fire and the bright lights of the city seen through the tall glass doors enlivened the semi-darkness of the rectangular room.

Jennifer watched Peter watching Michelle. His talking was high-pitched and long-winded. He replied and responded to her; he reiterated and was reminded. Jennifer knew all this without hearing his words. Voices had become melody for her and she lay and listened to the burning firewood's crackling rhythms rising and falling behind the conversation.

Nora had never seen Michelle talk so much. She had a way of saying something very obvious as though she'd just discovered it. Peter was quick and amusing. He told Nora about a play he'd seen in London the week before. The way he imitated Scottish accents and succinctly described the action in his sly way made Nora laugh. She leaned back in a soft armchair and when she closed her eyes she questioned the stability of her back against the soft permeability of the upholstery, which seemed to be constructed of a pliable too-elastic material. The chair felt both insubstantial and all-encompassing. Peter said the house had the original wood paneling and light fixtures from 1920 when it was built by a silent film star.

Nora felt a sudden wave of affection for her friends, especially Jennifer and Floyd who were sprawled on cushions near the wide stone fireplace, their faces gilded by the flames. A lump rose in her throat, which was all the unexpressed words she might use to say what she felt. They were all extraordinary, Nora thought, each young woman tender and lovable and the men open-minded and understanding. Her eyes misted over when she looked at Michelle who was leaning against Peter on the sofa. He had his arm draped over her shoulders. She hoped they would always be together. They were so vulnerable yet willing to trust each other and their hair shone in the firelight. Nora thought how like fur hair is, and she watched Jennifer and Floyd recline and stretch and arrange themselves comfortably like dogs in front of the fire. The thought of how like dogs they looked made her laugh and Peter asked her what she was laughing at and she said Jennifer and Floyd are curled up like two dogs by the fire and Peter asked spaniels ? and Nora said maybe Labradors and Michelle exclaimed ay Chihuahuas in a chirpy Mexican accent that made everyone laugh again.

Nora's chair took on the warm pliable consistency of chewing gum. She half-rose from the seat but was pulled back. She felt vaguely alarmed but knew that someone would help her if she needed to get up. Michelle and Peter continued giggling and talking for a long while, and when Nora tried to stand up and realized she was stuck in the chair, she leaned back and admired the ceiling which was not square but curved at the corners in an interesting and unusual pattern.

Peter knew a club just a few minutes away where a fantastic band was appearing for just one night, tonight. It was his intention to take Michelle there and Michelle wanted Jennifer to go but Floyd wanted to stay by the fire so he said why don't you all go and I'll wait here until you get back. Jennifer said she wanted to stay with Floyd.

"Please come," Michelle said, "you have to come with us, Nora."

Jennifer watched Nora slowly shift to the edge of the low chair where she'd been sitting and hold on to the arm of the chair and carefully stand up, supporting herself with both hands. Then Nora took a deep breath, opened the smooth black leather handbag she always carried and removed a gold compact and a lipstick. As the others talked, Jennifer watched how Nora stared at her face in the little round mirror and slowly applied very red lipstick to her lips, first the top, then the bottom. Nora's pale face and large eyes came to life in the firelight, suddenly vivid and defined.

Michelle knelt on the floor and gave Jennifer a big hug goodbye and she hugged Floyd too and they all, kneeling, hugged each other. "I love you guys," Michelle told them and they told her that they, both of them, loved her too.

"What about me?" pouted Peter and he was so slim and light-colored and sweet-smelling when he turned to Nora with a mock-abandoned expression on his mock-sad face that she embraced him as they stood watching the others and said "I love you, Peter," with an ironic exaggerated emphasis on the "I." Though her tone was insincere, Nora felt she was telling the truth.

…

As she and Michelle danced together on a platform below the blasting speakers, Nora tried out new movements, twisting her wrists high in the air and curving her neck from right to left. Michelle seldom looked at anyone as she involved herself exclusively with moving to the music. Nora wondered how long they'd been dancing. She felt the music like a buoyant wave rise from her ankles to the base of her spine, loosening her shoulders and arms. The white tennis dress seemed to glow in the dark and Michelle was damp with sweat like she'd just played two sets. Peter had disappeared but she felt certain that he was nearby. He had her jacket and her handbag, she realized suddenly with a fugitive jolt of paranoia. But there was something about Peter that inspired confidence; she knew he could be trusted.

Nora was aware that the drug had taken hold. The nausea had passed but she was suffering from what seemed to be an intensified sensitivity to people. A beefy sweating man wearing gold chains resting on thick chest hair actually caused her to involuntarily shudder when he brushed against her arm. The pressing heat of bodies jammed into a small space was overwhelming. Nora concentrated on finding new movements to dance with force and significance, abandoning herself entirely to the music.

Without any introduction, a boy in his early twenties began dancing with Nora. He seemed very young, he still had pimples for heavens sake, she noticed, and wore the bunched and clumped hairstyle that on some men looked casually tousled and on others looked clownishly tasseled. He said nothing to her, simply began dancing opposite her and smiled a greeting. Peter had returned and was dancing with Michelle so Nora smiled back at the boy who was eyeing her body as though transfixed. Nora attempted to meet his eyes but they never again rose above her neck.

The band members were English but lead singer Eddie Prance sang "Are we to be our own gods?" in an accent that sounded American.

Nora found herself singing along with the crowd to the line "you were my cash cow, but I've lost you now." At least, that's what she thought they were saying. Then, "are we to be our own gods, own gods, own gods? Are we to be exceptional?"

On the word "exceptional," as the last syllable spun out allllllllllll, over a prolonged buzzing guitar note, Peter Revel took Nora by the hand and led her over to an open space where Michelle was twirling like a dervish. He wrapped his left arm around Nora's waist and pulled Michelle in with his right and the three of them linked arms in a loose circle as Eddie wailed "you were my sacred cow, but I've got you now."

Peter, laughing and dancing, half-sang, half-spoke to both of the women: "I've got you now." Michelle's soft hand touched Nora's face and neck and Peter, who was a graceful dancer, kissed her somewhere near her ear. All three dancers were linked to the music as it reached an all-encompassing throbbing crescendo of feedback and percussion behind the keening preening voice of Eddie Prance, a skinny red-haired boy with crooked teeth and muscular legs. Nora admired his costume: shiny black skin-tight trousers and a ragged tuxedo shirt open at the throat and knotted at the waist.

"Isn't Eddie fabulous?" Peter shouted to be heard and Nora agreed that he was.

"He absolutely rules."

Nora felt an overwhelming affection and gratitude for Eddie Prance. For his skill and courage in singing his songs and working so hard on behalf of others because he obviously had important insights into life that illuminated and in fact paralleled her own personal beliefs. She also felt grateful to Peter for bringing her to hear Eddie because she had the feeling that tonight many problems that had been hovering over her for months might be resolved.

Eddie Prance had an expressive face with large green pink-rimmed eyes and damp blotchy skin. Nora couldn't help but stare at him when the band took a break and he climbed down from the stage. Peter hurried over to greet the musicians and Nora had the opportunity to tell Eddie what she thought of his music.

She heard herself saying "Your songs are wonderful. I'm so glad I came here tonight," in a voice she hardly recognized as her own.

Eddie was so hot and sweaty from performing that Nora felt like she was standing next to an electric heater. He reminded her of a basketball player interviewed coming off the court at half time. His nostrils and pupils looked dilated and his hair was soaking wet.

"Why don't you come up to the house later?" Peter invited Eddie, who said thanks man, maybe, and headed into a back room.

"Eddie said he might come over later," Peter told Michelle when they sat down at a table near the wall.

"He's great," she said.

"I've known him for a long time," Peter told her.

When the three club-goers did finally return to the house on Alta View Drive they found Jennifer and Floyd asleep in front of the fire.

Michelle yawned. "I'm so tired," she said, looking at Peter.

"In that case," said Peter, "we must all go to bed." He looked at Nora and Michelle with such an explicitly yearning expression on his smooth face that Nora, at least, thought his meaning was clear.

"Come with me," he said, and led the two women upstairs. Nora and Michelle followed Peter into a spacious carpeted bedroom. The bed faced two tall windows and a door opened from the far wall onto a bathroom. Peter pulled the heavy silk drapes closed and turned on a small lamp.

"The bathroom is that way," he indicated to Nora in the voice of a solicitous host and Michelle kicked off her shoes and bounced onto the large king-size bed.

"I'm sleeping here." Michelle said. "Is this your aunt's room?"

"Yes," Peter said, "my room is across the hall."

"I want to sleep here" Michelle repeated, in her little-girl voice, and proceeded to unzip her dress, pull it over her head, place it on a chair and get under the covers.

As Nora locked the door of the bathroom she caught a glimpse of Peter unbuttoning his white shirt and following Michelle into bed. The expanse of shiny black porcelain tile and mirrors was slightly intimidating but she was determined to have a shower. She longed to feel hot water on her shoulders and back. Nora took her time finding soap and towels and after covering her hair carefully to keep it dry, she stood under the shower for a good long time.

When Nora finished washing she wrapped herself in a towel and opened the bathroom door a few inches to survey the pitch-dark bedroom. She could make out two motionless bodies lying under the covers on one side of the oversized white bed.

With the drapes pulled, the only light was a blue-white glow through the thin fabric. It appeared to Nora that there was a wide expanse of bed that was lying unused, a space more than wide enough for her to fit in. She had a sense that dawn was fast approaching and this might be her last chance to sleep a few hours before it was necessary to begin a new day.

As Nora cautiously slipped under the covers she heard the regular sounds of Michelle snoring; apparently she had fallen asleep very quickly. Nora lay silent and motionless on her back and listened. She could hear a clock ticking, the distant hum of far away traffic and, close by, the sound of another body breathing. She strained to hear--was Peter awake ?

"Where are you from, Peter?" she whispered very softly into the darkness, as though they had just been introduced.

"I was born in Brno" Peter replied, "in Bohemia, where my parents were vacationing." He continued in a low confiding tone, "My father was Rumanian but his mother was Russian and my mother's mother was Czech and her father was a star of the Moscow ballet. Somehow, they all ran away to London. My father has ties to the most powerful men in Bucharest and Moscow. He's involved in international finance and filmmaking. He expects me to follow in his footsteps."

"Oh," said Nora.

"But let's not waste time with banal chit-chat," Peter said, deftly sliding out of his side of the bed and walking around and slipping under the covers on Nora's side. He barely jostled the wide mattress and Michelle's even breathing continued without a break. Nora nudged Michelle very very carefully away from the center of the bed towards the other side. Peter, on her right, smelled of Patchouli and wine. He was heavier than she would have guessed and the mattress sagged under his weight, causing her to roll closer to him.

"Tell me something about you," he spoke softly in Nora's ear.

"I'm new to this city," she told him. "I'm not at home here, my parents are dead. I belong in an older city where occasionally friends and acquaintances greet me when we meet on the streets. I have no family, only beloved friends. My car is getting old, and I need to find a new place to live alone. I just finished writing a screenplay for a film, a love story, and I want to see it produced. I miss snow."

As Nora spoke, Peter gently stroked her hair and his hand slowly strayed to her shoulders. "Are you involved with anyone?"

"You mean am I married or...?"

"Are you in love with anyone?" he asked. His hand found her hand and he rubbed it gently against his cheek.

Nora hesitated before answering. "I was, but now, I don't know."

"That won't do," Peter said. "Tell me the truth, please."

"No," she said, then "I don't know. Tell me more about you."

"I'm sick of talking about myself," Peter said.

"Tell me a story then," Nora requested.

Peter moved closer to her and let his hand rest carelessly on her thigh.

"In the royal courts of ancient Japan," he began, "the young unmarried ladies of the court lived in spacious quarters divided by delicate paper screens. At night they slept under silk quilts on woven mats on the floors of wooden pavilions overlooking exquisite gardens. Their heads rested on quaint porcelain pillows of elaborate design and one lady, whose name in Japanese means Laughing Cloud, dreamt always of her lover, Kenji.

"What does Kenji mean in Japanese?" Nora asked.

"I can't remember" Peter said. "Maybe Bamboo Sprout ?"

"Please continue," Nora said.

"Laughing Cloud could not sleep at night wondering about Kenji and whether he might contrive to sneak into her room and lie with her in her silken bed. You see, if he could manage to enter the palace and find her bed without waking the guards he could do anything he wanted with her."

"Really?" Nora said, "anything?" Peter shifted his arms and embraced her under the covers.

"As long as they were quiet and didn't wake anyone else--those were the rules. Possibly Kenji means Stout Cabbage Stalk. Anyway, late one night, as Laughing Cloud, or Leelee in Japanese, lay awake in her bed, she heard a faint rustling sound as the paper screen parted and she saw a male figure tiptoe towards her in the silver moonlight. It was so dark she couldn't see his face."

Nora waited for Peter to continue. "And then what happened ?" she asked.

Peter abruptly got out of bed and Nora heard the bathroom door open and close.

She felt Michelle stir and heard a choked interruption in her snoring. Nora closed her eyes and stopped breathing for a while. She lay in bed on her back without moving. When she finally took in air through her nose she held it for a second without moving a muscle then let it out noiselessly. She wondered how long she could remain utterly still, straining to hear the faintest sound. Nora calculated that she could affect the quality of the darkness by creating her own absolute stillness, a stillness so formidable and dense that it would envelope the entire room.

"Wha happen ?" Michelle started and slurred and veered back into sleep. Nora didn't answer, she waited for the girl's voice to retreat and then she heard soft snoring again and she allowed herself to breathe.

When she heard him open the bathroom door she didn't move a muscle. Nora's large eyes, wide open, saw only a shadow move in front of the draped windows. He uncovered her and still she didn't move or take a breath. His movements were slow and skillfully deliberate, soundless and certain, as though he could see Nora's pale body perfectly in the dark. Nora welcomed him like a guest into the darkness she had carefully guarded and circumscribed.

In the end, of course, they did wake Michelle, and she politely moved to the edge of the bed. Michelle was too tired to stay awake long enough to get involved, so she turned over and went back to sleep before her friends even thought of sleep. Sometime in the early dawn, Nora thought she heard Michelle whisper "Bamboo Sprout" in Peter's ear but she knew she must have imagined it.

CHAPTER THIRTY

J ennifer told Nora the next morning that she didn't want Floyd to leave town without seeing the La Brea tar pits, so Nora found herself driving through Beverly Hills down Wilshire Boulevard towards a line of towering palm trees planted in a precise row. Floyd and Jennifer whispered in the backseat as the L.A. County art museum came into view. Nora drove around the corner to park where the curved tusks of extinct mastodons could be seen behind the greenery on the landscaped grounds.

Jennifer was sure that seeing the tar pit with its life-size replicas of prehistoric animals and smelling the pungent oily aroma would be something Floyd would always remember. Jennifer already felt sad that Floyd was leaving; she wanted to prolong his visit as long as possible.

"Do you smell it ?" Jennifer's voice was inflected with a note of enthusiasm that Nora couldn't fathom.   Floyd nodded and squeezed Jennifer's hand as she hurried toward the fenced display and pointed out the animals and told Floyd "See, they thought it was water and they came here to drink."

Nora and Michelle hung back as Floyd and Jennifer peered through the chain link fence surrounding the largest tar pit. The stunted trees growing near the fence gave little shade and Nora felt tired and depleted in the glaring sunshine. She worried that she'd had no opportunity to apply sunscreen to her face in the hurried morning. She sat down beside Michelle on a bench facing the oily pond that looked roughly the size of an Olympic swimming pool, though it was actually a hole. The mid-day temperature felt like it was in the 90's. Nora wished she had remembered to keep a hat in her car.

Michelle hoped Jennifer didn't want to spend too long at the tar pits. She was eager to get home and check to see if Josh had called to explain his behavior last night. Michelle knew that Josh was the kind of person who worried all the time about what other people thought of him. Leaving his seat empty at Cal Portnoy's table was not something he would have planned to do. Michelle tried to think of what could have happened to Josh, why he would have abandoned her, but the Ecstasy had left her brain feeling tired and lazy; she found she couldn't conjure up even one possibility. Still, she couldn't help but feel concerned about Josh--he was always so tense and nervous. Michelle knew that if she involved herself in Josh's life she could help him and possibly make him see that worrying about what other people thought all the time was stupid. Because she was able to understand so clearly what Josh wanted and needed she realized a feeling of deep unfathomable affection for him. Michelle gathered her thick hair to pillow her head against the back of the wooden bench. She closed her eyes and leaned back, feeling the hot sun warm her face and neck and bare arms.

Floyd grasped the tall metal fence and gave it a shake with both hands. The sturdy woven steel was already heating up .

"Guess they don't want these critters to escape," he said to Jennifer and she rewarded his effort with a faint attempt at a laugh. Floyd could see how upset she was about him leaving but he knew there was no way he could stay in this city. He never could understand why March had stayed here all this time when she could have moved to New Mexico.

"Hey," Floyd saw some tears in Jennifer's eyes. "Now, don't you start that.

So she stared through the fence at the big mastodons with their smaller babies until curved white tusks became circles and then hoops and then white wheels rolling slowly into the oozing oily blackness of the tar. Jennifer saw, through her tears, the white wheels become bubbles of air and then children's balloons and finally clouds, amorphous against the blue sky.

"I'm glad you came when you did Floyd" Jennifer felt there were things she just had to tell him. "I'm really, you know, grateful."

Floyd put his arm around Jennifer's waist. Her fingers were hooked onto the metal links of the fence as she stood looking at the mastodons. He stood next to her and spoke softly into her ear. "Jenny, I'm the one who's grateful to you for helping me say goodbye to my sister. You were a big help to me."

"You promise to come back and visit me?" Jennifer was almost afraid to look at him for fear she'd start crying again.

"I'm not one to move around too much, you know. My work keeps me pretty busy. But don't forget, next spring when the cactus is in bloom we'll go out to the desert and scatter March's ashes."

Spring seemed very far away to Jennifer. "Oh Floyd," she said, though she wanted to say more, that's all she could come up with.

Once she was back in the house on Westborne Street, Michelle hurried to check the telephone messages. Josh had called at eight in the morning and said he needed to talk to her immediately and Peter left a message saying he had a meeting scheduled with Cal Portnoy for next Tuesday.

"Let's plan on getting together soon, Michelle" Peter's Russian British voice sounded excited; Michelle could hear the eagerness in it.

"Who's Cal Portnoy?" Jennifer asked. She walked into the kitchen as Michelle was listening to the recorded messages.

"He's a producer I met..." Michelle paused to calculate exactly when. "Last night," she concluded, though it seemed like two or three nights might have passed.

"Is he going to give you a job?" Jennifer asked.

"See, Josh wanted me to meet him but then Josh left, so Peter started talking to Cal and he had some ideas that Cal liked."

"What kind of ideas?" Jennifer asked.

"I forget exactly" Michelle tried to recall. "Something about a TV show about real people, you know, like reality."

"And you would be in it?"

"Peter said I could be like the hostess. You know, like I would say hello and goodbye to the real people who would come on the show--and they would be different each time but I'd be on every time."

Jennifer stared at the counter and didn't say anything. Michelle put her arm around her friend and nudged her into a chair.

"You can be on the show too! If Cal had met you he would want you for sure. We could do it together. It would be better with the two of us--I know Peter will want you to do it too."

Jennifer had tears in her eyes. "Michelle, Floyd has to leave pretty soon."

Floyd came out of the bedroom wearing a clean plaid shirt with his hair slicked back wet from the shower. Jennifer stood up and watched as Floyd took the cover off Leo's cage.

"Oh, I almost forgot about Leo," Jennifer looked sorry.

The parrot squawked and complained. Jennifer took his empty water dish into the kitchen to fill it and found a few cashews left in the bag.

"We'll have to buy some bird food," she said to Michelle.

"You'll look after this old bird now, won't you?" Floyd said. "He needs to be fed and watered every day."

Jennifer looked like she might cry so Michelle said "Don't worry, I promise we'll take care of Leo."

"I gotta go now." Floyd said simply.

Michelle kissed Floyd goodbye and waited in the living room while Jennifer walked outside with him. Michelle stood at the window and watched Floyd throw some bundles into the back of his old green pick-up. He stood talking with Jennifer for a long time and Michelle watched her friend brush away tears. Then Jennifer stood and watched Floyd drive away but she didn't come back into the house.

Michelle looked through her purse and found the business card Peter had given her. She examined it carefully. Piotyr Benivetscu Revelinsky was written in an embossed black script. Underneath this name was written "director" and under that "metteur en scene" and then another line printed in a strange alphabet unknown to her.

As Michelle was about to dial Peter's number the phone rang and the gruff voice of Cal Portnoy was on the other end.

"Is this Michelle ?" he asked.

"Yes, it's me--hi Cal," Michelle responded.

"So," Cal said, "how 'bout some tennis next Sunday?"

"That would be nice," Michelle said. "Can my girlfriend come too ?"

"Sure," Cal said, "it's casual--a bunch of people get together here at my place on Sundays; knock the ball around a little bit."

Michelle chatted with Cal for a few seconds and then mentioned..."We don't really have a car right now."

"I'll send a driver for you around eleven," Cal replied. He was, Michelle thought, a man who knew how to solve problems.

Jennifer didn't feel like going back into the house after Floyd drove away. She walked around to the back yard and sat down near the fire pit which was now a circle of charred wood and papery ashes. With Floyd gone, Jennifer felt for the first time that March was really dead.   But somehow the grief of death, the finality, was so very different than the feelings she had about Floyd leaving. She knew she could begin to forget March like she might forget a house she'd lived in or a place she visited. March was fast becoming a solemn quiet memory untouched by pain or regret.   March, dead, was solid and certain.   But with Floyd, whenever she thought of him there would be a question. This was something worse, this uncertainty-- Jennifer could feel it happening already. She would be wondering what he was doing and whether he would come back and if he wanted to see her and how much and when. She thought the prospect of this uncertainty might be more painful than death.

Jennifer wondered what it was about Floyd that made her care about him so much. She had never met anyone like him; she had no one to compare him to. She might meet a hundred men in Los Angeles who would all be somehow similar to each other but not one would be like Floyd because men like Floyd couldn't live in this city, she knew that at the same time as she knew she loved Los Angeles.

As she searched for her key at the front door of the house on Westborne Street, Nora noticed that the Volvo wasn't parked in the driveway, so she figured she had about three hours before Ginger was likely to return home. When Nora entered the kitchen she saw a fresh loaf of bread and a bouquet of flowers decorating the kitchen table.

Through the window Nora saw Floyd in his cowboy hat come out of March's house (Jennifer's now, she thought) and she watched as Jennifer kissed him goodbye. As Floyd's pickup truck drove away, Nora became aware of a heavy bruised aching feeling in her legs and arms. She couldn't recall the last time she'd slept more than a few hours. She intended to pack some of her clothes and drive up to Pam's house, and explain her situation to her sister face to face when she got there. She needed to get packed and out of the house before Ginger returned home.

When she walked upstairs and looked around her small bedroom with its single rectangular back window and inadequate closet, Nora felt a wave of depression. She sat down on the rumpled unmade bed which now seemed to belong to someone else. Nora felt disassociated from the room now, as if she were walking into a stranger's bedroom. To recollect and evaluate the events of the past days and nights required more clarity and fortitude than Nora was able to summon, so she reminded herself of her simple agenda once again. I'll pack just the few things I'll need right away then come and move everything else later, she told herself in an effort to make her plan seem simple. It seemed so much easier to think only of the future and ignore everything that had gone before.

Nora opened her closet and stared at the clothing hanging on hangers inside. She made an effort to discriminate between those items she might want or need in the next few days and those that would be better left behind. She stood staring for several minutes, absently touching some jackets and blouses, then sat down on the bed. She took off her shoes and lay back on the pillow. After I rest for a minute I'll be able to work on this, she thought. I'll wake up and pack and leave, she told herself. I have plenty of time for a nap, then I'll pack my things and drive to Pam's house.

CHAPTER THIRTY - ONE

When the last of the late lunch crowd left Troppo, Dan finished counting up the afternoon receipts as he sat at the quiet bar waiting for Ginger. She had invited him to go with her to a benefit screening of a new David Lynch film and he was looking forward to this evening. Earlier in the day, Dan had some doubts about whether Ginger still wanted to go with him because of what had happened the previous morning, but when he telephoned her office she sounded very friendly and reasonable. Dan tried to offer an explanation but Ginger told him it wasn't necessary-- she knew they weren't a committed couple. Dan was relieved to know that Ginger understood how complicated his relationship with Nora was; how difficult to define.

Dan couldn't remember hearing the phrase "committed couple" before Ginger used it, but it sounded like something she probably said often in her therapy work. It was a conveniently neutral way to define a relationship without specifying gender or emotional issues or legal status--and it had a solid adult sound. Dan thought that a commitment was more or less the same as a promise, maybe a long-term promise or a permanent promise--maybe a kind of public promise. Not that Dan wanted to hide anything from anyone, but after all, Ginger understood that he and Nora were...and he had made no promises, no commitments, to either Ginger or Nora. Nora happened to be renting a room in Ginger's house but that didn't mean...Dan wasn't sure what it meant or didn't mean. He assumed that Ginger or Nora would let him know if there were boundaries that he should observe because he wasn't entirely certain about... Because women, Dan thought, were much better at setting boundaries than men were. Boundaries was another word Ginger used often, and Dan saw it was a way to describe people's behavior without making judgments, without saying that doing something was wrong, for example--or right. Boundaries implied a line or a barrier which separated what was allowed or expected from what was not allowed. Dan knew that these lines shifted all the time and he assumed it was up to the women involved to decide where the lines were located.

As the sun set in the west, Ginger could see slices of the vivid lavender and orange sky between the tall buildings as she drove down Wilshire Boulevard on her way to Troppo Restaurant. She had bought two tickets for this evening's event from her friend Marcie who worked with the Cambodian Mental Health program. Many of Ginger's friends attended this annual benefit, possibly even Tim, though she had no way of knowing whether he and his new wife...Ginger reminded herself not to focus on areas of anxiety which made her feel powerless but to assert her own beliefs and needs instead. She needed to work on being more assertive. The day had been especially stressful because a client had called right at four o'clock with a problem and she'd been obliged to see him at four-thirty, which left no time for her to go home before she went to pick up Dan. She looked in the rear-view mirror as she stopped at a red light: behind her slightly damp pink face, more cars were lined up as far as she could see. Ginger saw that she'd forgotten to put on lipstick and she reached into her bag to find the silver tube she carried with her.

Ginger noticed with surprise that her hand was shaking as she tried to apply color to her lips. Ruling out neurological causes, she diagnosed the problem as nervousness and determined that it was the prospect of going out with Dan that was causing this exceptional shakiness. She reminded herself again that her relationship with Dan was based on mutual respect and friendship, they were not actually dating in the usual sense of the word.

289

Going to bed together had not been premeditated and was not the primary focus of their relationship. He had never said that he...Ginger hit the accelerator to speed up to prevent someone in the right lane from cutting into her lane but she was one second too slow and a wide van pulled in front of her.

"Asshole!" she yelled, though the windows were all rolled up and she knew he couldn't hear, she shouted so loudly that her forehead began to throb.

Not that tonight was a real date--it was just an event that she went to every year and Dan happened to be a huge David Lynch fan so it was a way to thank him for his hospitality and...It seemed suddenly very difficult for Ginger to follow any single thought to its logical conclusion. She tried to focus on driving through the treacherous traffic and at the same time do some yoga breathing exercises. She checked her hair in the mirror and reminded herself again that she did not have an exclusive committed relationship with Dan.

...

When Michelle finally talked to Josh on the telephone, he said he wanted to come right over. " We need to talk. Let's go out to dinner tonight," he suggested, "just the two of us."

"I'm really tired, Josh" Michelle told him truthfully, reclining and extending her legs on the cushions of the soft couch. "I was out really late last night."

She could tell that Josh did not expect this reply to his invitation. She could hear his shallow breathing during a long pause while he considered what to say to her. Michelle felt vaguely sorry for his discomfort but knew that Josh deserved some punishment for what he had done the night before. In fact, something in his voice suggested that he expected punishment.

"Please Michelle, I need to see you so I can explain what happened." Josh maintained a convincingly repentant tone of voice. "My uncle David needed my help and he had...There was a problem with...Listen, please don't think I wanted to leave you at the... believe me, it was the last thing I wanted to do but I had to...I did come back, but everyone was gone by the time I..."

"What did you expect me to do, Josh, wait there alone?"

Michelle asked the question in her little-girl voice-- equal parts needy, wanton and helpless.

Josh's voice betrayed real fear now. "Please Michelle, don't think I did this on purpose. You know I would never..."

"I'm sorry Josh, but I just don't think I can see you tonight." After saying this, Michelle hesitated--should she hang up now and give him a good scare ? Might as well, she thought, and put down the receiver.

Jennifer, making a sandwich in the adjoining kitchen, heard the telephone ringing and ringing.

"Aren't you going to answer that?" She called to half-naked Michelle, who was wearing March's peach-colored Japanese kimono sprawled open in shameless negligence across the red and purple flowers of the faded couch.

"Will you get it?" her friend requested. "Tell him I can't come to the phone."

Jennifer picked up the phone and Josh said "Listen, Michelle, I'm really really sorry, okay? Tell me how I can make this up to you."

"You can buy me a new car and have it delivered to the house." Jennifer quickly replied in a stern voice, then stuck out her tongue and winked at Michelle.

"Jennifer, can I talk to Michelle please." Josh was whining. Jennifer hated whiners.

"I'm sorry, she can't come to the phone right now. Can I take a message ?"

"Tell her..." Jennifer heard Josh's long sigh and a pause like he was thinking. "Tell her I want her to call me. No wait, Jennifer...tell Michelle I really miss her okay?"

"Okay," Jennifer used her most businesslike voice "will do. Anything else ?"

After Josh hung up, Jennifer couldn't help but shake her head at his lack of imagination, his cowardice. She found it hard to believe that she had once thought he was someone who could help them. It was obvious to her now that Josh was a total waste of time. She related this insight to Michelle.

"No, he's not." her friend replied. "I can tell he really cares about me. I'll call him back later."

"You must be kidding." Jennifer flopped down on the end of the couch near Michelle's tan sprawled legs. She encircled her friend's tiny ankle with her thumb and forefinger. "What do you see in him?"

Michelle shrugged sleepily and tried to form the sentence that would answer this question but she was just too tired. "I don't know, he's sweet."

"I don't know what makes you think so," Jennifer said, giving her leg a shake, but Michelle's eyes were closed; she had already dozed off.

Jennifer went over and opened Leo's cage. "Come on out, bird brain, come on," she said, extending her wrist for the parrot to perch on.

Leo cocked his head one way then another. His talons were like a rope pulling on Jennifer's forearm. She turned off the television with her free arm and walked to the front window. Jennifer felt very restless; the house seemed stuffy and crowded. She was filled with a desire to go somewhere but realized they no longer had a car. She thought of March's old Ford Valiant totaled in the accident and towed off to a dump somewhere. Jennifer walked into the back yard with Leo on her arm, thinking she would light the lantern in the tent and sit for a while to consider and imagine.

Nora woke up when she heard the sound. She thought at first it was a truck motor idling, then she thought it was a group of people humming. She fell asleep again into her dream of boxes and sorting and a stairway she wanted to walk down so she could leave the house but all the steps were cluttered with cardboard boxes half-full of her belongings. The partially full cartons were waiting for one or two more things to be added before they could finally be closed and moved out of the way. As she attempted to make her way downstairs in the dream, Nora saw her one naked body fragment into a parade of many thighs and arms and feet--a series of consecutive poses corresponding to each step down the stairs. Nora woke up from the dream and thought of Duchamp's "Nude Descending a Staircase." She recalled the painting clearly-- the unnatural flesh tones, the multiple body parts delineated in sharp black angles, the animal-like expression on the triangle face.

Or was it faces ? She lay in the dark contemplating this image of her body fragmented into abstraction, irreparably mutable. Or was it Picasso, she questioned herself, who painted that ? A succession of movements of a particular velocity piled inside a square picture. She imagined a long strip of film, each frame containing the same photographically diminished body with its tiny increment of frozen movement. She saw flesh-colored replicas like shadows follow her body as it moved through rooms. She saw her most significant gestures instantly and subsequently abandoned. She saw the solid forms of herself disappear behind the flow of new movement and end in a still place where the body, she, stopped moving through the world and dissolved into it again.

Nora slid open the rectangular metal window in her bedroom to hear where the music was coming from--it was like a choir but without melody or measure, only harmony which rose and fell in volume. Nora put her shoes on and walked into the back yard where white petals floated on water pooled near piles of fresh dug earth. She was drawn to a light in March's tent in the adjoining yard which glowed inside the thick cloth walls like an ember.

Jennifer greeted Nora from her curled up seat on pillows near the small table. She was shuffling a deck of oversized cards and Leo the parrot was perched on a small three-legged stool. Jennifer was glad to have company.

"What's going on," Nora asked Jennifer. "Did you hear that music ?"

"When ?"

"Just now, it was like humming or singing or something."

" I hear that sometimes."

Nora sat down on a pillow near Jennifer and called Leo's name with clicking kissing sounds. To her surprise he immediately came and perched on her wrist which she held steady so that his sharp talons didn't dig into her skin. Nora couldn't help but smile at how the presence of the bird on her arm pleased her. Leo felt heavy but fragile like a teapot made of flowers. He was weighty with potential flight and sound. A sudden fondness for the cunning face and eye-catching feathers of the parrot touched Nora.

"Hello Leo."

"Hello." Leo squawked back immediately with the hoarse mocking voice birds use to imitate humans.

Jennifer and Nora laughed to hear the recalcitrant parrot respond so obediently. "He must like you," Jennifer told Nora.

Nora looked into the vigilant eyes of the bird and gently patted his shiny head as she returned him to his perch.

"Pretty bird," she said, "you are so nice."

"Nice cream" the bird said, then again, unmistakable "ice cream."

"Leo's talkative tonight." Jennifer said.

"You didn't hear anything out here ?" Nora questioned Jennifer. "I know I heard something; it was like humming or chanting."

"No."

"Must have been somebody in the street playing their car radio." Nora leaned back on the cushions.

"When are you moving to your sister's house ?" Jennifer asked.

"Tonight. I just have to pack a few things." Nora looked at her watch to see how late it was. She'd slept several hours. Ginger hadn't returned as expected.

"Hey, if you want, you know we have an empty bedroom you could use. You could pay us whatever you can afford, I mean, it's low rent. You can change March's room around any way you want--paint it, whatever." Jennifer was thinking, too, that if Nora stayed with them, possibly she could use her car occasionally, until she got one of her own.

The flame of the kerosene lamp on the table threw flickering shadows against the curved interior of the tent. Nora had the odd sensation that she hadn't completely woken up yet. Possibly I won't move in with Pam and Van after all, she thought, with a sense of relief that wasn't quite real, as if it were happening in dream time.

"You know what Henry David Thoreau said?"she told Jennifer. "I would rather sit on a pumpkin and have it to myself than share a velvet throne."

Jennifer nodded but she wasn't sure if Nora meant their room was a pumpkin or what. "Let's go get some ice cream" Jennifer suggested. "We'll take Leo."

"Can parrots ride in cars ?'

"Sure, I guess so."

The closest ice cream place was down on Santa Monica Boulevard near La Cienega. Leo hopped to Nora's shoulder when they got out of the car and she walked carefully past glass storefronts on the wide sidewalk. Jennifer opened the door to Steve's Sweet Shop which was lit up like a refrigerator inside with large pictures of ice cream cones and sandwiches on the shiny white walls. At eleven o'clock at night there were several male customers occupying the small round tables. The men all wore variations on the standard West Hollywood uniform--t-shirt, shorts, jeans, tennis shoes, sandals. The prevailing costume choice, Nora thought as she glanced at the clientele, was young athlete at play.

Jennifer took one look around the place and said "Let's go somewhere else."

Nora didn't argue. Apparently Jennifer felt strongly about it. Back on the sidewalk, Jennifer told Nora she thought the place was too cold.

"The air-conditioning was turned down so low I was afraid Leo couldn't take it. He should be protected from sudden changes in temperature."

Nora and Jennifer continued walking past a shoe store and a loud bar where the sidewalk was blotched and sticky with spilled drinks. A large group of men were gathered outside the bar smoking but none looked at the two women and the parrot as they walked by. Nora realized she hadn't eaten all day and thought about finding a restaurant; but Jennifer seemed to be preoccupied.

"You know what, Nora, I think we have to go back home." Jennifer said.

Nora had never seen Jennifer so serious. "Why ?"

"I think we're going to have a visitor tonight. I feel it." Jennifer said.

Nora was aware of a sharp sense of anticipation but she didn't know why or what to expect. As they turned the corner and walked purposely towards her car they were silent. Leo fluttered into the air, then landed again on Nora's shoulder and she said "good bird, nice boy."

Jennifer said nothing during the short ride home and Nora didn't question her. When she turned on to Westborne Street, Nora noticed that Ginger's car was parked in her driveway.

"Ginger must be home now." Nora said.

Jennifer said "I need to wake up Michelle."

Nora followed Jennifer into the house, Leo's sharp elastic claws clutching her shoulder; she felt unbalanced by the bird's weight. Michelle was no longer asleep in the living room. Jennifer called her name and there was no answer, then she found a note on the table, "Went out with Josh, back later." Jennifer quickly crumpled up the paper and threw it away.

"We have to go outside" Jennifer looked intently at Nora as if trying to gauge her stamina. "Are you tired ?"

"No." Nora felt strangely like it was morning instead of night; her long nap had disoriented her.

The two women walked into the back yard. Nora sat down on a stool near the dark tent and Jennifer spread a blanket on the ground beside her. From where she was sitting, Nora could see into the window of the kitchen next door where she saw Ginger's head pass in front of the round light. Ginger's up late, Nora thought. Then there were two heads visible in the window and Nora recognized Dan standing next to Ginger in the kitchen. He had a glass in his hand and seemed to be drinking something.

"Maybe we should make a fire," Nora said.

Jennifer felt glad she was with Nora and she wasn't sorry Michelle had gone off with Josh. She liked Nora because she was a woman who never acted without thinking—she seemed to have a good reason for everything she did, Jennifer thought, she is careful and smart. Jennifer felt lucky to have met another woman as careful and smart as she herself was; possibly more careful.

Jennifer knew what to expect but there was no way she could prepare Nora. She seems very relaxed, Jennifer thought, if it happens she'll be fine. A sound like a large truck backing up was coming from the street--a rhythmic beep beep beep beep that maintained a perfectly pitched unvarying sequence. An engine started up somewhere down the block and some small gnats or tiny fruit flies buzzed.

"What's that sound ?" Nora questioned Jennifer as she moved from the stool to sit beside her on the blanket. She tried hard to listen, half-closing her eyes. Nora's face looked as if she had stopped seeing and breathing and was only hearing.

Jennifer moved closer to Nora as soon as they felt it. Nora braced herself with her hands on the blanket and Jennifer rolled onto her stomach with her arms over her head. It didn't last long.

The music rose in volume and the rich creamy scent of the last overripe magnolias on the tree mixed with the odor of damp earth to create a sensation that married the odor with the sound. The music blossomed pungently in the damp soil of the night and the women smelled a crescendo of pianos and cellos and sweet high-pitched violins.

Jennifer heard Nora calling her name and she reached out to her. Once the rolling motion stopped, the light dispersed and the sound seemed to ascend into the air.

"Look" Jennifer pointed and Nora looked towards the sky and she saw it too.

It wasn't as if you could see music, but you could see its passage, its grandeur, the spirals of its movement and color. Nora struggled to form some description even as she was looking, but she was pulled into the moment, the witnessing, which was beyond words or apart from word-making. She simply heard and saw and felt the full force of the event--which was both visitation and blessing, illustration and mystery. Nora saw how by seeing the beauty of the mystery and accepting it, she herself became filled with it. They were both breathless and elated with astonishment at the potential for sharing in what was eternally possibility.

CHAPTER THIRTY - TWO

"**O**kay, Nora, move closer to the tent just a couple of inches. Good ! Now Andy, move in tighter on the bird. Try to keep Leo from jumping around, okay Nora ?"

Candy stepped back beside the oleander bushes and nodded her approval as the cameraman moved in to film a close-up shot of Nora with the parrot on her shoulder.

Candy was pleased with how smoothly things were going. The women's faces looked like they were glowing in the soft morning light with the sun casting long shadows behind the house. After a few minutes, the cameraman stopped filming to ask the blonde newswoman a question.

Nora relaxed when the camera stopped and handed Leo to an assistant who carefully returned the bird to his cage.

Jennifer had telephoned Candy immediately after the previous night's incident and the television crew with their brightly painted van showed up first thing in the morning. Since the Angel Lady story had become something of a favorite with her station's viewers, Candy was eager to cover new developments. There were some indications that the network people were looking at the story and she wanted to make sure she was first on the scene. Candy interviewed Jennifer in depth; but Nora proved to be even more photogenic than the younger woman and she was able to contribute a new perspective to the story. They could close the segment with a shot of the bird, Candy thought, maybe with electronic music behind it. She also planned to interview a number of people in the neighborhood to find out if there might be others who had seen something unusual or heard the unexplained musical sounds. The Angel Lady story was beginning to look like it might turn into a special report.

From her window over the sink, Ginger watched the television crew carrying equipment to the orange and brown van parked on the street. As she put water into the coffee maker, the doorbell rang. Candy Cummings greeted Ginger like an old friend and asked her if she'd noticed any unusual sounds the night before.

"Sorry, I can't help you."

Candy lingered at the front door but Ginger didn't ask her to come in. Dan was almost finished showering in the bathroom. Ginger was anticipating an intimate breakfast for two; she was planning to cook bacon and eggs and French toast. She didn't want any uninvited guests in her kitchen this morning.

"This is my cell phone," Candy told Ginger, writing another number on the card she held out to her. Ginger responded with an impatient nod. "Please call me if anything happens...you know, anything that might be of interest."

Ginger took Candy's card, then hesitated--should she tell the newswoman what she really thought ?

"You know, Candy, I believe Jennifer and Michelle need professional help to deal with their abandonment issues. It's very possible that they are delusional. I suspect possible sexual abuse and we can't rule out substance abuse. If these issues can be resolved, the delusional episodes will stop."

"I respect your opinion, Ginger," Candy said, "but I have a responsibility to my viewers. You have to realize that what happened here is news and people have a right to know."

As she watched Candy return to the van, Ginger couldn't help feeling that she'd done the right thing by telling the truth. Dan walked into the kitchen then with his hair damp, smelling of aftershave and toothpaste and Ginger felt a warm flush of satisfaction and well-being.

"How do you like your eggs ?" she asked him.

Nora decided to take a walk. She had never really explored the neighborhood around Westborne Street and she felt the need for some exercise. Jennifer had gone to sleep after the TV crew left but Nora didn't feel tired, though she'd been awake all night. She knew Pam would be calling to talk to her after the television interviews were aired and she dreaded having to explain to her half-sister what happened last night. It would take time to digest the experience, to go over it in her memory until she could claim what happened and keep the important moments for herself. Nora felt singled out and lucky—there was pride involved, and greed, she didn't want to share what happened to her. She wanted it for herself, untainted. Nora knew that when it became necessary to explain and describe what happened she would be forced to reduce last night's events to some kind of story--a story in the shared vocabulary of common experience. To find words she would need to find herself; to locate herself firmly in a new context of awareness. She knew that no matter how diligently she tried, she was doomed to fail at this description, this communication, because understanding last night's event required something called belief or faith.

Nora now understood faith as a transforming certainty, an element of awareness that had nothing to do with language or logic, a wholly different faculty. What had changed, she wondered; what was new, what was finished ? Have I changed because of this new knowledge or was the understanding given to me, granted to me, born in me, precisely because of who I am? More likely, she thought, it changed how I think about what's possible.

What was entirely unexpected, Nora realized, was the feeling she had that everything would be okay. This feeling of well-being seemed to be rooted in an awareness that the events of last night and this morning were somehow part of a longer, older story. In fact, Nora no longer felt worried about questions of truth and doubt or even the problem of where she should live. She would probably stay with Jennifer and Michelle for a while until she decided on the next step to take with the screenplay, the title of which, Nora thought, could be "The Unexpected Woman."

Nora found herself walking through the quiet residential streets of West Hollywood with genuine enjoyment. The sun broke through the morning haze and small well-watered gardens glistened with the polished greenery of camellias and boxwood and pitosporum. Jade plants and eccentrically shaped cactus occupied sunny spots; roses and lilies and impatiens colored the corners and borders. Nora saw how quiet and orderly most of the houses looked from the sidewalk. She wondered about the people behind the windows and doors. She couldn't remember the last time she'd taken a long walk and she continued west without a destination in mind.

As she walked, she considered the events of the past few days. She recalled the night she and Dan finished the last scene of their screenplay. In her remembering, Dan became mixed in with the characters they had written about, the invented dialog. But Dan was nothing like the urbane characters in the novel who lived on another continent in another time in rain-soaked London. She thought it was an odd quirk of her imagination to confuse Dan with those invented characters they'd imagined together, who had become somehow real to her. Real, she thought, because they are passionate. Passion always draws us in--even a passionate desire to kill a large fish or bury a relative or find the source of a river. Even if we don't share the desire we care about the outcome. Because, Nora thought, passion requires struggle which involves suffering, and patience, which requires time. Struggle and time shape a beginning, a middle and an end. And we always want to know what happens in the end. Is the desire satisfied or does the struggle continue and then what. Who wins and who suffers ? And everyone suffers, there is no one alive in the world who doesn't. Maybe only pain draws humans together, Nora thought, not love or sympathy but the commonality of suffering which, in the end, engenders compassion.

They had not yet agreed on what to call it. The woman in blue, she thought, there's a title and how sad that sounded, like blues music; lanquid, peaceful, floating in air or water. How different from the woman in red, who would be flirting or angry or dancing a rhumba. How a color could mean...white, she thought, the woman in white, a bride, a virgin, a saint...all the same woman.

Before she realized how far she'd walked, Nora found herself turning onto Santa Monica Boulevard. She had frequently driven past these treeless blocks of dusty old repair shops and dingy dry cleaners, liquor stores with metal bars protecting the windows and gradually bigger and cleaner clothing boutiques and greeting card shops and pizza parlors and crowded cafes scenting the air with the roasted odor of steaming coffee. The walking satisfied Nora's need to remain unfocused, unquestioning, a need to be in the open, not pinned down.

After a while she came to the edge of a busy supermarket parking lot. A very tan homeless woman with matted sun-bleached hair rested by a metal shopping cart full of her belongings.

"It's gonna rain." the woman announced loudly to Nora who pitied the forlorn creature wearing a dirty pink sweatshirt whose prediction was so obviously mistaken. Nora found no way to avoid meeting the woman's eyes. She scooped a handful of change out of her purse and dropped it into the empty paper cup the tan woman held.

As she dodged cars driving heedlessly in and out of the supermarket lot, Nora felt awkwardly invisible. She hurried to catch the green light at the next intersection and quickened her pace. She had walked further than she intended when she saw the shield-shaped sign reading Beverly Hills posted at the edge of the sidewalk. It was then that Nora thought about walking to the beach. She simply realized that the possibility existed and there was nothing stopping her and the weather was sunny and slightly breezy and it felt good to be outdoors. The idea of walking across L.A. was inconceivable; no one ever did, it was never by anyone ever considered as a possibility. Nora smiled at the absurd simplicity of walking which lent a mock heroic quality to the idea. Somehow being under the sky gave her a different perspective; gave her time to think, away from all the questions and expectations and decisions she knew were waiting for her.

The new perspective involved only movement, nothing more; only that she continue without stopping. And walking didn't involve too much effort, she reflected, just one foot in front of the other, a pleasant rhythm. She didn't think about how long or how much time, only that if she kept on walking west and didn't stop she would eventually reach the edge of the city where it touched the ocean.

Now that the storefronts were behind her and she faced several blocks of walking beside the relatively deserted surroundings of the grassy park that bordered Santa Monica Boulevard in Beverly Hills, Nora felt alone for the first time. An unsteady figure carrying a shabby bag bulging with his belongings stood up from the paved path in the grass and began shuffling towards Nora. She could smell his rank odor before she read his expression, which she did very quickly, avoiding direct eye contact. She saw a blur of wary eyes set deep in a blotched face surrounded by gristly hair.

"Hey miss," the filthy vagrant shouted at her. "Hey ! Cut the gloved call ! Be the surprised world."

Nora was almost certain that was not what he said. But that's what it sounded like. He spoke in the imperative, directly to her as she hurried past him. It sounded like. Cup the beloved cell. Be the surprised fool.

Is that what he said ? She hurried past him, putting as much distance as possible between them. He was tall and broad but didn't seem dangerous; he was walking with a shambling unsteady gait; there was no chance he would chase her. I can run faster, she thought. She glanced back and saw the man continuing on his way east.

To her left, six lanes of traffic rushed by like a furious deaf river of fumes. It struck Nora that the only people who had spoken to her so far had been homeless beggars, as if perhaps she had inadvertently entered their territory, a sub-city that existed in a different space-time continuum than the Los Angeles which she drove through daily. Other pedestrians had taken no notice of her as they hurried in and out of shops and cars. Nora felt the first pangs of fatigue and began to have doubts. What if I get too tired, she thought. What if I can't make it ? Nora knew she was only dramatizing her situation to avoid thinking about the ending. She knew that her final destination would be Dan's house; and if he wasn't there she knew where to find a key. By reassuring herself that she had a destination, Nora was able to avoid the queasy insecure feeling she always got when she contemplated her own homelessness.

Nora found herself thinking of Jennifer like someone she had known for a long time. Much longer, it seemed to her, than she'd known Ginger who remained somehow, after two years of living in the same house, an acquaintance. She thought that intimacy couldn't be measured in years but possibly in another way, like fruit ripening or flowers blooming, she thought, but couldn't follow that image, it evaded her, evaporating on the bright street.

After crossing the six-lane intersection at Wilshire, Nora saw she was approaching one of the blocks in Los Angeles that appeared to be almost impassable on foot. The huge Beverly Hills Hotel parking garage was separated from the busy boulevard by a marginal strip of sidewalk barely wide enough for two feet. The curb buckled and narrowed to a faint ledge until it was lost in the gaping oil-stained entrances to the block-long garage. Nora felt like a trespasser as she held her breath to avoid inhaling exhaust fumes and watched nervously for heedless drivers making rapid swerves. Once past this long gray block, Nora knew that the worst was yet ahead. She would have to walk under the overpass on-ramp to the 405 freeway, one of the busiest intersections in the city.

Nora calculated that if she turned around now she could be back in time to pack her things and drive to Pam's house before dark. If she walked back to Westborne Street, she would have the advantage of covering familiar territory. Nora wasn't entirely certain if it was even possible to walk under the freeway overpass she was approaching. Though she had driven past it hundreds of times, she never noticed if there was a sidewalk at the edge of the street under the dark freeway. She had certainly never seen anyone walking there. If there was no sidewalk she would have to make a wide detour in an unknown direction, but she couldn't be sure until she got closer. She was also uncertain as to just how long it would take to walk the rest of the way to Santa Monica.

If it's not too late I'll stop and rest, Nora thought, checking her watch. She was annoyed to discover that her wrist was bare. She remembered taking her watch off when she was holding Leo, as his talons got caught in the band. As she walked beside the busy boulevard, Nora tried to guess the time of day. The sun was high overhead and it was definitely late afternoon, but how long had she been walking and how long would it take to get to Dan's house? It was essential, Nora thought, to reach her destination before dark.

For the first time, worry attached itself to Nora's walk. She feared walking through an unknown neighborhood after dark. As it was almost November, the days were short and the sun set early.

Help me, she found herself asking. Please help me, though I am unworthy I put myself in your hands. I trust that you'll watch out for me.

After these requests were put into words, Nora realized that she felt a new certainty and a sense of relief. Who is it I'm asking, she questioned herself. And the question seemed pointless suddenly, as she knew the who to be something far beyond one entity—it was a presence large enough to envelope the earth, with power enough to light the world's suns and stars. It seemed to her that words would only diminish the idea of this divinity and define it into a stale construction when in fact it remains always limitless and she part of it. Nora continued walking.

CHAPTER THIRTY - THREE

J ennifer got into bed and tried to sleep after the TV crew left but she couldn't lie still. She closed her eyes but she felt like she might never be tired again, she was so full of energy or spirit or maybe it was desire--a word that rhymed with inspire, like inspiration. Though Floyd was gone she still felt his presence like an odor left on her skin and it was all mixed up with what happened last night. It got so bad she couldn't rest until she found a vacuum cleaner in the hall closet and cleaned the whole house and washed all the dishes. Michelle didn't get home until after noon.

"Look what Josh gave me last night." Michelle showed Jennifer a sparkling heart that hung around her neck on a thin gold chain.

"He probably felt guilty," Jennifer told her.

"It's real gold and diamonds," Michelle said.

"Listen," Jennifer's voice was eager "We have to talk to Peter. He called several times. I think he's got some good ideas and we need to ..."

"What happened last night ?" Michelle interrupted her. "how...I mean, was it the same as before ?"

"The feeling was the same," Jennifer told her friend, "but it was different--I mean it wasn't so much of a surprise and I wasn't so scared. Nora seemed to be..."

"Wish I'd been here," Michelle interrupted. "What did you say to Candy ?"

"Don't worry, you'll see it all in the news later tonight."

Jennifer felt impatient. There was so much to be done. They would meet Cal Portnoy tomorrow. There was no time to think about yesterday. Even Floyd was beginning to recede into the past. Jennifer tried to hold on to his voice, his smell, his careful way of walking; but he was beginning to wane like a full moon gradually loses its symmetry and becomes a deflated ball, an empty bowl, a crescent and then a sliver, then darkness. She didn't want to be always thinking about him; she saw that it would take some effort, but she had to distract herself. Her thirst for him made her feverish, impatient, reckless. She couldn't look back, had to immerse herself in something that would wash the memory away quickly. She had no aptitude for missing and mourning; she didn't enjoy it; she had to go on to the next thing.

"We have to call Peter Revel immediately." Jennifer told Michelle.

Michelle seemed overwhelmed by the many new developments of the past 48 hours. She flopped down onto the sofa and fingered the little heart at her throat.

"I'm tired," she said.

Jennifer had seen this happen before: Michelle at times became cow-like, unthinking and inert. Jennifer had seen it happen whenever her friend had too many new things to deal with-- especially good things. Michelle was more comfortable with failure--when good things happened she slowed down and resisted the change. Jennifer knew she didn't mean to, but she couldn't help it.

"I'm calling Peter," Jennifer told Michelle. "We have to get together with him today."

"Can't we do it some other time ?" Michelle closed her eyes and sprawled on the sofa.

"What's wrong with you ?"

"Nothing, but I can't go out with you tonight. Josh and I are having dinner with his uncle."

Jennifer knew better than to try to change Michelle's mind--she was stuck on Josh now. Michelle could only be loyal to one person at a time, Jennifer knew that as she knew all her friend's abilities and limits.

Jennifer dialed Peter's number and left a message. "Why don't we get together soon, okay Peter ? Looking forward to seeing you. Call me."

"He's not home ?" Michelle felt somewhat hurt at being left out of the television interviews and wondered if Jennifer had plans that she wasn't telling her about.

"Look," Jennifer wanted Michelle to pay attention. "We have to be prepared for tomorrow--Portnoy is a big producer, he can make things happen for us."

"I know." Michelle remembered that she was supposed to play tennis tomorrow. She had never played tennis in her life.

As she cleared dirty glasses off the kitchen counter, Jennifer found a silver key chain with a BMW key on it.

"These must be Nora's keys" Jennifer said, picking them up and feeling the heft of them in her hand. "Where did she go ? Is her car still here ?" Michelle shrugged, she was preoccupied with her own thoughts.

When Jennifer saw that Nora's car was still parked on the street, she thought she should move it closer to the house. Once she was behind the wheel, it occurred to Jennifer that Leo needed bird food and the refrigerator was empty. The supermarket isn't far, she thought, Nora won't mind if I drive her car to get some food.

When Jennifer went back into the house to get her purse, Michelle was lying on the sofa talking on the telephone in very low tones. Jennifer shook her leg to get her attention.

"Do you have any money ? I want to buy some food."

"Just a second Josh," Michelle said into the phone.

"Look in my purse." Michelle turned her head away from Jennifer and continued talking to Josh in a whispery voice.

Jennifer pocketed a twenty-dollar bill. "I'm going," she said loudly, to interrupt Michelle who waved her hand in a dismissive gesture.

Jennifer adjusted the seat in Nora's car and made sure the mirror was at the best angle. It occurred to her as she headed towards the supermarket on Sunset Boulevard that she might find Peter Revel at home if she drove up there now. It's only a few blocks further, she thought.

...

The rose-tinged rays of evening cast a faint pink glow upon the beige walls of the spacious bedroom in the Hollywood hills. "Revel," Peter was explaining to Jennifer. "is lever spelled backwards. Give me a long enough lever and I'll move the world. Didn't Archimedes say that ? Or was it fulcrum or... ?"

Peter paused and tried to concentrate. "What in the hell was that ? Give me a long enough something and I'll move the earth."

"What are you talking about ?" Jennifer asked him.

"Leverage, darling, that's physics. You know, leverage. "

Peter continued licking Jennifer's elbow which tasted faintly of strawberries. They were both lying face down in a criss-crossed position on his aunt's king-sized bed, having just emerged from a long warm bath in her Jacuzzi after ingesting some of the London Brand X. Peter noticed that, in fact, their nude bodies formed the letter X as they lay on the bed. We are literally X-ing, he thought. Literally. His belly intersected with the concave curve of Jennifer's lower spine. He knew this was deeply, religiously significant or pre-ordained by god.

Jennifer's hand reached back and touched what she was looking for. Without turning over she told Peter, "I'd say your lever is ready for anything."

Peter then rose on his knees and contemplated Jennifer's unspeakably perfect back. The delicate wing-like shoulder blades, the flesh on either side of her spine curving around her twig-like ribs, narrowing to a slim waist then swelling into two pink mounds, dimpled on either side of the tail bone. He marveled at how unmuscled, how perfectly yielding a woman's body could be, yet still look sculpted.

"May I kiss you here ?" he asked, drawing a circle upon her body with his index finger as if it were sand. As if her skin.

"Yes," she said.

"And here ?"

"Yes."

"Here too ?"

"Yes."

He lay on his back then and they talked. Jennifer told him about her mother's abusive boyfriend in Texas where she went to grade school and then moving to Omaha where her father married a woman named Tiffany who worked in the Nebraska state prison.

"He calls her Tuffy," Jennifer told Peter. "Can you believe that? She has three kids."

Jennifer suspected that Peter couldn't fully appreciate the significance of this information, yet she had never before revealed this shameful fact regarding her father's wife to anyone other than Michelle. Speaking of it now allowed her to contemplate the vast geographical and psychic distance that existed between herself and the world her father inhabited. She realized as she lay there that she need never go back to Omaha. Ever. Jennifer felt hugely relieved and comforted by this sudden epiphany.

"Are you closer to your father or your mother ?" Peter asked her.

Jennifer considered the immense stupidity of her mother and the flagrant uselessness of her father.

"Neither one, really." She told him. "How about you ?"

"My mother, ah," he sighed, "she died you see."

Jennifer saw her die, a brief flash, and felt it too. The tragic brevity of her maternal affection like a star falling from a night sky. She felt for Peter who had lived through it. Something terrible.

"And your father ?"

"Never home." Peter explained without bitterness.

Jennifer rolled over on the large bed and caressed Peter's smooth face with all the sympathy and tenderness she felt.

"Tell me more about leverage, " she requested, as the tall windows rattled and the first raindrops of the season blew against the glass.

CHAPTER THIRTY - FOUR

Dan heard it before he left the restaurant: the rattle and flap of the canvas awning over the entrance, the intermittent swish of tires on wet pavement. When he opened the door he felt a blast of cool air and saw the sidewalk outside Troppo slick with water. Dan inhaled a moist lung-full of rain-soaked air. The steady downpour was drenching the streets and rooftops and cars of Beverly Hills. As Dan approached the street in front of the restaurant he thought about his old Mustang. He eyed his empty parking space with regret, knowing the wet weather would mean slow taxi service and a long wait to get home.

When Dan finally slipped into the back seat of a yellow cab and told the driver his address he was greeted with "Which way you want to go ?"

Dan knew from the way the driver answered that he didn't know where the street was. "It's in Santa Monica" he told the driver. "You can take Beverly Boulevard."

When the taxi turned left on Wilshire, Dan's fears were confirmed. "No, not this way. You need to go west."

"What is best way ?"

The driver's accent sounded middle eastern, possibly Russian or Armenian, it was hard to tell. Dan peered at the faded printed sign to the right of the taxi's meter. The name seemed to have an unpronounceable combination of vowels and the photo didn't match.

Dan was tired after a long day at the restaurant. This is his job, he thought, he should know where streets are. "You don't know where Pacific Street is?"

"Too many streets in this city," the driver sounded aggravated, he shrugged his shoulders.

"Take Santa Monica Boulevard" Dan directed the taxi-driver, as he leaned back in the cold taxi and stared out the rain-spattered windshield awash with the frenzied lights of Saturday night traffic. He thought about missing things and what it meant to feel the absence of a particular car or friend. He wondered if Nora would miss their writing sessions. We need a title for the screenplay, he thought. "Pursuit of Darkness" maybe or "Catch a Falling Star." Dan already missed talking with Nora, though it had only been two days since... He thought of his old Mustang then, to distract himself. He knew he could never stop hoping. On the wet windows of the taxi, neon lights blurred in the night like spilled paint.

"You wanna take freeway ?"

The taxi was stopped at an intersection somewhere near a freeway on-ramp. Dan looked out the window and tried to get his bearings but the mini-mall on the north corner looked identical to so many others. He saw nothing that conclusively identified his location. Was that the bank where he...? No, it was further east. Dan turned to read a rain-swept street sign in the dark. The rain was coming faster now and the storm drains were backed up. Taller vehicles drove by the taxi, spraying yard-high wakes of water off their wheels.

The taxi driver was nervous about continuing on Santa Monica Boulevard. Sometimes the first rain of the season caused storm drains to overflow and the busy streets were flooded.

"I don't want to take the freeway," Dan said, "it takes longer."

Dan didn't know where to turn. He peered through the streaked windows of the taxi to consider how far they had yet to travel. On the sidewalk he saw people huddled in the doorway of a bar. The temperature had dropped significantly since sunset. They appeared to be waiting for the rain to let up before they walked to their cars. Dan told the driver to turn left and the side street seemed less flooded but darker and abandoned at this late hour. They drove past auto parts stores and plumbing suppliers and block-long low warehouses without sidewalks or landscaping. At the next traffic light Dan saw that they were twelve blocks away from his street. One huge building occupied most of the short block ahead. The low windowless warehouse was marked with an old illuminated sign above a narrow entrance lit by a bluish fluorescent light. A single slim figure paced in the sheltered doorway.

As the taxi sped by, Dan took a careful look and then shouted "Wait" to the driver. "Stop!"

How had he recognized her ? It must have been the red jacket, he thought. She was soaked with rain and her hair was plastered to her head. She looked frightened and stood warily against the wall of the building when the taxi stopped. When Dan walked toward her, Nora stared as though she didn't recognize him. She said nothing.

"Nora," Dan said "what are you doing here ?" He knew it was her but there was no reason it should be or could be her. Nora had no reason to be in the doorway of an electronics supply warehouse at this hour on a rainy night. There was just no way, no possible explanation.

She embraced Dan; he could feel how cold she was.

"Take me home" was all she said.

He helped her out of her wet clothes and into his bed. He brought some extra blankets and said he'd make tea. He didn't ask questions. She seemed so different...her usual poise and patter was missing. Nora had nothing to say.

The rain kept up a rushing staccato racket on the thin roof of Dan's bungalow--the sound blanketed the room where Nora lay waiting while Dan put water on to boil and made sure Greta was fed. He bent down and rubbed the fat face and ragged ears of the old boxer, who seemed restless because of the rain. She didn't lay down in her usual place by the stove but stayed near Dan, causing him to almost trip over her when he made some tea for Nora.

"Easy Greta," Dan said, "lay down girl."

Nora heard Dan moving in the kitchen of the small house and the clicking whirring sounds of the furnace igniting and heat circulating; but the din of hard rain drumming on the thin roof drowned out all other sounds. When the rain started Nora had walked for blocks looking for shelter, but she couldn't remember how or where. She felt stiff and overwhelmed by fatigue. Though she knew she was in a warm bed the loud rain seemed to be penetrating the room and Nora shivered because she imagined that she could still feel stinging drops of water on her skin.

Dan entered the bedroom with a cup of tea. "I put honey in it" he said and that made Nora cry, a soft sob of gratitude.

He sat down beside the bed and watched her drink. She took a long sip and finally looked at him, at his eyes, for the first time. She said nothing.

"Are you cold ?" he asked.

Then he uncovered her and began with her ankles and feet, rubbing his hands against her skin in a steady rhythm, working his way up her calves and knees to her thighs, warming her skin with the friction of his palms. He worked with a dexterous businesslike thoroughness, not stopping to ask questions, keeping a constant vigorous movement.

Dan had seen hypothermia cases in Wyoming; friends caught without shelter in snowstorms. He knew that when a body loses a certain percentage of heat, the brain is affected. Nora's skin felt very cold, as if she'd been exposed for a long time.

"Turn over" he ordered.

Nora turned onto her stomach and Dan continued the procedure, rubbing each portion of her body vigorously with both his hands. She lay quietly, obediently offering herself to Dan's ministrations. He pressed his strong hands firmly on each shoulder, massaging towards the spine and neck and head, running his hands through her smooth hair with gentle strokes.

Nora's eyes closed and she curled onto her side.

"You go to sleep now," Dan gently kissed her head, touching her face carefully with the tips of his fingers.

…

Pam and Van watched the news at eleven from the white sofa in their beige and white living room. On the large television screen they saw Candy Cummings talking to her anchorman at the television news desk.

"Yet another sighting of the Angel Lady in West Hollywood." The handsome man with the bright necktie reported. "Candy Cummings spoke this morning with the women on Westborne

Street who made contact with the mysterious being who appeared in their backyard."

Pam let out a high-pitched shriek when she saw her sister on the screen.

"That's Nora !" she exclaimed, grabbing the remote device to bring the sound level up higher. "What is she DOING ?"

Nora looked calm and centered in front of the camera. "The experience was really intense but almost indescribable" Nora explained to Candy. "I feel that my understanding of visual reality will never be the same."

When Candy turned to Jennifer for more clarification, she spoke with a mixture of confidence and exhilaration. "All I know for sure Candy is what we were told : this particular moment in time, this day, this season, is blessed. We should all be aware of the sacred impermanence of life, every day we are given is a bountiful gift."

"She warned about selfishness," Jennifer said. "We must think of ourselves as part of something larger and more important than our own desires."

"So," Candy looked at both women "we aren't in for another earthquake in the near future ?"

Jennifer smiled and shook her head because Candy wasn't serious; she didn't really think that, it was just to get people's attention. Then the news team came back on the screen and there was a commercial break.

Pam hurried to dial her phone. "Hi Ginger," she said "Can I talk to Nora?...Oh, Since when ?" Pam covered the receiver and told Van, "Nora's not living at Ginger's any more...You were asleep ? I'm sorry ! I just saw the news and... No...I don't know where she is. Ginge, I'm really sorry I woke you up. No, really doll, go back to sleep. I'm sorry, okay ?"

Pam hung up the telephone and reported to her husband. "Ginger doesn't know where Nora is. She thought she was staying here."

"That's strange,"Van agreed. "Doesn't she have a cell phone ?"

"No. Hope she calls me." Pam tried to remember her last conversation with her sister. "When did she get into this spiritual thing I wonder ? She's been pretty depressed lately. You think she's taking medication ?"

"You mean like pain-killers?"Van asked, "or anti-depressants?"

"Look," Pam pointed at the TV screen, "there's more."

Candy was standing on a sidewalk with a 30-something African American man and a red-haired woman, both looked well-dressed and relaxed.

"Did you hear or see anything out of the ordinary last night ?" she asked them. The woman answered first.

"We were both at the Comedy Club on Sunset until two o'clock or so. I do stand-up every Friday after midnight. When we drove home Carl said he heard something that sounded like music, like a chorus singing. We live right over there." The woman pointed east on Westborne street. She had a nice smile and a great haircut.

Candy thanked the young couple and greeted another neighbor. A small knot of people gathered in the background. "What can you tell us, Mr. Tebby ?" Candy asked a paunchy senior citizen in a stained zipper jacket.

"There's all kinds of people coming and going at odd hours and that big puddle of water is still there." the old man said. "Not a thing the city can do about it."

The screen filled with Candy's confident smile.

"Well, as you can see, Jim, there is more to this story than meets the eye. Does the Angel Lady have something important to tell us ? You'll hear it first on TV 8."

Van went into the kitchen. He came back to the sofa holding a fried chicken leg in his hand. Pam sniffed the air.

"Where did that come from ?" she asked her husband.

"The Colonel," he answered as he chewed.

"Who ?"

"Colonel Sanders. There's more in the refrigerator."

CHAPTER THIRTY - FIVE

Nora awoke from a deep sleep under the warm pile of blankets Dan had heaped on top of her the night before. She slid out of bed in the cool of the quiet morning and walked down the hall in her bare feet to find the bathroom flooded with the burnished sunlight of early autumn.

Nora was eager to start the day. She slipped into Dan's flannel bathrobe left hanging on a hook behind the door. She didn't see her clothes; Dan must have hung them somewhere to dry. As Nora walked softly past the room where she knew Dan was still asleep, her body felt unusually light and empty. The rain had changed everything. When she opened the front door, fresh air wafted inside charged with the rich scent of wet earth. The sky seemed washed in blue and the shrubbery near the house sparkled with moisture. Nora lingered for a moment in the crisp air, then saw the car parked in Dan's narrow driveway a few feet away--a blue Mustang. Nora stared at it for a long time, then approached it, disbelieving. She got close enough to look inside the car and tried the door. It wasn't locked.

Nora didn't want to open the door and get inside the car. She felt afraid, suddenly, and looked carefully up and down the street of two-story apartment buildings and narrow porches to see if anyone was watching; then she hurried back inside the house. Nora walked quickly through the living room into the kitchen. She poured a tall glass of water from the faucet and stood in her bare feet and drank it all. Then she went to the window and looked again--the Mustang was still there.

Greta was curled up at the foot of the bed where Dan was sleeping. The dog got up and rubbed against Nora when she entered.

"Dan," Nora shook his shoulder gently. "I have to show you something."

Dan woke up slowly, saw Nora's face come into focus, smiled and stretched his arms over his head. "You okay ?' he asked.

"Yes, I think so," she replied. "I have to show you something, you have to come outside."

As she waited impatiently he pulled on a pair of jeans and followed her, barefoot, to the front door. She opened the door and pointed.

"Look."

When he saw the Mustang, Dan inhaled sharply. He bounded down the stairs, opened the unlocked door and sat inside with his hands on the steering wheel. Nora waited and watched him roll down the window.

"They left the keys on the dashboard," he called to her in a high excited voice she'd never heard before.

The engine turned over and the car came to life. "Hey!" Dan called to Nora, "Let's go for a ride."

Nora, wearing only the oversized bathrobe, slid into the passenger seat beside Dan who was bare-chested and barefoot.

"A quarter tank of gas!" He exclaimed in the same high boyish voice.

Dan glanced over at Nora and kissed her on the mouth with a sudden direct fierceness that took her by surprise. He draped his right arm around her shoulders as the Mustang pulled onto Ocean Park and headed west.

They rolled through the quiet Sunday morning streets, then impulsively Dan headed down the long concrete ramp that connects the edge of Santa Monica's widest street to the Pacific Coast Highway hundreds of feet below. The wide foaming edge of the ocean sparkled in the sun. He was amazed at how well the car was running.   Was it possible that someone took it for a joyride and then returned it without damage ? It was unbelievable but possible. He looked over at Nora whose hair was blowing out the open window in the breeze. The sea air smelled briny and had a touch of winter in it that made his eyes water. She turned to him and smiled. She wore no make-up and seemed younger. He had never seen her look so radiant.

What Nora wanted then was to ride and ride until the day ended and another day began and to continue riding for several days . She contemplated Dan's profile against the morning sky and the gleaming Pacific. His hair had grown longer and he had a stubble of beard that made him look reckless, rough around the edges. She saw how he was, possibly, a more complex person than the Dan she thought she knew--mysterious and robust, capable of tenderness and insight. Riding down the steep incline towards the ocean filled Nora with a giddy buoyant joyfulness.

She remembered then what she'd forgotten-- the simple ease of allowing the present moment to be everything, without thinking backwards and forwards. She felt whole, fully present and alive. Now that she remembered she wouldn't forget again, Nora told herself, and she became aware of an intense gratitude that pressed against her throat and weighed on her chest near her heart. Nora tried to pinpoint the moment when she first found this joyfulness and made it her own; but her memory was hazy after her deep sleep and the dreams that filled it-- and she wondered if this too, this ride with Dan in his car, might be a dream.

...

Jennifer stood in her bedroom in front of the closet and wondered what to wear to the party at Cal Portnoy's; then she turned to consider Michelle, who was still sleeping. Jennifer had gone to bed early and didn't hear her come in, but she knew Michelle had stayed out late with Josh the night before. In fifteen minutes I'm waking her up, Jennifer planned. She was eager to start the day.

When she let Leo out of his cage and gave him some food and fresh water, the bird squawked "Let's go, let's go." in his shrill peckish voice.

Sleepy Michelle finally got up and joined Jennifer at the yellow Formica table.

"Jen, guess what happened last night ?" Michelle waited for a second until Jennifer looked at her.

"What ?"

"Josh told me he wants to like, get married."

"Married ?" Jennifer questioned, at a loss. "Married ?"

"Yeah. Me and Josh."

Michelle looked very pleased with herself, Jennifer thought. But Josh couldn't be a husband, he was so slight, so insignificant, so easily frightened.

"Is this a joke ?" she asked Michelle who answered by shaking her head like she had a big secret.

"How old is Josh ?" Jennifer asked Michelle.

"He's twenty-seven," her friend replied. "Last night his uncle David told us about how he got married when he was twenty-five years old. He's like Josh's mentor, you know, like he gives him advice and stuff. He thinks Josh would be happier if he was married and I have terrific career potential. That's what he said."

Jennifer had trouble making sense out of the words that were coming from Michelle's mouth. It was like she'd been abducted by aliens and taught a foreign language.

"Yeah but Michelle, Josh isn't...I mean, how can you get married to Josh ?" Jennifer couldn't even begin to confront this new reality. Michelle would come to her senses before long--she had somehow fallen under some malign influence that would soon wear off, like a bad drug.

Michelle was thinking about a long lace dress and a white veil. She thought about a diamond ring, two rings, she thought, and pearls. At her uncle's wedding she remembered the two small figures on top of the pastel cake; a doll couple in black and white, smooth and decorative. Michelle aspired to that state of sweet perfection.

"We have to get ready for the party" Jennifer reminded Michelle.

"It's not a party, it's a lunch or a brunch or something. And I can't play tennis."

"Don't worry. I have a feeling it's gonna rain again."

Michelle went to the window and looked at the sky.

"Are you sure ?"

"There's a fifty per cent chance of rain." Jennifer told her. "What kind of odds do you want ?"

Michelle knew from past experience that Jennifer was often right about weather. It was one of those things she was lucky with. Josh had impressed upon her the significance of this unexpected invitation from Cal and she knew how important it was for her to make a good impression on the aging producer, even though Josh wasn't invited. These concerns, however, did not occupy the forefront of Michelle's mind.

What absorbed Michelle and fully occupied her imagination was the idea she had of herself as a bride, dressed in a long white dress and veil, walking down the aisle in a church where she would say "I do" to Josh. It was a scene she had often watched in television shows and movies featuring a bride beautiful and demure coupled with a bridegroom whole-hearted and sincere. The wedding would be staged in front of large scale architecture with romantic music in the background. Abundant pastel flowers, well-dressed attendants, distinguished authority figures pronouncing formal vows and universal approval expressed at a lavish after-wedding feast completed the scenario. Michelle had never before thought of herself in the role of bride, and in fact had attended but one wedding in her entire life, but now that the possibility presented itself she could think of nothing else.

Michelle wondered why everybody thought it was such a big deal that they were going to visit Cal Portnoy at home. It didn't seem like it would be any fun at all to have a party so early in the day. Michelle didn't know anybody who played tennis but she had seen it on TV and the games seemed long and boring. Still, Josh said Cal was a very famous TV and movie producer.

"Do you think Cal Portnoy will hire us to be on a television show ?" Michelle asked Jennifer.

"It's not that simple," Jennifer explained. She'd learned a lot from talking with Peter and she had a much clearer picture now of how the system worked. "I'll explain some things to you later, but you have to get ready. We have to look our best."

Later, sitting at a round table shaded with a striped umbrella on the lawn beneath the well-trimmed palm trees in Cal Portnoy's back yard, Michelle saw that Jennifer had been right. The Portnoy home wasn't like a place where people lived; it was more like a park or, Michelle thought, a resort hotel. The waiter had just brought her another glass of orange juice mixed with champagne, a concoction Michelle found delicious. She was waiting for Mrs. Portnoy, Judy, to return.

As Michelle sipped from a fresh glass of the bubbly drink they called a mimosa, she watched Jennifer playing croquet with Cal Portnoy and several other men on the wide expanse of lawn which surrounded the house and extended for a long ways towards the tennis court in the distance. Cal limped slightly as he had twisted his ankle the night before and couldn't play tennis today. A sudden brief rain shower just before noon had interrupted the first match between Peter Revel and David Samuels. After that, there was some talk about waiting for the court to dry off but no one seemed eager to try a game. Michelle was glad that she didn't have to make excuses about not playing tennis and she was especially glad that she had met Mrs. Portnoy, who she had to remember to call Judy. Judy had seen Jennifer and Michelle the very first time they'd appeared on Candy's news show and she was really nice, Michelle thought. Judy wanted to know all about the Angel Lady and what she looked like.

Michelle saw a familiar face in the group of guests approaching on the wide veranda and she recognized Donna Samuels waving and hurrying towards her. After kissing her enthusiastically on both cheeks, Uncle David's wife, as Michelle thought of her, took a seat at the table and exclaimed "Judy told me you were here--I'm so glad to see you." Then Judy came back to join the other women and Donna told her "I met Michelle after the premiere of...what was that Hawaiian film you were in ?" she asked.

"The movie was called Bound to Deliver but I wasn't..."

"You're too modest, sweetheart," Donna interrupted Michelle, "you did a great job even though you had a small part."

"There is no such thing as a small part," Mrs. Portnoy said knowingly and Donna nodded agreement.

"The first time I saw Michelle and her friend on Candy Cummings' show I just knew they were special" Judy told Donna. "Did you see them when they predicted the earthquake ? Unbelievable-- I get goose bumps just thinking about it."

Donna had not seen that particular show or the follow-up, but Judy had and she was eager to claim Michelle as her discovery.

"The very first time I saw her I thought, this girl has something," Judy stated emphatically.

"You know Michelle's been dating my nephew Josh," Donna Samuels told her sister, not to be outdone.

"Really ?" Judy took off her sunglasses and opened her eyes wide to display her astonishment. "You mean, Michelle might be joining our family ?"

Michelle looked carefully at Judy and Donna. "Are you two sisters?"

"Didn't you know? We're twins, not identical but fraternal."

Michelle had not known; but her genuine surprise and delight at learning of it was gratifying to both women.

"Isn't she adorable ?" Donna said to her sister, with a proprietary gesture. After all, she thought, I met her first.

Judy saw some new guests heading towards her. "Oh, here comes Rita Bellows and that English playwright she wants to introduce to Cal," Judy Portnoy abruptly left the table and hurried over to greet a couple who had just walked through the large double doors that led from the living room into the garden.

Jennifer looked across the lawn and saw Michelle was still drinking and talking with the older women. Lucky I learned to play croquet in Omaha, Jennifer thought, remembering the long summer afternoons with nothing to do but join in endless boring games with the kids across the street. Jennifer felt pleased that she was the only female playing croquet with Cal. Josh's uncle David, Peter Revel and Cal's assistant, Spencer made up the rest of the competition.

Spencer had just begun working for Cal as an intern. Jennifer chatted with him while they were standing around on the lawn and learned that Spencer had graduated from some Ivy League college and was eager to learn from Cal about producing films. Jennifer noticed that Cal never missed an opportunity to remind Spencer of his low status. The younger man looked slightly abashed whenever Cal put him down, but there seemed to be a mutual understanding that such abuse was tolerated, even expected, in exchange for the privilege of being included in Cal's life. In fact, with his short legs and chubby baby face topped with a head of hair so thin it was almost colorless, Spencer might have been pathetic had he not been unfailingly sarcastic and contemptuous of everyone he met--he believed this attitude prevented him from being thought a fool.

"Come on" Cal was saying to his intern, "let's see you knock my ball through for me. I know you can do it."

Earlier in the game, Spencer had inadvertently hit Jennifer's ball through a crowded wicket, allowing her to pull far ahead of the others. Spencer's pink face radiated annoyance as he took his turn. The other players attempted to match Cal's intensely competitive style of play but Spencer allowed it to be known that he considered the game boring and a waste of time. The more attitude Spencer displayed the more Cal enjoyed provoking him.

"Don't hit the ball out of the park now, Spencer." Cal emitted a snort of derision at the puny distance covered by Spencer's ball. "You see, the movement should come from up here."

Cal planted his feet on the grass and swung the wooden mallet back three feet and brought it forward with a solid plunk to connect with his red ball which rolled ten feet in a straight line towards the next wicket.

It was Jennifer's turn next and Cal didn't like the way she was addressing the ball.

"No, don't bend your elbows !" he exclaimed. Cal took the game very seriously.

"Look here" he said, and bent over Jennifer's back, placing his arms atop her arms and his hands over her hands.

Jennifer could smell the pungent cologne Cal wore and the sour scent of wine on his breath. His freckled arms felt damp against hers. She saw Spencer watching them with what looked like disgust or amusement, with him you couldn't tell the difference. David Samuels observed his host with a polite smile. Peter was busy chatting with one of the other guests. Cal saw the other men watching and moved his hands down onto Jennifer's hips.

"Stand like this," he told her, looking over her head to observe Spencer's reaction.

Jennifer could tell that Cal felt no attraction to her at all. His attentions to her were calculated to prove something to the other men. She was aware that since she was a stranger, and young, she was an object of more than usual attention. The other women at the party were wives and familiar faces. She and Michelle were the new girls.

Jennifer turned and looked squarely into Cal's eyes. "Where'd you learn to play this game ?" She asked him. "You're pretty good."

Cal grinned happily and looked around to see if the other men had heard. "Feel the weight of these mallets," he said. "Perfectly balanced. They're made to order in northern England with specially aged Scottish maple; an old family business. They only make a few sets a year, hand-carved and initialed."

Jennifer fingered the handle of the croquet mallet appreciatively and smiled at Cal, who was watching two white curly-haired dogs run swiftly towards them. "Who let the dogs out ?" He asked no one in particular. "Hey girl," Cal spoke in a babyish voice to the dog as he bent down to pet and ruffle, "how's my girl ?"

"Spencer," Cal's voice rose to a curt command, "take Napoleon and Josephine back to the house, will you ?" The producer stood up and dusted off his hands. " Spencer is great with animals," he told Jennifer as Spencer rounded up the dogs obediently. "He's an expert with the plastic bags--you know, the ones for picking up dog shit."

Peter and David chuckled appreciatively at Cal's wit and Spencer gave Peter a hate-filled look as he called "Poley, JoJo" in his flat bored voice and the dogs followed him towards the back of the house, which was a five minute walk from the croquet lawn. Spencer walked stiffly and deliberately, without glancing at the frolicking dogs.

"Those bichons frises are beautiful dogs," David said admiringly.

"Judy found a breeder in Maine," Cal explained, "those damn dogs cost me more than my Mercedes last year."

Jennifer walked closer to Peter who was reaching for a drink from a tray the waiter had brought to them. Jennifer felt thirsty so she had one too. "You're a first-rate croquet player," Peter said to Jennifer.

"I need to work on my backswing," she said.

"I think Cal likes you," Peter said in a low voice as they stood talking on the lawn in the sunshine. They made a handsome couple--the tall well-dressed man with shiny hair and fashionable sunglasses beside a smiling young girl with exceptionally long slim legs wearing a short skirt.

"No, Cal has the hots for Michelle."

"Michelle? Does she like him ?"

Jennifer looked at Peter's eyes to see if he was serious. His upper lip stiffened into mock propriety and he lifted his eyebrows in a look of exaggerated curiosity. Jennifer couldn't help laughing; Peter liked to make her giggle.

"Doubtful-- she's talking about marrying Josh."

"Josh Samuels?" Peter looked genuinely horrified. "How could she ?"

"How could who what ?"

Spencer had returned and thought nothing of interrupting their conversation with his question. Though he was never rude to people he thought were important or famous, he looked for opportunities to intimidate others.

"Jen was just telling me about David giving Cal a blow job in the kitchen this morning while Judy was greeting the guests." Peter replied to Spencer in a sincere friendly voice. "Or was that you ?"

Spencer's downy cheeks flamed red. "I'll ask Cal about that," he replied. "He's always interested in what his guests say about him."

Jennifer saw that Spencer was insecure and lonely. She felt sorry for him. He reminded her of her little brother in Omaha. He had the same colorless hair.

When the croquet game was over, Peter followed Cal who was drawn into conversation with his wife and her friends. Jennifer joined Spencer, who was gathering up the croquet mallets and putting them into canvas bags. "How long have you been in L.A., Spencer ?" Jennifer asked him in a friendly voice.

Spencer seemed reluctant to look at Jennifer. He picked up a croquet ball and put it into a box. "Almost a year," he told her.

"You must be learning a lot about the film industry." Jennifer said.

"Are you an actress ?" Spencer replied with bland contempt.

"I'm new here too. I don't know very many people and I was going to ask you if you wanted to go with me to a movie sometime," Jennifer said.

Spencer shrugged. He seemed to be unsure as to how to respond. Jennifer knew he wanted to say yes but he doubted her sincerity.

"I don't have that much free time," Spencer told her.

"Can I call you some time?" Jennifer asked and Spencer wrote his phone number for her. Jennifer thanked him and said she'd call tomorrow, then joined Michelle where she was sitting and drinking with Donna Samuels.

"Oh, this is your friend," Donna cooed when Jennifer sat down at their table. "You two are both so adorable." Michelle was having another mimosa and Donna was on her second.

"I was just telling Michelle that I was an actress when I was your age," Donna smiled at the recollection. "Did you ever see 'Emergency Landing'?"

"Which one were you?" Michelle said.

"That was a great film," Jennifer hastily added. "Was that your first role ?"

"My second," Donna said, "then I got married."

At the mention of marriage, Michelle sat up straighter and leaned forward with suddenly focused attention. "Tell me about your wedding" she asked Donna, with such sincere interest that the older woman immediately launched into a detailed description.

Jennifer slipped away, keeping her eyes open for Peter, who seemed to have disappeared in the knot of people hovering around the stone terrace near the house.

At a crowded table, Judy Portnoy introduced her husband to Ralph Guilford, a distinguished English poet who had just written a play about Queen Victoria that was a critical and popular success at the National Theater.

Peter Revel pulled up a chair and said "I loved 'Majesty in Black' it was awesome."

"Awesome ?" Ralph Guilford repeated, half-turning his large frame awkwardly towards Peter, as though caught off guard.

The playwright was a man of above-average size who, in his 60 plus years, had never been known to indulge in physical exercise. He had long-fingered fleshy hands as soft as a girl's and tiny pointed teeth.

"Dame Helen is marvelous in the lead of course." the writer replied in his mumbling way, as though he didn't want to disturb anyone with the sound of his voice, "Not sure it would have worked without her, really."

"You are far too modest, Ralph. The play is absolutely brilliant," his companion Rita remarked emphatically in a ringing, confident voice, then turned to Cal and told him "It was a sensation last season in London and they're talking about bringing it to New York."

"What's it about ?" Cal asked.

"Queen Victoria, of course, and her life immediately after the death of her husband." Rita supplied helpfully.

"Grief, really," Ralph muttered, "how it transcends the daily, illuminates the mundane, that sort of thing."

Judy nudged her husband and spoke to him in an encouraging tone. "You know-- Queen Victoria ! You really should read it, Cal, everyone's talking about Majesty in Black."

Judy was always enthusiastic about the latest things. Cal thought he might have his secretary give it a read. Story sounded like a downer but Bob Brockman made money on that Brit history drama last year. Shot it in Ireland with huge tax incentives and used English crew people who all worked for scale. Might be the kind of costumey thing the academy went for.

Cal got up from the table abruptly and headed for the house. His pills were in the bedroom and he felt a migraine coming on. As he entered the door he saw Carrie Topper across the room walking towards him. Cal needed to take his pills but he couldn't avoid greeting her and she'd want to talk. They were promoting Carrie as a likely Oscar nominee this year for her role as a pregnant welfare mother with AIDS.

Cal's head was beginning to throb; if he didn't take the pills immediately he'd have a full-fledged migraine. Just before the actress got within greeting distance, Peter Revel caught up with Cal.

"Judy asked me to..." Peter began but he stopped when he saw Cal's face.

"What's wrong, Cal ?"

"I need my pills" Cal explained, perspiration beading up on his broad forehead. He motioned towards his bedroom and then indicated Carrie.

Peter grasped the situation at once. He hurried to the actress and stood in front of her. "Carrie Topper--I am such a huge fan of yours, I've always wanted to meet you. I saw "Tragedy Magee" recently and it is without a doubt the best movie of the year. You must be really proud of that."

Carrie had once been a successful fashion model. Slim and lithe, she was frequently photographed in revealing gowns by Versace, Gucci and Dior. She nodded impatiently at Peter and looked over his shoulder to see where Cal Portnoy had gone.

"Is Cal avoiding me ?" Carrie asked Peter, crinkling her perfectly shaped eyebrows in an exaggerated show of dismay--making it a joke. Peter laughed with her at the sheer impossible absurdity of anyone ever wanting to avoid Carrie Topper.

"Cal had a conference call. He'll be back out in a minute."

Carrie looked around for her agent Mel Cummings, who had accompanied her to the party, but he had disappeared. Peter found Carrie a seat at a palm shaded table away from the others.

"Are you working with Cal ?" Carrie asked him.

"We have some ongoing projects," Peter answered, then, looking intently at the actress he said "You truly are a goddess, you know that ? You are even more beautiful in person than on the screen. Are you working on something new ?"

Carrie smiled. "I've been reading some scripts, but Mel says it's time to do something completely different than my other roles, you know, stretch myself."

One of the most powerful agents in Hollywood, Mel Cummings had guided Carrie's career from the beginning, expertly picking roles that suited the talents of his client who had evolved from being considered only a pretty face into a serious dramatic actress.

"I'm getting tired of playing prostitutes and rape victims," Carrie said.

"Don't forget bereaved beauty queen in "Scream for your Supper.""

"You saw that ?" Carrie seemed surprised. "It went straight to video."

"I've seen all your films." Peter assured her. "You are my cinema queen."

Carrie leaned back in her chair and smiled benevolently as Peter continued.

"Listen, you didn't hear this from me, okay ? But there's a good chance Cal's going to do Majesty in Black next year."

Carrie had not seen the play or read Majesty in Black, but she'd heard about it. "That's the kind of thing I want to do, something with class." Carrie told Peter. "What's it about ?"

Peter signaled the waiter for drinks and began to tell Carrie the entire story. The beautiful African-American actress listened with rapt interest.

Michelle hadn't moved from the table near the house where Donna also stayed seated, drinking and chatting. Donna was explaining to Michelle that the Portnoys' Sunday afternoon tennis games took place almost every weekend in the summer months. Many of the guests simply dropped in to say hello and left after a short visit. Michelle had become quiet and content to watch the ebb and flow of guests and greetings. She could see Jennifer at the edge of the wide lawn sitting on a bench in the rose garden.

"Haven't I seen you on television ?" Jennifer looked up at the thin older man who asked the question. She knew he had been watching her for the past few minutes.

"That's possible," she replied when her eyes met his.

Mel Cummings introduced himself and added, "I'm at I.T.and I., innovative talent, international." Mel couldn't remember if he'd seen this girl on one of Cal's TV series or if she was in a current film. But her face was definitely familiar, he should know her name. She had a distinctive look, and she was really young; Mel hadn't talked to anyone so young in years.

Jennifer explained to Mel that she had left her last agent. "He calls me all the time but I'm not going back with him, no matter how much he begs."

Mel tried to make his voice seem sympathetic. "That's a shame. What happened ?" he asked.

"Some people just aren't tuned in, you know what I mean ? I didn't feel he appreciated me; he didn't understand me." Jennifer explained.

"What didn't he understand ?" Mel asked her.

"I'm able to get to the heart of things and learn what I need to know lightning fast. My conscience is clear and my instincts are voracious. I fear nothing and no one, my talent is monstrous."

Mel moved closer and said "I totally understand, Jennifer, I really do appreciate ... Can I ask you something Jennifer ?"

"Go ahead."

"Here's my question: How much money would you like to make in the next year? Or say, the next six months?"

"Which ?" Jennifer asked, "A year or six months ?"

"Okay," Mel said, "let's say in the next year."

Jennifer looked around the garden and thought for a minute, then looked directly at Mel. "One million, five hundred thousand dollars."

"Bingo," Mel said. "That's the right answer.

CHAPTER THIRTY - SIX

May 11, 1999

Ginger heard a car door slam and hurried to look out the window over her kitchen sink but she saw no sign of Jennifer's car on Westborne Street. The clock above the stove showed ten minutes after six.

"I hope Jennifer gets here soon, I don't want to be late for the shower," Ginger told Nora while she poured what was left of the coffee into her cup.

"It took forever to get out of Manhattan this morning," Nora was talking as Ginger sat down opposite her at the round oak table. "There was a big thunderstorm and the plane was delayed for two hours at LaGuardia. I was afraid I might have to take a later flight."

"I think Mercury must be in retrograde," Ginger offered as explanation. "But I'm so glad you got here in time." Ginger checked her watch again. From the table, she picked up a beribboned box wrapped in bright patterned paper and moved it to the counter near the door. "I can't believe you've been gone almost six months. It doesn't seem possible."

"No, it seems like just last week," Nora agreed. She had moved back to New York just before Christmas, and so much had happened since then.

Ginger opened the back door and let Greta into the kitchen.

"What have you heard from Dan ?" Nora asked Ginger who sat and scratched the old boxer behind the ears.

"He's staying in Alaska for another month. First it was spring skiing, but then he called from Mount McKinley. I guess he wants to do some climbing there. I said I'd keep Greta while he's gone. I like having a dog around, she's good company."

"Dan told me he wants to write another script," Nora said. "Something about mountain climbers."

"There's Jennifer now," Ginger said at the sound of the door bell, and both women stood up and prepared to leave.

"Nora !" Jennifer greeted Nora enthusiastically with a warm hug. "You made it ! I'm so glad you got here !"

Jennifer's hair had been dyed black for her latest role and the new implants had changed her figure significantly, Nora noticed.

"How could I not come ? I've been looking forward to this for weeks," Nora replied. "Let me look at you," she said affectionately and Jennifer obediently twirled around to display her new dress which was cut very low to show off her recently augmented bust line.

As the three women walked outside in the damp spring evening, Jennifer watched Nora's reaction when she opened the door of her brand new silver Jaguar SL 580.

"Wow, is this your car ?" Nora asked, clearly surprised.

"Yeah, I've had it for a couple of months," Jennifer said, opening the trunk of the sleek sedan and placing Ginger's gift beside other brightly-wrapped packages.

Ginger slid into the soft leather of the back seat. "You ride in front, Nora."

"This is so luxurious, Jennifer." Ginger admired the polished wood dashboard and the gleaming instrument panels and the clean animal perfume of the white leather upholstery. "What a beautiful car."

"I love this car," Jennifer said as she eased the car into gear and drove towards Sunset Boulevard. "How's New York ?"

"Do you know where we're going ?" Ginger asked from the back seat.

"New York is great," Nora said.

"Bel Air, Bellagio Road, right ?" Jennifer said. "I was there once before."

Ginger was always impressed with Jennifer's sense of direction. She never had a problem driving anywhere.

Nora wanted to find out about the plans for tomorrow. "You and Michelle are meeting Floyd in Joshua Tree tomorrow morning?" she asked Jennifer. Where is that exactly ?"

"We can all go in my car if you want." Ginger offered.

"I don't mind driving," Jennifer said, "but I'll probably spend the night there."

"We're definitely going to scatter March's ashes tomorrow ?" Nora asked.

"Definitely. We've been planning this for a while. Floyd will be coming from New Mexico." Jennifer said. At first, Floyd wanted to have the memorial on March 21, the spring equinox; but Jennifer and Michelle were involved in shooting the first six segments of "Father Knows Better" and couldn't get any time off.

"So, Michelle's having a girl," Nora said to Jennifer. "What's she going to call the baby ? Did she pick out a name yet?"

"Michelle told me she wants to name the baby Guadalupe, after her mother," Ginger said.

Jennifer shook her head. "But Josh doesn't like that name. He wants to call it something else-- Meryl or Melissa or something."

"I'm sure they'll work it out," Ginger said optimistically. She was looking forward to the evening. Ginger hadn't seen Michelle since the wedding in December, but she knew the young couple had moved to a three bedroom house in Sherman Oaks after returning from a honeymoon in Bali.

Jennifer sped through the green lawns of Beverly Hills and slowed down and turned right at the Bel Air gate off Sunset. It was easy to find the address on the empty curving street because hired parking attendants in red and white uniforms were stationed at the curb.

"Who is it who lives here ?" Nora asked.

"Donna is Josh's aunt," Jennifer explained. "Michelle met her before they were married. Ginger and I wanted to have the shower but Donna insisted, and she has a bigger place, so..."

"This looks like a big party." Ginger said, as they waited behind a line of cars for scurrying men in uniform to open the doors of Jennifer's Jaguar.

David Samuels himself greeted the shower guests and waved them into the crowded living room which opened onto a patio beside a large oval swimming pool surrounded by tree ferns, palms and ficus trees draped in strings of tiny white lights.

"You'll find Donna and Michelle out near the pool somewhere," he told Jennifer.

Nora was surprised at the large number of guests at the baby shower. They must have invited the entire agency as well as family friends, she thought, wondering how many actually knew Michelle.

Michelle was sitting near the pool but when she saw her friends she stood up and hurried towards them with an excited smile. Nora was amazed at the size and shape of Michelle's body. She looked almost twice as wide as before. Michelle opened her arms to Nora and embraced her and Nora could tell she was genuinely happy to see her.

"I'm really glad you came, Nora, thanks for flying all the way out here. It wouldn't have been the same without you."

Sudden unexpected tears filled Nora's eyes when she hugged Michelle. "I missed you." was all she could say. She was going to say something more, something upbeat like 'I couldn't let you have a baby and not be here to celebrate' but Nora had a lump in her throat and couldn't speak.

Nora realized at that moment how much she truly did miss Michelle, the soft-hearted, lazy, giggling girl with trusting eyes. That girl had changed into a pregnant woman and she would never see her again-- the girl who had been Michelle was gone. For a split second, Nora felt a sharp visceral sense of loss, as though someone had died, but she knew this was a happy occasion and quickly brushed away the hot tears that blurred her vision.

Ginger told Michelle how beautiful she looked and Michelle said "I've gained thirty pounds already."

"That's normal," Ginger assured her.

Jennifer pulled Nora's arm. "Hey, I want you to meet somebody, come over here."

"Luke Selway, Nora Gregorian."

"Oh." Nora was momentarily flustered. "We've met before."

"How are you Nora ?" Luke wore a trendy light-colored suit and his permanently amused expression. "You look great. I saw your sister last week. She told me you'd moved back to New York."

"Yes. A friend of mine offered me his apartment." Nora told him. "Where did you meet Jennifer ?"

"We're working together on a TV show for Cal Portnoy Productions; I'm producing the soundtrack. She's a real talent, that girl. I hear she's up for the lead in the new Brad Nathan Ellis movie." Luke continued. "Did you see her the other night on the Don Pryor show ? He was asking her about 'seeing ghosts' and making jokes about supernatural powers and she totally blew him away telling about her abusive childhood in Omaha and the way she found a spiritual path. I find her very refreshing."

"Yes." Nora said, "Yes, she definitely is."

"Tell me what you've been doing." Luke had the knack of looking interested, Nora thought. He really appeared to be genuinely interested.

"Well, I finally got my screenplay 'Girl in Green Moonlight' set up over at Facetime Films," Nora told him. "We have a producer, Peter Revel, who got Ian McClash signed to direct it. Now it looks like Kim Barrington might do it. She said it's the most intelligent female role she's seen in years."

"Peter's producing your film ?" Luke seemed to be on a first-name basis with him. "You know he bought the rights to Majesty in Black and he's got Carrie Topper to play Queen Victoria ?"

"Carrie Topper ?" Peter hadn't mentioned this project to Nora.

"Of course, he's getting all kinds of free publicity just because of the casting--Peter's no dummy."

"No," Nora said.

"Ian McClash is a fantastic director," Luke said, "I loved Playground of Morpheus, and Delectable Corpse was great too."

"Yeah, Ian won the Palme d'Or at Cannes in '89. We still don't have all the money, but Peter's raised over five million already."

"What's the budget ?" Luke asked.

"Around eleven."

"Well good luck with that. Sounds like a great project," Luke said with what really sounded like genuine enthusiasm. "We should get together sometime, have lunch or something."

"Thanks, I..." Nora found herself nodding to the air as Luke's attention was suddenly diverted.

"Hey sweetie !" The thin red-haired girl in stiletto heels embraced Luke in an enthusiastic greeting that became a full-fledged embrace so Nora hurried towards Ginger. She saw her standing alone near the bar with a martini in her hand. "You should try one of these cosmopolitans," Ginger gestured with her glass towards the bartender, "the pink ones, they're delicious."

"Did you see where Jennifer went ?" Nora asked and Ginger shrugged as she looked around the poolside patio full of people drinking and talking. Michelle and Jennifer were nowhere to be seen.

"She told me her agent Mel Cummings might be here. I want to talk to him because he also represents Kim Barrington and we need her to sign the contract to play Iris in "Girl in Green Moonlight.""

"You mean she's going to play the lead in your movie ?" Ginger grabbed a miniature quiche from a passing tray. "That's great Nora, Kim Barrington is a big star."

"Kim says she's interested but she hasn't signed a contract yet," Nora explained. "Until she does, we won't be able to get all the financing we need to make the movie. But her agent won't let her sign the deal until the full amount of money is in the bank."

"But you can't get the money you need to make the film until she signs ?"

"Right." Nora had recently learned some of the fine points of independent film financing.

The area around the pool had become crowded with men and women talking and drinking. Nora and Ginger walked towards the open doors leading to the living room and found Michelle and Josh sitting on a pink sofa with two middle-aged women. Josh also had changed, Nora thought he looked older, heavier, more assured.

Michelle indicated the older women and told Ginger "Did you know these two are twins ?"

Ginger said "You have a beautiful home, Donna."

"We've been here almost eighteen years," the hostess replied.

"Would you ladies like another drink ?" Josh asked, standing.

"I can't," said Michelle ruefully, then excused herself to go to the bathroom.

Ginger moved closer to Judy and asked if she had children. "I have one son who's in art school in Tallahassee, Florida," Judy told her.

"My daughter's in Toronto," Ginger said. Judy nodded sympathetically.

Jennifer and Michelle made sure the door of the bathroom was locked and Jennifer reached in her pocket and pulled out a hard white cylinder with a brown tip designed to look exactly like a filter cigarette. As Jennifer filled the end of the little pipe and lit up, Michelle switched on a loud fan that created a resounding whirr in the powder room off the hallway near the Samuels' kitchen.

"Where'd you get this ?" Michelle asked, inhaling deeply as Jennifer held another match to the burning end.

"It's from Humbolt County; Spencer got it for me," Jennifer said. " It's really strong."

Michelle held the smoke in her lungs for several seconds then exhaled. She thought she could feel the muscles of her face relax. "My face hurts from smiling so much," she told Jennifer, passing her the cigarette pipe.

"I know what you mean," her friend nodded as she attempted to speak without allowing smoke to escape from her mouth. It sounded like I-oh-wa-chu-ean.

After Jennifer coughed and exhaled she asked Michelle "Like when is your actual due date?"

She knew Michelle had said July, but there was some question. Michelle opened the little window in the room and waved at the smoke. "The doctors can't be like exactly certain, but they think it could be July or June."

"What do you think?" Jennifer moved her face very close to her friend's face. "Come on, you can tell me."

"I think June." Michelle said. "Like it's not a big deal. It might even be early June." Jennifer thought Michelle looked ready to have the baby at any moment, her belly was huge and her breasts had almost doubled in size.

"I wonder if the baby will look like you." Jennifer said. "I hope so."

"You know, I'm the same age my mother was when she had me." Michelle said, "I think about her, you know, she told me her mother and father, my grandparents, were from Guadalajara. I never got to meet them but I'd like to go there some time. "

"Did you tell Manny about the baby ?" Jennifer remembered Michelle's stepfather in Oxnard. They visited him once on their way to L.A. from Santa Barbara. He'd given them some pointers on freeway driving.

"No, I tried calling him when we got married but the number I had was no longer in service. He only lived with us four or five years before my Mom died. We weren't that close. I also thought about calling my Aunt Teresa.

Jennifer nodded, remembering the quiet woman who had opened the door the first time she met Michelle.

"You know, she wasn't really my aunt, I just called her that. She was my mom's friend and she had five kids of her own—but she took care of me. They moved to Monterey last year. Maybe I should write to her or something. I don't know."

Jennifer could see this family talk was making Michelle feel sad. Having a baby seemed to make people start thinking about their relatives, which was always depressing. Michelle had never known her father and Jennifer thought it might have been better if she had never met hers.

There was a knock on the bathroom door and Jennifer felt a shiver of panic, as though they might be discovered. She enjoyed the rush of adrenalin but knew they were in no real danger.

"Just a minute," Jennifer called to the door, maybe a little too loudly.

Michelle looked at her friend flushing the ashes from the cigarette pipe into the swirling water of Donna's pink toilet bowl and wiping the residue off with a lacy pink guest towel and she began to giggle. There was a high helpless note in Michelle's laughter, Jennifer thought, which somehow bridged the dizzying gap between who they had been and who they were becoming and Jennifer couldn't help but laugh herself.

"Hey, I know you're in there." The voice on the other side of the door sounded familiar.

The two friends giggled even harder at their predicament. "Who is it ?" Michelle asked Jennifer, then in a louder voice, spoke to the door "Who is it ?"

"It's Mister Revelinsky" came the voice and Michelle opened the door for Peter. "What kind of mischief are you girls up to in here ?"

Michelle and Jennifer hugged him, giggling, and all three walked out of the bathroom, Nora met them in the hallway.

"You look exceptionally beautiful, darling." Peter said by way of greeting Nora. " I'm so glad to see you." Peter kissed Nora very warmly and deliberately on each cheek. " How long will you be in town ?"

"Just this weekend. We're all going out to the desert early tomorrow for the memorial, then I have to fly back on Sunday." Nora told Peter.

"I'm driving," Jennifer explained to him. "Come with us if you want."

"I'll be staying at Ginger's house." Nora told him.

"Are you two friends again ?" Peter loved gossip and always wanted to know how people were getting along.

"Yes, we patched things up. Oh, by the way, is Mel Cummings here ? I really need to talk to him about Kim."

Jennifer shook her head. "I haven't seen him. Have you, Peter?"

"I think Mel is in Australia," Peter said.

Nora was going to ask about Carrie Topper but just then Donna came to tell them that Paul Tormay, the famous singer, was about to perform, so they followed the rest of the guests towards the white piano in the living room.

The audience responded enthusiastically as Paul launched into a low-key rendering of "I can't give you anything but love, baby," then he sang, in his celebrated mellow baritone, "You belong to me," and finally, to applause and murmurs of approval, "Pretty Baby."

Nora saw Michelle glance happily at Josh who stood beside her with a smugly satisfied expression on his face. Then she noticed Jennifer's face-- her eyes were blinking rapidly and she seemed to be self-consciously fighting back tears--or was it laughter ? Nora couldn't tell for sure but she joined in the prolonged applause as Paul Tormay finished playing and planted a big kiss on the mother-to-be.

CHAPTER THIRTY - SEVEN

The next morning, minutes before her alarm went off, Jennifer was awakened by a telephone call from Floyd.

"You know how to get there, don't you ?" his calm voice was surrounded by quiet. "There's a little gas station on highway 62 north of Joshua Tree, you can't miss it, I'll be waiting there."

"We should be there by eight o'clock," Jennifer assured him.

"I'll be waiting for you," Floyd told her. He didn't talk for long. Almost half a year, she thought. So much had happened.

Jennifer enjoyed being up early, it was rare that she rose before the sun.

When she took the cover off Leo's cage, the parrot looked surprised to be awakened before the room reached its usual brightness.

"Erk," he said. "Ark ? Squaw ?"

"We're going to the desert this morning, Leo," Jennifer explained to him.

"What should I bring ?" Jennifer was in the habit of talking to Leo when she was home alone. She tried to think ahead to what she might encounter. It was still dark outside but there wasn't much time before they had to start out. Candles and matches she thought, and tobacco and water.

Nora arrived at the door exactly on time and told Jennifer "Michelle called, she's running late, she said she'd ride with Ginger and they'll meet us there a little later."

Most of the citizens of Los Angeles were still sleeping when Nora and Jennifer drove south on the empty freeway through the deep shade of tall office buildings then mile after mile of identical flat suburbs interspersed with industrial sites so vast and unpopulated it was impossible to tell what had been or was being manufactured. They watched the sun rise in a pale orange shimmer over the range of mountains to the east of the tangled freeways and by the time they traversed the sprawl of Orange County's beach towns, the day had begun and they were driving through the sandy scrub on the western edge of the Mohave desert.

Nora had never seen Joshua trees before. They were outlandish, as though designed for a different planet than the one inhabited by stately oak trees and graceful maples. They looked like a cross between a tall cactus and a small tree struck by lightning. Human-sized limbs exploded into random sprouts of spiky leaves and dusty blossoms. Instead of branching out evenly from a central trunk they seemed to reach for the sky off-kilter, inebriated; they leaned and lurched.

"Do you know what we're going to be doing-- I mean, what will Floyd want to do with the ashes, do you think ?" Nora asked Jennifer.

"He has a plan; I guess we'll find out pretty soon," Jennifer said, her eyes searching the roadside for a sign.

SAnTAnna SToreE was hand-lettered on the front of a stucco building where old tires and greasy tools leaned against bleached tan walls. Two dilapidated gas pumps in front showed numbers in glass windows.

"This must be it." The storefront was cube-shaped, with a flat roof and a wide front entrance framed by rust-eaten advertisements for Budweiser and Coca-cola. Floyd's old green pickup truck was parked in the dusty lot behind the store.

When Nora got out of the car she became aware of an agreeable stillness across the entire 360-degree beige panorama where telephone poles held up miles of invisible wire and a few half-rotted cars slept on the sand; as though noise couldn't penetrate the limpid air that seemed to have weight, like water.

Floyd walked around the corner of the building and stopped.

"Is that Jennifer?" His long blue shadow stretched across the dusty lot.

"I hardly recognized you, girl."

Nora could feel Jennifer's nervousness--it traveled through the dry air like electricity.

"Oh Floyd," Jennifer ran smiling into his arms and Nora saw him kiss the top of her head, then her face and lips.

Nora stood quietly apart as they embraced. She couldn't hear what Jennifer said but she spoke for several minutes in a low voice to Floyd, as if she'd been waiting a long time to say whatever it was.

"The thing is," Floyd was explaining, "you can't do anything in the desert in the middle of the day. You either do it early in the morning or at sunset." Nora and Floyd were sitting on stools at the counter in the gas station store. Nora thought the name should have been written Santa Ana, which she knew was the name of the mountains in the distance and also a hot wind which blew across Los Angeles. Possibly this is where the wind originates, she thought as she sat observing the leather-faced proprietor of the gas station, a wiry, desiccated man with small hooded eyes. Nora wondered if he painted the crooked sign and whether he looked like someone who would be a poor speller.

Jennifer had to open the windows of her car because Leo had been left in the front seat and she was afraid he would get too hot. The solid block of shade cast by the gas station was shrinking as the sun rose higher.

Jennifer kept trying to call Michelle, who was assumed to be on the road, but the reception was bad. Finally, behind a crackle of static on the line, Michelle answered. "Where are you ?" Jennifer greeted her. "Are you lost ? We've been waiting for you."

"I'm sorry Jennifer, I tried to call but...," Michelle sounded pained. Her voice came intermittently with deep holes of silence in it. "I couldn't get in touch..."

"I can't hear you. What ?" Jennifer shouted and pressed the phone to her ear.

"It's Josh, he doesn't want me to leave. He's really sick."

"What ?" Jennifer yelled.

Leo awked and fluttered his wings, startled at the sudden loud noise. Jennifer sat in the car listening to Michelle talk and explain and explain how Josh was in bed with a high fever and she didn't feel she could leave him and Ginger decided she didn't want to drive out there alone and Jennifer had nothing to say.

"Please don't be mad at me, Jen, I really wanted to be there, you know that, but I can't leave Josh like this. I know he really needs me."

"Well if that's the way it is, what can I say ? We'll miss you."

"I know," Michelle said, "I'm really really sorry. Please don't be mad at me, Jen. March would understand, you know ?"

"Sure," Jennifer said, "that's it then." She closed the phone without saying goodbye. Then she made a fist and held her arm out to Leo, who hopped adroitly unto her wrist without slipping.

Jennifer asked the man behind the counter, whose name was Jack, for water for Leo. The man didn't seem surprised or interested when he saw the parrot, but he brought the water to the counter carefully, in a thick tan coffee cup, as soon as Jennifer asked for it. Then the four people watched the parrot drink. Leo dipped and jittered his beak into the cup, then lifted his head as if to ease the water down his glittering green throat.

The gas station store had a grimy machine that dispensed coffee and another appliance which cooked hotdogs by rotating them slowly between heated steel rollers behind a grease- spattered window. A slow fan hanging from the ceiling stirred the odors of gasoline, bitter coffee and old grease.

"We can't expect to do anything in the middle of the day," Floyd was explaining. "We've lost the shadows now, we'll have to wait until later." Without shadows, Floyd said, there was no use in beginning anything.

He appeared to be disappointed but resigned. He accepted the responsibility of doing what needed to be done but he stopped short of explaining what he planned to do or what the intended outcome might be.

Floyd knew where to go. "We can drive up on the old Pearblossom road, it's not too far from here."

"Wait," Nora said, "I want to get a picture of you two."

Floyd was wearing his cowboy hat and Jennifer had big sunglasses. He casually put his arm around her and she lifted her chin and struck a nonchalant pose.

"Now Nora, don't you plan on taking any pictures once we get started with the ceremony," Floyd warned her.

"Why not ?" Jennifer asked.

"That's an important rule," Floyd told her, "No cameras."

"What difference does it make if we take pictures ?"

Floyd shrugged, he didn't invent the rule. "I s'pose it makes a difference in the way we pay attention-- what we do here happens between us and the spirits only once and only we see it and only we know it."

"Should we take two cars ?" Jennifer sounded reluctant.

"No, the road's not paved all the way, you don't want that shiny new car of yours to get all banged up and dusty. You can leave your car here and we'll go in my truck," Floyd said.

Jennifer sat beside Nora in the cab of the pickup with her legs slanted to the right to allow Floyd room to shift gears. Leo perched on the edge of the milk crate Nora held in her lap and at first, the bird squawked about the pitching and lurching motion of the truck. But as the journey continued, all the passengers gradually became quiet, as though the massive silence of the desert absorbed them, too, in its silence.

Floyd's truck didn't have air conditioning and the temperature increased as the sun rose higher in the sky. The old pickup bounced and rattled, very slowly following the rutted dirt road which climbed a long gradual incline into a forest of Joshua Trees interspersed with rocky desert brush.

After an hour or so, Floyd pulled off the road near a huge horseshoe-shaped outcropping of brown sandstone, bigger than a house, steep-edged and solid, which loomed over the ragged desert flora. Around the main rock, smaller boulders of the same gray-brown color had gathered, as though drawn into community with their own kind. The rock acted as a wind break and the massive weight of it held moisture in the ground, establishing a haven for the few scrappy green plants clinging to the edge of shade.

Jennifer carefully placed Leo's crate beside the rock. Floyd got busy carrying some wooden poles from his pickup to a flat spot nearby and constructed a makeshift tent, securing the poles with rope, then spreading them to create a sturdy umbrella-like structure. He draped some old blankets over the top, and tossed another blanket on the ground inside.

"You can sit in here with Leo if you want" Floyd told Nora.

Nora appreciated the comfort of the shade in the mid-day heat. "How do you like the desert, Leo ?" Nora asked when she sat down inside the tent. The sound of her own voice seemed foreign and strained. The parrot said nothing.

Jennifer leaned against the side of the truck and watched to see what Floyd would do. He looked at her with his steady wide-set eyes and motioned with his head towards the distant mountains. In the fierce silence, surrounded by the furnace of mid-day sun, Jennifer felt uncertain and clumsy. Floyd brought out an old leather pack and loaded it with supplies and tools from his truck. Jennifer saw him place a heavy metal canister in the pack; she knew it contained March's ashes. As Jennifer followed him through the dry brush, Floyd picked up dry sticks and branches dropped from Joshua trees.

Nora wasn't sure how much time had passed while she waited in the tent with the parrot. When she stood up she felt dizzy, and the bright heat reflecting off the sandy ground stung her eyes when she stepped, light-headed, out into the sun. She looked around for Jennifer and Floyd but she saw no sign of them in any direction. Nora considered going to look for them but decided it was better to wait; she wanted to stay within sight of the car and the tent.

She eyed the tall rock outcropping and tried to estimate its height. Though she was wearing thin sandals, by pushing and pulling herself up a vertical cleft in the rough stone Nora managed a slow climb to the flat area on top which seemed to be about the height of a three storey building. When she stood to look around, she was amazed at how far she could see. Miles away, under the blue dome of desert sky, the Santa Ana gas station shimmered in the heat, a sugar cube beside the brown snake of a road.

Nora searched for a sign of her friends in the dry terrain, but not even a leaf moved in the still afternoon. Only a lone hawk floated high in the air, absolutely noiseless, close to invisible. Nothing to do but wait until Jennifer and Floyd come back, she thought, feeling transparent and empty, as though she had no memory. With an effort, Nora recalled that just three days before she'd walked down Fifth Avenue in New York among throngs of people in a cold wet rain. She experienced a shiver of vertigo as she gauged the distance to the ground far below; she could see where she climbed up but she couldn't see a foothold, no way back down. A wave of panic washed over her as she thought about going down, and she sat on the flat summit of the rock, her heart pumping.

Jennifer followed Floyd as he walked into a dusty creek bed, a scattered trail of pebbles marking a long-dried-up stream of water. She wanted to embrace him but he turned his back to her.

"Floyd," she said, "I missed you."

"Missing people is a waste of time," Floyd said as he worked, he didn't look up and Jennifer could tell he was annoyed. "Why did you do that to yourself?" he asked her.

She was going to ask what; but she knew what he meant. "I guess I look a lot different than the last time I saw you," she said. "I thought it was an improvement."

"You're not the same girl I knew" Floyd said. "It's not only your shape and your hair, there's something else too."

"I am me," she said, "inside, I'm the same."

"When I met you I thought I knew what you wanted or what you needed-- now I don't know." There was no anger in his voice, but no understanding either.

Jennifer felt the dead weight of the heat and the silence pressing down on her like it could flatten her. It was an effort to stand upright. She hated how empty and pointless the desert felt-- like all expectations, all plans, all ambition evaporated here. She couldn't think of anything to tell Floyd, to convince him, nothing she wanted to share. Still, she couldn't help it; she wanted to be near him.

Floyd knelt down to pick up a fist-sized stone, then one like a tongue, then an ear. Jennifer watched him. She stooped to pick up a white stone and he stopped her.

"I'll take care of this myself."

"What can I do?" Jennifer asked him. "I'm sorry." But Floyd didn't answer.

"Do you know how much I care about you?"

"Yes," he said. "I know."

"I think about you all the time," she said but he kept walking away from her and didn't turn back.

The smoke made Nora's eyes water and she turned over on the warm rock. When she opened her eyes, Nora realized that she had fallen asleep for most of the afternoon and the landscape had changed--the desert was now full of shadows— blue stains pooled around the ragged trees like spilled ink. Her dream was still with her, warm and potent; Nora reached back to retrieve it but it stayed out of reach, eluding her. She was bowing, that was it! There was a Chinese man smiling and he bowed low to her and she bowed to him. An altar, she thought, entering into the dream, trying to pull it back to her. We were in front of an altar and we bowed to each other. The dream then was released into waking memory and she held it intact and complete, recalling the feeling of respect, reverence, the meaning of a bow, lowering the head, honoring someone above you. Above yourself. The acknowledgement of reverence, a formal movement, full of grace.

From her high vantage point, Nora looked east towards the mountains. There was a fire burning in a clearing not far away and she could see Jennifer and Floyd standing near it. Suddenly, as she thought about joining them, Nora remembered her predicament— how to get down. She'd made it to the top but she couldn't go anywhere else. Suddenly, she saw how foolish it was to get stuck, trapped, when she was surrounded by nothing but open space. It was absurd, really, Nora realized, and she made a low bow in the direction of the mountains; a gesture that made her laugh as she did it. A quiet spasm began in her throat when she bent down and exploded in a soft ha when she stood up. While she was at it she bowed in the opposite direction, towards the misty west where the sun was beginning to decline, a purple veil over the blue sky. To be thorough, Nora bowed to the north and the south as well, then she cupped her hands and shouted. She saw by their movements that her friends heard her, and Floyd immediately began walking towards the rock, waving a slow calm greeting with his thick arm. He climbed to the summit of the rock without hesitating.

"You woke up."

"I couldn't figure out how to get back down. Then I went to sleep." Nora was so relieved at the effortless way Floyd climbed the rock to join her that she embraced him and kissed him on the mouth, almost without thinking, as though he were an old friend. He tasted of apples and wood smoke.

"We could see you sleeping up here," Floyd said. "Did you have any dreams?"

"Yes," said Nora, surprised, "Yes, I did."

Floyd said nothing more about dreams and the two of them stood and watched the desert sky as it dissolved into gaudy, generous pools of color-- lavender with streaks of lush rosy pink and peach. Nora had no idea of the time. It seemed the evening might go on for as long as the entire afternoon, a lengthy diminishment of the day, each minute meaningful in its illumination. Floyd seemed in no hurry. They watched Jennifer tending the fire, occasionally throwing small pieces of wood into the flames.

Floyd climbed down first, helping her find footholds in the rock face, now colored sunset pink. Nora followed his steps as she descended, wary but eager to see what would happen next. When they reached the campfire, Jennifer seemed preoccupied.

"I'm ready to start drumming," Floyd told them. "But first we need to give Nora some water."

Until that moment Nora hadn't realized how thirsty she was, her tongue felt like cotton. Jennifer immediately ran to the tent and came back with a bottle of water. In the rosy light with her black hair she looked like a different girl than the one Nora had known; this new girl was reserved, uncertain. Floyd made himself comfortable beside the fire and began a simple rhythmic pounding on his small drum. Jennifer sat near him on a blanket, motionless. The desert air cooled as the sun sank and the wind stirred. Nora stood near the fire; beyond the orange flames she could see the terrain of active shadows. The big rock seemed taller sitting on its violet shade.

As Nora surveyed the horizon she saw a pair of headlights on the dirt road leading to their encampment.

"Looks like somebody's driving up here."

Jennifer stood up to look, but Floyd didn't stop drumming. A cloud of brown dust was progressing steadily up the slow furrows of road. It was a dot of bright red color, the approaching vehicle, and traveled the rough road at a dangerously high speed.

"Everything is almost ready." Floyd was still softly drumming, watching the fire. "What about Leo?" His voice was stern.

As Jennifer walked to the tent to get Leo, the red vehicle came close enough to be heard, the engine noise loud and disturbing in the quiet place. Bright headlights swept the rock and suddenly they saw that it was a Jeep, the dune buggy kind with big tires and an open cab. Nora could hear loud music and saw Peter Revel behind the wheel holding a video camera to his eye and Ginger riding beside him.

The desert silence returned when the motor was switched off. Peter trained the camera on Jennifer's face as he leaped out of the Jeep.

"We found you!" Peter announced as Ginger beamed. "We've been driving for hours."

"Peter wants to record the whole event," Ginger explained breathlessly, "like documentary-style—a native American ceremony."

"We're now entering the Joshua Tree National preserve," Peter held the camera and spoke in his British television voice. " Can you explain what you plan to do here this evening, Jennifer?" he moved in closer to get good sound quality.

"Peter, I think you should ask..." She indicated Floyd, who had stopped drumming and was watching.

Peter walked towards the campfire and aimed his camera at Floyd and Nora, a wider shot.

"No cameras Peter, no pictures are allowed." Nora was turning away.

"What's the problem?" Peter looked momentarily annoyed but he lowered the camera from his eye. "This background is perfect--we're going to lose the light soon, let's get on with it." He moved toward Floyd with the camera running, "Floyd Redhill, native American, is about to begin a memorial ceremony in the Joshua Tree National Park."

Floyd jumped up and pushed Peter's camera away from his face and took Jennifer by the arm and walked around to the other side of the rock. Peter tried to follow them but Floyd stopped him with a look so fierce he shrugged and focused his lens on the campfire.

"Don't you care about this?" Floyd asked Jennifer. "I thought you understood something about what I'm trying to do here."

"I do care but I don't see why we can't be more open about it, I mean Peter is a friend of ours, what harm can..."

"You have to listen to me, Jen. We can't record this. He has to stop."

"Just a few shots of us in the landscape is all he wants. I don't see how that could hurt anything." Jennifer was surprised at how adamant Floyd was. She realized she hardly knew this man, he was sweating and his jaw was tense.

"Tell them to leave now," Floyd said, "we'll lose the shadows. we don't have much time."

Jennifer didn't see why Floyd couldn't be more flexible; the location and the ceremony would look great on camera and Peter knew someone at the BBC who was interested in Native American things.

Leo flew out of the tent and landed on Nora's shoulder as she stood beside the fire.

"Oh, I have to get that shot." Peter said, hurrying towards the fire. "stay there, Nora, just as you are, don't move a muscle. This is fantastic," Peter exclaimed. "You look fabulous ! These cactus or trees, whatever, they are amazing! What a place!"

"I told Peter where we planned to meet you," Ginger explained to Nora in a conspiratorial voice, "then the man at the gas station told us which way you went."

Peter kept the camera running. "Stay right where you are, don't say a word," he repeated to Nora, then he made his way over the uneven terrain and panned across the Joshua Trees to where Floyd and Jennifer were talking.

"Floyd Redhill, Native American, is at home here in the Mohave desert." Peter focused his camera on the black silhouettes of the spiked trees against the orange-pink horizon.

"I really have to meet with my director in the morning," Jennifer talked to Floyd as he moved away from Peter. "I don't think I can stay."

"You're going to leave now?" Floyd asked Jennifer in a quiet voice. She nodded, she didn't try to touch him.

"Floyd, I'd like you to keep Leo. I'm working all day and he gets lonesome. I think March would have wanted you to have him." Jennifer looked sorry but she also looked impatient.

Floyd stood and watched as Jennifer went over to talk to Peter, who shrugged and put the camera away. Leo flew up to perch on a crooked branch of a Joshua tree.

Jennifer and Peter got into the jeep and prepared to leave.

"You're not coming with us, Nora?" Ginger looked surprised when Nora went back to her place beside the fire.

"No. I'll stay here," Nora waved goodbye as Ginger got in the back seat and the jeep headed down the road towards the highway.

"I'm thinking that it's so late now that we might just want to spend the night here and wait until dawn tomorrow," Floyd looked at Nora.

"That's fine with me." she said.

Leo dug his talons into the soft skin of the little tree and watched the noisy red car speed away with Jennifer. The bright lights disappeared gradually into black and the hush returned, the dense silence he remembered from a long time ago.

Two of the people stayed by the fire, which was bright orange now and growing hotter. Leo watched as the black-haired man made music with the drum and the woman's arms moved like wings as she began to dance.

THE END

Susan Roether